The
Alabaster
Concordat

J. Armand

www.jarmandbooks.com

ISBN: 0997002808, 978-0-9970028-0-5

Cover illustration by Greg Opalinski

Table of Contents

"It is easier to build strong children than to repair broken men."

— Frederick Douglass

Prologue

Emily's positive vibes were exactly what brought me back to her Manhattan hideout where I had stayed for a short time before running off to slay a demon lord in the Middle East. Her and her fellow Outsiders had taken refuge in a rundown apartment building uptown. I had started to help renovate it to accommodate the entirety of their undead coven in the city along with any homeless humans who were desperate enough not to ask questions.

"Thanks for letting me come over, Em. I know it's been a while since I bailed on you guys."

"Don't worry about it! This is your home too, isn't it? I'm sure you had a good reason. I heard you've been busy saving the world." Emily always saw the best in every situation, no matter how bad it was in reality. When we had first met I considered her naïve. Now, it was the loss of my own naivety after years of struggling to survive that left my soul disquieted and mourning the days when I didn't know better.

"This place has really changed since I was here. I was kind of hoping that you'd have something for me to do, but it looks like you have everything sorted." A few months ago I was helping put up sheetrock and assemble cheap beds; now the building had been transformed into something more closely resembling a decent hotel chain. "How'd you get all this done?"

The Outsiders were not the most organized bunch. They were runaway teenagers, cast-outs, throwaways, and vagabonds turned undead and then turned away. There weren't any rules or hierarchy that kept them at the top of the food chain like the other three covens. As a result, they often became fodder and cheap labor to carry out the dirty work that the other covens needed in their war games.

"It just takes teamwork...you can bring that up to 5B, please," Emily said as she smiled and turned to face the hallway outside her room, where two teenagers in hoodies walked past carrying a flat-screen TV that easily weighed more than the both of them combined.

It wasn't easy to sneak up on me; I could sense objects and people all around using my telekinetic powers, even if they were invisible or cloaked by an illusion. Emily sensed these two coming long before I did and she hardly had any training that I knew about.

The same thing happened a few more times during our conversation until finally I had to ask.

"Have you been practicing telepathy?" I questioned, reasoning that it was probably the only way she could have pulled this group together the way she did.

"What's that?" she asked with a face full of innocence.

"Mind reading and mind control."

"Oh, no! It's just good manners. If you say please, people are always more willing to help."

I wasn't about to argue that. Whether or not she was consciously using her mental powers, at least it was for constructive purposes and the betterment of her people. I couldn't say the same for myself and my usual company recently, which was the reason I came here in the first place.

"Have you heard what's been going on in the world?"

"I've heard about the demons if that's what you mean. I hear they're taking over whole towns in the Middle East and making the people there disappear overnight. It's terrible, but I know you'll beat them!"

My heart sank and stomach hurt upon hearing her say that. The ones responsible weren't the Infernals from Hell; they were me and my supposed other half, Gianluca. It all started with a woman's voice he had heard while in a coma after our recent battle against the forces of Hell. Since then he hasn't heard the voice or spoken of it, but still he searches, carving a path of destruction along the way.

We had defeated most of the remaining demons left over by Demon Lord Ma'al's invasion, but it didn't stop there. Gianluca continued silencing the chaos by slaughtering human terrorists in droves. It eerily resembled the legends of his ancient past, when he stalked the Earth conquering civilizations for the Infernal Kings that gave him his dark power until finally breaking free from being in their service.

"What would you do if someone you know was involved in that bad stuff though?" I asked.

"Well, when you love somebody it's up to you to stand by them and guide them on a path of light should they stray."

"I don't even know what love is outside of family. What if it's just somebody you care about?"

Gianluca was someone who meant a lot to me. Unfortunately, the feelings of falling in love had been slipping further away before they ever crossed that threshold of actually *being* in love. Our chemistry and attraction to one another were undeniable and even overwhelming at times. We managed to make plenty of good memories—like teaching him English—in between fighting for world peace but it wasn't enough to prevent all the blood he spilled from getting to me.

I had killed plenty of times. It was arguably justifiable, but I never felt good about it afterward. When I closed my eyes, my nightmares were tormented by fire and the faces of my victims. On the other hand, Gianluca seemed to revel in it.

Entire villages were engulfed by darkness that left only the empty shells of buildings. For him, every decapitation, every corpse crushed beneath his step were just testaments to his glory.

"We should all love each other, even our enemies. That's what the word of the Lord teaches us." I expected her to say something like that; it didn't solve my problem, but wasn't too far off.

The situation would have been much clearer if it wasn't that his victims were the bad guys. I wanted evil to lose, but not at the cost of losing one of our own to the bloodlust. Every attempt to dissuade Gianluca had failed. He understood that I didn't enjoy war like he did and made every effort to remove me from the frontlines, but that only made it worse. Instead of both of us fighting, he dove further into the carnage on his own.

I tried to be his other half by balancing his destruction with my own powers of creation. I have never been the philosophical type, but I had hopes that it would also bring balance between us and our effect on the world. My plan didn't last more than a few weeks at best. While I was floating in front of a pile of rubble and deciding the best way to rework the shattered remains of a military compound into homes for innocent civilians, Gianluca had already stampeded through two more besieged villages. I had no way of keeping up with his pace and as a result we had nothing to show the innocent that we were on their side and not another evil force vying for dominance over the last.

People grew scared as word spread of the creeping darkness. They didn't know if they would be next. My best friend Lyle—the leader of a military organization called PROJECT: UNITY that was tasked with keeping the peace between the supernatural and mortal world—was scared. Gianluca was unstoppable and nothing in their arsenal, or mine, could slow him down should the need arise like it had once before. I didn't want to discuss it with Lyle, partially out of embarrassment that I hadn't heeded the warnings I was given about this very thing happening. I also was never able to discuss it without being concerned that Gianluca would overhear. Every shadow was at his command to see, hear, and move through.

I was afraid.

I was afraid of the person that I should have been falling in love with. I was afraid of what he might do if he felt his allies were conspiring against him. I was afraid that the lines between good and evil would blur for him as his bloodlust increased, and that he would only see people as obstacles.

Most of all, I was tired of being afraid.

One thing became clearer with every night that passed: Gianluca had to be stopped. It had to be done carefully and without force; violence was pointless against him. Somehow, I had to get him to take a step back and look at what he was doing and what he might become again with his good sense overtaken by the thirst for battle.

There was one person I could always go to when I wanted insight into my problems, but he wasn't always the easiest to track down.

"Is Octavio around?" I asked Emily. "I haven't said hi to him yet and he's always got something interesting to say."

Octavio Jules—"Grampy"—might have seemed like a senile old undead coot, but his tidbits of clairvoyance were always accurate if you could figure them out.

"I think he's still playing hide-and-seek with Mia if you can find him."

"Oh good. That should be fun and take my mind off things." I stepped out into the hall, keeping all my senses on alert to help me see through Octavio's trickery. *Now where could that old codger be hiding?* Mia was usually easy enough to find so it might be better to start with her. The little imp had a habit of making her presence known with her mischievous ways. I couldn't blame her; being an immortal undead child and knowing you would never grow up had to be frustrating.

I was halfway down the freshly painted hallway admiring their choice in molding when a potted fern slid out of an opened room and turned a few times before stopping in the middle of the floor.

Well that was easy. "Hey, Grampy," I greeted the suspicious houseplant, which promptly transformed into the mangy lazy-eyed hobo I was looking for. He was quite a bit cleaner and lacking the pungent aroma that I had grown accustomed to.

"Welcome home, sonny," he said with a smack of his gums and licked his lips. "Yer not the lil' girl I was seekin', but a friendly face is a friendly face all the same."

"Excuse me? If you were doing the seeking why were you camouflaged? Badly."

"It's what's on the inside that counts!" I couldn't stop myself from staring at his new method of accessorizing by tying tin cans around his waist as a makeshift fanny pack.

"Yes, we're all special in some way. A very valuable lesson. Thanks."

"Verily."

"I came by to ask for your insight about something—"

"Would you like a candy?" he asked, noticing me still staring at his tin cans.

"No... definitely not," I tried to back away, but he took one from a can and shoved it into my hand.

"Anyway, my question is about someone I've been traveling with; big guy, Italian accent, controls darkness... Octavio this is just an empty wrapper." I looked down at the crumpled wrapper he had given me and in that moment he was already hobbling away as fast as he could.

"It's what's on the inside that counts!" he shouted back. I rolled my eyes and opened the candy wrapper to humor him when a chill set in and the light in the hallway faded into blackness.

As the light returned, a heavy ebony gauntlet rested on my shoulder from the shadows behind me. I looked down at the wrapper in my hand where only a single word was written inside: run.

Chapter One

I looked out over the rolling hills of sand where Gianluca had brought us through the shadows.

"Do you like it?" he asked.

"Like what?"

"This land is for you—to build. I think you do not like the ruin places so I make it clean for you."

"What was here before?" I inquired rather warily as a large flock of birds flew overhead.

"A city, but I conquer it in our name. Now you can make a new one, maybe... in the Roman style?" He smiled. It was difficult not to find the passion he had for his heritage endearing, along with his attempts to please. Yet there was so much more beneath the surface that didn't sit well with me.

"Are you sure everyone that lived here was all evil? Humans can change you know. Evil is a choice for them, unlike with demons. We were just supposed to set an example, not commit genocide—"

"No, we are to help the balance for good. There is still very much evil in this world to clean. I do this and you heal the land to give a new hope to the people." I turned in the air to survey the area.

"What does my little chick want to build first?" he asked as another flock of birds passed in the same direction as the last.

My reason for scanning the area wasn't to see what I had to work with—I was only half-interested in that because once Gianluca built momentum again I doubted it would make much of a difference.

My attention fell just outside of natural sight where voices mumbled to each other. I knew that other supernaturals were watching us from the edge of the shadows. I didn't know who or what they were; demons, undead, maybe something else entirely, but I knew that they were there and had been for some time—whenever I accompanied Gianluca on one of his crusades during the previous few months, in fact. He never seemed to notice though, and if he did, he never mentioned it.

I realized that the undead were most likely seething from all the attention we were drawing to supernaturals. Most of them worked hard at keeping their existence a secret, but there was little to nothing they could do to stop such an incredible force as the dark knight at my side.

If our watchers were Infernals taking a peek from the bowels of Hell, they may possibly have uttered words of praise. Gianluca and I had both been prime targets for the Kings of the Inferno to use as weapons of mass destruction on Earth. We may have slipped through their grasp, but did it matter when their work was already being done for them so willingly?

"Maybe it should be rebuilt to how the locals had it before. This is their land after all."

"No. This is yours," he argued.

"I don't want it."

Gianluca knelt before me and took my hand. "Little one, why does it not please you? There will be more. I promise the whole world if it make you happy."

"I don't want the world or any of this. We were supposed to be helping the locals take back their homes from terrorists, not taking their land for ourselves."

"To conquer is the greatest glory, it is always this way. But now I do this for you, for us."

"That's only going to cause more problems, Gianluca. Can't you see that?" We had been over this plenty of times and he always interpreted my disapproval as not wanting to do the fighting myself, or not having enough land to work with. Creating things was supposed to be fun and inspiring, but all I felt was despair.

"Why do you say Gianluca? Is always Gianni from you. You are angry with me?"

It was times like these I wished that *I* didn't see the bigger picture. I knew he must have seen it too; the fear being spread, the chaos being displaced rather than resolved. This wasn't a language barrier issue. Gianluca was far more worldly than I was, so much so that I began to think the conflict between us was more about him not respecting my opinion than not understanding it.

"I'm not angry. I'm worried you're doing more harm than good. I don't want to conquer, I don't want you to conquer. I want you to take a break and enjoy something else besides slaughter. Even if you're only killing bad guys, eventually there's going to come a time when you become one yourself...again."

He remained quiet for a moment before standing and putting his hands on my shoulders. "Okay. No more. I only want to make this world a good place like in my past when I am human."

"I know, but you can't force the world to change so violently or it'll change *you* first and it won't be for the better."

We were pulled back through the shadows as Gianluca returned us to the frigid north, to Greenland where PROJECT: UNITY had their base of operations. I spent most of my time there with Lyle and his co-commander Lisette Timmons discussing plans for the future of the organization. There were constant talks about how to handle the many supernatural threats in the world and the possibility of any apocalyptic scenarios that we had heard rumors of more than enough times.

Lyle wanted me to step up and be more of a leader, but despite all his words of encouragement that wasn't something I was comfortable doing. He did manage to bait me into speaking at some of our meetings after ignoring my threats of retaliation.

Lyle used to be a police officer for the NYPD. He was familiar with teambuilding situations and dealing with the public in an authoritative manner. I, on the other hand, used to feel that I was a nobody; an ordinary kid with extraordinary powers that never got the chance to do anything with his life aside from trying to survive on a day-by-day basis. Leadership wasn't in my nature. Still, Lyle thought my connection to the supernatural world was invaluable and each time he forced me to step up to the plate and take charge it became a little easier.

"Hey, man. You're back early," Lyle greeted me while Gianluca went back to our room to rest. We were in the new library that had been added on to the base after receiving a hefty donation from a wealthy ally. PROJECT: UNITY had some of the most advanced technology on Earth, stuff that most major governments could never even dream of, and the library was no exception.

"Yup, I think I was finally able to put a stop to things for a while."

The sleek ultra-modern aesthetic of white molded plastic and stainless steel that pervaded the rest of the base was just as prevalent in the library. There were thousands of physical books in various languages organized in rotating cubes that lined the walls. Finding what you were looking for was easy; all you had to do was go to any flat-screen terminal around the room and ask the artificial intelligence program PARAGON to illuminate the cube and shelf your book was on. Another innovative mechanism of the library was that digital books could be loaded onto tablet devices or projected anywhere in the room as three-dimensional interactive holograms from a wristband. The AI could cross-reference any word or phrase with millions of resources and create simulated images of them to make research effortless.

"What are you doing in here?" I asked him. "I thought you stopped pretending to read books after Rebecca dumped you."

"She didn't dump me. We agreed that it wasn't the best time to be working on a relationship right now."

"You sure it wasn't because you were rusty in bed?" I joked.

"No way. The sex is still on the table according to her," Lyle said, grinning. "Now stop trying to be funny and come check this out."

Lyle pointed to the tablet in his hand that he hadn't looked up from for more than a quick glance. "You know how the U.S. military along with their allies *and* their enemies have been crawling all over the locations in the Middle East wiped out by... *him*?"

"Yeah..." I knew he was referring to Gianluca vaguely on purpose.

"Now an entire city is gone, buildings and all. They saw the whole thing on satellite imaging like this one. The U.S. is moving in to check it out as we speak."

"I was just there."

"I know." Lyle showed me what he was looking at. It was a bird's eye view of me and Gianluca in the desert from a few minutes ago. Speaking of birds, those flocks that went by were missing from the video. Odd.

"I look good."

"Do you have any idea how bad this is, man? Even if we erase the evidence, a small *city* is missing. It was one thing when it was only some terrorists that both sides thought ran off during the night and we could hack the tapes and jam the live feed to cover up. Both sides thought the other had hackers that were blacking out surveillance so they could move from town to town unnoticed, but now there's not even a town left! They know you two are involved and something unnatural is going on." I watched the rest of the replay from moments ago. Right after we left the deserted sands, jeeps drove up with troops to start investigating.

"Can we get anyone to start erasing memories?" I asked. The undead coven called the Archios was usually on top of these situations.

"A *city* is *gone!*" Lyle restated. "What are we gonna do when they look on a map or go by there again? Get him to put it back!"

"There is no city to put back. You want to make a change, but you both are scared to make it." Gianluca approached from a darkening shadow in the corner that was the source of his voice. I jumped, but Lyle seemed more angered than nervous. I knew Lyle wanted everything to be in order before any big plays were made and right now the terrorists weren't the biggest threat to world peace, Gianluca was. It wasn't that we all didn't want human terrorism abolished, but doing it by supernatural means when the world isn't even officially aware of our existence would just cause more chaos many degrees of magnitude greater than anything the humans could do on their own.

"We're not scared," I said. "We're concerned you're taking this too far like I told you. The humans have solid evidence of our involvement now." I took the tablet from Lyle to show Gianluca, but he didn't care.

"Then I will go speak to them so they know there is no secret."

"That's a really bad idea," Lyle interjected.

"Why? These are just humans. They are skin and bones with toys trying to play a soldier. It does nothing to me. If they want to be a friend then we have no problem and I protect them too. No more hiding. You say this, Dorian, no?"

"Gianni," I switched to my term of endearment for him to hopefully appeal to his emotions and keep him from doing something else rash. "Taking on the world isn't the answer if they're acting out of fear. What about the other supernaturals who've been hiding for so long? Many of them are really powerful and have invested a lot in keeping secrets. Even if by some miracle the humans set aside their fears, which they're notoriously bad at doing, we'd still have the other supernaturals to deal with. We have to take things slowly."

"Then I go talk to them," he said. I sighed a silent breath of relief from his willingness to compromise. It would buy us plenty of time even for him to find all the supernaturals out there to consult with. "I will go to the Ancients. They can give the most help."

Dealing with the Ancients pretty much never worked out, but Gianluca always maintained some amount of faith in them. Maybe it was a basic level of respect, as he viewed them as being among the few who were his peers. I knew well enough by now that there was nothing the Ancients loved more than to twist everything to their benefit at the expense of everyone else. If I had to pick one that was worse than all the rest...

"First, we go to see Aurelia."

... it was her.

Chapter Two

Not far from the streets of Paris a winding road lays bare through a wooded grove. At the end of that road and further still, a copse thick with brush and pine obscures a paradise like none other known to Earth. Beyond this heaven's gates of wrought iron and roses lies Eden's envy, where a palatial chateau stands watch against the moonlit sky. Cloaked in beauty's angelic veneer, a wretched monarch resides inside the divine fortress of glass and gold.

"Can we maybe skip this Ancient and go to the next?" I asked Gianluca as the shadows cleared a path for us to the bustling ballroom where Aurelia de Saint-Pierre sat upon her throne in an extravagant lilac gown and watched the merriment with a look of general apathy. The warm candlelight radiating from the column-mounted sconces around the room did little to soften her expression.

I followed behind Gianluca as he strode through the parting crowd and up to the throne with confidence. He donned his shadow-forged armor, sans helmet, to show he meant business. I was always hopelessly underdressed whenever my adventures brought me around the Archios. I remembered the times of yesteryear when it actually mattered to me. Now I floated amongst the undead socialites in my jeans and hoodie without a care. It did make me miss the Outsiders' casual nature.

Gianluca addressed the brunette vixen on bended knee. In most cases, Gianluca's formality in these situations was endearing, but now I couldn't have rolled my eyes harder. Aurelia sprung to life, melting away that icy façade like a doll given breath with a touch of pixie dust. The two of them rose to greet each other like old friends and began to chat in Latin.

I cleared my throat and bluntly stated, "In English," to remind Gianluca I was still there and had no clue what they were saying. He turned and put his arm around my shoulder, bringing me up closer from behind him with an apologetic smile. I would have much rather preferred to stay where I wasn't so close to the Queen of the Archios coven. Even for someone like myself who was nearly immune to the telepathic effects of the undead, getting caught in Aurelia's spellbinding allure was enough to mess with your mind and bend your will to hers.

The two of us had hardly interacted with one another in the past, but it was still enough for me to despise her. In the beginning, I thought she was an ally, but her sweetness was only skin deep. When she was done needing assistance she ordered my execution, only to never follow through with it. I supposed I should consider that downright amicable in this world, but I was far from grateful. Her reputation of enslaving and torturing my friend and her servant, Noah, was enough for me to wish her dead.

"Can we speak more... alone?" Gianluca asked her, indicating the gala event that continued on around us.

"Certainly," she responded with a nod and the most pleasant smile imaginable. A soft clap of her dainty porcelain hands emptied the room in a breeze as her guests vacated immediately upon her command. "What wondrous fate brings you to me this night, Gaius? And in such a manner? There is no need for armor like that here. You might hurt someone more delicate than yourself if not careful with your touch." She placed a hand suggestively above her breast. I narrowed my eyes at her in displeasure, but then pushed out my disgruntled thoughts to avoid any possibility of her reading them for amusement.

"I come for your strength this day, not weakness," he said. I could feel her presence taking hold in intoxicating waves that even lowered Gianluca's eyes to where her hand rested.

Something in the shadows around the darkest edges of the room where the candlelight couldn't reach stirred, taking my attention off of

Aurelia momentarily. It didn't seem Gianluca was the cause.

"What could I possibly have of interest to someone as strong as you, Gaius?" she asked, again referring to him by his Roman name.

He left my side to approach her. With a finger he raised her chin so her eyes met his and said, "This beauty is enough." She feigned a coy expression and responded to him in Latin. That started the two of them whispering to each other. I wanted to throw something or bring the ceiling down on them both, but he soon stopped as if suddenly remembering they weren't alone.

"I will like your help with the humans," he told her and took a step back. "You know there is much trouble today in the world. Soon we have no more time for a party like here tonight."

"I do not measure the passage of time by man's transient civilizations, but by my own footsteps. The Archios will continue to dance even when man is no more."

"Why hide to dance?" Gianluca asked. "A queen so beautiful should be seen by the people."

Aurelia's face turned grim once more, not taking kindly to his questioning. "I hide from no one. My people gaze upon me in worship at every chance as you have seen here tonight with your very eyes. *I* do not retreat into the shadows, my dear knight."

"Hm, only this many people? I do not think it is very much for a queen." I had to hold back a laugh at his assessment of her underlings. I thought she would be fuming from such disrespect, but if she was she didn't show it.

"My kingdom is the Earth itself. My reign is eternal. My people countless. Do not try to manipulate me, Gaius. I will not tolerate such naughtiness in the presence of royalty." She wagged a finger at him playfully until he took her hand in his like he had done with me so many times. It was getting more and more difficult to stay silent.

"No, never. I wish what you do: to see this world ours again."

"What?" I finally spoke. This wasn't part of the plan, not that I was sure I knew what the plan was before this.

"The world has always been, and still is, mine," Aurelia laughed off his proposal.

"You do not fool me," Gianluca continued without acknowledging my interruption. "Your kingdom is more dark every day. The humans and monsters are at your door, for me too. Only you can control the humans though. Make them fall in love with your beauty again and I will make the monsters fall with my sword."

"Gianluca, can we talk about this...?" I tried breaking in again. *Encouraging* Aurelia to take over? He's completely lost it.

"I have been in control of mankind for centuries," said Aurelia. "They are of no cause for concern to me. I alone have held back the tide of our extinction at their hands. Their *cities* may crumble, but like a weed in my vast garden they will return only to fall under my heel again."

"It is not the human themselves," Gianluca said. "It is what they bring. Things much greater, even more than you: demons. Only you have this power, this beauty, to calm their soul and to control the minds."

"We're not trying to control the humans. We just want their memory of us erased at most," I spoke up in vain once more.

"Hell is beneath me for good reason. I do not fear the Infernal-kind any more than I do the worms that sift the dirt of my land," Aurelia said.

"They start to walk this Earth. You know this, yes? They will come for the strong soul in this castle. Only I think I can protect you if you will let me."

I would rather the demons got to her and then we deal with them after.

"And what would you have me do for this service, brave knight?" She traced a finger along the curves of his pauldron. "What of the others who would see me dead for such a righteous act as protecting the humans from themselves?" She looked straight at me over his shoulder, sending me into a daze. Clearly, she read my mind. Not that she needed to. It was probably quite obvious by the look on my face that I couldn't tolerate being around her.

"No one will touch you," he replied.

"No one?" She kept her eyes on me.

"No one. I promise to you." Gianluca's promise was punctuated with more movement in the shadows. At first, I thought it might have been Noah. I couldn't feel anything with my powers though and knowing him he would have wanted me to notice him if he was being this obvious. Maybe it was Gianluca, but it was rather odd behavior for him to randomly stir up the shadows during what was to be a peaceful conversation.

"Then, so be it. You will have the Archios' full support." Aurelia returned her attention to Gianluca and sat back down on her throne. "When the time comes I will assume command of those mortals who may seek to foil your plans."

"We will make a treaty for the good of this world; you, I, Dorian, and the other Ancient Ones. If they do not agree then it is my blade they answer to. But for the humans, they will know only peace. To help them is to help us."

"Absolutely," Aurelia agreed with a sincere smile. "You may think me indolent, or even cruel, for sitting upon this throne in quiet each night while the world weeps blood. But what you desire, I have already worked toward long before you opened your eyes for the first time.

"You are a brave and valiant warrior that speaks boldly with his sword, yet I am a queen whose sharpest weapon is her tongue that must be used with subtlety, lest it be cut from her mouth. My strength is only as great as my finest warrior and without the help of one such as yourself I fear a more significant change could not have been possible until now."

"Speaking of your finest warrior; where's Noah?" I asked. The way she was speaking I was beginning to worry something had happened to him.

When Aurelia saw that Gianluca was also waiting for a reply, she decided not to ignore me. "Running free in the wilds of Thailand, I suppose. You would know better than I." Free. An interesting choice of words to use for her slave, unless he somehow leveraged his freedom from her since we last spoke months ago.

I could see her not wanting to bother putting up a fight if someone posed an actual challenge like he would with his cursed sword, Muramasa. She did forget about the execution she ordered for me and Lyle, and all we had to do was escape back to New York. The once or twice I saw her after that was never an issue.

I didn't get a chance to ask any more questions. Gianluca sealed their agreement with a tender kiss to her hand and whisked him and I back through the shadows to our bedroom at PROJECT: UNITY. "What was all that about?" I asked him as soon as the darkness cleared.

"I do not understand?"

"You understand just fine," I snapped. "You acted like I wasn't even there. You went ahead and made a deal with that devil. You want her to *control* all the humans?"

"I see." He nodded and put his hands on my shoulders. "You are angry with me for the kiss. I tell you before only you are for me. This Ancient is one you must dance with to warm the cold heart. I still think you are the most beautiful, very much more than her. You know this."

"This has nothing to do with you being all over her!" *Not that it helped the situation either.*

"She should be destroyed, not danced with or made treaties with."

"The Ancient Ones must live or their soul will give great power to the demons. To destroy someone as her is not so easy with only a sword. Is better to make more ally than more enemy."

"I don't see why you can't just cut her head off and throw her into the Nether Realm."

"Her sister will bring her back and they will both make many more problem for us. A woman's revenge is worse than the fire of Hell. Two woman... I would not want to see."

"What are you talking about? Her sister is gone. You banished her to the Nether when she betrayed us." Aurelia's sister—Rozalin—used to be an undead like Aurelia, only she manipulated several of the covens to help her cheat death along with her necromantic powers and become a phantom of immense strength.

"She escape when I am weak after our fight in Hell. I know this and I see her in the castle tonight. The treaty I make is with both. They think I do not know, but there is nothing in the darkness I do not see." So it was Rozalin lurking in the shadows. I'm not sure which sister was worse, but at least with Rozalin there was no pretending that she wasn't a murderous psychopath. "You are so young. There is still many thing for you to learn about this world—"

I shoved away from him and pointed in anger, causing the plastic-coated room to tremble. "Stop treating me like a child! For someone who claims to only be a soldier you sure know a lot about playing politics."

An emergency alarm went off and the computer generated face that was PARAGON's avatar appeared on the terminal screen in the room. "Do you require assistance?" it asked.

"No!" I barked and hit the touchscreen harder than I should have to shut it off.

"I have seen many things and many people, little one. You need to trust me." *How could I trust him? How can I trust someone who doesn't respect me?* "I only try to make you happy, to heal this world from all the hate so we can have a peace."

"Of course," I resigned, knowing that this wouldn't be settled by force—verbal or otherwise. "Let's just go to bed." Whether or not his intentions were still pure, it was clear that I would have to find a way to stop this plan before it got any more out of control.

Chapter Three

Atop a mountain peak, nestled between the dire crags, once sat a castle of mythic splendor. Atop a mountain peak, once beyond a forbidden path, sat a castle whose spires once pierced the heavens. Atop this mountain's peak now sits the shell of a long forgotten grandeur. Atop this mountain's peak a castle sits more alive than ever...

"Why are we here?" I asked. It was a new night and for the first time in a while it didn't start out in the desert. We were in some sort of overgrown courtyard enclosed by high stone walls. Above and in the distance I could see flying buttresses lined with vultures watching us and towers rising up against the backdrop of a low hanging moon. "Where *is* here?"

"The mountains, little one. To visit a friend, the Carpathian."

"I don't have any Carpathian friends." The Carpathians were a savage, almost feral, coven of undead that lived in the appropriately named Carpathian Mountains throughout Eastern Europe. I didn't enjoy having to play nice with one of them recently and now looked forward to it even less than being in the company of Aurelia.

The Carpathians were responsible for a parasitic plague that threatened the population of Manhattan in their bid for world domination. They were also responsible for the death of my parents after infecting them to get to me. Both Ancients of their coven that I had known were destroyed, so I wasn't sure why we were here.

"Hm," Gianluca seemed puzzled once we were transported past the arched gate to enter the castle keep. There was no light except for the small amount provided by the moon through opened windows and damaged walls. He had no problem seeing in the dark though and I did rather well myself by feeling out my surroundings with my powers.

"What's wrong?" I asked. From the little I could see with my eyes it appeared as if this place had been abandoned and left in ruins centuries ago. Heavy gothic stone and ironwork was bent, broken, and in need of restoration. The old wood doors and furniture were rotted out and the entire building smelled of must and decay.

"It is so busy here. More than I think before we come." Gianluca was right. From the darkness came faint sounds of crawling and scratching on the stone. Dust occasionally fell from above from something moving along with an intermittent whooshing sound. This place wasn't as abandoned as it first looked.

"I do not know where to find our friend," he said and chose to continue on foot through the ruins instead of by shadow.

"Who?" I felt around for any roughly human shapes with my tactile-telekinesis, but the only objects even close were shattered busts and gargoyles.

"Vyrlakalos."

"That thing died—" I was halfway through my sentence when the ceiling above started to cave-in, giving me awful memories of our time in Hell when we were almost trapped for eternity.

The extra moonlight that poured in from the new holes in the high vaulted ceiling and walls showed what was making those sounds earlier. Between the cracks and crevices of the stone were veins growing like roots in the soil. They were pumping blood up to a gigantic mass that throbbed and twitched from its bony anchors.

A protective membrane slid back to unsheathe the pulsating monstrosity and allow a series of enormous fleshy petals to unfurl and reveal the emaciated torso of our "friend".

"I see now," said Gianluca. "It is not busy here like I think. Is the castle that moves, not many people in it. The castle *is* the Ancient too."

Four huge spindly hands and four equally large spider-like appendages came in from the windows around the room. They were attached to the main body through the openings in the ceiling. This whole castle keep was one big Carpathian.

"How are you still alive?" I asked. "I saw you turned into charcoal down in Hell."

"I tell you, little one; the Ancients are not so easy to kill," Gianluca answered.

"Your disappointment in my survival amuses me," Vyrlakalos hissed from its slavering maw. "I am omniscient. I am omnipresent. The body of mine you were so fortunate to have aid you was but a mere fraction of a more magnificent whole. Even what you see before you is but a piece of my great being." The floor heaved and sighed as tentacles slithered up between the stone.

It might not be fair to judge Vyrlakalos as harshly as I did. It, or "she" as some referred to her by, did make good on her end of the deal to help us in our mission to take down the demon lord in Iraq. It wasn't out of the kindness of her heart, however. As an exception to the rest of her normally dimwitted coven, she was well aware of the consequences to us all if demons were allowed to roam the Earth unchecked.

"You know why I come, Vyrlakalos," Gianluca said and approached her with the same confidence as he did with Aurelia. I, on the other hand, was preoccupied trying to float high enough away from the tentacles below but low enough to not be in reach of anything gross on the ceiling.

"I know all," she answered. "Your work in the desert lands has been... admirable... impressive even. But you hold back. You have concerns."

"My little chick has worry the chaos will spread out from fear even when the evil is killed."

"To be human is to be imperfect, chaotic. You must kill *all* the humans to achieve true peace. But then I would grow hungry and I will not allow that." One of the skeletal hands from the window came a bit too close, making me grab on to the back of Gianluca's armor. It wasn't easy to disgust me anymore, but Vyrlakalos was an exception.

"What if they are too sick to fight? The evil ones with a demon inside. Then I will not have to kill them. The humans will think is a natural thing. You can make a poison like this, yes?"

Asking a Carpathian to start biological warfare using weapons of mass destruction. Great.

"You insult my intellect, Dark One" Vyrlakalos shrieked. "A pox to strip this world of flesh would take only moments for me to concoct. Yet still you forget the matter of such petty grievances from those whom hope to prolong the arrival of the apocalypse with mind games and hiding like children. They will not let their precious herd be culled without meddling in my grand design."

"I will deal with the other Ancient Ones," Gianluca asserted. "The Archios agree to a treaty for this."

Vyrlakalos let out a horrid, sinister laugh that shook the keep along with her. "The impotent

Archios are of no concern to one such as me. They are meat for the slaughter. Should the paranoia-stricken Strigoi turn their magicked eyes toward me, however, there could be delays in our plan."

"Hm," Gianluca mused. "I will be sure they do not bother you."

"Gianni, this is a terrible idea," I whispered into his ear. On the other hand it sounded like an efficient way to get rid of any stray Hell-touched and possessed humans left over from Lord Ma'al's invasion. It could also deter more demons from taking it upon themselves to possess humans for a while too and give Gianni a reason to stop the slaughter while trying to find them himself.

"We only make our enemy sick to weaken them so they cannot fight." He patted my hand still on his armor and whispered back. "Then no more will join them and they will focus on a healing not war. This is better than so much killing, no? The good humans will not look for us if they do not think it is supernatural."

"I guess." It wasn't *much* better, but he was starting to make a change in the right direction. I had to assume that this would quickly spiral downward when the disease spread to innocent people unless we had a cure ready.

"There is another matter," Vyrlakalos hissed again. "I have tasted the humans' technology. They have the means to harness the sun in the form of weapons. This could be... troublesome should they wish to eradicate the lepers."

"You mean nuclear missiles," I said. "Yeah, I could see that being a little bit of a problem."

"Oh, if only a little then we will not worry for now," said Gianluca.

"I was being sarcastic. I don't think *any* of us could live through one of those. Once one country starts using them, they all will until nothing is left. There will be no more Earth. It'll be a wasteland of death and radiation—bad stuff."

"Only few have access to such weaponry," Vyrlakalos said. "It will be easy enough for even the incompetent Archios to see them eliminated."

"You would trust the Archios with that power?" I asked, hoping to cause some dissent before this plan could get underway.

"Those sniveling cowards would destroy themselves before they could do true harm to me. They pride themselves on living amongst mankind. They have known of these weapons before even I, yet they are too clumsy and arrogant to think to use them."

"I will come when it is time for your poison," Gianluca told Vyrlakalos. "First, I go be sure no one will interfere."

"Your plan amuses me. My pestilence will be made available to you when you seek it. But do not fail me, for even the darkness cannot contain all that is The Old One of Boundless Flesh."

Gianluca and I returned to base having closed out our second diplomatic endeavor in two days. I wrestled with what limited options I had to deal with what was about to happen. I wished I could have talked with Lyle in more depth about this, but still I couldn't trust that Gianluca wouldn't find out and go even more over the edge.

The Ancients were vain beasts that all loathed each other. In my short time dealing with them, I realized how they all survived for so long despite their hatred for one another: they kept their distance. They didn't try to eliminate one another like they did their other obstacles. The most the Ancients did was make meager passive-aggressive attempts at disrupting the others' efforts.

This plan of Gianluca's relied on the fact that the Ancients believed he would do whatever was necessary to keep everyone away from one another. Either they believed he was idealistic enough to really be fighting to save the world, which would benefit them, or they believed it was all a ruse and they wanted to ensure their survival by playing along.

I could try to get them to distrust Gianluca, but I didn't want them to hurt him. I still felt that Gianluca wasn't doing this out of evil intent, but rather was employing a heavy-handed approach at world peace that came natural to someone who prided himself on being a warrior. I had to get the Ancients to hate each other so much that they would try to sabotage the plan and take the focus off of the humans.

I sucked at subterfuge, but I knew it was a necessary life skill for the supernatural. I didn't see any other way so I had better learn fast. First, I needed to bide my time until an opening presented itself.

"You are so quiet," Gianluca observed, breaking into my inner monologue and petting my cheek from his place next to me in bed.

"Sorry, I'm just tired."

"I let you take a rest." He kissed my forehead and turned down the lights before leaving the room. I waited twenty—maybe thirty—minutes before I also got up to leave. I checked the PARAGON terminal in the room first to track where Lyle was. A map appeared showing him upstairs in the common area so I headed straight there.

I floated down the softly glowing cerulean halls. Everything here was built with improving the human condition in mind, and the walls were no exception. Behind the translucent plastic paneling was a lighting system that changed with the time of day, emitting a frequency to either facilitate relaxation during the nighttime or to help energize someone in the daytime.

I was turning the corner to bring me to the central atrium when a tiny colorful bird whizzed past my head and straight up to the top floor.

"Excuse me! Mister!" A woman called from ahead. "Can you help me?" She held up a bird cage as she ran over. I remembered her from some of the recruits from Nigeria. I think she was on the research team, or maybe it was medical. "I was cleaning the cage when the little thing flew off on me! I know we aren't allowed to have pets outside our rooms, but please don't tell the commanders."

"Um, okay. No problem." I didn't really understand the no pet rule. They had brought werewolves on base before. What was a dog or a cat going to do that was any worse?

I flew up to find the canary, which wasn't hard with all the cheeping. It sat perched on the railing around the elevator and as soon as I got near, flew right into the cage I was given.

"Here you go," I said, returning the caged bird down to its owner.

"Oh, thank you! I don't know what got into her. She's never done that before. Now to go hide her back in my room before I am reported!" She smiled and ran off with as much energy as her feathered friend.

I continued on until I found Lyle in the common area with a bunch of PROJECT: UNITY members crowded around a big screen TV playing video games.

"Hey, I need to talk to you," I said.

"Go for it," he responded in a daze without taking his eyes off the screen.

"I meant in private." The game was so loud I almost had to scream over it.

"'Kay, just give me a minute."

"You're playing a fighting game where two superhumans beat each other up. You see that almost every day in real life." He wasn't listening so I sat on the floor next to the couch and waited. I started to use my powers to break the rocks at the base of one of the potted trees into cubes and spheres when I looked up and saw the tiny bird from earlier popping up and down the branches. It was a good thing the TV volume was so loud that no one could hear it chirping.

I got up to see if its owner was around, but the woman was nowhere in sight. I checked to make sure that Lyle was still in a trance so I could return the bird without getting anyone in trouble, but when I turned around it was gone. I went back to the atrium and searched for it until the shadows converged around me.

"What are you doing out here, little one? I look for you in bed."

I guess I wasn't going to be speaking to Lyle alone after all...

Chapter Four

Across an emerald meadow down a lazy country road... Where dreams now shattered drift along on whispers old... An English garden nature claims guards a sleeping manor far from tame... Where shattered dreams caution of a waking madness within. A nightmare slumbers, now the veil grows thin.

"How do you know Castile?" I asked Gianni upon arriving at Castile's Somerset estate the next night. The last time I was here the mansion had sustained heavy damage during a battle with a spirit that was pursuing Noah and I. Castile was presumed dead as a result, but I had strong suspicions that it wasn't true and it looked like I was right.

The elegant abode appeared as pristine as the day it was built and the fresh candlesticks burning inside the window told us someone must be home. Aurelia's own chateau had needed repair several times due to supernatural occurrences and it was always meticulously restored almost overnight as if by magic. I knew that wasn't the case with her however; she simply commanded her pawns to make the necessary restorations even if it meant enslaving an army of witless humans.

Castile was another story all together. I don't know if I would call it magic or illusions of the mind, given his aptitude with telepathic powers. It seemed as if he projected whatever was in his memories around him down to the very last detail. But when taking something from this lucid dream world out of the area, it faded as if it had never existed to begin with.

"I know many of the Ancient Ones," Gianluca answered. "There is nothing I cannot find in the darkness."

Out of all the Ancients, Castile Belanger was by far the easiest to deal with. He could be a tad off-putting from his overly stiff and polite mannerisms, but was still someone I would much rather be with as opposed to Aurelia or Vyrlakalos.

That's it!

Castile hated Aurelia with a passion. There's no way he would be involved in anything that was to her benefit. He was one who could read my mind too so I might not even need to say a word for him to know my plan.

We approached the walnut doors of the Elizabethan mansion, for once not taking a path through the shadows directly inside as we had on our other two visits. "Maybe... you wait here," said Gianluca with his hand on the door handle.

"I survived Vyrlakalos. This is a vacation by comparison." *Did Gianluca know what I was up to? He couldn't read minds, but if he knew Castile could then maybe he was worried that our recent disagreements would complicate diplomacy.*

The door swung open.

"Come in, come in!" an elderly maid ushered. "Don't get caught in the rain. It would be rude to track water through the house. Master Belanger must not be kept waiting."

"It isn't rain—" I started, but as soon as the door closed behind us the maid vanished into thin air and a storm began outside.

"Good evening, gentleman," the polished Englishman in his Victorian finest welcomed us from a seat in the parlor where he sipped his tea. There were no other servants around like the last time I was here—not that they were anything more than some sort of illusion anyway. I felt around the room with my powers, but it all seemed real enough.

"I come with news," said Gianluca.

"News would imply it to be something *new*, would it not? But, I already know why you are here."

"Then I come with an offer for friendship," Gianluca tried again.

"You do not *offer* friendship, you build one. Is that not true?" Castile directed his question toward me with a stare that pierced right through my soul. He set down his teacup on the saucer so gently there was hardly a clink of the china touching.

I felt bad for Gianluca who was struggling to speak in English and wasn't dealing with someone about to pretend to be wooed as Aurelia did. "He wants to make an alliance," I said, coming to Gianluca's aid against my original intentions.

"Ah. When one seeks cordial relations it is common decency to tread lightly in tongue and foot. Your purpose is betrayed by coming dressed for war." Castile's honey-colored eyes glowed in Gianluca's direction, changing his shadow armor into his usual casual attire: a black pinstripe button-down, half unbuttoned, with matching slacks and shoes that he had copied from an advertisement he saw in Italy.

Gianluca appeared just as surprised as I was that someone was able to affect the darkness only he was thought to control.

"Don't be too startled. You are in my world," said Castile. "Come, sit and discuss what you will with me now that you are properly dressed."

"Go outside," Gianluca said to me without turning his head so he could keep his eyes on Castile.

"There's no need for that," Castile retorted. "He is in no danger. Not that it would matter much. My domain does not end at the door. Besides, you wouldn't want him waiting out in the rain, would you? That would make me a most ungracious host and I would not allow it. I have a reputation of civility to uphold."

I was beginning to feel a little on edge. The Castile I remembered wasn't so aggressive. Maybe it wasn't a good idea that I had insisted on coming.

"There is a war with Hell coming," Gianluca said without taking Castile up on his offer to sit. I stood by him, unsure now of how I could steer this back on track.

"Yes, the cycle of apocatastasis that you started ahead of time. Or maybe right on time, depending on your perspective, I suppose." Castile fiddled with the fireplace trying to light it and mumbled to himself, "I'm still no good with starting this thing." He extended a hand out to beckon someone over who wasn't there a moment ago. Another maid appeared from empty space like a ghost, only quite solid, and lit the fireplace for him. He thanked her and she excused herself from the room where she disappeared once around the corner when I checked.

The fact that this was probably all coming from his imagination made it even more unsettling.

"You know this war will come," Gianluca continued. "It is better when we are in control."

"And by 'we' you mean to include me in this alliance with the Archios?" Castile asked. *He already knew, or did he read my mind from outside?*

"Yes. We have a same enemy."

"My enemy *is* the Archios or, more specifically, that rotten whore of a queen they worship. It would do you well to know whom you speak with before offering an alliance. That two-pence courtesan is responsible for the death of my beloved."

Ha! This is perfect. Now if only he'll help me dismantle this plan and maybe Aurelia along with it.

The parlor lighting changed from a warm hue to cold grayscale. I thought I had gone severely colorblind and then the wallpaper started to peel up the walls and the rug beneath us sizzled into charred embers. Under the exposed floorboards fire licked at our feet and the rain outside the window stopped in midair.

"I know you," Gianluca said, unfazed. "I need the Archios for the humans, but only you can watch the Archios, most important: Aurelia."

The room reverted back to its comfortable glow, returning along with the wallpaper and rug as suddenly as they had vanished. "Well, you should have spoken up sooner," Castile stated calmly and refilled his teacup from a pot that was not there before. "It isn't polite to prattle on when there are such serious matters at hand."

"Then you will help us?" Gianluca asked. "No more of this, this dream. You cannot hide here in this forever."

"This is no dream, my good man. My mind plucks delicately at the strings of time and space to weave a reality to my liking. I think one where that slovenly wench's reign ends is about due, don't you?"

"I have no wish to harm anyone who help save this world," Gianluca said. "This is our survival. All our protection is my word. I will not see her make you hurt either." He was trying so hard. I was having doubts about my own plan to sabotage his.

Castile stared at the ceiling with his eyes glowing again. "What would the gods have me do, hm? My eyes are opened."

"Castile, is there any way you can keep watch on the Archios so they don't totally take over?" I asked. "I'd imagine no one on the outside knows them as well as you. I think Gianluca wants someone as a system of checks and balances. Someone powerful enough not to be swayed by them... or killed."

"Yes, for the balance," Gianluca agreed, happy that I got his point across for him. This might be the best outcome I could hope for at the moment.

"A watcher...sees faces where there are no traces, listens to words lost to time, messages found in rhyme," Castile recited, still staring at the ceiling with intent. "The call is strong. I hear your voice."

"Uh, okay, so that's a yes?" I asked. He was reminding me of the way Octavio acted at times. The walls around us faded from sight as the maids had. The entire mansion was gone, leaving us outside in the garden with Castile in his chair fixed on the full moon.

"I see the light of yesterday now here tomorrow. I see what I must do," he said and disappeared. Rainy night turned to clear day before our eyes, replacing the pale moon with blinding sunlight. It was early evening when we had arrived. We weren't in there that long.

Birds sung their morning song from trees and statues covered in vines, watching their brethren pluck breakfast from the dirt at our feet. Gianluca's armor returned, not by his usual command with swirling shadows but with the same fading effect as from Castile's reality.

"I wanna go home..."

"Life was more better in Roma," Gianluca sighed after almost an hour of silence while watching cooking shows in Italian in our room. We had spent a better part of the day listening to Lyle have a legitimate panic attack over the situation in the Middle East. I shared his worries but also felt disconnected from the human side of things while I focused on the supernatural side.

To think that I could look back at all the battles I had fought and find them less demanding than navigating these flimsy truces. Against my disdain for fighting, being immolated was easier to endure than faking peace with Aurelia and that was saying something. Worst of all was scheming against the person you shared a bed with.

Until today everything was relatively business-as-usual while the governments involved with investigating the mysterious disappearing city were busy scratching their heads. Rumors began to spread though, as they always did, but with a twist. The officials were fixated on pointing fingers at each other rather than suspecting the more "obvious" supernatural cause.

So far, the current most popular theory was that either the U.S. or Russia developed some sort of small scale underground traveling nuke, or "sand torpedo", tested it on the unsuspecting city at night, and then carted away or buried the aftermath. Both sides also swore that they had solid evidence implicating the other. The human imagination scared me almost about as much as Castile's. Gianluca remained confident that Aurelia could clean this up, but she had better hurry.

"I'm sorry," I said with genuine feelings of sympathy for his struggle. "I have to be honest... I don't trust this plan. The world is *different*, not better or worse. Humans can't be controlled and intimidated like in the past. There are too many and they're too strong as a group. Maybe I don't know as much about war as you do, but I know this world and I know we can't change it using old methods."

"The world is the same, just more difficult now. When is many little pebble or a one big rock on the road, it still must be moved. This does not mean you do a different thing to fix it."

"We're dealing with a lot of people's lives though, including our own."

"I know this."

"And the Ancients..."

"I do not like them much, but is good to make the enemies work for you as friends even for a short time."

"Castile is the only one I would begin to trust at all and even he's not what I had thought."

"That madman wears the sheep's clothes," said Gianni. I laughed. He smiled. And for the first time in a month the knot in my stomach loosened just a bit.

"What are you planning on doing about Vyrlakalos?" I asked. She was slightly more trustworthy than Aurelia and Rozalin; at least she kept her word when helping us during our last battle and then returned to solitude. However, I knew the Carpathians despised mankind, and giving one as powerful as her the chance to inflict misery and sickness on a small population of the possessed could be seen as too tempting to show restraint.

"I see if the Strigoi have that answer." The Strigoi were a coven of undead sorcerers, some of whom were responsible for my creation as a living weapon and subsequent involvement in the supernatural world. They had used a combination of forbidden rituals and advanced gene manipulation to create me and several others to serve them. That plan fell through and many of them died when they tried capturing me so since then they had decided it best to leave me alone.

I had never met a Strigoi Ancient before though. The coven itself was secretive and generally cowards that hid from everything, even if an argument could be made that their magic gave them a significant advantage over most opposition.

"Are you trying to get the Ancients to kill each other off so we won't have to?" I asked. "First Castile and Aurelia, then the Strigoi after Vyrlakalos specifically mentioned that they could give her trouble."

Were both our plans the same all along? Were my thoughts of deception unnecessary? Now I was starting to feel guilty for plotting to conspire against him.

"Is for balance like you say. On my honor I will not let any do harm to the other, but they must know there are reasons to cooperate. If they feel the danger, they will not be so quick to betray. To see your enemy when you cannot hide from them is when people are very willing to make a peace.

"The Ancient Ones feel safe because they hide. They think they are *invictus*, they cannot be stopped, but we all have a weakness."

Let the Ancients keep each other in check like they have been for centuries and bait them into using their specialties to protect the Earth by appealing to their egos and need to survive. He's kept his word and hasn't lifted his sword since this started either. *Maybe I shouldn't have doubted your ability to make this work after all, Gianni, but I'm still reserving judgment for now.*

Chapter Five

Betwixt the wyrd and wilds in a distortion of space and time, exists a microcosm, a fragment of man's mind. A realm of magic all its own where deep within reigns the eldritch throne. The scholars toil by silver moon. They hide their sins, they ignore their doom.

"Hm, I think I make a mistake," Gianni said as we peered out from the shadow world onto Earth. The shadow world—or Nether Realm—went by many names. It was a dimension of total darkness that connected to every shadow in existence and from which Gianni drew his power. Much like the other dimensions I had been to, it didn't follow the same rules of reality. There was no light, yet we could see each other perfectly; there was no air, yet we could speak just fine.

At the moment, we were looking out at somewhere in Munich, skating through the shadows to find the Strigoi's sanctuary, also known as an *arcanum*. They tended to fester underground, in repurposed and reinforced military bunkers and abandoned sewers for maximum security and seclusion, but Gianni was adamant that they were right here above ground in the heart of the city. It wasn't like him to have this much trouble finding people and places though.

"We've been at this for a while," I said. "Maybe we should pull over and ask for directions."

"I can almost hear the voices. They are here. I know it."

"All I hear are cars and pedestrians speaking German. How do you know what the Strigoi sound like specifically?"

"Because the voices is not here or out there. It is in some other places, another world maybe." I would have tried to convince him to give up if we didn't now need the Strigoi Ancient to keep Vyrlakalos in check.

I had some degree of rapport with one of the Strigoi. Vance was one of those responsible for not only creating me but also saving my life when I had become infected with a soul-eating parasite. Most of the time, only genuine threats led him to pull his nose out of a dusty tome and do something helpful. But I knew there was a tiny semblance of humanity left in that cold, undead heart.

When I last saw him he had sent his apprentice here before coming to help with a plan to defeat Lord Ma'al. He had snuck off again once the job was done, so presumably he would be here and could help mediate things.

"Here. I find it," Gianni announced.

"That's a manhole cover! I told you to check underground!"

"Shh, no. Is between like I say." The cover was partially paved over, but Gianni was right. We weren't going underground, not completely. Between the layers of road, between the pavement and the sewer ceiling, was a shadow we traveled that kept expanding until we were in another world entirely. "You see? Victory for Gianluca! Where there is the dark I always find the way."

"Good job, Gianni." I smiled.

"Oh, I am Gianni again?" He smiled back. "Very nice."

We left the shadows behind to enter a desolate and gloomy mid-eighteenth century city. The cramped buildings here were a hybrid of colonial and Dark Ages architecture with heavy wrought iron and gargoyles guarding delicately styled brick and wood. The gothic features here were much more intricate in their design than the crude version present in Vyrlakalos' castle.

There were no lights on in any of the houses and only a few of the oil streetlamps along the cobblestone road were lit, but we could see clear as day from the giant moon coming up over the horizon.

In the distance a warped version of the *Frauenkirche* cathedral loomed over the city where

Gianni pointed. "There," he said. "But I do not hear the voice of them anymore."

"They must know we're here by now." I kind of wanted to explore the rest of the city. It was one of the more interesting places I had been that wasn't full of things trying to kill me. The only inhabitants of any kind that had made themselves known so far were a murder of crows lining the streetlamps.

"Something is wrong here," Gianni said as the sky rippled like water. He grabbed me and pulled us through the shadows and into the cathedral-like arcanum.

Any surface not covered by mystical scrolls and scriptures was filled with lit candles of varying sizes and years of melted wax built up around them. Where pews would be stood multistory bookcases brimming with arcane knowledge. Statues of religious figures in alcoves were instead replaced by whom I could only assume were high-ranking members of the Strigoi.

"No one's home." I floated through the bookshelves trying to read some of the literature, but it was all in some eldritch language. "Knowing the Strigoi they probably ran off scared when we invaded."

A strange altar of inanimate tentacles lined with eyes was erected on a wooden stage at the head of the room. It was far too tall for a normal-sized person to read from, if it was reading material meant to be placed on top.

"I do not think so." Gianni bent down and put his fingers to the floor. "Ash. Much of it. Come, we must hurry."

We rushed through a dark corridor that exited out to the right behind the altar. There were so many ways to go at each intersection, each of which seemed to loop back around until Gianni found a way to bring us through a wall and cheat the endless maze.

"Wait! That's Heather, Vance's apprentice," I said when we got to the next room. She was just leaving through another doorway as we got there, but I recognized her rather out of place formal collegiate attire that clashed with the robes and tunics of most Strigoi.

The room was in shambles. Only shattered desks and bookcases remained with papers strewn about the mess. Torn vestments similar to what Vance wore were caught on the doorframe.

"Heather, wait! Where's Vance? What happened here?" I shouted as I chased after her down a flight of stairs and into a crypt.

"He's gone," she said, stopping with her back to me in front of five stone sarcophagi mounted in the wall. Above them were stained glass portraits of who must have been in each.

"What happened?" I asked with Gianluca appearing by my side.

"I killed him."

"What?! How? You're just a—"

She held her hand out to the side.

It glowed. Green.

Then it ignited in flames. Green flames.

The flames of hellfire.

She looked over her shoulder at me with a smile as the back of her blazer ripped open revealing a pair of crimson bat wings. Her auburn hair turned gray and curved horns sprouted from the sides of her skull. "There is no Heather. There never was," she said in a different, but familiar voice when her eyes changed to bright red with vertical slits for pupils.

"You..."

"A demon? Here? How?" Gianni asked. "This is not Hell."

"How observant," she sneered and turned around. Her transformation was complete and there was no mistaking who she was now: Minerva.

Minerva—Vance's aunt and former Strigoi herself—was the reason for my creation. She tricked the arcanum of Strigoi she ruled as archmage into thinking that the experiment was to protect their cowardly hides during the inevitable apocalypse, when in fact she had planned all along to use myself and the other results of the project as the perfect vessels for the Infernal Kings. Demons were unable to survive on Earth—the atmosphere was toxic to them—they required a vessel to possess. The stronger the demon, the sturdier the vessel needed to be to contain their power. The Ancients would have seemed to be the perfect receptacle except for their fatal flaw to sun or holy light.

"The ambient magic in these arcanums was just barely enough for me to harness so I could keep that pathetic body in one piece at the cost of restricting my power to a mere sliver." She flapped her wings and took flight to look down her nose at us.

"Where is the Ancient One?" Gianni asked and pointed his sword at her.

"You're looking at what's left of the fool." She nodded to the empty sarcophagi lined with ashes. "Vojislav thought he could split his soul into five separate bodies to hide from notice since each piece would appear weaker than the whole. It didn't take long for someone of my intellect to track down those missing from here and send them all to Hell. One Ancient down, four to go."

"What makes you think we're gonna let you? I've already sent you back to Hell twice and I'm stronger now."

"Oh, yes! Save the world. Quiet the chaos, right? You're doing such a splendid job of it too. The mortals are in a frenzy and you think killing a few rotten eggs will calm all this down and make our Infernal host just give up.

"Please. Even with Lord Ma'al's power you are still an insect and a failure."

"What are you talking about?" I asked. "Ma'al is dead, lady. We killed him for good and if I have to hunt you down in Hell to stop you from coming back myself I'm more than happy to do it."

"Dead, yes, but to say *usurped* may be more accurate. The Ma'al you know may have been defeated, but lives on in you along with billions of other souls."

"Enough of this!" Gianni shouted. He went to attack, but I stopped him.

"Wait. I want to know what she's talking about."

"You think this 'great power' of yours is helping save innocent lives?" she laughed.

"Just tell me what you mean!" I yelled and tried to attack her with a telekinetic push. The force reflected off of a barrier surrounding her and back into me, throwing me into the wall with a brutal crunch.

"Did you think I wouldn't be prepared for something like that? I *made* you," she laughed again until Gianni bound her in darkness and put the tip of his sword to her throat. "My, yes, the knight. Another mass murderer looking for redemption through damnation. The Infernal Kings send their regards. They are pleased to find the chaos you spread in your wake is everything they had hoped for."

Gianni believed that he defeated the Infernal Kings centuries ago, or rather the Nether Lords we think they posed as when turning him into their instrument of destruction. Lord Ma'al mentioned them being one and the same, but Gianni had dismissed it when I told him.

"Tell me what you meant about Ma'al and the others!" I screamed after having peeled myself from the wall and healed my broken bones.

"My nephew spared your worthless life by merging you with that soul-eating parasite from the Rift you were infected with years ago, but did he forget to tell you that the ritual never severed the connection with the Rift itself?"

"No, I knew that. It's what made me immortal. So what?"

"Are you that blind? You *are* the parasite now. Your powers, your immortality, your regeneration all draw from the Rift now that you have been made one. You are absorbing the power gathered by the other parasites that travel countless worlds looking for souls to feed their native dimension.

"The Rift is a void. It has no ambient energy or elements like other dimensions and needs to draw on the raw power of souls to fuel itself and the creatures there so it does not collapse. The parasites were made for this task. They are harvesters. Only now there is a new part of the equation: You.

"All those souls taken from endless worlds and other dimensions that the parasites drain funnel into you. Whether innocent like your parents, or not, like Ma'al when they were infected. You aren't just taking spare energy out of thin air like channeling a lightning bolt. You are doing the very same thing that all demons do: devour souls for power."

"NO!" I yelled. "You're lying!"

"I don't have to. Why do you think Hell has not retaliated against you for destroying one of their most infamous lords? You have taken up his mantle whether you realized it or not. Even this pathetic creationism ideal you have is just building over a graveyard with more spilled blood! Exactly what Lord Ma'al was known for.

"You should be thanking me. When I struck you with hellfire during our last encounter it crippled your soul, weakening you significantly. Ma'al must have done the same, as I can see the aura of your soul and notice your growth has been stunted compared to what it should be. If left unchecked, I delight to imagine how many souls you would need to reap to feed your full potential!

"In just a few years you have probably erased more innocent life from existence than your precious dark knight has in centuries!" she cackled. "And let me tell you, it is a far more painful death to die from the parasite than it is suffocate in the shadows. You are working out wonderfully for your intended purpose as a weapon of chaos after all! You may be my greatest failure, but even my failures give merit to my great genius!"

Gianni went to swing his sword across her neck when she exploded in smoke and vanished into a glowing pentagram on the wall. Her laughter echoed throughout the crypt.

"This whole time I was trying to do the right thing and everything I did was just the opposite."

"She is a demon, it is all lies." Gianni put his arms around me.

"I don't think so," I said. "I think part of me knew that it was a possibility, but I never sat down and thought about it. I was more comfortable in believing what was convenient to get me through each day; that it was some magical energy reserve I was drawing from—or only the energy from that *one* parasite I was merged with—not that I was actively depriving people of life."

"You are still good. This is a choice, remember?"

"But, it doesn't matter what I choose. Even just sitting here, my immortality comes from other people's demise. What's the point of saving a city if it takes the sacrifice of a planet?"

"We do not know how much souls it takes for this. Maybe only one gives you many powers. You take the demon lord soul and that is very strong, maybe it gives you power for a long time to save other people."

"I have no way of knowing and that's just as big a problem..." And to think, before this I thought that Gianni was the one we'd have to worry about. "I should've been dead so many times by now. I'm only alive because of other people's involuntary sacrifices."

"Just do not use your powers much until there is a big purpose. Everything in life needs each other to live. Animals eat other animals, and humans eat those animals, and the undead drinks their blood. You do not need to eat the food because you are immortal, but you need the energy from something so you can be strong to protect this world."

"I...I don't know. When I became immortal I worried that in the future I wouldn't have any purpose to my life when everything settled down, but now that just changed. Then I looked forward to having nothing to do when all I did was fight. Now I feel like if I'm not doing something every single second and making the most of my energy I'm sacrificing innocent people with no reason."

"That is life, even if you are mortal. Only the mortals do not pay attention to what is sacrifice for them every day."

Chapter Six

"Is it safe to assume that this Minerva is a credible threat to the other Ancients and therefore, ourselves?" Commander Timmons asked.

Back at PROJECT: UNITY I had Lyle call a meeting with as much of the base as was available to discuss what was happening and offer some transparency into the supernatural side of our problems. This was out-of-character for me. Public speaking made my hands sweat although I did know pretty much everyone here. But if there was ever a time to suck it up and get over it, now was it.

We gathered in the atrium with everyone looking over the railings that circled the several floors above. PARAGON screens around base televised the meeting for those who couldn't see. I had told Lyle everything—except what I had learned about myself—ahead of time so he could do most of the talking, but the questions kept getting directed back to me. Gianluca was present in body, but absent in mind. It was clear that he was troubled by the latest developments and his thoughts were thousands of miles away.

"Yeah—I mean yes," I said. "The plan was to have them help us calm the public, conceal our presence to the officials, and neutralize the chaos caused by the terrorism threat the possessed humans pose by making it look like natural causes, like Ebola, or malaria, or something else I guess.

"Even if they aren't going to help us, we don't want them dying because their souls will give a lot of power to the kings, enough that they would send someone like Minerva to go fetch them. Right now the Ancients are the lesser but necessary evil."

"A lot of this activity from Hell increased after one of the Carpathian Ancients died due to the actions of Minerva during the parasite plague in Manhattan," said Lyle. "Now they have another Ancient's soul from this Strigoi we never got to meet so we should expect things to get even crazier."

Gianni left through the shadows without saying anything. Lyle gave me a look but I didn't know any better. "We need to start protection detail for the remaining Ancients," Lyle continued.

"I don't mean to sound like this, but how do you plan on protecting Ancients that are more powerful than entire human armies?" I asked.

"They're more vulnerable during the day but we're not. You and I took down Ma'al—*in Hell.*" There were some cheers in the crowd from those who were part of the team back then.

"I don't want to lose anyone," I said. "We've already lost Vance..." It didn't quite hit me until now that he was gone.

It wasn't like Vance and I had a close friendship or anything like that, but he had become a sort of constant in my life that was often severely lacking in stability. Vance had saved me in the past by betraying Minerva and risking his life to do it. He was our problem solver and involved in most, if not all, of our victories through the years in some way. The more I thought about it the more it started to hurt.

"How many Ancients are there?" Timmons asked.

"Four if we're counting Rozalin, who's with Aurelia," I said.

"You and Gianluca can take one location each, our troops will take the third," said Timmons. "As long as this Minerva can't be in more than once place at a time, Gianluca can transport you two to where she shows up. Demons can only last a very short time on Earth without a host vessel so even if we can't beat her we can stall her out fairly easily I should think."

"Sounds good," Lyle agreed. "She wasn't so tough back in New York. With all this firepower the balance is even more in our favor."

"I wouldn't get too cocky," I said. "She still killed two Ancients and took their souls without any trouble."

"Yeah, but we were trying to kill the Carpathian one too back then and didn't know what we were dealing with. It's a totally different game."

"What defense do any of us have against hellfire?" I asked. This would be where we would hunt down Vance for a solution. "It's instant death to mortals and most supernaturals."

"The Blackbournes have that demon leather armor that protected Owen from it when we invaded Lord Ma'al's lair," Lyle said. The Blackbournes were an organized crime family of skilled hunters that preyed on supernaturals across England. As a group, they were some of the finest megalomaniacs and sociopaths the mortal world had to offer, but we were able to make nice with a couple of them by appealing to their lust for blood sport.

"Get in touch with him and see if he can locate a few more sets of armor," I told Lyle. Owen Blackbourne was a professional boxer and MMA fighter that joined the family in his teenage years to escape an abusive father. Owen was a decent guy if he could keep his pants on and hands to himself whenever a woman was around. After getting kidnapped and experimented on by a corporation that the Blackbournes were looking to do illegal business with, he changed his tune toward hunting for pure sport and helped us in our fight against Hell with his superhuman augmentations.

From the lab reports we collected on him where he was being held, and PROJECT: UNITY's examinations, we learned that he had been pumped full of a steroid synthesized from werewolf hormones that gave him enhanced strength and reflexes, but also the means to endure the brutal operations. Without anesthesia, both of his eyes were swapped with superior versions from an unknown supernatural "donor" that could also see auras. His heart and bone marrow were replaced with a werewolf's to improve his cardiovascular system and ability to heal. Most of his tendons and ligaments were exchanged for a genetically perfected set meant to synergize with his artificially improved anatomy.

"I'll call him right after this," Lyle agreed.

"Can an Ancient really erase everything that's happened from the public?" an engineer from the R&D lab asked. "That whole 'disappearing city' situation has already been leaked online for days and intel in the Middle East says that terror networks have spread the information to their cells around the globe."

"What if the Ancients panic and command the supernaturals to just start killing off people when they realize how far this has spread?" one of our pilots interrupted before any of us could answer the first question.

"How do we know they won't turn on us when we try to help?" someone else shouted.

"The U.S., Russia, the U.K., Israel, India, and Pakistan are all threatening nuclear retaliation because they're blaming each other for what's going on," another engineer broke in. "I still have family in India. What are we supposed to do if someone pushes the button? There's no way everyone can be kept under control. There's too much room for error."

"The truth is going to come out sometime. We should be dealing with it not covering it up! Turning the human race into mindless zombies isn't solving anything!" another person yelled. "I joined PROJECT: UNITY to spread peace, not enslave people!"

"Quiet! All of you!" Commander Timmons stood up. "No one is being enslaved. You aren't helping anything by acting like this. We called a meeting to share ideas, not spread fear."

"Our priority should be the governments," came another shout. My stomach started to turn along with the crowd's demeanor. "We should be the ones to meet with officials and lay everything out on the table."

"Keeping the public from rioting is more important. Politicians will feel pressure from them to take action and it's harder to erase the memories of billions of people than a few government officials. There's no putting this back the way it was now that the lid's been blown off." The shouts just kept coming. There were some good ideas mixed in, but Lyle and I couldn't even talk to each other over all the noise. All we could do was look at each other and sigh. These were supposed to be our allies, but we had a better reception from the Ancients.

Lyle and Lisette were starting to get the crowd to calm down when the shadows under my chair swallowed me and spit me out next to Gianni.

"Are you okay?" I asked.

We were in Yomi, in front of the Shrine of Spring to be more specific. The four elemental guardian spirits that resided here along with their leader the Great Dragon Guardian of the East—Empress Kamakura—were allies of ours. They never wanted to get involved in mortal affairs so it was rather worthless coming to them for help.

"Yes, of course."

"I heard a good idea at the meeting," I said as we walked up to the golden doors of the shrine.

"Okay, later." He patted me on the head. Empress Kamakura had appeared before us in her human form. Her voice chimed in our heads, speaking with thoughts not spoken words.

"Greetings, Dark One." As usual, Empress Kamakura only ever addressed Gianni directly.

"Empress, we need your help," said Gianni. "There is much chaos on Earth and a demon now returns to hunt the Ancient Ones for their souls. I try to cut the evil from Earth but only fear comes."

"That demon may have been the woman's voice you both were hearing trying to trick you into coming and causing chaos in the Middle East to look for her," I chimed in.

"The humans need a god to have faith in and to lead them again," Gianni continued. "They will only fear me, but you and the pantheon here can be this for them. They will call out to you with prayers if you show yourself when we take their weapons away and stop the fighting."

"But you are a god, Dark One," Empress Kamakura replied. "You are one of the Ascended. Had you not been, never would I have granted you audience."

Gianni seemed as confused as I was. "What does this mean? Ascended? I am no god."

"Your mortal soul has transcended its limits," she explained.

"What I do to have this? I... do not understand."

"Every mortal soul has their own path to transcendence. Rare it is for the mortal body to last the duration of the trial. It is possible that after cleansing the stain that once marred your soul you were able to transcend." When we had fought in Hell, Gianni was overcome by the dark side that had festered within him since the Infernal Kings gave him his powers. He defeated that dark side when it had manifested and attacked us, nearly at the cost of his own life. He said his mind was clearer and he felt more powerful, but... a god?

"I am only a man that knows darkness. I do not wish for prayers. I am a soldier, no more."

"Prayers serve you not," Kamakura's voice tinkled with the sound of bells in our minds along with the luminous runes covering her skin. "Only True Gods transcended by spirits, not souls, harmonize with human prayers. Our being is a dynamic myriad, yours is not. You shall never fade nor fall to slumber as we, but your power is finite while ours is bound only by our followers worship."

"This change nothing. Humans will never trust the darkness. They will fear me because it is their nature. They are born to do this."

"Gianni, if we show ourselves to the leaders of the human world and talk to them—"

"Shh, little one," Gianni dismissed me and put his arm over my shoulder then continued on talking to Kamakura. I scowled at him, but he didn't take notice. "My plan is for the Ancient Ones that still live. There is one I know who has the power to make the people worship her. This will not be enough if the demons come."

"We won't *need* Aurelia if we talk to the world leaders on our own to show them we're good," I said, but Gianni just shushed me again and put his hand over my mouth. Whether he was being playful or not, I was pissed. *When was he going to take me seriously? Why am I even here?*

"I can offer you no assistance at this time," Kamakura said, as she always did. "My oath stands to not interfere with the mortal world until the Heavenly Ones awaken once more. Only if this land is threatened shall I rise to strike its foes. I sense that time may soon come, but it is not now."

"I have hope it does not come to this," said Gianni with a bow and took us from Yomi.

"Why wouldn't you listen to me?" I asked back on base. We were in the atrium, where there was enough of a crowd left over from the meeting to make our discussion less conspicuous.

"I need to show strength or she will think I am a fool." He leaned in to kiss me, but I turned my cheek and backed away. "No, do not be angry. Tell me."

"One of the team here suggested they talk to the world leaders. I think it'd be better if we did since we're the supernaturals and the ones that have been seen in the Middle East. We can go to the U.N. and let them know we're the good guys."

"U.N.?"

"United Nations. It's where most of the leaders of the human world meet. I don't see any human just walking in there, but you can get past security and all that."

"They will only know to fear the darkness as it always is, little one."

"It's better than anything else we've come up with. We need to just cut to the chase. Some of them will have to believe us that we're the good guys."

"Hmm... Maybe not us," he said and carried us back through the shadows. My head was starting to spin from traveling like this.

"Oh, no! Not her!" We were once again in Aurelia's chateau and faced with yet another unexpected reunion.

Chapter Seven

"Rudgar? What the hell are you doing here?" The middle-aged German man standing at attention beside Aurelia's throne was Lars Rudgar—formerly Commander Rudgar of PROJECT: UNITY and Lyle's mentor—who bailed on the team before our mission to Hell. He ran PROJECT: UNITY more like an aggressive military than a peace corps, which now after witnessing the uproar at our meeting may not have been so bad except for his use of double agents and dirty secrets. He had good intentions, but like Gianni his application of them could have used some work.

Aurelia nodded from her throne to allow Rudgar to speak, although he hadn't looked over to check for permission first. "I had made the acquaintance of the lovely lady that sits next to me quite some years ago while still in the German

Special Forces unit that monitored the occult and paranormal. One of her people was a target I had been assigned to monitor.

"When I was ordered by my commanding officer to eliminate that target I couldn't follow through. There was no justifiable reason to end the life of such a beautiful and peaceful creature. Instead, I introduced myself and in turn was brought to meet Ms. de Saint-Pierre who commended me on my chivalry.

"After realizing my leadership in PROJECT: UNITY was flawed and the situation was bigger than any of us, I thought to return to her for guidance as she has always been a favored and generous ally."

Aurelia had Rudgar in her pocket this whole time... Just how "generous" was she? Did she have the rest of PROJECT: UNITY at her disposal too? Does Lyle know?

"This is good news," Gianni said. "The more ally is better. The Strigoi Ancient has fallen to the demons."

"Pity." Aurelia circled the rim of a blood-filled champagne flute with her finger. "So much knowledge and still the poor thing couldn't smell the rat beneath his nose."

"You knew?" I blurted out. She concealed her smile by taking a sip from her glass.

"Please. Tonight is a night for celebration between friends! Let us dispense with these unpleasant topics and continue the festivities with another introduction." The ballroom was sparsely populated with small gatherings of Archios spread out chatting among themselves. When the doors opened and the sound of heavy footsteps on the marble floor approached, everyone stopped to turn their attention to who had entered. "I've taken precautions to ensure my safety in these most dangerous of times so that I am never without guard."

A man who was easily Gianni's size and looked like he could wrestle a rhinoceros and come out winning came forward to stand on Aurelia's other side. He had striking, handsome features similar to... Noah's... masculine ruggedness. *Did she really replace him?*

There was no mistaking that this man was an Archios, but he lacked the added hypnotic allure common to them. Or maybe it was just overshadowed by Aurelia's presence.

"Kenneth, greet our guests," Aurelia commanded in a sweet tone.

"Well met." He offered only a modest nod without a trace of a smile. Kenneth had a very thick Scottish accent so much so that it was readily apparent with only having spoken two words. Along with his beard and almost shoulder-length brown hair he resembled something of a well-groomed Viking. Still, he was not the typical company I'd expect Aurelia to keep, though Noah wasn't exactly a highbrow socialite either.

There was something else about him that stood out even more than his hulking physique and possible Viking heritage: his Old World looking armor. I was used to the undead mixing and matching various styles in their dwellings and outfits that they picked up throughout the centuries, but there was something recognizable about this particular armor. It resembled the Blackbournes' armor— or, more specifically, the armor of a certain Blackbourne.

William Blackbourne, Emily's now deceased boyfriend, wore a more antiquated style of hunting armor than the others' all-black executioner garb. I had joked that he dressed like King Arthur because as a thin and unassuming human it looked more like he was dressing up in an out-of-context costume.

Kenneth was not someone I would venture to tease. On him, the armor was a match he filled out well. Everything was adorned in fine detail with stitching and etched metal trimmings. It was more colorful than what I remember of William's. The little cloth that was visible was a tartan sash around his waist. There were red accents to the brown leather and bright silver buckles adorned the many straps. Getting in and out of it seemed like it would be annoying.

His boots were greaves made of metal, which attributed to his loud footsteps, along with a single matching pauldron on his right shoulder and one gauntlet. It was strange to only have one gauntlet and this one was quite interesting. A ruby gem was fixed to the back of the hand and each finger was clawed. The etchings on the gauntlet were different than the rest of the armor. It wasn't a matching set, and something about it reminded me of the arcane scrawlings I had encountered in the past.

"We celebrate later. We must act now," said Gianni. "My idea is for you to speak with the Unity Nations."

"United Nations," I corrected. "And it was my idea... that I took from someone else... and it *didn't* include—"

A droplet of blood rolled off the tip of a claw on Kenneth's gauntlet and onto the floor. Aurelia gave him a look of displeasure out of the corner of her eye that could have shattered steel like glass.

"Shh," Gianluca shushed me for the final time. "This is not the same."

"Fine, *Gaius*," I snapped. "Do whatever you want. I'll be outside." I tried not to look too bitter over the whole ordeal as I walked out. No one followed after me and I was fine with that.

I left the opulence of the gilded marble halls behind and ventured into the night. I would rather freeze out here than listen to anymore of the bullshit going on inside. The estate was so expansive that the paths trailing around the property needed intermittent streetlamps, as the light of the chateau didn't come close to reaching halfway across. The massive tiered fountain on the front lawn was still running, despite winter coming soon, so I decided to sit by it and listen to the sound of water for a few minutes to calm down.

Let's try to think about this rationally. I want supernaturals to not have to hide anymore and it also seems like the best way to clear up what's going on in the world. Even if Gianluca and the terrorism situation is resolved or covered up, it sounds like the demons' schemes are inevitable.

Dealing with humanity now and getting them accustomed to us before everything goes to hell will only help us in the long run.

Aurelia already controls what she wants to behind the scenes and I don't see Gianluca turning on her unless she does something so horrible he can't ignore it. With supernaturals out in the open and her as the figurehead dealing with the world leaders, she would constantly be under a microscope with everyone watching her every move, not just Castile or Gianluca or Rudgar who she feels she can manipulate. Right now she's okay with it because she feels protected, but if anything goes wrong when it's all out in the open, it's all on her.

It might not be so bad to let her play queen for a day during the transition. From now on I should go back to focusing on what I do best: kicking ass and trying to build things.

I was enjoying my self-imposed time out when the incessant cheeping of a sparrow on the fountain interrupted. *All right. I'll bite. What's with all the birds this week? Do they not sleep at night anymore or am I missing something?*

The bird kept tweeting from one spot without moving or drinking the water. A couple of Archios strolled by but were too busy talking to notice. I slid closer until... the bird flew away.

Feeling stupid, I checked that nobody saw me trying to sneak up on a bird and got up to go back inside. Gianluca had to be done by now or close to it. I was going to tell him that I didn't want to be brought along anymore if I would just be ignored.

I was at the doors to the chateau when my hand grazed something sticky on my pants. It had been a while since I ruined my clothes but if I sat in bird poop there would be hell to pay... The stickiness came from something dark red though. *Blood?*

As soon as I thought that, the cheeping started again. It was coming from the grass behind me. *Was the bird hurt? Maybe I could bring it to that woman on base who kept one as a pet.*

I crept closer trying not to startle it, but it flew further across the lawn. Sure enough, there was blood where it had been sitting. Its flight seemed strong, but it made me feel bad to leave it when it was injured. I could use my powers to pick it up without getting close—but did I want to sacrifice human souls for that?

I approached again, as slowly as possible and without caring about the Archios giving me dirty looks as they passed. *More blood.* This was a lot for such a small animal. The sparrow kept flying off, leading me further and further away from the chateau to more blood stains until I started to get the feeling that it wasn't the one who was hurt.

We played this game of cat and mouse, or idiot and bird, until I stopped checking for the blood and just followed obediently. It became too dark to see as I wandered into the woods around the side of the chateau and then the bird left me.

The last time I stumbled out here on my own I got kidnapped by... Minerva. *Shit.* This seems like a pretty weak attempt at luring me away from my allies, but then again it did work.

I could have felt around in the dark using my powers, yet decided against it. I actually welcomed the chance to fight Minerva. It would be even better if she brought me to Hell with her so I could kill her once and for all.

My late night excursion continued to the edge of the woods. *I had to have been walking for half an hour by now. How much bigger could this property be?* Once through to the other side, I was in a sweeping meadow of tall grass that must have gone on for miles. To my right in the distance was a small building with a light on. I wasn't sure I was even on Aurelia's estate anymore, but I had nothing else to do except check it out.

I reached a dirt road that led to the small building in one direction and back through the trees in the other. *There was a path I could have taken this whole time.* Once I was close enough I could see that the building was a stable for horses with a lantern hanging outside. There was a cottage and a ranch house along with a second, larger stable across from them.

I walked toward the first stable and stopped at the sight of more blood on the ground. There was significantly more here than I had seen on the way. I removed the lantern from its hook to carry with me so I could see where the trail of blood would end. I was starting to get a terrible feeling in my stomach as the blood stains turned into smears that painted the way a deep red.

"Hello?" I called into the stable.

No one answered.

I tip-toed in, debating with myself what would be the appropriate level of threat to respond by using my powers. This could just be a horse or something that a wolf got to. I was expecting to see dead animals in the stalls yet there was still nothing but a trail of blood leading out the other side of the stable.

Outside again, there was a short path covered over by grass that led to a barn. The barn was snuggled within a dense gathering of trees that made up this perimeter of the woods. The door was closed although the bloody trail continued up to it, which meant whatever happened in there couldn't have been done by an animal, unless there's one that knows how to slide a barn door shut.

I opened the door.

The lantern afforded me a clear view of the inside of the tiny barn. Pools and streaks of blood were everywhere. There was so much of it that you could tell it settled at different depths by how it dried along the edges.

"Is anybody in here?" I called out. The barn was so cluttered inside with farm tools, saddles, and bales of hay that even in full light I couldn't see around it all from my spot at the door. I didn't want to keep this up. Whatever was hurt was probably dead and I didn't feel like going out of the way to make myself sad by finding it. The thought ran through my mind that Aurelia probably had her servants serve pigs blood to guests she didn't like.

I closed the door and started to walk back when I heard something from within the barn. Had I not been trained to keep my senses sharp I never would have heard something so faint, but I learned to listen for patterns in my surroundings to better pick out when something changed. I knew what the grass sounded like beneath my feet, what the bird sounded like when flying, the branches scraping against the barn outside, and that it creaked inside even from a gentle breeze. This was none of those sounds. It was a light rustling. I wouldn't have been able to hear it with the door closed if it was a mouse—I wasn't *that* good—and there were no other ways in except a small window above the door.

"I know you're in here," I said upon sliding the door open a crack so whatever it was couldn't run out without me getting a good look at it first. No more rustling, but a bale of hay had moved from before.

I circled around, giving whatever it was a wide berth. It moved again and this time I saw it, or rather I saw the hay on the ground moving. There was half a shoeprint that appeared in it. Whatever it was... was invisible?

"Noah?" I took a shot in the dark.

"Hey."

"Noah, what the hell? What's going on?" I asked as he came into view. "Oh, my god..."

Chapter Eight

Noah. He's kidnapped me, stabbed me, thrown me off a roof, beaten me, and yet somehow, the big idiot had managed to become my closest friend aside from Lyle. I could say with confidence that as much abuse as Noah had put me through I came out of it for the better. He had given me a crash course in the supernatural world with self-defense training so hardcore that I thought my immortality had reached its limit more than once.

"What—what happened?" I asked.

"I tripped."

"On what? A landmine?" His left leg was broken so badly that the shin bone was poking out through the skin, as was his forearm on the same side. He was covered in lacerations and his nose was busted. I had seen him cut up like this before, but never along with the broken bones.

One of the reasons I hated Aurelia so much was because of how she treated him. On top of tricking him into becoming her undead servant, she would have him bled dry to drink or serve his blood to her guests.

"Don't worry about it." Noah was a sarcastic jerk, but I knew his arrogance was an act to shield himself. He always came through for me when I needed help, although he would never admit to needing it himself. I had to give him the same tough love he gave me to ever get anywhere with him.

"Here, take my blood," I offered my wrist without getting closer to make him work for it.

"I'm good," he declined. He hadn't moved his head to look at me and his broken arm was holding his side.

"Stop being such a big baby and take the blood." When he still didn't budge I knew something was wrong. I sat next to him and put my arm to his mouth, looking away while I waited for the bite until eventually he gave in.

Any bite from an Archios sent the body and mind into a state of pure ecstasy. They couldn't help it, and I knew it felt just as good on their end, but when it was one of your best friends and in a life-or-death situation it always made it awkward.

I lost track of time as my mind wandered while he fed, trying to divert my attention elsewhere.

"Thanks," he mumbled after he was done. "She's been pretty pissed since she found out Vyrlakalos turned my blood to poison."

The deep slices covering his skin had already begun to seal, but he was cringing in pain more than before.

"What is it?" I noticed he was trying to move the broken arm that was covering his side. He wouldn't answer so I lifted it carefully, ignoring his warning growls.

"Oh g—" I started, turning away and trying not to dry heave.

"If you throw up on me I'll beat the shit out of you." His arm had been holding in his intestines that were spilling out. The skin was healing around it making it even more painful as it squeezed shut. I pushed his insides back into place and shoved my wrist into his mouth, forcing him to bite for both our sakes. At least the pleasant sensation would take my mind off that.

I set his broken bones back in place, something I had learned to do while helping out in the medical ward at PROJECT: UNITY, and fed him again to get them started on healing.

"Why didn't you say anything when I called in here the first time?" I got up to grab a blanket I saw by the saddles.

"I wasn't sure it was you. You didn't smell as bad as usual."

I threw the blanket in his face. "How long have you been out here like this?"

"No idea. What day is it?" He said from behind the blanket over his face. He still wasn't moving. I knew it took longer for the undead than for me to heal from serious injuries.

"Tuesday." I wrapped the blanket around him and sat back down.

"Then four days, and I wanted the blue blanket, by the way."

"Do you mind if I set it on fire after wrapping you in it?"

"That would not be to my liking, no." We both started to laugh. "Where's the Italian?"

"Don't worry about it." I used his own dismissive answer against him. "You were right about love being a weakness though."

Noah had always preached that love and relationships were a distraction and left you vulnerable. It was one of the first ways that Aurelia had broken him down to obey her. Any of the women he fell in love with were put to death by his own hands at Aurelia's command to prove she had total control over him.

"Wish I could say it sucks being right all the time," he said. "The guy was a douche anyway."

I didn't say anything in response. I was pissed at Gianluca for constantly dismissing me and the way he went about his plans, but I didn't want to start a war between us if he overheard. "I mean, the guy is so full of himself and it's creepy how he's always just dropping in or hiding in the shadows."

"You're always doing the same thing and you couldn't be anymore full of yourself or you'd explode," I pointed out.

"Yeah, but I do it with style," he grinned. I flicked him on the nose, now that it had healed. Surprisingly, he didn't lash out, but maybe he couldn't yet.

"How was Thailand?" I asked. It was a sensitive subject because he wanted me to go with him after he helped in Hell but I had opted to stay with Gianluca.

"Never went." So Aurelia lied. Big surprise. Now I felt guilty for not going with him. Maybe if I had he wouldn't have been stuck here to be tortured. I was always under the impression that Aurelia allowed Noah to hang around me so that she had me under her control by proxy.

"Let me help you—"

"Drop it," he cut me off. We had had this conversation plenty of times in the past. He refused to accept my help freeing him from Aurelia.

"Vance is dead," I told him after a moment in silence. "*Dead* dead."

"No shit?" Noah loved to bully Vance almost as much as he did to me. I knew Noah respected him though. Noah respected anyone who showed bravery and Vance helped take down his own master when she was after us.

"It was Minerva. She was posing as that protégé of his."

"I'm still hungry," he said after another minute of silence. "Gimme more of your blood." He opened his mouth like I was expected to serve him.

"I think you're just milking this for attention now." Most of the more grievous wounds had been taken care of and were healing steadily.

"Do you really wanna find out? Because if I am, and I *can* get up, I'll make sure it won't be pleasant when I come after you."

"Fine." I figured he was bluffing, but it did take a lot of blood to heal and also use his powers if he needed to defend himself so I let him have it. By now my regeneration had definitely kicked in from all the blood he had taken, if not only for the puncture marks he had left in my wrist too. That meant I was using energy from the Rift, but I couldn't leave a friend in need like this. *It probably wasn't very much energy*, I hoped.

I debated telling Noah about the soul stealing problem—for an egotistical, muscle-bound brute he was actually very wise—but before I had the chance I was pulled to my feet.

"Come." It was Gianluca. "We leave now."

"Wait," I said, rubbing my arm where Noah's fangs had ripped the skin from being jerked out. "He's hurt and needs blood."

"Then he go to get it himself." Gianluca put his arm around me to take me into the shadows with him, but I backed away.

"You can go. I'm staying," I said.

"I do not want his lips on you, for blood or any reason. You are mine."

"It's *my* blood and I can do what I want. He's *hurt*. It's not like your lips haven't been places I didn't want them before for lesser reasons." I went to sit back down by Noah in defiance but he had disappeared from the barn when my back was turned.

Gianluca brought me back with him to our room on base. He acted like nothing was wrong and we hadn't just been arguing a second ago. Maybe I should have let this go because of some greater purpose, but I couldn't.

"I am *not* yours." I glared at him with his back to me. "You can't tell me what to do and treat me like a child, then expect there to be something between us. You'd rather listen to that monster in a fancy dress than me."

"You do not know what you are saying." He turned to me. "You are still angry for the kiss. I know. I care for you with my whole heart, but you are very young and I am the man. I will make the decision. It is my duty. To speak this way during a visit only hurts my honor as a man."

"What?!" I shouted, trying to contain my anger before my powers flared up. "How is any of this about *your* honor or being a man? Maybe you haven't realized but I'm a man too and I don't have to be two thousand years old to be one. We're supposed to be *equals*."

"You do not understand the world because you are very young. You only see a little piece. How can you make a decision for the world you do not know so much yet? You trust me and I will give you the world and anything you want to be happy."

"I don't *want* the world! What I want is to be considered an equal!"

Gianluca shook his head. "You do not listen. This happens every time you see this friend of yours I tell you is bad."

"Leave Noah out of this. At least *he* respects me."

"He is a child. It is two child playing to be a man. He knows no respect and make you act this way when I try to give you better."

"You weren't a child when you were our age, were you? At my age you were a soldier and called yourself a man."

"Yes and I know many more things now than when I am human. I did not act this way like you when I was this age. You are angry because you do not understand. This is why I try to teach you, but still you are angry and do not listen. Everybody have a place. Here, I am the man and you are my little chick. I make the decision that is best for us."

"Don't call me that. I'm not your anything anymore. You're trying to make stuff from a dead empire two thousand years ago work today. And if that's your plan for saving this world in the end, I don't want any part of it. Things *change*—it's called progress."

He stared at me before saying anything. "I will let you take a rest. I think so much happen these days your mind is not clear."

"It's crystal clear." I left the room and headed for Lyle's. The look on my face was enough to part the gathering in the hallway. I couldn't believe

Gianluca was still clinging to such antiquated, condescending views and had such a lack of remorse when he always seemed so caring and sympathetic.

"What's going on?" Lyle asked when letting me in and noticing the anger on my face.

"I just ended whatever it is that Gianluca and I had. Why are the beds pushed together?"

"Rebecca was coming over, but... I guess I'll tell her it's a bad time."

"Sorry."

"How bad was this break up?" he asked. "The base is still here so that's good, but he's not gonna cause some global catastrophe is he?"

"I don't know, Lyle. I don't really care right now either." I slid the beds apart and took the one I used to sleep on when we roomed together.

"What happened? You guys seemed perfect for each other. I never saw you so happy, although I haven't seen a lot of you lately I guess."

"He wasn't what I thought he was." I didn't care if Gianluca was listening in by this point. "He's got some weird reverse ageism and sexism mindset. I'm not man enough in his eyes to make decisions and I'm too young to know any better about a world I've been *currently* living in. He thinks he can ignore me and brush me off all the time because his 'honor' is more important than respecting me."

"Well, he does come from a totally different time where relationships weren't exactly equal partnerships, but I don't agree with anybody being treated like that."

"I feel like all the good times were an act because he never really thought of me as anything more than a plaything," I sighed and tried not to let my emotions get to me.

"I don't know, man. He seemed pretty genuine to me but he also seems like a lot more of a complicated guy than I thought at first. Sometimes people don't work out after they get to know each other better." Lyle sat at his computer sending a message, presumably to Rebecca to cancel their plans. I felt bad about barging in, but had no one else to talk to. If I was alone, I figured Gianluca would feel as if he could return when I didn't want to see or speak to him.

"Yeah, I knew something was up when he wouldn't listen to me about the situation in the Middle East," I said. "But I was trying to be the voice of reason. He just doesn't want to accept that things change, the world is different and doesn't work the way it used to. He insists that his way and the way things were, are the right way and the way it should all be again. He's not going to cause the end of the world through evil like some thought; it'll be through being a stubborn idiot."

"You're kinda really stubborn yourself."

"No, I'm not!"

"Wait. Let me suit up before we continue this," Lyle laughed.

"Shut up. You're supposed to be on my side."

"I am, but I'm just being real. The two of you butting heads are like an immovable object meeting an unstoppable force."

"That's not what I want from the person that's supposed to be my other half," I said. "We should be in sync, not one holding the other back and making them feel like they don't matter."

"You might be a magical flying creature, but this isn't a fairy tale. Some relationships suck like that once you're in them long enough to find out more about the person. You can either try to work it out or move on if you feel you can't.

"You should be happy you're having normal problems for once. Rebecca and I decided to put the brakes on taking things any further because of the war. We might pick up where we left off when things calm down, or we might not. You never know what could happen or who you might fall in love with."

Chapter Nine

I woke up the next day thinking that it was morning. It was never easy to tell when you lived underground and had the lights off. Before even opening my eyes I rolled over and the side of my face was met with something unexpected. At first I thought it was crumbs, which after I remembered I was in Lyle's room wasn't all that unexpected.

When I did open my eyes and I saw that I was lying in sand. It wasn't just sand in my bed, but I was out in the desert.

"Gianluca!" I shouted. *If this was his idea of giving me a time out...* My rage was put on hold by a sparrow that flew down in front of me. It stood there in the sand tweeting at me until I got up.

The bird flew away over my head and I realized I was dreaming. The bird had flown across a daytime sky that was behind me. Straight ahead in the other direction where I was facing when I awakened was night. I started in the direction toward the bird as I lost control over myself in the dream and began flying.

There was something in the sand below me that stood out, something small and ivory. I kept passing over it as the dream repeated until one final time when the bird appeared sitting on it like an egg.

"Hey. Hey! Wake up, man." Lyle jolted me from my happy place under the covers. "It's five in the afternoon, dude. We got stuff to do."

I remembered a time not long ago when I couldn't sleep through a night. I used to get frequent nightmares and wake up drenched in sweat. This strange dream was interesting though. I wanted to go back to it. "Get dressed fast. We have, uh, a meeting in my office."

"Why'd you say it like that?" I asked and untangled myself from my cotton cocoon. "There *are* crumbs in this bed!" I looked down at the sheets.

"Yeah, sorry. I had a pizza-bagel before you came over last night."

There was a white rose and a chunk of alabaster on the nightstand next to my bed. *Maybe the dream was just a dream.* "This better have been from you."

Gianluca used to love giving me gifts of white and referred to my pale skin as alabaster. He always said how attractive he found my complexion in comparison to his olive tan, which was more common to Romans from his time. He would bring me dozens of white flowers and clothes, but the most thoughtful gift was a piece of white marble for me to use my powers on to create something with. I shared his love for Greco-Roman architecture and he encouraged my interest in it by supplying me with marble and alabaster to practice being creative since he knew I disliked all the fighting.

"Afraid not, sorry. We do have a meeting though and he's going to be there so try and be civil. Timmons is off-base for the night so it's just you and me."

"Yeah, yeah…" I dragged myself out of bed, not too thrilled with the idea of having to talk war with the person I just broke up with over that same subject. "Oh, I never got to tell you: I saw Rudgar last night. He was at Aurelia's kissing her ass."

"Funny you should say that."

"Oh god, what? Don't tell me this meeting is with them."

"All right, I won't tell you. Just get your ass downstairs." Lyle fled the room in a hurry like I had never seen. I knew he took his position as commander seriously, but jeez it was only Aurelia. It wasn't like she was going anywhere anytime soon.

"Oh, no, this is much worse," I said under my breath upon entering Lyle's office. The big screen along the back wall of the office was a live-feed with Rudgar. In the background, Aurelia was on her throne with Kenneth standing stalwart at her side. It was a different throne though, and they weren't in the ballroom but elsewhere in the chateau. I suppose I should have known that just one throne wouldn't be enough for her.

Better still, four shadowy portals lined the office wall, two on either side of the screen. From left to right, Castile, Aurelia, Gianluca, and Vyrlakalos all had their own two-way window from their residences, with Gianluca in the Nether, so we could communicate safely at a distance. I never knew Gianluca could do this with his shadows, but then again I didn't know he was such an opinionated jerk either. I regretted not bringing the rock with me so I could have thrown it through the portal at him, or better yet a flashlight to make his shadow go away. I knew only supernatural light could affect his darkness though but the thought was amusing enough to keep me from walking out.

Lyle was about to speak when I sat down next to him. "I tried to get Owen Blackbourne on the call, but he wasn't available." Lyle scribbled a note on a paper on his desk for me to see: "Hung over". "Unfortunately, he told me the demon armor they use isn't in supply to purchase even one for our troops. Cost aside, the other members of the Blackbournes aren't willing to give up their own for us to use, although Owen expressed interest in joining us personally."

"Maybe we're better off without it," I said. "That armor can corrupt you if you wear it for too long."

"Infernal hide would make a fine defense, but the human maggot within is unnecessary," Vyrlakalos hissed. "I am unable to replicate the magicked properties I once had while assuming their demonic form in Hell. I shall lie in ambush and await this assassin to strip their flesh without need of any pitiful mortal escort."

"And what of daylight?" Castile asked. "What contingency would you offer should this fiend act while we sleep?"

"I can exist within the living meat of my creations to shield me from the sun's gaze."

"They won't have the strength to combat such a demon," Castile retorted.

"Worry not for my soul but your own wretched life," Vyrlakalos screeched. "You will be the first to fall with not more than a frail dream between you and death. Your paltry astral bastion will be all our undoing when your soul is used to stoke the flames at our doors."

"The monster speaks true," said Aurelia. "The weakest will need to be watched with greatest intent."

"How could one ever focus on me when you are so desperate to make such a spectacle of yourself?" Castile said. Vyrlakalos burst into heinous laughter and shapeshifted into a nude version of Aurelia, making a mockery of her by adding eyes to her breasts and rotting the skin in putrid colors. I started to laugh too until Lyle hit me on the arm.

"My concern is increased due to the fact that two precious little souls are drawing all of the attention," Castile continued.

"Does the loneliness still eat at your heart, dear?" Aurelia asked with just a hint of a smile.

"Maybe the monster can create you a fresh bride from what remains of your old one."

Castile stood with his eyes burning red and looked like he was about to jump through the portal at Aurelia when Gianluca closed it on him. Rozalin finally made herself known, rising up from the shadows around Aurelia's throne. The raven-haired specter's ghostly hands appeared on the back of the throne followed by her long hair animating in the air as if swept up in a fierce gale. Her blood-curdling laugh rang out with such force that it shook me to the core.

"No more of this," Gianluca said and returned Castile's portal to rejoin the conversation. "We must put the old times away in the past."

"Funny hearing that come from you..." I said, to which Lyle hit me on the arm again.

"I could not agree more, Gaius," said Aurelia. "The time for pettiness has passed. We must look toward the future, together, if we are to survive."

I rolled my eyes at all the hypocrisy.

"I've been assessing the threat from the governments," Rudgar said. "While most, if not all, countries with interests in the Middle East are on higher alert than usual, the actual threat of nuclear warfare is minimal to none. No one is willing to start nuclear war in the Middle East. Most of the land there and the targets are not worth what a nuke would cost and the backlash of retribution to the homeland that fired it.

"The United States and allies have significantly increased their military presence in response and you can only expect it to grow even more. Fortunately, no major world powers will be willing to fire nukes at a single target such as a lone supernatural either—or at least they would not be willing to do so until it was too late. Those types of last resort plans are greatly exaggerated by the media as propaganda. The real threats are the government-run and vigilante witch hunts that will crop up quickly and spread just as fast once your presence is known and made public. It can interfere with our plans and put millions of lives in danger, both mortal and supernatural alike.

"My suggestion is to grant Lady de Saint-Pierre an immediate audience with the United Nations with our full support so that she may negotiate an international treaty and lay the groundwork for peace before any more moves are made that may draw attention to us. Without this, Hell will not hold back by sending only a single assassin for the Ancients, as the amount of anarchy on Earth will be more than enough to open dimensional gates globally."

"Very nice," said Gianluca. "Then we will do this right away when Aurelia is ready."

"I will have my speech prepared before dawn," Aurelia said.

"How dutifully magnanimous of you," Castile scoffed.

"We must work together," Gianluca reminded everyone. "No more battle between us. I will guard Aurelia during the day. Half the army will go to Vyrlakalos with Rudgar. Lyle, go with the other half for Castile."

"I'll take Blackbourne with me too," said Lyle. "We're going to need to rotate out a lot since we have no idea when anything is going to happen. It could be weeks."

"Or years," I added.

"Understand this is a treaty for us," Gianluca said. "There will be no harm to come from our allies. Any who betray will know only darkness. Only together we are *invictus*."

"We're in," Lyle spoke up first.

"I guess so," I sighed. It wasn't like I had much of a choice.

"Aye," Castile agreed with a nod. "This should prove to at least be quite... entertaining."

"We accept," said Aurelia.

Vyrlakalos returned to her original horrid skeletal form bathed in flaps of meat. "I am already invincible but your offerings of flesh may prove useful in my hands." Saliva dripped from her gaping maw.

"There is no offering," Gianluca clarified. "Rudgar and the men will go to Aurelia, and I to Vyrlakalos so there is no mistake. Your poisons will not be needed if we can make the humans understand and only need a fight with the demons. After the war you and your kind will not have a need to hide and can have a peace. This is what you want, no?"

"The cattle are of limited concern. I accept only on the grounds of that none present will interfere with my plans to survive the conclusion of this cycle. I am not so foolish as to believe Hell can be defeated outright. Only those intelligent enough to see this will survive the rebirth of the world."

"What the dear Carpathian says is true," said Castile. "The end is nigh and many humans will perish, if not pushed to the brink of extinction, regardless of our actions. Our best hope for this alliance is to reach the other side of this apocatastasis as intact as possible so that we may start the cycle over again. This former Strigoi Minerva is only the first of many problems to come for our personal survival and barely a beginning to the humans' annihilation."

"I'm not just going to hunker down and let billions of people die because it's been foreseen," said Lyle.

"No one is stopping you from joining them in the afterlife," Castile said. "If you are smart, you will focus on defense, not offense, and live to be a progenitor of your kind in the new world with whomever else may remain. Somethings are simply inevitable."

"As much as I despise their kind," Vyrlakalos started with a screech, "the humans must endure to procreate and repopulate the Earth like the vermin they are. Their survival is linked to our own, as is their demise. It is as basic as the necessity for sustenance. A larger population that survives means a greater gap between boundaries that we will not need to cross when we grow hungry."

Once the egos were put aside and the real, dark subject was on the table, it seemed that the Ancients were a lot more apt to work together, or at least not openly *against* each other. I would even go so far as to say they seemed a bit scared or aware of the possibility they might fail. Rozalin was the only one with nothing to lose, and potentially something to gain in the form of a surplus of souls flooding into the Underworld if humanity was wiped out. However, I doubted that Aurelia would be so blind as to let her sister ruin her plans to survive the war and claim a great deal of recognition for it.

"It sounds like we're all more or less on the same page," said Rudgar. "This will be a treaty not soon forgotten by history."

Chapter Ten

The meeting concluded without much fanfare.

Lyle sat with a sullen expression on his face. "Don't be so upset. It's only the extinction of *most* of the human race," I joked to cheer him up. "Repopulating the Earth is a pretty sweet pick-up line if you ask me."

"I'm worried about our team. We have no defenses against Minerva. All offense, just like Castile said. I have to be honest, it crossed my mind to just... *requisition* that armor from the Blackbournes."

"That doesn't sound like the Lyle I know."

"That's what bothers me. We've barely started and it feels like we're already so desperate to agree to things we never would have before unless it was a last resort. I don't know a lot about war, but I know that people usually get this desperate at the final push, not the first. This doesn't feel like an alliance. It doesn't seem like we're fighting to win. It feels like we're fighting not to lose before the person next to us."

"Do not think with a limit." Gianluca appeared in the room with us. "You are a leader and this is a war. Your men need armor. It is your duty to get this, even if you must take it by force. I will help if you need."

"I'd prefer not to make any more enemies," said Lyle.

"Then speak with a sweet tongue."

"That's more Aurelia's specialty."

Gianluca put a hand on Lyle's shoulder in a display of camaraderie. "To be the hero of your people you must do what they cannot. Do what must be done for victory."

I narrowed my eyes at Gianluca. Lyle's biggest obsession was to be a hero and walk in his father's footsteps to make him proud. It wasn't by mistake that Gianluca chose that wording to encourage Lyle to confront the Blackbournes. PROJECT: UNITY and the Blackbournes were at opposite ends of the spectrum when it came to the law and only our recent friendships with them made any sort of relations possible.

"People should do things in their own way," I said. "Especially when they're trying to put the past behind them."

"Can we have this room?" Gianluca asked Lyle, motioning toward me.

"Sure, just... keep it cool. I don't wanna lose the base."

Lyle left us against my silent protest shaking my head at him.

"Do you like your presents?" Gianluca asked once we were alone.

"No," I said.

"I see. My stubborn little one is still angry."

"I'm not yours, so stop saying that."

"I know you say this because of anger, but love does not go so quick."

"We're not in love. We've never once said we loved each other. All I did for months was follow you around and try to clean up your mess as you caused problems. Then you'd give me these presents to make me think you cared when all you were doing was keeping me quiet."

"You do not have to say this word to know the feeling in the heart. Is not good to start war with a bad feelings between the one you love. In tradition we make love before battle for strength and good luck."

Gianluca put his hand out to touch my face, but I moved away.

"Well I *don't* love you and I'm not making *anything* with you. You don't respect me and you pushed this war ahead a lot sooner than it would have been on purpose," I said. "You *like* to fight and conquer like you're back in Rome adding to the empire."

"The world will be better when this is over. When I meet you, you say I cannot show my feelings because two men cannot have love. When I look at this world, I see the wars that never end. They do not fight for an empire or glory, only to kill for blood. I try to fix all this. I will. You will see the world will be happy with peace like when it is my Roma."

"With you as the ruler."

"Maybe, for some if they like to follow."

"So much for only being a soldier."

"I am a man first and I will do what I need for my honor and the one I love. A soldier duty is for battle, a man is for his family and state."

"But only you're the man, not me. Right? You've never thought of me as an equal."

"Because you are too young. You are a man, yes, but not the same. You do not need to have such a duty if you are mine. This is for me to worry."

"And what about the others that aren't 'men' to you? With this treaty does that mean Aurelia can no longer treat Noah like she does since we aren't allowed to cause harm to each other?"

"He is a property. Is her decision how to give him discipline."

"Property?!" I yelled. I didn't know what I wanted to scream at him first. "It—he—how can you say that?! He's a *person*! People aren't property. You have a *lot* to learn about current times. She tortures him and he can't escape! How is that okay with you? Your first love was a slave wasn't he? Didn't you ever want him to be free?"

"No. He is happy and had honor and pride for his duty. He was in service to Roma. Noah has no respect. He would be given death many times with another master."

"He deserves to be free! If this treaty doesn't protect him then I'm out. I don't want to be part of it."

"If he is free, he will not join and be an ally. You know this. He is a wild dog. Your eyes are so closed to this world. This is why we are not the same. Humans everywhere still have a slave; many supernaturals also do. I see with my own eyes even today. Only because where you live there may be no slave you think everywhere is free.

"This is how the world live before even I am alive. Some serve and some lead. When you know which place is yours, then you know peace. He is lucky Aurelia give him even a little peace for his bad loyalty. I do not see the others in her service say the many bad things like him or wish to hurt her."

"I'm done," I shouted, my hands shaking in a blind rage. I clenched my fists to try and hold back from involuntarily using my powers due to my anger. "I've stood by and tried to justify everything you've done and told myself your intentions were pure, but I can't be with anybody who thinks the way that you do. It's just been getting worse and worse the more I get to know you. You haven't been the same since Hell, or maybe this really is who you are."

"Because I see much more evil now in this world than I think was here before. I tell you I try to fix it. The humans need a strong leader, more than only me. Alone they cause more chaos. This is the reason for a treaty too."

"A stronger leader like who? Aurelia?"

"Yes. For the politics is no one better. Together we make a new Roma, our Roma, where there is peace. I will fight all the evil and you will build the new empire across the world, little one."

"Stop calling me that. I'm *not* your little one. I hope you enjoy all your glory because you can fight this war that you started without me. I'm not going to stand in your shadow any longer."

"I know you do not mean this," he said with annoyance in his voice. "I will make Aurelia promise Noah does not die if this is important for you—"

"Just go..." My words finally got through to him. Gianluca marched out of the room through a darkening shadow on the wall. I left the office and tried to calm down on my way to take the elevator back up to the barracks.

"Where are you going?" I asked Lyle upon running into him on the way.

"Blackbournes'. Everything good with you and Gianluca?"

"No. He thinks Aurelia has the right to torture Noah and keep him as her slave and that it's his fault he 'doesn't know his place'. I know you and Noah don't get along, but he only acts the way he does because he's hurting." I sat with Lyle on one of the ergonomically molded plastic benches that lined the walls of the atrium.

"The guy *is* kinda the biggest asshole on Earth," he said. "But just because I'm not crazy about him doesn't mean I condone slavery and torture. Gianluca has a really archaic way of thinking. The guy just woke up after being asleep for hundreds of years. All the changes are probably freaking him out and he's trying to hold on to what he knows and remembers. I'm sure he'll come around, but it might take some time to really adjust."

"Stop trying to make me feel bad."

"I'm not. I just don't want you mad or hating him to the point that you make bad decisions about anything, not only your relationship together."

"There is no more relationship," I stated firmly.

"All I'm saying is: I think he's a good guy at heart. He'll come around when everything that's been going on is under control. You two are immortal. You guys won't even remember this a thousand years from now."

"Don't start talking like you won't be around. If I have to live forever so do you."

"No way, man! One life is all I got and I'm gonna make the best of it. After that I'll be on my fluffy cloud watching sports, eating pizza and drinking an unlimited supply of cold beers with some sexy angel ladies."

"I'll fly up there and drag you back to Earth if I have to."

"I don't think they let your kind into Heaven."

"What is *that* supposed to mean?"

"You know…" He stood up. "You've gotta be this tall to ride the cloud." Lyle put his hand out just above my head and laughed.

"Shut up, human!" He loved making fun of me being shorter than him. I wasn't *much* shorter; only an inch or two, not like with Gianluca or Noah who dwarfed me. Since I got more comfortable with my powers I used to levitate all the time to make up for my height—just bringing myself slightly off the floor to seem more intimidating—but not anymore.

"Don't go to the Blackbournes'. Gianluca was trying to rile you up. You want to build bridges not burn them. He's a god now or something according to Kamakura and wants to rebuild the Roman Empire. He and all the Ancients don't really care about civilization crumbling. You heard them. They're counting on it. As long as they survive and a handful of humans they consider it a win. You just gotta do things your way."

"Yeah, man, I know. I wasn't really gonna go there guns blazin'. I didn't plan on leaving until I got something though either."

"I'll come with you. Maybe with both of us—"

PARAGON's global red alert system broke into our conversation, lighting up the base with flashing warning lights and blaring sirens. The screens and terminals mounted everywhere showed the feed from one of the satellites we had been monitoring. Lyle and I ran over to the nearest terminal where others that had been passing by joined us.

"What—what is that?" someone asked. "Pyramids?"

We had an aerial view of a cluster of pyramids in the desert. I didn't know why we were watching this until one started to shine like a star in the sky and out shot a beam of light into space that cut our transmission.

"Was that lightning?" another person asked. "Lightning doesn't reach outer space," someone replied.

"What the fuck was that?" Lyle looked to me like I should know.

"Don't ask me! Where was it?"

"PARAGON, where was that last video from?" The AI brought up a world map highlighting Egypt then zoomed in to show Giza. Lyle quickly found another hacked satellite feed in the area with PARAGON's assistance for all to see. "Whatever that was knocked out two other satellites in the area."

Alarmed shouts and gasps could be heard around base from all those who were watching. The Earth had split open in fault lines radiating outward from the pyramids. A whirling sandstorm whipped up around them, growing rapidly in size and magnitude.

"Get another satellite! Zoom out!" I yelled over the panic breaking out on base. "How far does this go? There's a city *right* there."

The raging storm sliced right through buildings like a knife, and the city that had been there was gone by the time Lyle got another clear shot. Cars and buses were thrown into the air like toys only to be shredded into nothing before they could land again.

"There are almost three million people that live there...," said Lyle as he looked it up in another window on the screen.

"I... I'm not sure many could've survived that." The base had gone quiet as everyone was struck hard with disbelief at what they were witnessing. The sandstorm was so fierce we couldn't see through it by satellite anymore.

"Giza is gone," Lyle confirmed. "Another city just gone. This one was fully populated with civilians too..." He pulled up a news station reporting from Cairo, which wasn't far from the storm's edge. Horses, camels, people, vehicles, skyscrapers—all were being sucked across the Nile and into the lethal hurricane. Tremors erupted the ground and split the Earth as the fault lines still continued snaking their way out from the pyramids. "Cairo is half gone... It's been three minutes. How is this happening?"

"Commander, look!" One of the troops ran up with a tablet device watching another satellite. Lyle put the video up on the big screen in the hall so we could all see.

"What is *that*?!" he shouted as a serpentine shadow descended down toward the pyramids.

"No... fucking... way." I couldn't believe what I was seeing—even more than a storm and earthquake that in tandem just killed millions of people. "That's Kamakura... the dragon I told you about. We have to get over there right now!"

"You said it was a woman!" Lyle yelled as we ran for the hangar.

"I *said* she turns into a dragon. I wasn't lying!"

"That thing is huge! I thought she was on our side?!"

"She is, she said she'd only help if it really meant the end of the world!" I contemplated calling to Gianluca to take us there, but as I thought it Lyle stopped me.

"Wait. Look at this," he held up the tablet. "I got a feed from a military post on the ground just outside the storm. The picture's bad, but it looks like that dragon is attacking the pyramid—Gianluca is there!"

"She's attacking him?" *Had he caused this? No, if anything it was her. She had the combined powers of the five elements; wind, earth, water, fire, lightning. The first two of which were wreaking havoc before our eyes.*

"It looks like they're both after someone that's standing on top of the pyramid. I'll go back to the satellite view." We got a good shot inside the eye of the storm. It was close enough that I could just make out Gianluca in his full armor. When his helmet was on I knew this would not be resolved through diplomacy. Kamakura was flying down from above. We saw her scales glow and she opened her mouth, presumably to roar but we had no sound, and like that, the razor-sharp tempest was replaced by torrential rains.

"Come on. We have to go." I pulled Lyle along with me. Everyone on base was scrambling to get into gear.

"Is that a Demon King?" Lyle asked. "It looks like one of those pharaohs." I stopped to check one of the screens on the wall. Whoever had caused all that destruction from atop the pyramid was bigger than Gianluca.

"Zoom in closer!" I shouted. It wasn't a "pharaoh guy", but a man with dark skin about eight-feet-tall and the head of a weird dog, wearing nothing but a decorative loincloth and a lot of gold jewelry. He was wielding a staff in one hand, a sword with a hooked sickle blade in the other. They were about to face each other down with Kamakura looming overhead when there was a bright flash that came from the staff.

"Where'd the dragon go?" Lyle asked when the light dimmed. The rain had stopped and allowed a clear view of the scene. "Why isn't Gianluca moving? This better not have frozen on me."

The video wasn't frozen. The Egyptian dog-man was still moving, circling Gianluca. Then we saw why he had stopped. Gianluca was turning to stone, armor and all. Down at the base of the pyramid was another figure that must have been Kamakura returned to her human form. She was turned to glass.

I was scared, horrified, and emotional all at the same time as I watched. The strange being waved his staff in the air and Gianluca and

Kamakura sunk into the stones of the pyramid. He looked around and then straight up at the camera, making us all panic that he knew we were watching. He raised his golden staff toward the direction of the camera and the video cut out.

"He destroyed the satellite... This is it," said Lyle. "This is happening and we just lost our two strongest allies and five million people in under ten minutes."

"I should've been there," I said. "I—I said really terrible things to him. The last thing I said was that I didn't want to be with him anymore and I wouldn't help him."

"Commander, what are your orders?" I didn't realize we were still surrounded by troops ready to go. There was nothing left to go to though.

"Ditch the weapons and armor," Lyle ordered. "There's no way we're engaging a Demon King on our own. Rendezvous outside Cairo city limits in civilian clothes and start searching for survivors. Get the whole medical team and have them set up camp to treat the wounded. Dr. Sullivan is in charge at camp while I lead the rescue team. I'll tell Commander Timmons to meet us there if she isn't already."

Lyle turned to me. I was surprisingly lucid, but I knew I was in shock and it would wear off soon. I had been down this road before. "I didn't want him to die," I said with tears in my eyes.

"I know. There's a good chance he's not gone though. Maybe he just got turned to stone because he couldn't be killed."

"I'm going to get them out. I'll rip the pyramid apart one stone at a time if I have to."

"Dorian, listen to me. We *can't* afford to lose you. You have to get to the Ancients. I'll hit up Rudgar to get Aurelia to the U.N. right away. We need her there at all costs to make sure we aren't fighting a war on two fronts. I'll have a pilot stay behind to take you to Castile and Vyrlakalos."

"And what happens if that demon pops his head out again?" I asked.

"This is war, dude. We do what we need to do."

"I don't like that answer, Lyle! I'm not losing you or anyone else for this. It's my fault that Gianni—"

"Hey! It's not your fault! But you gotta take care of your end for us to even have a chance. Find out what we're up against first."

"Oh, I'll do a lot more than just that."

Chapter Eleven

"You can drop me off down there in the courtyard," I told my pilot. "Be ready to get out of here as soon as I come back."

We made it to the Carpathian mountains from Greenland in just under two hours by taking one of PROJECT: UNITY's new mini-jet hybrids with vertical lift takeoff. It could only hold two people and was smaller than some crop dusters, but the thing was *fast*.

During the flight I had been going over what I'd say to the Ancients while trying not to think about what was going on in Egypt. I had to be firm, I had to push buttons, and most of all I had to use their ego against them like I had learned. They needed my help as much as I needed theirs.

Once we landed I ran to the huge doors of the castle keep and entered, wary of being snatched up into some hideous meat trap. "Vyrlakalos!"

No answer.

I walked around in the dark hoping I wouldn't have to go far before she made herself known. This was a lot more foreboding without the use of my powers to sense the surrounding area. I couldn't feel anything moving, but I could hear it. Dawn was coming soon so I had to hurry.

I climbed the enclosed spiral staircase that circled up the left corner of the main hall, calling for Vyrlakalos the whole way. The entire second floor was one big master bedroom. The walls and floor were in as much disrepair as the rest of the keep. I could see where Vyrlakalos hung down through the ceiling downstairs by the holes in the stone floor. The place was filthy, with weather-stained rugs and bedding covered in grime and matted leaves that had blown in over the years. Antique furniture was piled in a rotted, splintered mess against a wall. Some pieces had a cloth thrown over them, as if that would help the condition of the dwelling.

"How does she live like this?" I said to myself.

"You arrive not on the heels of your master," Vyrlakalos rose up from a hole in the floor on a pillar of flesh. "Perhaps unwise."

"He sent me," I lied and bit my tongue before I could argue that I had no master. Let her think that I represented Gianluca. I could potentially use the archaic mindset of the Ancients to my advantage in calling them to arms. I was pretty sure

Vyrlakalos couldn't read minds like Aurelia and Castile.

"A difficult task for one set in stone," she hissed.

Never mind that plan.

"Then you know the first Demon King has risen."

Vyrlakalos let out a howling, raspy laugh. The room began to shake as parts of her body slithered out from between the cracks of the floor and attached to her, forming one large monstrosity supported by four spider-like legs coming from her back. "That was no Infernal King. You would have been left trembling in your icy metal cavern had there been."

"I don't tremble." *Not anymore.* She roared in my face to test me but I stood strong. "Who was that on the pyramid then?" I asked and wiped away the spit that Vyrlakalos had sprayed.

"There was no meat on its form so it is of no interest to me."

"No meat? Like an illusion?"

"Take your questions elsewhere and be thankful I do not hunger. I will not waste a moment of my time on such trivia."

"The treaty still stands. Whether this is an Infernal King or not, it's a huge problem that's going to pave the way for more trouble."

"A treaty with no one to enforce it means nothing," she hissed again.

"I'm here to enforce it," I said, glaring straight into her soulless eyes.

"You are a speck that could be squashed without effort if I so choose."

"Then go ahead. Make your move." We stared each other down in complete silence for what felt like an eternity. It was so quiet I could hear the dust that had shaken free from the walls settling. "You won't. Not because of any treaty, but the same reason you didn't try to the other time we fought. You're scared my regeneration is too much for you. Is that it? I might just be the superior being that takes over *your* body if you try to eat me like you do all your victims. You read my file at PROJECT: UNITY and you know the parasite from the Rift I've merged with will devour your soul and you'll be nothing."

"You *dare* to threaten me?" Vyrlakalos screamed and shook the keep.

"If I have to treat you like an animal then I will! Only intelligent creatures can understand the concepts of treaties and alliances."

"I could rip you to pieces and watch with pleasure as they try to regrow!" A pair of bony clawed hands came in through the windows on either side of the room but stopped before touching me. "But it will be more fun to watch you chase a false hope and just maybe be of use to me in the process."

"Whatever you want to think to make this move forward. Do you have any information on this guy we saw or not?"

"I have nothing to tell you." She reached into her chest and pulled out a folded parchment from between her ribs. "Return this to the dreamer in England and leave my sight. My tolerance of your company has expired."

"Castile? I was on my way there next." I took the paper she threw on the floor and opened it.

"Is this supposed to be some sort of joke?" I asked. The paper had nothing on it but a bloodstain.

"It is nothing for your blind eyes to see. Now do as I command."

I casually strolled back downstairs and out the door to maintain appearances, but bolted for the jet once I was in the courtyard.

"Let's get out of here," I said to the pilot.

"Where to next?" he asked.

"Somerset, England. I'll mark it on the map. Have you heard anything about what's going on in Egypt yet?" I didn't know my pilot's name. I think it was Jeffery or Jordan, but I was too embarrassed to ask after waiting so long. He had his helmet on the whole time so I couldn't get a good look at his face to help me remember.

"It's made a big splash on social media and the news, but I haven't heard anything from Commander Turner or Commander Timmons. Seems like no one got a good look at the guy who caused all this, but I'm sure that the government or group whose satellites picked it all up also saw."

My worry was that Aurelia wouldn't go through with her speech at the U.N., instead taking refuge in her chateau like always and waiting out the storm since this wasn't an Infernal King. The public would go insane with panic, further speeding up their return.

Then there was Gianluca. I wanted him to be safe; I didn't hate him. We weren't compatible like I thought we were, but I still cared about him. *He couldn't really be dead, could he?*

We arrived at Castile's manor with plenty of time to spare before daybreak. I knew he could read my mind better than anyone else so this would be tricky. Honesty would be the best approach. Brutal honesty.

Upon entering the mansion I noticed a distinct change of atmosphere. There were no make-believe servants and the interior lighting made it look like trying to watch a 3D movie without the special glasses. Within a few seconds, I started to get a headache from being here; the rooms started to flicker.

"Castile?"

He appeared before me without a word, rather frenzied in expression, and sat down in his usual chair by the fireplace in the parlor. "Are you feeling all right?" I asked.

Castile extended a hand toward the sofa to offer me a seat and I obliged. The foyer I had come in from disappeared into a black void. Outside the window was the same nothingness. I supposed this meant he didn't want me to leave.

He took a sip of tea from his bottomless teacup that always appeared and the room's lighting returned to normal. "Quite well," he said. "I see a burning star in you where a candle once stood when we had last conversed. Something has changed... You have something for me?"

"Yes." I wasn't going to pretend I was astonished that he knew what I was carrying without showing it to him first. I handed him the parchment from my pocket. He didn't even unfold it before smiling and nodding in response.

"Vyrlakalos. Always one to find the humor in the most dire straits."

"She wrote you a joke?"

"You could say that, in the loosest sense of the word. I take it you sought his aid in favor of Aurelia's. A wise, if not amusing choice."

"I thought Vyrlakalos was a 'she'?"

"I've known him by both. It matters not. You seek answers to our troubles in the east. Ask." He tossed the parchment into the fireplace to dispose of it. "Honesty would be the best approach."

"Who, or what, is the man with the dog head that just wrecked Egypt?" I asked. "Vyrlakalos said there was no 'meat' on him, but I don't know what that means unless he's an illusion."

"You would not draw blood should you stick him with a sword."

"What does that mean? I don't have time for word games. Neither of us do."

"Then do not waste mine when you already know the answer."

"If I did then I wouldn't be asking. Maybe I should have gone to Aurelia. It seems she's the one to go to when you want results."

Castile's face turned sour. "I had higher hopes for you but should you wish for me to insult your intelligence I will be more direct. The being you saw was a deity with the head of a magicked beast not native to Earth, although more closely mistaken as a jackal. He is known by many names as most Ancients are. You may be most familiar with the name Set."

"How was I supposed to already know that?"

"Because you have encountered such beings before when you led one to my residence in the past." The room went black and then a Chinese warrior with long black hair and a spear on his back that crackled with electricity was standing before me.

"The guardian spirits from Yomi? Oh, yeah, they didn't bleed either. Empress Kamakura is a deity too and this Set turned her to glass. How could he be so powerful without the prayers of his followers? Nobody worships the Egyptian gods anymore... do they?"

"That I do not know," the image of the spirit spoke in Castile's voice and then returned to himself. "Seek knowledge and you shall have your answer."

"I thought I was by coming to you—" In the midst of the blackness a sparrow flew down between us and looked up at me. "The bird—that's been you this whole time? What's it supposed to mean or were you just spying on me?"

"This is your mind, not mine. I am not the one showing you this."

"You're projecting what's in my mind? But I wasn't thinking about birds." The sparrow disappeared when I reached out to touch it.

"Then someone else is and they are putting their thoughts inside you."

"Who else can do that? Aurelia? I doubt she would be showing me birds." I remembered the one on her property that lead me to Noah. She wouldn't have lied and said he was in Thailand only to bring me to him later to give him help.

"The better question is who would want to?" Castile asked. "When one has want, little else matters. Deepest desire will always trump skill. In light of current events it may be an ally if it has not already led to your death. A possible relation to our Egyptian adversary, perhaps?" He disappeared leaving me in the dark room. I felt the sofa fall out from under me and as soon as I hit the floor it came into view only much different than before.

I was on a black and white tile floor with each tile about three feet across. When life-sized statues of black chess pieces appeared opposite me I realized what was going on. "I wasn't thinking about chess."

"No, but I was and now you are too." Castile's good-natured chuckle echoed in the emptiness surrounding us. "It is a game of kings."

"We don't have time to play games."

"Then don't waste a move."

"I don't have any pieces on my side," I said, playing along.

"You are one. I thought that would be obvious." I was standing on the white king's square and the statue of the black king across from me turned into Set. Maybe I should have been honored that Castile didn't make me a pawn.

"You can't expect me to win when I don't have any other pieces to guard or attack. All I can do is run away, but eventually I'll lose no matter what."

"Then you had better find more pieces." The chessboard went dark and we were back sitting in the parlor once the light returned.

"What you're saying is that I need to find more help than what I have now to beat Set? You could have just said so."

"To say or to show, the lesson is the same, but what transpires after rarely is. I have shared all I know with you. We each have our own part to play in this. Not all of us were born to be kings, even if those who were are limited in movements and vulnerable for the time being." Nice bit of reverse psychology there to motivate me into resolving all this for him. It was more appreciated than the usual threats from others.

"One last thing. Can you tell me if Gianluca... is he dead?" I asked, not knowing if I wanted the answer.

"His existence is no more. Dead? I do not know. For that you would need to ask one in tune with Death itself."

Chapter Twelve

I dashed back to the jet where the pilot was stretching his legs. "Sorry for the wait. Let's get back to base."

Only one person I knew had a more intimate relationship with death than anyone else. Rozalin de Saint-Pierre. The sisters were over four thousand years old, the eldest of the known Ancients, and with Rozalin's knowledge of magic she may know something about this Set. She was a phantom and also a powerful necromancer that used her magic to cheat death over and over.

She was as treacherous as they come, but knowing that upfront evened the playing field a bit. I couldn't ask about Gianluca's fate directly, of course. I had to show her our goals were the same and let her take me to the answer in her own way, like Gianluca had taught me in the past. The problem was that I was still unsure if her sister could read my mind so I had better play it safe.

"Commander Turner contacted me while you were away. He's returning to base for supplies now that more international aid arrived."

"Did he say what the situation was like over there?"

"Quiet from what you'd expect. Most people are too afraid to come out and are hiding in their homes. There are only a handful of survivors in the areas that were hit. The team has mostly been trying to corral whoever they can so they can redirect them, keeping them from wandering through the streets away from the direction of the pyramids and toward the camp they set up for medical treatment. It didn't sound like the camp was that full, so it looks like this is more of a recovery mission than a rescue."

Vance, Empress Kamakura, and... Gianni were all gone. The numbness from shock began to wane and was replaced by the weight of depression as we flew back to base. I blamed myself. Gianluca wouldn't have gone into battle distracted if it weren't for me. *I should have been there.*

With everyone away, the base was downright spooky in its emptiness. Once inside I headed right for the library while the pilot took care of maintenance on the jet in the hangar. I needed to find out more on Set and any possible correlation with the birds I had been seeing.

Rudgar?

The former PROJECT: UNITY commander was taking the glass elevator in the atrium down when I walked by. He was already on the floor below and didn't see me.

Rudgar had disconnected himself from PARAGON when he left the team so I was surprised to see him walking around without setting off security. *Why was he here and who let him in?*

I took the stairs to follow Rudgar down to the armory. "Rudgar, what are you doing here?" I called after him. He could be useful in finding out what Rozalin and Aurelia might know about Set without having to deal with them myself.

"Re-establishing my uplink to PARAGON and picking up a firearm."

All human members of PROJECT: UNITY had a flexible plastic implant the size of a grain of rice embedded in the backs of their necks that PARAGON used to identify them and monitor their vitals. It was necessary to fire any PROJECT: UNITY weapon, but also used to jam telepathy by scanning individuals for intrusive brain waves. According to Lyle, PARAGON was set to run multiple bio-scans for Gianluca and I using its sensors around the base since we didn't have the implants and were considered an exception. Although it did take up a much larger amount of PARAGON's processing power to constantly be scanning us while on base, the effects were minimal.

"How'd you get in here without already being connected?"

"Turner never changed the override passcodes." *Jesus Christ, Lyle...*

"So, you're back now? Just like that?" I asked.

"Leaving the base didn't mean I left the team. My absence brought those who remained closer as I had planned. I accepted the fact that my presence caused distrust during a critical time. I only disconnected from PARAGON so no one would be tempted to follow, although I supposed Gianluca could have found me in the shadows if I were really needed."

"And now that your 'absence' is over, who are you back here for? PROJECT: UNITY or Aurelia?"

"I wasn't aware that they were on different sides."

"She's always on her own side. It's interesting how you forgot to bring up the fact that you were in such good standing with her."

"There was no reason to bring it up. Besides, the last time I was here Mr. Burckhardt was too. I didn't need to create another reason for him to give me trouble, seeing as how they aren't on the best of terms."

"You think she's going to treat you any differently after this than she does with him? You'll be lucky if you're alive. I don't get what you have that she's interested in to begin with."

"It isn't too hard to figure out. I am acting as her liaison to the mortal world, or more specifically to PROJECT: UNITY. Most of what you see here on this base was paid for by her bankroll, directly or not, after we cut ties with more formal government funding."

"Now I feel dirty sleeping here." I cringed. Come to think of it, that could have been why she let Noah stay here for so long when we were fighting Hell and Vyrlakalos came for an uninvited visit. He was there to protect her investment whether he was aware of it at the time or not.

I had always thought that she let Noah roam free when he wasn't needed and just called on him to go kill someone she didn't like. This week put things in a new perspective. He never went *anywhere* that she didn't have a stake in and when he wasn't useful for the moment, she made him pay with his blood.

"Regardless of your feelings toward her, when the new world is born you won't have an easy time finding a place that our queen *doesn't* own."

"Our queen?" I raised an eyebrow in question. The Rudgar I remembered was fascinated by supernaturals, but that was a tad much. "You sound like you're ready to let her take over the world."

"Supernaturals already *do* own the world. They always have. It wasn't a human that rose up from the pyramids and murdered five million innocent people. It wasn't a human that swallowed a city into the abyss overnight. Humans are led to believe that they have the power to change the world, but it's nothing more than a convenient lie so those who truly rule can be left undisturbed.

"I would much rather back a benevolent monarch that appreciates beauty than serve under the madman or the monster. Gianluca is dead and you are far too inexperienced—"

"He's not dead, he was just turned to stone," I insisted. "And I would rather live in a world run by Castile or Vyrlakalos any day than one under Aurelia's rule. Everyone is expendable to her and she has no value for life or freedom. Even Vyrlakalos can be reasoned with and shown the value of an individual."

"There is no use in debating whom we are subjugated by at the moment when we can't be sure we'll live to see it."

"Has Aurelia made her speech at the United Nations yet?" I asked.

"No. These things take time. Our fair lady has made the arrangements for an emergency session in Geneva to discuss the current events and will be arriving there herself before dawn. The world leaders are expected to travel there during the day, giving us time to prepare security and our own arrangements."

"Make her fly coach," I laughed, but Rudgar ignored me. *Noah would've loved that one.* "What do you know about Set? Have either of the sisters said anything?"

"He is the Egyptian God of Chaos. Gods are nourished by the worship of their followers, or in more secular terms: the resulting energy emitted from a resonance between souls that harmonize toward a specific image or ideal. Although, I'm unaware of any modern sects with enough numbers to make him rise.

"If what legends and supernatural history have to say are true; a fully empowered deity can rival that of the Infernal Kings. The gods who are of the highest order are supposedly those who created the universe in their larval forms as spirits and made Earth so that it would be toxic to the Infernals."

"Set might be a good guy then? Or maybe the enemy of my enemy?"

"It's possible. Back when many of these polytheistic pantheons were worshipped, the populations were a fraction of what they are now. If a deity that can shape the Earth with only a few thousand devotees comes back to a population of *billions*... I don't want to imagine what destruction they could bring with them.

"I do have good news from Rozalin to pass on, however. She can sense the flow of spiritual energies between dimensions and it would appear that for the moment Set is weakened after his big entrance. At least we know that he won't be putting on a show like that again for some time, though we have no idea how long that could be.

"Now, before you get any crazy ideas of rushing in there, he could get his power back without warning and we'd lose you like we did Gianluca. Set must know he is weakened and wouldn't go unguarded after drawing so much attention to himself." *I thought of the chessboard at Castile's.* "We can assume whoever went through the trouble of raising him wouldn't leave anything to chance either."

"This might be good news for everyone else, but it doesn't help me get Gianluca out of there. I still need to gather more information so I know what I'm dealing with when I do go in after him."

"He's gone, Benoit. As soon as you accept that you'll make yourself a lot more useful around here.

"We'll see about that." I left Rudgar and continued on to the library where I dove right into my research.

Set, Seth, or Sutekh, God of Chaos and Storms, Lord of the Desert, slayer of the serpent Apep, son of Geb, God of the earth and Nut, goddess of the sky, usurper to his brother Osiris, betrayer to his sister Isis, husband to his second sister Nephthys, father to Anubis, rival to his nephew Horus.

"Well, that's an interesting family," I thought out loud. I had dug up as many books, articles, legends, and research papers on Set's mythology that PARAGON could find. Information was in no short supply, but weeding out the folktale from the truth was made that much more difficult. Without anyone to confirm any of this I had to look for repeating themes and concepts and hope that some ounce of accuracy trickled down through the years. "Everyone knows the undead fear sunlight, werewolves are hurt by silver, demons hate holy objects... what are the weaknesses for a chaos god?"

"Are you seriously talking to yourself in here?" Lyle's voice came from the doorway. I almost jumped out of my skin. I didn't realized I had been so engrossed in reading that hours slipped by.

"No, I knew you were there."

"Yeah, right. Tell me you found something we can use. Novak told me it didn't sound like the Ancients were much help."

"Who?" I looked up at him bewildered.

"Novak. Bobby Novak? Your pilot...? Don't tell me you were flying around with him the whole time too embarrassed to ask his name because you forgot it."

"No, I knew... I just didn't know his last name."

"I'm gonna follow up on that with him." Lyle collapsed into a chair beside me, looking haggard and dirty.

"Please don't, and no, Castile was sort of helpful. Nobody is jumping at the chance to go beat up the God of Chaos though, if that's what you're asking."

"Figured as much. I got a bit of a run down from Rudgar when we were flying back. Not much of a secret *who* this guy is, as much as what we can do to stop him or why he's here now."

"Yeah, I saw Rudgar here," I said. "Great job changing the password to get in here by the way."

"We don't get many visitors that would have need to use it, so it hasn't been high on my to-do list," Lyle defended himself.

"I'm not sure how I feel about Rudgar after he bailed on us before our vacation to Hell and now he's turned into Aurelia's lapdog," I said.

"At this point, I don't really care, man. You should have seen Cairo. It's like someone just split it right down the middle and erased one half. We didn't even go near Giza. People are saying they saw a giant flying snake that caused the storm."

"Poor Kamakura. She was always really strict on her oath of noninterference. She was able to stop the storm and then she gets turned to glass and blamed. If it wasn't for her who knows how much worse that could've gotten."

"Injuries were either cuts and scrapes from those far enough away to run, or total dismemberment from those caught in the winds. No middle ground. If this guy wasn't so close to what's left of Cairo, I'd actual be in favor of dropping a nuke."

"He'd just come back again though. Gods don't die, they just fall asleep in their dimension until they're worshipped again... so maybe that is his weakness. We're not fighting him, we're fighting whoever brought him back."

"We'd better find them fast then before the God of Chaos causes enough chaos to bring the Infernal Kings into this world and then we have that to deal with too." Lyle was on to something.

"Holy shit. That's it! It's not *who's* worshipping him, it's *what*. The demons! Set isn't affected by the atmosphere on Earth like the demons are. They found a way to summon him to do their dirty work. When they don't want him anymore, they just stop their prayers to him and poof, he's gone and they're in charge."

"Demons pray?"

"I guess they can. It's about having a soul, when enough souls resonate toward something, like a god, the energy released empowers it. Demons are made from evil souls, right? And the lords have tons of souls—like Ma'al had in his domain when we fought him."

"All we have to do is go to Hell and kill every single demon there." Lyle didn't hold back the sarcasm in his voice. "We'd be better off evacuating what's left of Cairo and having Aurelia convince the governments to drop a nuke on Set every time he wakes up."

"That's not solving anything and it would only be a very temporary solution. I'm sure if they wanted to they could raise other gods in other locations or just move Set around each time to wipe out a city before he can be stopped again. The residual radiation would leave the place uninhabitable after a while too.

"We don't even know if a nuke would work on him. In this legend, Set supposedly rides Ra's solar chariot, which is supposed to represent the sun, to defeat this evil serpent Apep every night to bring the dawn. We know this isn't to be taken literally, but if he has anything to do with the sun you've gotta figure he'd be pretty resistant to the heat of a nuke."

"Too bad we can't just ask one of them."

"One of who?"

"The other Egyptian gods. You were saying when I came in about knowing other supernaturals' weaknesses because we actually know some to find out what's true."

"How would we do that? Who would we even pick if we could?" I scrolled through the page of Egyptian gods as PARAGON rendered each of them in holographic form. There were dozens to choose from and all had their own legends.

"I don't know, man, but this mortal needs a shower and a nap. Timmons took over in Egypt so I could regroup with half the team and split us between Castile and Vyrlakalos. I don't like sending my men there after what Vyrlakalos did the last time, but we got no choice with Gianluca... not around." The last time he was referring to was when we first met Vyrlakalos as an enemy who invaded the base and killed almost everyone.

"We're really spreading ourselves thin and only a few months ago we thought we had too many new recruits," I said. "I know I'm contradicting myself by saying this because I'm always complaining about all the fighting, but I'd like to go and beat Set's face in right now."

"You better get some rest then," Lyle said on his way out. "Never know when you might get your chance." Lyle was right. I needed to be at the top of my game and there was no room for error.

Chapter Thirteen

On my way back to my bedroom a colorful streak whizzed by my head in the direction I was going. It was that woman's pet canary from the other day. The bird's owner was nowhere around, but I wasn't about to use my powers to catch it. Lyle had plenty of other things to worry about than the no-pet rule.

If I have to fight Set I'll need my powers... How much can I really hold back against a god?

I got to my room and as soon as I opened the door the canary flew in from behind me and landed on the chunk of alabaster Gianluca had given me. I didn't remember bringing it in here. I had left the rock along with the white rose in Lyle's room.

This is like that dream, in the sand, the bird was sitting on something white.

"Excuse me, mister." It was the bird's owner at my door. "My bird, I think it—oh, there you are!" She walked right up to it and carried it in her hand. "So sorry. This little thing is so much trouble!"

"Wait," I stopped her as she went to leave. "Do you know anything about Ancient Egypt? Birds maybe?"

"No," she smiled apologetically. "Maybe you can try the library?"

"Yeah, I did." I held up the tablet I had brought with me to show her.

"What about this one?" She pointed to the screen I had loaded. "A bird like this?"

"That's Ra. He's more of a falcon or a hawk," I said, but by the time I looked back up the woman was gone along with her canary. I checked out in the hall to be sure no one was messing with my head. The bird woman was already several rooms away and turning the corner.

What other bird gods are there? "PARAGON find me Ancient Egyptian gods with bird heads like Ra." PARAGON had a voice command feature that I always felt uneasy speaking with. The computer-generated face of a woman that was meant to make the program seem more human crossed the line into the uncanny valley. Some of the other PROJECT: UNITY members, like Lyle, would carry on whole conversations with the AI.

Thoth, the ibis-headed god of knowledge. Often associated with the moon and balance between the forces of good and evil. Sometimes represented by a baboon in place of an ibis.

"What the heck is an ibis?" PARAGON showed me a picture of a bird that looked like a stork with a long, curved bill. "Oh. Go back to the Egyptian bird gods."

Ra, the hawk-headed god of the sun. Known as the chief deity of the Egyptian pantheon. More accurately represented in some contexts as the mythical Phoenix than an actual hawk.

Horus, the falcon-headed god of the sky and war. One of the oldest known Egyptian deities and protector of the pharaohs. The Eye of Horus, or Wadjet, is a symbol of his royal protection.

"Hm, this was the one that's Set's nephew and rival. PARAGON cross-reference Set and Horus."

The legend of Set and Horus is a tale recounting the conflict between uncle and nephew for the right to rule all of Egypt. Set, lord of Upper Egypt, and Horus, lord of Lower Egypt wished to prove their superiority over the other before the gods. Set attempts to rape and humiliate the young Horus to prove his dominance, but was outsmarted with the help of Horus's mother, Isis. In some versions, Set is successful in raping his nephew, but is ultimately outsmarted when asked to prove this act to the gods as his evidence of superiority.

In other conflicts, Set has torn out one of Horus's eyes during battle and in retaliation Horus castrates Set.

"Okay, that's... enough of that. Back to the bird gods."

Geb, god of the earth and vegetation. Often associated with the goose. Said to have laid an egg from which the world itself was hatched. Isis is sometimes referred to as hatching from one such egg.

I looked over at the alabaster chunk. Isis didn't come up as a bird god. She was mentioned as outsmarting Set though...

"PARAGON, show me the Egyptian goddess Isis." The AI complied. "What the hell? She has wings! Stupid computer." Isis appeared as a human woman, but with brilliant feathered wings coming from her back. She reminded me of an Ancient Egyptian interpretation of an angel.

Isis, goddess of light, life, and magic. Often associated with the sparrow, kite, vulture, and cow. Known for thwarting her brother, Set, on several occasions. Her following extended into the Greco-Roman era and is sometimes identified with Aphrodite and Demeter.

"PARAGON, how did Isis beat Set?"

When her husband Osiris was dismembered at the hands of Set and his body scattered throughout Egypt, Isis collected the pieces and tricked Ra into telling her his secret name by inflicting him with a poison for which only she had the cure. By invoking the true name of Ra during an incantation she was able to resurrect Osiris and bear him a son to defeat Set.

In some accounts, after Set had raped Horus she helped to remove the semen. She then tricked Set into eating lettuce—his favorite food—that also contained Horus's semen. When brought before the other gods it was seen that Set had received Horus's seed and not the other way around.

Set also attempted to rape Isis, but was unsuccessful—

"Okay, PARAGON, that's enough," I said in disgust, putting the tablet on the nightstand and turning down the lights. "We're not doing any of that and none of it helps me actually stop this sicko from leveling anymore cities." There's no way I could defeat a god on my own, but another god could and I bet if anyone knew how it would be this Isis.

I slept for only a couple of hours. I was lucky to have gotten any sleep at all. I hadn't eaten in days, but I had started getting used to not needing to anymore. It was a few years that I had been immortal without any real need for food, sleep, or even oxygen, but some habits were harder to shake than others.

I rolled over to grab the tablet and continue my research when I saw the chunk of alabaster had changed. It was now in the shape of an egg. If that wasn't a sign I was on the right track, I didn't know what was.

I picked up the alabaster egg to inspect it. *This looks like my work. Had I done this in my sleep?* It was perfectly smooth and the debris left over from rounding it out was still on the nightstand so it wasn't likely that it was some sort of illusion or switched with the original.

I had been trying to use my powers less and now they were acting out on their own.

"PARAGON, find me more information on Isis," I instructed the AI using the tablet. Maybe my luck would continue and PARAGON would find me an easy guide on how to awaken a sleeping god.

Then again... if the images of the birds were coming from her, she must already be awake in some capacity. That would change my goal from waking her to trying to find where she is currently. Gods lived in different dimensions though, like Empress Kamakura in Yomi. I had no way of traveling to other dimensions. The only one who could do that was Gianluca... or Rozalin. I'm not sure if Rozalin could bring others across dimensions and if she could I wouldn't trust her to, so I needed to find my own way.

I checked out what else PARAGON found for me on Isis.

Isis, or Aset, is known as the "mother goddess" for her nurturing of Horus and her followers. The image of Isis nursing the baby Horus is said to have inspired later works of the Blessed Virgin Mary doing the same with the baby Jesus.

The name Isis is closely related to the word "throne" and represents her importance as a protector of the pharaohs. As her following grew she absorbed aspects of other goddesses into herself, such as Hathor, the goddess of love, fertility, and more, whose solar crown she can be seen wearing in many depictions.

Because of her maternal role and that of a protector, her name was often invoked in Egyptian healing spells and rituals. She was known as a powerful user of magic, protecting not only the living but also the dead, and most widely recognized for her act of resurrecting the fallen Osiris.

"PARAGON, find me temples or places of worship related to Isis." I didn't know much about Ancient Egypt, but I did know that the pyramids in Giza where Set rose were meant as tombs for the pharaohs and not temples for the gods. There was a definite connection between the afterlife and these deities.

When a person died it seemed that their soul went to whichever underworld was associated with their religion and not just one big waiting room for everybody to be sorted out. The prayers from the souls of the dead that stayed in the afterlife must be what kept the gods of old religions from fading away completely. I saw this during my first two visits to Yomi.

The Kiyomizu Temple in Kyoto that I transported from into Yomi was a big tourist attraction. True, it was not still a place of active worship, but the passing on of legends and traditions to so many people at the site seemed to keep the veils between worlds thin enough for me to pass through with a little magical help prepared ahead of time by Vance.

The pyramids of Giza were also a major tourist location that had to draw much more of a crowd than an individual temple of Set's and just so happened to be linked to the afterlife as a collection of tombs. It was probably very easy for someone powerful enough to contact him from there. Too bad I couldn't do the same to see Isis.

Demons had the advantage of being able to move between dimensions freely with the exception of Earth, which was toxic to them in the absence of a high enough level of chaos. When Gianluca stayed behind to defend Yomi after Kamakura was weakened from our battle, he said that he had fought many demons that tried to invade and snatch up the souls there.

PARAGON found me seven results for temples of Isis, not only in Egypt but also Greece, Pompeii, and Hungary. "PARAGON, can you narrow results down to the most important?"

Philae Temple is one of the most notable places of worship for the goddess Isis. Its original location sustained heavy flooding from the Nile River so the temple complex was relocated piece by piece to Agilkia Island in Lake Nasser.

"PARAGON, call Lyle." Talking to a computer wasn't so bad, I guess. "You're already up?" I asked. Lyle was in PROJECT: UNITY's standard issue armor. It consisted of a sleek motorcycle-style helmet with a visor connected to PARAGON and an all-black suit of high-tech SWAT riot gear made from polyfiber mesh with a high-density plastic alloy that could stop high-caliber bullets at close range. Lyle and I tested its durability by having me use my powers against him while wearing it. I was impressed that it could protect him from a casual telekinetic hit about equal to what I'd use to toss a car a good hundred feet.

"Yeah. I showered, slept for an hour, and had something to eat. We're heading out to the Ancients'. I'll be going to Vyrlakalos with some of the team and letting the others go to Castile since he seems less hostile."

"Careful she doesn't eat you," I warned.

"We're taking the drones to survey the castle while we set up camp down near the entrance so she doesn't get tempted. Did you come up with anything?"

"I need to get to a temple on a lake in Egypt down by Sudan. I've been getting what I think are omens of birds from the goddess Isis. It may be who Gianluca heard calling out to him for help too now that I think of it."

"I'll tell Bobby to fire up the jet. Aurelia's speech should be in about four hours, so make sure you're available."

"Why? I couldn't care less about her or her speech."

"I'm not totally sold on the whole idea and want to make sure we have someone around in case things don't go smoothly."

"Were you aware that she's funded most of this base?" I asked.

"No...? Her name isn't on anything that I've seen."

"Probably laundered through her many other investments and minions. I wouldn't be too surprised if she wants PROJECT: UNITY as her personal army."

"That's not going to happen. We're peacekeepers and we can't be bought. Besides, the implants protect us from all of that mind-control stuff."

"Those things don't mean squat against someone like her. I'm still not sure if she can read *my* mind and most other supernaturals can't, except Castile. If she wants to, she'll find a way. She always does."

"One problem at a time, man. Right now she's on our side and that's all that matters. We can't worry about tomorrow if we can't get through today. I just messaged Novak so get your ass to the hangar in the next ten minutes and good luck."

"Thanks, you too." I logged out of our call and took the world's fastest shower before running to the hangar where my ride was waiting.

"We're off to Egypt," I told Novak. "I've got a date with a goddess and that's probably the first and last time I'll ever say that."

Chapter Fourteen

I watched the world fly by out the window of the cockpit as we passed over Europe. I kept getting the feeling that I should have gone with Lyle. He was tough, hell he was tougher than me sometimes, but he was still human. Should Minerva show up, he and his small team would be caught in the crossfire between a demon and an Ancient that would have no qualms about eating them to keep herself alive.

Then I started to think about Noah and wondered why Isis led me to him. "Can we stop at Aurelia's on the way?" I asked Bobby. She should have left for Geneva before the sun came up and I doubted she took Noah with her.

"Sure thing."

We were there in no time and I headed straight for the barn where there was a noticeable display of sparrows lining the roof. I didn't know if that was good or bad. *Why would the birds keep leading me to Noah if they were related to the trouble in Egypt? Did he have answers about Set? Or was he just a missing piece on my side of the board? And if that was the case then why didn't Lyle show up as one?*

Noah was nowhere in sight and the interior of the barn was spotless. I tried to leave and check elsewhere, but as soon as I slid the door back open I was smacked in the face by the birds flying in to sit on the rafters.

"It would help if you could talk. Why does everything have to be so cryptic when the world is ending? I'm kinda in a rush," I said. In the midst of my ranting and shuffling hay about the floor, my foot got stuck in something—possibly a handle to a trap door.

I descended down a ladder into a small well-lit cellar. The lantern that had been hanging outside on my previous visit was down here... and so was Noah.

He was hanging from the ceiling shackled by his wrists, his face bloodied and broken, every inch of exposed skin covered by third-degree burns and lacerations that cut right to the bone. His mouth was gagged with a riding bit used for horses and beneath him was a bucket that his blood dripped into from his bare feet. *I guess Aurelia found a use for the poison in his blood.*

I climbed up on a barrel next to the one the lantern was on and freed Noah's mouth and then used my powers as little as possible to break the shackles. That was when I noticed his throat was slashed and fangs were smashed out. Helping him down without the use of my powers was no easy task being that he was double my size. The source of my power preyed on my mind, and I kept asking myself if I really had the right to use it, in spite of Noah's severe injuries.

Without his fangs to bite me I had to find another way to keep a steady flow of blood down his throat. I went back up to the barn and got some rags and a nail from a toolbox by the saddles, then grabbed a pail from the stable and crossed my fingers as I tried to get water from the pump around back. Thankfully, it worked right as I was about to give up.

I hurried back to Noah and wrapped one of the rags around his neck where it was slit to stop the blood from pouring back out. I took a deep breath and stuck the nail in my forearm, wincing and trying not to yell out in pain. I let the blood drip into his mouth and regretted the times I complained to myself about the awkwardness of him biting me.

"What... are you doing back here, little shit?" he asked once he had enough blood in his system to regain consciousness. He was good. He knew it was me and his eyes had yet to open. I didn't even smell bad like I usually did from my adventures. But who else would care about him enough to do this?

"I was worried about you, dummy." His body finally had enough blood in it to start healing and eventually he managed to open one eye. The other was so caked with dried blood that the lids were fused shut. He looked up at me for only a split second and then stared straight ahead at the wall in silence.

Bone and teeth were always the last to regrow (anything hard or calcific always came last in the process), so his fangs weren't back before he had begun to recover from most of his burns and cuts. Once he was in decent shape I removed the nail from my arm and the rag from around his neck before wetting another one with water from the pail. I watched for where the wounds had healed the most and cleaned off the blood and burnt skin starting with his face.

He still hadn't said another word and neither did I. There was nothing else to say that I hadn't already. I didn't want it to turn into a verbal shoving match between us, with me telling him how he should handle this and accept my help when I wasn't in his situation to know better.

I was in genuine disbelief at how he still said nothing by the time I was done cleaning him and washing out what I could from his matted hair. Not so much as a growl or sarcastic quip. The water in the pail was black and smelled fowl from the mixture of blood and burnt flesh.

There wasn't any way that I could take him with me right now even if I succeeded in coercing him. It was daylight and the jet only held two people. If he turned to mist it used up a lot of blood and he could wind up reverting back in the sunlight and dying. It was doubtful anyone at PROJECT: UNITY was available to come get him and even if they were, Aurelia would call him right back to suffer some more.

With the pail in one hand I got up and went to climb the ladder when Noah spoke. "Stay," he said. I closed my eyes and told myself not to look over at him. I didn't know how to answer. Everyone I cared about needed me and things kept getting worse.

I couldn't do it though. I couldn't leave him here alone. "If I stay, I want to talk."

"About what?"

"I don't know where to start. An Egyptian god called Set came down and destroyed two cities. Gianluca and Kamakura went to stop him and... well, they're... gone."

"Good," Noah said and spat dried blood on the ground after licking his lips. "That guy was an asshole."

I ignored him and continued.

"Before he left, Gianluca got the Ancients to agree on a treaty for when something like this happens. I've already spoken to two of them to get as much information as I could. After all this talk about the end of the world I never expected it would happen this way. I thought we had a good ten or twenty years and there would be some sign first that the war was starting."

"There needs to be at least two sides with a fighting chance for it to be a war, otherwise it's called a slaughter." Noah leaned over to pull his boots out from behind a barrel and put them on.

"So, you're taking the same cowardly way as the Ancients then? We don't stand a chance so just hide and ride out the storm?"

"I never said that, but my options are kinda limited if you haven't noticed. I'm swept up in the wind like everybody else until that changes."

"When will that be?" I knew he meant to kill Aurelia and gain his freedom. I wanted her dead for his sake too, but now I was starting to wonder if she was necessary to retain any amount of peace during what was happening. Then again, Castile could do her job...

"I don't wanna talk about it."

"I'll help you—"

"I *don't* want to talk about it," he repeated with anger in his voice.

I stood there not knowing what else to say. This was always a sore subject and it frustrated me that he wouldn't let me help him. "I guess I'll let you rest."

I started to climb back up the ladder when he spoke up.

"Where the hell are you going?" he asked.

"Egypt. I have a lead to follow."

"I didn't say you could leave. Where's my blanket?" I rolled my eyes, grabbed a blanket from the barn and tossed it down to him. "What am I supposed to do with that? I still can't move."

"I saw you put your boots on. Are you kidding me?"

"Do you hear laughter?"

I sighed and went back down. "You're such a big baby," I said and threw the blanket on him.

"Do it like you mean it," he grinned and his tone softened.

"Bye, Noah."

"Why are you always in such a rush to die?" I knew the pilot was waiting for me and I needed to find Isis and her connection with these birds, but they *did* lead me here. It was obvious that Noah wanted me around too for whatever reason.

"Have you been noticing a lot of birds lately or anything strange with them?" I asked.

"Not from down here."

I sat next to him without saying anything else to see if he would let something slip without my prodding, but he just kept staring at me out of the corner of his eye.

"What?" I finally asked after several uncomfortable minutes.

"Something's different about you," he said. "Why aren't you buzzing around like a stupid bee?"

"You mean why aren't I levitating? Floating?" I laughed at his description of me. "You're the first one to notice."

"Because I know you better than anyone."

"I'm trying not to use my powers as much." Noah had wanted me to learn restraint when he trained me so he should understand. He kept staring at me though, waiting for me to say more. "Stop looking at me like that."

"You could've gotten yourself a blanket too. I'm not sharing mine."

"I'm fine." It was chilly in the cellar, but I was too distracted thinking about everything going on to care.

"You have goosebumps." He went to poke my arm but I pushed his hand away. Twice. Three times.

"Get away from me!" I shouted at him, trying not to laugh again.

"God, you're cranky. You'd think someone chained you up in a cellar and beat the crap out of you."

"I'm worried about everything going on. Millions of people died, Gianluca was turned to stone..."

"Turned to stone? I thought he was dead— you want to save him, don't you?"

"It was my fault. It happened right after we were arguing about you. I told him I didn't love him. I don't see us together, but it doesn't mean I wanted him to get hurt."

"You were arguing about me? What were you saying?"

"Don't worry about it."

"Probably how much better looking I am than him," he smirked and put his hands behind his head. Most of his remaining injuries had healed, save for a few of the deeper ones that were reduced to red marks and a bit of his fangs.

"I need to get going," I told him and made another attempt to leave.

"Wait."

"Noah, just come with me once the sun goes down," I said, after having enough of his stalling. "I'll have a plane come get you."

Was his spirit that broken he didn't want to be alone? He was never like this. Was he giving up on trying to fight back? "I need your help," I added so he wouldn't feel I was pitying him.

"I *can't*. And you don't need my help, anyway. You're nothing like you were when we met a few years back. You're smarter, stronger, braver, more focused. If anybody needs help it'll be your enemies."

"Thank you. That's... the nicest compliment I think I've ever heard." I don't know if it meant so much to me because I was surprised that somebody felt that way or because I was caught off guard hearing it from him in particular.

"It was meant for me being able to make something out of you."

"You really are my favorite douchebag, Noah."

"I'm everybody's favorite."

"Maybe it's time you finally learned it isn't a weakness to accept help," I said as I climbed the ladder. "I promise I'll come back after I'm done in Egypt."

Chapter Fifteen

Philae was nothing short of breathtaking even if it was only a fraction of its former glory in this state. As with most of my other journeys, I wished that I had been here under more pleasant circumstances. It was hard to believe that this whole complex had been kept intact through the process of being taken apart and put back together. What looked to be simple, boring slabs of limestone from afar were actually decorated with hieroglyphs and enormous carvings of the gods. I recognized depictions of Thoth and Isis on the outer walls immediately.

There were plenty of columns, which were my favorite architectural element. Some were toppled over or possibly had never been reassembled after transport from the old island, but many remained intact. I preferred Corinthian and composite style columns from Greco-Roman architecture, but these were nice too. Many of the surfaces here were covered in hieroglyphics and pictures of various religious scenes. The Egyptians wasted no space when it came to telling a story.

The island itself was tiny, with sparse patches of desert plants growing along the shore. You could see across to the mainland from any side, which made the complex feel more like a grand stage in the center of an aquatic amphitheater than a remote location hidden away in an oasis. What I didn't know was that the historic site was opened to the public. I had assumed that once sacred places like this were under some restricted access to prevent the ruins from being further destroyed. I came at a good time, however, because visitation was prohibited after October and it was already November. I didn't need any interference while trying to commune with the goddess on site.

I roamed the paved grounds for a bit, not knowing exactly which direction I should be headed or if this was enough to reach out to Isis. There was more than one building here and I figured there would be a shrine of some type in one of them that would have the closest connection to her. I had hopes that a bird would appear and take me right to where I needed to go, but it looked like I had run out of lucky omens.

Without any obvious signs to follow I wandered through the first two buildings I came across and tried to clear my mind from all the noise of my whirling thoughts. I had never prayed before, but I imagined that I would need to be clear-headed to let in whatever was trying to communicate with me from the other side. I didn't like abstracts and concepts that needed to be read into. I was a cold hard facts guy, even after all the time I spent dealing with the metaphysical.

"All right, Isis, I'm here," I said, trying a direct approach. "Hopefully it was you that I was supposed to come see—" A gust of wind carrying sand from outside blew past me and took a sharp turn into one of the chambers I hadn't explored yet. I was quite certain that I had heard whispers in the wind and that was all I needed to know.

The room I was led to was unremarkable. I was expecting a grandiose shrine with statues and gold everywhere, but it was just four walls and a ceiling with a hole in it that let sunlight in. There were hieroglyphs, but that was nothing new. None of them seemed of greater importance compared with any of the others I had seen to this point. Two waist-high stone pillars stood side by side in the middle of the room. I tried touching them, pushing them, and pressing down on them, thinking maybe they were weighted pedestals that would open a secret passage like in the movies, but nothing happened.

"...help...the light...find..." a whisper rode down on a gust of a wind from the shaft in the ceiling.

"Help find what?" I asked back. The room started to change. The hieroglyphs carved into the sandy colored walls became filled with vivid colors and signs of disrepair vanished. In the four corners of the room lush ferns in beautiful pots appeared and torches lined the short hall I came in from.

"...find... treasures...return to me..." The whisper grew loud enough to confirm that it was a woman's voice, so this must be Isis. Along with the whisper was the very faint sound of birds singing. I realized now that these sounds weren't coming from the wind, but sung to me in my head the same as when Empress Kamakura spoke and her voice was projected with the sound of chimes tinkling in the background between syllables.

"Okay," I agreed. "What treasures and where can I find them?"

The sunlight grew brighter. I covered my eyes from the glare above and then saw two items made of gold come into view on the pedestals in front of me. One was easily recognizable. It was an *ankh*—a common symbol associated with Ancient Egypt.

The other treasure I couldn't even begin to guess what it was. It looked like it may have been some sort of tool. The mystery item was the same size as the *ankh* and roughly the same shape. It had a part coming straight down like the bottom of the *ankh*, maybe used as a handle. The top was a wide loop with three straight rows across that each held small rings. It reminded me of a handheld abacus in a way, but that couldn't be it.

The vision faded and the room was returned to its present day state. I felt reassured that I was on the right track and ran back out to meet the pilot. Instead of sandy, monotone ruins, I had walked out into a mirage of what the temple complex must have looked like so many centuries ago on the old island.

There were palm trees just about everywhere to offer shade from the African sun. Brightly painted murals with rich reds and blues like back inside the room took the place of the worn away artwork. Flags billowed from their poles mounted in the grooves among the carvings of the gods. The cracked and crumbling statues and structures were turned whole and the sparkling cobalt water around the island was much higher along the coast where wooden boats were docked.

I had never pictured any of this being so vibrant. I always imagined Ancient Egypt as a barren and dreary desert with nothing to offer but sand and heatstroke. The Egyptians' ingenious use of irrigation systems branching off from the Nile provided needed relief from the harsh environment. It spoke to how clever the people were back then to meet their needs in ways we take for granted today.

Back on base I went straight to the library, almost leaping from the jet before it came to a complete stop. All the globetrotting in the past week was getting to me now more than ever. I didn't know whether I was coming or going and the recent visions messing with my head weren't helping, but I had to stay sharp. I needed to concentrate on finding what and where these treasures were.

The temple had been moved, so there was a chance that those working on it took whatever artifacts were inside to a museum where it would be public information. That meant PARAGON should have a relatively easy time tracking them down. Of course, the treasures could have been looted by vandals at any time over the centuries, making this the worst game of hide-and-seek. It would be close to impossible to find them then, even for Gianni... if he was here.

"PARAGON, find me anything on artifacts or relics taken from Philae Temple."

Two pink granite obelisks were taken by collectors in the early 19th century. Only one remains intact where it stands today in its new home in Dorset, England.

"PARAGON, is there anything about an *ankh* taken from Philae Temple by these collectors?"

There are over twenty results for ankhs related to Philae Temple. The ankh is a symbol of eternal life and is common to both royalty and deities. It is still used today in pagan cults and religions.

"Over twenty?! PARAGON, are any of those results made from gold?"

Pottery, bronze, iron, and a variety of stones including granite and alabaster.

"Alabaster, huh?" This wasn't going as well as I had thought it would. "PARAGON, are there any *ankhs* made of gold anywhere?"

In present day, gold or gold alloy is a common material for the ankh symbol in jewelry. In the past, an ankh made of wood and overlaid in sheet gold was created as a mirror case for the Pharaoh Tutankhamun's tomb.

PARAGON brought up a hologram of the mirror case, but it was nothing like the *ankh* that Isis had shown me. Maybe hers had never been found or maybe it had never been made yet. *What if I made one? Maybe what she wants is an offering.*

In the meantime I drew a picture on the screen of the second object hoping that PARAGON would be able to tell me what it was.

A sistrum is a rattle used in religious ceremonies or as an instrument during festivals. It has been associated with the Ancient Egyptian goddess Hathor, but after being assimilated by the more prevalent Isis the sistrum was incorporated into her depictions as well. It is said that Isis played the rattle for the infant Horus.

"This is probably a long shot. PARAGON, find me any gold *sistrum* related to Isis, Hathor, or Philae Temple."

The Egyptian Museum of Antiquities in Cairo has one of gilded wood on record. It is currently on loan to the British Museum in London, England. PARAGON showed me a picture of the *sistrum* from the museum's website. It was close in appearance to the one I saw at Philae and the best chance I had at something authentic. If I was able to get the *sistrum* and present it to Isis, maybe she could tell me more about the *ankh.* Now I just needed a plan to get it.

The Blackbournes had most of England in their pocket and rich people loved donating to museums and art galleries. I wouldn't put it past them to know someone with connections at the museum or some society with ties to it.

I was about to have PARAGON call Owen when I received a transmission myself. It was Lyle calling from his helmet uplink. "You watching Aurelia's speech?" he asked.

"I didn't know I could watch, not that I'd want to. I'm back from Philae and—"

"I thought I told you Rudgar was gonna have PARAGON hack security to stream the speech for us? This is history being made, man. It affects all of us and I wanted you on call in case something goes down to stop it."

"I'm sure Aurelia has got herself covered. I gotta go, Lyle. Important history lesson happening on my end too. I need to go visit our favorite Brits."

"Oh, yeah? See if you can convince them to cough up a few sets of that demon armor. Maybe they'll listen to you. And don't forget to turn on the—"

"You're breaking up Lyle, I can't hear you. Must be a bad connection!"

"This isn't a cellphone, dude. It doesn't work like that. I can also see you through the camera on the tablet—"

I hung up before he finished. He was going to get me back for that somehow, but I really did not want anything to do with Aurelia's big night out. After she made the leaders of the mortal world adore her it would be more difficult than ever to get rid of her for good. If she was killed, word would get out who did it and no where would be safe because those responsible would be persecuted as the evil ones. She knew how to stay ten steps ahead of everyone.

"PARAGON, put me through to Owen Blackbourne." Somehow I pictured there being a lot more fighting and a lot less desk work required to save the world.

"An anonymous call from an untraceable number. What can I do for you, Yankee?" Owen answered right away, thinking that I was Lyle.

"It's Dorian," I said.

"Oh, the flying bloke. How are you, mate?"

"Could be worse, I suppose. I'm sure Lyle's told you what's been going on. I need something from the British Museum—an artifact—and I was hoping you'd have the connections to help me get it."

"What kind of artifact are we talking about?" he asked.

"Egyptian. It's a rattle or an instrument I need to bring back a goddess that should be able to help us stop what's going on in Egypt."

"A goddess, eh? What does she look like?"

"I don't know. I haven't seen her yet, just omens so far, but there are drawings."

"A blind date with a goddess? Mmm, yeah I'm in."

"Owen, seriously, can you help me or not?"

"Amy's father was on the Board of trustees for thirty years before passing. I'm sure something can be worked out. Come by tonight and we'll get it sorted over drinks."

Chapter Sixteen

"*Friends, compatriots, beloved chosen of humanity, I—Aurelia de Saint-Pierre—stand before you a humbled messenger of peace. It is my sincerest wish in addressing this room to present to you a mutually favorable solution to our most recent and direst of woes.*

"*Long has it been since I have walked amongst your kind, but be assured not once have you left the tireless compassion of my heart. I have done all in my power during the many years of my absence to guide in silence and care for you as I would my own children. Now, with prosperity and good fortune within reach at last, our enemies grow ever more sinister in their attempt to halt our progress.*

"*As you may well know, the cost of true success runs high. I alone bear a heavy burden by simply appearing here tonight, but it is a burden worth bearing to see my dream of a true utopia among our people come to fruition. I am unlike you and for that your ancestors drove me and my kind into hiding. They scorned our charity and persecuted us in a jealous rage of our beauty. The world fell into an intolerable darkness that grows ever darker still, but should those of today pay the price for the mistakes of their forefathers?*

"Do you not deserve a chance of your own to bask in the soothing caress of my divine blessing? To right the injustices and undo the terrible fate dealt to you by those no longer here? Why should you suffer, my beautiful creatures? Allow us to walk forward, together, out of the darkness. Let me comfort the wounds of this ailing world, and of those who live here, so that we may know peace again.

"It is true, there are monsters in this world. My people have shielded your kind from these evils for centuries despite our cruel exile and have asked for nothing in return. Those worthy of your concern are not the ones whom seek to join you in openness, but those whom endeavor to steal your freedom and rule you from their ivory tower. They slip their bonds from a place most hellish, one torn straight from the pages of holy scriptures meant to warn you. The first of many has risen in the Egyptian sands with more soon to follow. You have already seen the unbridled destruction of but a single beast twisting nature to its despicable whims and tasted bitter sorrow at the loss of too many sweet, innocent lives as result.

"But there is no need to fear your saviors, should you accept us into your hearts. We, the

Archios, were made for this world with the sole purpose of your salvation. Our very form brings pleasure when you gaze upon us. Our fangs are diminutive and purposeful, not meant to inflict pain, but bring you a sense of rapture long lost to mankind. Our resilient bodies and sharp minds are here to protect you from evil like that which stirs out there in the sands of a fallen empire.

"I beseech you, do not err and shun us, for we are your caregivers with the power to let you glimpse Heaven in our embrace. Strive for more than archaic savagery. Cast off the shackles of this mortal coil and ascend to your rightful place by my side in everlasting harmony. Allow me to guide you in the liberation of both our kind because only together may we become—undeniably—invincible! Stand with me now and unite in the light of a greater tomorrow!"

"That's enough of that," I said, stopping the recording right as everyone had risen from their seats to applaud. I had taken one of the tablets with me to watch the speech during the flight to meet with Owen.

"You have to admit, she gives a good presentation and looks hot doing it," said Bobby. "And that was only the part in English. She continues in five other languages!"

"People said that Hitler gave some impressive speeches too. The only thing I'll admit is that she probably looks better in a dress." Her gown was more avant garde red-carpet fashion than something appropriate for addressing a gathering of world leaders, but this was Aurelia we were talking about. The violet dress took up most of the staging area and was designed to give the appearance of rose petals encircling her. It would have been more accurate if there had been thorns.

I understood from the little I watched why she was the right person for the job. Although it was possible I hated her even more when she was pretending to be nice, I couldn't see anyone else I knew putting on such a dramatic and effective performance. She didn't stand behind the podium looking down at a script, only to occasionally glance around the room when taking a breath. Instead, she fluidly swished and swayed her way past the front row of diplomats and back, strategically placing one of her porcelain hands on the shoulder or the cheek of a captive audience member to immerse them even further in her bullshit. She trailed her finger across the desk in front of them as both men and women salivated in hope that she may grace them with a touch.

Aurelia didn't need a microphone and she couldn't be bothered putting any effort into projecting louder than her normal volume. Even in her soft yet authoritative voice, she had the crowd's undivided attention. It was their job to listen to her. They craned their necks and rose from their seats to keep her in their glazed-over sights—and to be sure they didn't miss a syllable that passed her lips.

Had it been anyone else giving that same speech, the reception would have been much different with constant questions and outbursts, most likely including "Who the hell are you and how did you get in here?" The words she spoke didn't matter. She could have read nursery rhymes backward or recited the alphabet in the wrong order and still elicited the same enamored response. The main reason she gave the speech at all was for her own ego. As Lyle had said, this would be going down in history. It would be another moment to add to her scrapbook of times she manipulated the masses of humanity.

There was also the fact that others outside of her influence may have drawn further suspicions of foul play had she used brute force and issued direct commands to try and win over her audience. The humans would be more apt to rebel should they feel they were being controlled, not lending a sympathetic ear to the pleas of a beautiful young lady who has only the best intentions for the modern world in mind.

The whole thing made me sick, especially since we were so desperate that it was our only choice.

"We're here," Bobby announced. "Does it matter where I drop you off?"

"He's the last house on the right." The Blackbourne's estate was a group of villas in the English countryside. Each residence was built in a semicircle around a central courtyard and belonged to a different member of this chapter.

The estate was quiet unlike most of my other visits. Two of the houses were dark inside; a mournful reminder of those in the family that had been lost in recent nights. Only Owen, his best buddy Micah, and house matriarch Amy were left.

"Hey, mate." After I rang the bell three times Owen answered the door in his boxers with a cigarette hanging from his mouth.

"Hey...am I interrupting anything?" I asked and shook the hand he offered. Owen was tall, blond, and incredibly attractive. The accent didn't hurt either. He had earned his celebrity status in the ring, but could have easily done the same as one of the world's top male models if it provided the same rush he was so addicted to chasing. When I was in high school I used to have a celebrity crush on him, but after meeting and getting to know him as well as I did it killed that for me. There was still a good guy in Owen buried deep beneath the many layers of British swagger, alcoholism, drug abuse, nymphomania, bloodlust, and all-around daredevil showmanship.

"Was just about to get dressed," he said. "Come on in. Fancy a drink?"

"That's all right. It doesn't do anything for me, remember?"

"Should I?" he asked, leading the way upstairs to his room.

"You guys tried to roofie me so you could dump me in the woods and hunt me when we first met."

"Sorry, not ringing any bells. It sounds like something we'd do though. Good times, eh?"

"I've had better. I've had worse too, but I've definitely had better."

"I was hoping you'd bring the Yankee with you," Owen said as he started suiting up in his hunting gear. I almost took a seat on his king-sized bed while I waited until I realized I'd probably stick to the sheets. "He's been dodging my invites ever since that last party a month back."

"Yeah, Lyle told me about it. He thought you guys were gonna play cards and have a few beers. He's not really the type to get it on with a bed full of escorts. He's more... traditional."

"It wasn't like we were going to kill them after. And it was hardly a full bed. I gave him what I call a 'Blackbourne starter pack'. There was some fine tail in the pack too, let me tell you. I would've been jealous if I hadn't wound up taking them all for myself anyway."

"Really charming," I laughed. "I'm glad some things never change."

"I wish that were true," he sighed and pulled up his hood. "My career is pretty much finished now. I'm in retirement."

"Why? You heal almost as fast as I do. It can't be an injury?"

"That's the problem, not the healing, but when I can throw a guy three times my size over my head with just one arm...there's a bit of an issue. What's the point of fighting for sport if you have to hold back so much you aren't breaking a sweat?"

"I see. So what are you thinking of doing now then?"

"Probably settle down, find myself a good girl to marry and bang out a few kids, get a desk job playing with numbers like Micah—" He started to grin and before I could call him on that never happening he came clean. "Could you imagine? I'd rather put a bloody bullet in my head. All I need to find is a bigger thrill, something to really get the heart pumping like that time we had in Hell."

"You were impaled through the chest and almost died of a collapsed lung and blood loss," I reminded him.

"It was the best time of my life. I need that again. This whole mess about the end of the world sounds like the perfect climax, really. Let's just be out with it, I say. Come fight me without all this bullshit and cover up nonsense."

"You're sick in the head."

"So I've been told, but it's just that I like to enjoy the time I've been given. You and the Yankee are so bloody stiff. You live forever, right? God, I would fly myself right into the sun and hope to end it all if I was that boring. No offense."

"None taken, but let me ask you: why are you dressing up for a hunt if we're just getting one of your connections to give us the artifacts?"

"You can never be too prepared. What if the world splits open on our way and I'm in my knickers? I like to dress for the occasion. Good taste is an English thing, I wouldn't expect you to understand." Coming from the other Blackbournes I might have taken that as an insult, but Owen had a way of making you laugh along with him. "I don't suppose your ride could take us to London?"

"It's only got two seats, although I guess he could make two trips," I said. "It would probably only take twenty to thirty minutes both ways."

"It's a three hour drive otherwise, a little shy of two hours with my driving in the Lamb."

"I'll talk to the pilot then since time is a factor."

Chapter Seventeen

Bobby made the round trip flights in under an hour, dropping us off not far from the British Museum. There was no way to get around the jet being seen above a city as busy as London, even at night, but at this point it didn't matter anymore.

"Where are we meeting your contact?" I asked as we wandered around to the side of the museum. It didn't seem that Owen knew where we were supposed to be going.

"This looks about right." We were standing in the staff parking lot by a padlocked metal cellar door. He bent down and when he broke off the lock his plan became clear.

"We weren't meeting anyone were we?"

"Nope," he said, swinging the doors open and heading inside. "If you're waiting for an invitation from Her Majesty I don't think she's coming either."

"If I knew we were just going to break in and grab what we needed I would've busted in here myself," I said and closed the door behind us. "I was trying *not* to cause more trouble than needed."

"See, you American blokes have no style," he answered as he put in the correct code to disable the security alarm. "I always wanted to be James Bond when I was a lad, pulling of a big heist, getting the woman at the end of the movie."

"He was the good guy... He didn't do heists."

"Then like Robin Hood. Take from the rich, give to the poor."

"But you're rich... and museums mostly work off donations, so it's like the rich is stealing from the poor."

"Fuck it. I just want to steal something and shag some women. Is that so wrong?"

"I don't know anymore, but isn't knowing the security alarm code ahead of time kind of cheating? It takes away most of the risk."

"Life is all about cheating. You ever take vitamins? You're cheating death."

"How drunk are you right now?" I knew I was probably better off not asking.

"I remembered the security code Amy had gotten for me, so not enough by my standards. Now keep your voice down."

We had entered into a small trash collection room. Such a room would have low priority on any security route, easy access to the alarm as most exits and entrances have, and a slim chance of running into anyone working here afterhours. It was a smart entry point and enough to make me think that Owen did actually put more thought into this than just picking the first door out of view that we came across.

"Any idea where we're going?" I whispered before we went out into the hall.

"None. All I know is that there are three vaults close by and one of them is where they keep what's on loan." It had been a while since I was in what would be considered a "normal" present day building. I was always in some old castle, or mansion, or PROJECT: UNITY's ultra-modern base.

We made it past a row of offices unnoticed until a guard on patrol came out from one of them. Owen was quick to react. He charged the man with a rising knee strike and put him in a chokehold until he was unconscious. He dragged the guard back into the office and stabbed him in the neck with a dart he retrieved from a pocket in the chest of his armor.

"Meant to be thrown, but just as well I suppose." Owen held up the dart for me to see before putting it back in his pocket. "Chokehold only puts a man out for a minute at most, but this'll keep him down a good few hours. Great in low doses for helping you get royally pissed at parties if you've got a tolerance like mine. Come to think of it, I should leave this wanker a bill. This stuff doesn't come cheap. Might've been cheaper to pay him off."

"There's a fire escape plan here," I said, ignoring him while I read the map posted by the door. "The hallway branches off up ahead, so we've got to take a left. The vaults are over there, but they're only numbered on the map." I was just about to leave the office when someone from the overnight cleaning crew walked in on us wheeling a trash can.

Owen threw a second dart over my shoulder and into the man's neck then leapt for him before he could make a noise or hit the ground. "I've got myself quite a collection," he said and hid this guy in the office with the guard.

"I'm glad you're enjoying yourself."

"Always." Owen posed the two men in a compromising position and then took out his phone to snap a picture. "Micah ought to get a good laugh out of this. Poor lad never leaves his desk anymore. We have to send the girls in under it for a little stress relief when he needs a break." Owen winked at me from behind his mask as we went back out into the hallway.

We made it to the correct hall without any further interruptions, but something was wrong. "What good fortune, one of the vaults is opened. Now if it's the one we need, I'll be suspicious."

"Wait up," I stopped Owen. "Something's wrong. I can feel it." I could *smell* it, to be more accurate. It was the pungent odor of sulfur along with a very subtle rise in temperature. I froze and tried to come up with a plan for what I had a feeling was awaiting us in the vault, but my nerves got the best of me. I charged in ahead of Owen and was proven right.

"I'm impressed," Minerva sneered down her nose at us. "You figured out to come here all by yourself, or did you have a little divine inspiration?" She was holding the golden *sistrum* in her hand. "You're still too late, but at least you can give yourself credit for *almost* keeping up with me. Maybe if you had that Archios brute with you that you're always following around, you would have made it here in time."

Owen went to leap for the *sistrum*, but was blasted out of the vault by a gout of balefire. Minerva lit the hand holding the artifact on fire. I tried to tear it from her grip with my powers, but her shield was up and reflected the force back at me. "By all means, why not try using your surroundings to attack me?" she mocked. "Maybe you can destroy all the other relics here in your frantic throes. This is just one big temple of forgotten relics of the past after all. Go ahead, doom a few other pathetic deities to eternal slumber."

All I could do was watch as the *sistrum* turned to ashes and fell from her hand. I was seething in a rage like no other. I focused all my energy and fought against her shield to compress the space surrounding her, but she was too strong and the vault began to shake violently from the immense vibrations caused by the recoil.

"Looks like I'm out of time," she said, and with a flick of her wrist sent pale green fires down both sides of the vault to incinerate what was left of the artifacts. With a bang and a poof of black smoke she was gone.

I rushed to scoop up the ashes of the *sistrum* and used my powers to pull the rows of shelving from the vault and into the hallway so they would be out of the fire. Owen ducked out of the way as half the contents of the room sailed past him. The fire alarm triggered and the overhead sprinklers turned on, but water couldn't extinguish otherworldly fires. "Sod it, we have to go," he said. "Close the vault. You got most of it out."

I still couldn't speak I was so angry. I grabbed an ancient pot from the collection and put the ashes in it. There were several ankhs, none of them gold, but I grabbed five of them and bolted for the exit.

"I take it you two have history?" Owen asked. I didn't care about holding back on my powers or anybody seeing us at all anymore. I tore through the air with him over the city to get back to the jet despite his startled screams for the first mile or two.

"You could say that." I answered when we landed.

"I've never struck a woman, even pissed off my arse, but she was real close to being my first and that's not something I get to say often." Owen took his mask off and lit up a cigarette. "Now I have been known to spank a few of the naughty ones, but something tells me that demon bugger wouldn't have been up for it—"

"Get me to Philae," I told Bobby and got in the jet without another word.

"Just because you're off to save the world doesn't mean you can't be a gent about it and have some bloody manners!" Owen shouted. "You're welcome!"

"Thanks," I said, thinking how much better that may have gone if it was Noah with me instead. "Have Micah pick you up. I'm going to be a while."

"Are you going to be all right in there by yourself?" Bobby asked as we landed at the temple complex a few hours later. It was morning here and the sky was a scintillating amber hue across the desert landscape and sparkling azure river. My mood still had me seeing only red, however. "I only have a sidearm with me in case that demon comes back, but the buddy system works."

"I'll be fine," I said. I had yet to calm down during the flight to the temple, but I managed to tell Bobby what had happened in the museum. It was more so I could vent than me wanting to share my humiliation.

I sped from the jet, half-running, half-skimming across the ground mid-flight. With artifacts in hand I headed to the largest temple of the complex where I had encountered the omen from Isis. There were no birds or visions or anything to signify success as I entered the chamber.

I placed the five ankhs on one pedestal and emptied the ashes of the *sistrum* onto the other.

Nothing.

"Isis, I don't know what else to do," I spoke to the shaft in the ceiling where light was streaming through. The vision of the golden *sistrum* appeared again overlapping the ash pile. "It was destroyed by a demon. This is all that's left."

A sparrow flew down from the shaft and landed on the ashes. I tensed up, afraid it would scatter them and that's exactly what it did. This wasn't helping my anger. I wanted to smack the little feathered monster away. "You could've just said it wasn't good enough! I got you a whole bunch of ankhs for extra credit. What about those?"

There was still no verbal response, but the bird was chirping away and flapping its wings in the ashes making a bigger mess. "You talked to me before, why can't you at least give me a verbal hint?" I asked.

Nothing.

The bird vanished, leaving me with the mess it had caused. I scooped the ashes back up and put them on the pedestal in the shimmering vision of the completed golden *sistrum*.

"Are you expecting me to put this back together?" I petitioned again.

Nothing.

The light from the vision dimmed. "I can't do that if that's what you're trying to get me to do..." I *had* rebuilt a whole village before, after the triumph in Hell. This wasn't the same though. That time, I had put the pieces of building back together, but they were still recognizable as pieces of buildings. This wasn't even gilded wood anymore; it was cinders.

I was also in a different state of mind when I rebuilt the village. I had felt this overwhelming positive force bubbling up inside me like a song being sung directly to my soul.

I could try to put the sistrum *back together. It's not like I have any other options. The good part is that there's a guide for me to follow as long as this vision doesn't fade anymore.* I used my hands to mold the basic shape within the outline on the pedestal. *Now for the hard part...*

I got on my knees so I was eye level with the cinders. My first thought was to work on making it three-dimensional so I held my hand above the pedestal as a guide of how far up to go. My head just wasn't in it though and I was having difficulty getting Minerva out of my thoughts. The cinders swirled around and jumped like iron filings being pulled by a magnet. The more I pressured myself to concentrate, the worse I did.

I had to relax and find some positive vibe to rekindle my creation powers. This was another time I wished Noah was around. That big idiot loved to antagonize me but he always knew the right buttons to push to get me on track. My usual reaction was wanting to clobber him, but that was part of his charm.

I started to smile and then laughed to myself as I remembered the time Noah taught me to fly by throwing me from the roof of Aurelia's guest house and catching me an inch above the ground. It wasn't funny back then; in fact, I don't know what it was that made me laugh about it now. At the time I thought I was going to die, and it must have looked pretty funny to Noah that I was flailing around given that he knew I wasn't in any real danger.

It was amusing how screwed up he was that he got so much entertainment from throwing people off of buildings and then catching them. He couldn't help himself and even did it to Lyle a couple of times to get a rise out of him. Maybe that was his messed up way of bonding with someone new, but that bridge had been burnt pretty badly between the two of them.

There was a light coming from the cinders now. I hadn't been paying attention, but while I reminisced I proceeded to fashion the cinders into the shape of the *sistrum*. If I let go it would have crumbled again, but it must have been enough for what Isis needed because it solidified on its own and was restored to its golden luster.

Escorted by a flock of sparrows, the hazy image of a woman's silhouette floated down the beam of light from the ceiling and placed a hand on the *sistrum*. The ghostly figure picked up the artifact in one hand and one of the ankhs in her other. She crossed her arms over her chest and then raised both artifacts into the light above. The ankh transformed into gold and with that she appeared before me in full view. *I'm glad I decided to bring those with me after all.*

"Greetings and many blessings upon you, Young One. I am Isis."

Chapter Eighteen

The goddess was not quite what I had been expecting based on all the hieroglyphics and artwork dedicated to her. She still had long black hair with bangs and was wrapped in a scarlet linen dress, but she was of average human height when in my mind I had pictured her to be closer to Set's size as in the pictures.

Isis's crown that was always shown as a flat circle framed by two horns was instead a miniature sun hovering between upward reaching wings from the sides of her head. I couldn't tell if these wings were a part of her or her headdress as the Norse Valkyries wore, but the feathers matched the full-sized slender wings from her back with colors and hues including browns, creams, and reds.

Her milk chocolate complexion glistened gold in tune with the warm radiant light of her visible aura. Just gazing upon her evoked the most pleasant feelings of curling up beside a roaring fireplace after being out in the cold. If I had been asked what a maternal presence was before this moment I wouldn't have been able to put it to words, but being near the goddess gave me the answer. It was a very specific feeling, one that took its rightful place in the highest echelon of nurturing comfort and acceptance. She made every fiber of your being feel at peace like only a mother could, without a word or the slightest change in expression.

"Hello," I said, not knowing the appropriate greeting protocol. Empress Kamakura always acted like I wasn't there so she made it easy on me. I realized I had still been kneeling and got to my feet, then rethought that and kneeled again, but when she didn't react either way I slowly stood back up. "It's very nice to finally meet you... I'm sorry if I came off disrespectful."

I had met plenty of "all-powerful" supernaturals, including another goddess, but Isis was special. I couldn't describe what it was about her.

"There is no need for you to fret, Young One," she spoke verbally in English and telepathically at the same time, unlike Kamakura, who only projected her thoughts into our minds. I had to focus to be sure that the faint sound of birds was still coming from Isis and not our avian audience around the chamber that had entered when she did. "My strength is limited and I can only muster the energy to communicate with those at peace."

"I guess the angrier I got the harder it was for you to contact me... I thought you were trying to test me."

"There was no need to. You have already proven yourself where another has failed. I had called out to the Dark One for his strength when I foresaw my brother's rise, but he closed himself off from me to seek other ambitions until I could no longer get through." *So, she was the voice Gianni heard, not Minerva trying to trick him. That meant his actions for glory and conquest really were his own...* "I had also made a plea to the Empress of the East, but she was bound by oath to another."

"Yeah, she... says that a lot."

"We are all bound by something. What matters is that you have succeeded where others could not. With these artifacts I can once again manifest to lend you my aid against my brother."

"I'm glad the magic in them wasn't lost when that one got destroyed."

"The artifacts themselves are not magic," she explained. It was so nice talking with her. Her voice was soothing and made me want to take a nap right here. Best of all, she was direct. "Spiritborn deities such as myself require prayers of worship to exist and draw strength from. We inspire our followers to create these icons as supplement to active prayer. The gods are not eternal, even we may fall, and so we prepare. While our flock may no longer hear our calls, these icons and temples stand as anchors in the material world to keep us from fading away forever while we sleep."

"Oh, that's pretty clever." *I had figured it was just for vanity, but this made a lot of the history behind religions even more interesting.*

"Soulborn deities such as yourself and the Dark One that have transcended—"

"Whoa, wait a minute. Back up. I'm not a deity. Gianni, er, the Dark One, maybe, but I'm just a freak of nature that finally found peace with that."

Isis smiled a knowing smile. "And that is why you have transcended."

"Because I'm okay with who I am? There would be millions of gods out there then. Tons of people have self-confidence." This was freaking me out. I'm sure most people would love the notion of godhood, but already being supernatural all it meant to me was more responsibilities and an even slimmer chance at ever being left alone. I had hopes that after some time during which the supernaturals would be integrated into the mortal world, I'd be able to lead a boring life again yet still be myself.

"There is nothing to fear, Young One. You possess a beautiful soul with immense power. There is more to transcendence than peace with one's self. You have endured trials that few others in history have. Take my hand and I will show you your deeds through the window of your soul, one not obscured by the prejudice of the mind's perspective and pride." She approached me and took both my hands in hers before I could refuse. There was a warm, tranquil feeling that filled me, and in an instant my trepidation washed away.

My eyes hadn't closed, but I felt as if I were in a dream. It was not an illusion or a vision of any sort, but that disorienting sensation you get when you know you're dreaming and can only watch events unfold.

"A trial by fire." I heard Isis's voice in my dream as I watched. It was the time Vance and Noah had saved me from the parasite I was infected with. Vance had merged us into one being and part of the ritual had me trapped in a magic circle burning to death, but I came out of it immortal... at a cost.

"But my power takes from the souls that the parasites in the Rift are sent out to eat," I said. "If anything wouldn't that make me evil by nature, but just good by choice? How does that make me eligible for transcendence? The Spiritborn gods only take the energy that resonates from the souls. Demons and monsters eat them."

"All things exist in balance, Young One. The harvesters from another world are a neutral entity only driven by the same simple instinct to survive as any living creature. Evil is a corruption of choice, not an impulse to live.

"The souls that nourish you are not forever lost, only returned to the cosmic cycle through you. Souls are a form of energy and energy can never be absolutely destroyed. The energy you release makes its way back into the cosmos to be collected again and reborn as a new soul in the heavens. Your choices and actions are important to guide that rebirth and maintain cosmic balance."

"I've seen what the parasites do though," I said. "It isn't pleasant."

"Nor is the process of a bird feasting upon a worm to one of its kin, but you exist on a higher level than the mortals of Earth now. Every soul that gives you strength is another that evil will not have. If you do not make the choice to bring peace with your power you will let it go for naught, a wasted sacrifice."

"I guess... that does make me feel better about it. If it has to be this way then you're right. I'd rather not let demons use souls to commit evil and if they're being reborn as new souls then maybe it isn't so bad." *The process of the parasites infecting people still stirred up so many emotions, especially when remembering my parents' dying from them...*

The scene of me burning to death ended and the next one started. "This was the battle with the Carpathians in Manhattan at the end of the parasite plague. I didn't really do much here. Why is this special?"

I watched as the swarm of Carpathians overtook Noah. I remembered this... he was being torn apart by them and I saved him by electrocuting them with nearby power lines and the water from a busted fire hydrant. This was before I could ash them with a single telekinetic strike.

I saw myself hesitating in the scene. I remembered not knowing if I should let him die because I knew Aurelia had sent him to kill me. He had said he wasn't going to, but I knew if Aurelia wanted she could have forced him against his will.

"A trial of mercy," said Isis. "You opened your heart to your enemy and spared a life."

"Do you know Noah?" I asked. "Why were you leading me to him? Was it for his speed to get the artifacts?"

"No. That is only a question you will have the answer to." The scene ended with Noah biting me to heal himself and then dumping me on the ground. That never really changed.

The next event was in pitch blackness until I saw my embrace with Gianni. This wasn't one I wanted to remember.

"A trial of humility," Isis said. "To let go of all ego and bare your soul to the void is an impressive feat most fail to accomplish in life and death."

I had only known Gianni for maybe a day or two *at most* when this had happened. It was more embarrassing for me now than it was back then. He got me to release all the pent-up anger and sadness I had been holding back since the death of my parents and cry in his arms. I exploded in a huge blast of telekinetic energy that I would later use again in battle. *I can't believe I cried in front of him...* "Is he going to be okay? Set—"

"My brother is draining them of their life-force, but I can restore them to their natural form once I gain more strength."

"Is he evil? Gian—the Dark One, I mean," I asked Isis. If anyone would know the real truth it would be her.

"No," she said with certainty.

"Others have said he is and sometimes I feel like he's leaning that way."

"Your souls are not in harmony and actions that feel strange to you can make it seem this way. His methods have made him desperate, so much so that my voice was lost to him. Only the future knows if this desperation will lead to acts of true evil, but love is not a question of good and evil." She knew what I was getting at.

I missed him, I cared about him, but our souls were definitely not in harmony. I didn't agree with anything he was doing or with his ideals. Seeing me cry on his shoulder after only knowing him for such a short time may have been a righteous act of humility to Isis, but it also showed me that I was looking to cling to someone in my time of need back then and willing to blind myself to the facts as we got to know each other. Being assured that he was "good" didn't mean we were compatible.

"What's next?" I asked, feeling more focused now that two of my biggest personal concerns were being put to rest.

"A trial of bravery."

It was the battle in Yomi against Kamakura's dragon form.

"I thought I was going to die," I laughed flippantly, sounding not unlike Owen for a moment.

I had flown right into her mouth and used that explosive technique which always left me weakened. I did like to brag a little that I had fought a dragon and not just any dragon, but a dragon deity. I could see that earning me points toward transcendence over the other events so far.

"A trial of charity," Isis announced and brought up the next scene. It was in Aurelia's chateau immediately after the battle with Kamakura. I had bargained with Kamakura, with Gianni's help, for the Muramasa to give to Noah. It was the weapon Noah was searching for to bring down Aurelia and win his freedom back. It was one of the first times I had seen Noah lighten up around me, even after knowing him for more than three years.

"I was just helping a friend in need. He would do the same for me," I said, my moment of elation starting to wane as I thought of him chained up and beaten...

"A trial of might." This one was the end of the fight with demon lord Ma'al in Hell a few months ago. I disintegrated dozens of the same type of demons that I had trouble fighting only one of in the past, and kept a mountain from collapsing in on us after the battle made the lair unstable.

"That seems more impressive now looking at it from outside my own body and not just screaming in the dark."

"A herculean feat at only a fraction of your strength. The trapped souls you had harvested from the Infernal allowed them to be reborn when their power was released through you. You also gained the insight of creation from the Infernal to use for a purpose other than evil, which brings us to the last trial: the trial of creation."

This was one I could agree with without any argument. I did feel kind of godly when I rebuilt the village in Iraq that had been ravaged by terrorism. I had felt an unstoppable flow of positive energy that did whatever I imagined to bring peace to innocent lives in danger and despair. It gave me chills—the good kind, like when you hear your favorite song and turn it up as loud as you can. I didn't want to be worshipped for it, though, and hid myself in a white sheet so nobody would see who I was, but word got out as it always did.

"What did you mean 'only a fraction' of my strength?" I asked as the chamber in Philae reappeared around us. Isis stood in front of me with her hands out in front of her holding a disgusting glowing puke green object that looked like broken glass with black hairy tendrils emerging from the cracks. "Um, what is that?"

I backed away and noticed one of those tendrils attached to me through my shirt. I went to pull it out when Isis commanded I stop.

"This is your soul, Young One. That strand is what keeps your body tethered to it. If it were to be severed you would die a true death."

"You called my soul 'beautiful' before. I didn't think you were being sarcastic." I recoiled in aversion and then slight panic. "Uh, can you put it back in me?"

"I will do more than that, but first I will explain. All souls are beautiful. Yours has been shattered and poisoned by the taint of hellfire. Do not look upon it in revulsion any more than you would a bird's broken wing. My power is limited, but

I can heal your soul so you may use its full potential and undo the chaos my brother has caused.

"When the wars in our land ignited some time ago my brother began to regain his strength, but it was not enough to awaken him. A demon sorceress then invaded our pantheon with the soul of a powerful ancient being as an offering. She told my brother she would revive him if he promised to return the world to Egyptian glory with him as King of the Gods in exchange for the souls of the heretics he slays. Anyone who knows of my brother, knows this has been his sole ambition since the dawn of time. It was not a promise that needed to be made."

"That's Minerva," I said. "She's the one who burnt your *sistrum* and... she's one of the ones that made me. If she gave Set the soul of an Ancient it was so that he would create so much chaos, her masters—the Infernal Kings—could march straight from Hell on to Earth. They don't care about reviving Egypt. They're just using him."

"Yes, it is as I feared. He is my brother, but he must be stopped at all costs."

"What about your son, Horus? He beat Set before right?"

"My son and the Ennead lent the last of their power to me so that I could seek help. Now it is up to you to do what Horus has before you."

"What is the Ennead?" I asked.

"The Ennead are the nine gods who preside over our pantheon and the ones that claimed Horus, and not Set, as the rightful heir of Egypt."

"Okay then, I guess it really is all up to me... I'm ready."

Isis's hands shined with a golden luminescence so bright it hurt my eyes. The broken pieces of my soul floated together and arranged themselves into an orb. The cracks sealed, leaving behind very fine black veins along the surface and the green corruption dissipated. My soul looked like a large white marble or a translucent alabaster sphere. It started to shine brighter and brighter until the light overtook the light from Isis. The last thing I saw was her gently pushing it back into my chest.

The sensation was like the vibe I had felt when rebuilding the village in Iraq, only magnified millions of times greater. I couldn't contain it. It was a happy feeling, but frightened me that I was going to explode. I was so amped that I was going numb and wanted to fly around the world to burn off energy.

"Before Set's departure from our pantheon to Earth he stole the Eye of Ra," Isis's voice was fading as my vision returned. The birds in the chamber were gone and she was disappearing back to her hazy state. "It is the stone on the end of his *was* staff and gives him incredible power. You will not be able to defeat him while he possesses it. He plans to use it to rewrite the reality on Earth in his own image. However, only those who know the true name of Ra can unlock the full omnipotence of the Eye. Bring it... to me... so... I may save... the fallen gods and... right my brother's... wrongs."

Isis was gone. The atmosphere of the chamber was so cold and lonely without her. There was something different about the room. Tiny, almost microscopic dots were covering every surface, including my clothes and the four ankhs that Isis had left behind. I shook my shirt off, but nothing changed so I peered in close to the dots on top of the empty pedestal. The closer I looked the more confused I became. The dots weren't moving and were the same color as whatever they were on. It was more like they were a different texture, like standing back and looking at a grain of salt on a white backdrop but even smaller than that.

I touched the stone with my finger, but it didn't feel like anything out of the ordinary. Then I used my powers to try and telekinetically lift one of the dots.

"What the hell..." The stone itself climbed up to a sharp point. I could manipulate solid stone with my powers as if I was molding soft clay. I pushed and pulled the dots along the miniature mountain I had made out of the pedestal, creating curlicues and spikes protruding from it. *Are these molecules I'm seeing? Am I able to affect something as small as that now?*

More power didn't necessarily mean bigger explosions, but better refinement of my skills and senses. No more breaking objects along a straight line dozens of times until I got the shape I wanted or whittling away at objects to make them smooth. My mind raced with giddy thoughts of all I could do. If this was what godhood would be about then bring it on.

This was my dream, my real one that I kept having to bury whenever conflict arose. I had wanted to be an architect to design and build houses and buildings with pillars and statues.

Gradually, my enhanced sight reverted to normal although I was still able to probe the stone with my powers and alter it with little to no effort.

"Thank you!" I shouted up to Isis excitedly, hoping she could hear me. "Sorry about your pedestal!" I started to reform it when a shadow swept over me from behind. I felt the chill of excitement imagining the possibility that it was Gianluca who had somehow broken free, but once I turned around that hope turned to horror. The shadow belonged to Set.

He loomed over me from the corridor and before anything else could happen, raised his staff with a blinding light.

Chapter Nineteen

Where... am I?

My head was pounding, my senses were skewed, and my body was stiff and soaked with sweat. I knew I was still somewhere in Egypt by the sandy limestone walls around me, but couldn't remember how I had gotten there. My arms were restrained out to the side and I was having trouble moving my head to look around. There was a collar around my neck attached to whatever I was lying on top of and a scorching reddish-orange light beat down on me from a shaft in the ceiling the same as in Isis's chamber.

Once I began to regain my composure I tried to break free of the manacles around my wrists, but some sort of spell protected them. In fact, everything in the room except my own clothes was warded with some magical shield. I could still feel the objects with my powers, but manipulating them was impossible.

I struggled physically trying to pull the chains out of the wall or at least slip my hands out, but it was no use. I was weak from exhaustion and still too disoriented. It was doubtful that even at my peak I would be able to free myself that way.

My eyes stung from the sweat dripping down into them. I was panting like a dog from the heat and dehydration as I kept trying to pull myself free. That was when I remembered what lead up to me being here.

The sound of something heavy sliding against one of the stone walls let in a choking wind that carried a torrent of sand about the chamber. Then a shadow was cast over me. I should have been indebted to it for the respite it gave me from the sweltering light above, but as the cause for the shadow stood over me I was anything but relieved.

"Should you value what little remains of your allies you'll give greater consideration to your struggling," Set's gruff voice boomed in my head with the sound of rabid growls and howling winds behind it. "The chains that bind are linked to the fate of the Fallen Ones behind you. An extra incentive for you to keep me company."

"I'm not afraid of you," I said with such fervor that it actually sounded believable. I attempted to blast him with a full-force telekinetic strike, but it failed to affect him in the slightest. Now I was beginning to be afraid.

"No, of course you're not. The sorceress told me you were too much a fool to fear your undoing and my sister has only added to that by filling your head with false tales of divinity. I have already taken captive the only two gods foolish enough to challenge me and turned their power to my own. Why does Isis insist upon such insults even now by sending children to defy me?"

"Maybe because it worked the last time? I heard the stories and how Horus kicked your ass and outsmarted you. I can't die so it's only a matter of time until I send you back into the history books to be forgotten again."

"No, you can't die," he snarled in my face, his lips turning up at the sides in a sinister grin. Set was even bigger and more imposing than Gianni was in his armor. "But, there are things many times worse than death that I shall enlighten you to. It is the only reason I have returned your flesh from stone so that we may experience them together."

"I've been set on fire, beaten unconscious, stabbed, and thrown to my death more times than I can remember and that was by somebody I consider a *friend*, so do your worst because you'll only be wasting your energy." I was hoping my confidence would dissuade him and buy me time to figure out how to get free. I didn't notice the staff anywhere or I might have been able to grab it with my powers and force him to release me, but I also couldn't move my head to see very well either.

"Horus may have gained the Ennead's favor with his mother's trickery, but she cannot interfere this time. With no other gods to defy me I shall use *you, Young One*, to prove my dominance over this world as its rightful heir and ruler."

"What are you talking about—? Get off of me!" I screamed and tried to kick him when his hand wrapped around the collar on my neck to squeeze the metal tighter until I choked.

"I should thank my sister for giving me this second chance to redeem my humiliation at her son's hands. I only hope the Ennead has enough strength left in them to see my triumph starting here with you."

I tried summoning all the power I could to tear him apart, but nothing worked. Isis said I couldn't defeat him while he had the staff, but he wasn't even holding it. I didn't want to detonate all my power and burn myself out. Not only would it leave me even more helpless, but I'd destroy the statue that Gianni had been turned into.

My heart was pounding uncontrollably as I kept my eyes shut so as not to look at him. I thought I'd pass out from my panicked attempts to breathe through the pain of the crushed collar, if not from the insipid heat only made worse by my desperate attempts to defend myself. I was powerless.

I can't die, but I can survive what should kill me. I will not be anyone's victim, their playing piece, their sacrifice. I did the last thing I could do.

I blew myself up.

When you can't control the world around you or the actions of others, the only thing you *can* control is yourself. No one can take that away from you if you don't let them.

As time slowed down around me and my body disintegrated into nothingness, I shunted as much of myself away from Set before it all went black.

The moment I came to I was made aware of my victory. I was floating across the room with Set covered in my blood, between me and the hallway he came in from. "Sorry, but I'll have to pass," I said and summoned my tattered shirt to wrap around my waist as he recovered from his shock.

The statues of Gianni and Kamakura were letting off a dim glow to my right that had been unnoticeable when under the burning red sun. The shaft in the ceiling was too narrow for me to escape through and went up so high that I feared I would be stuck halfway up if I tried my trick again, which would make me an easy target.

I needed to get the others out, but couldn't move their statues for the same reason that I was unable to move anything else in the room. Set lunged for me, but I outmaneuvered him and flew under his arms toward the exit. I had almost made it into the hallway when Set hit me from behind with a blistering gust of sand. He threw me back in the chamber and up against the wall.

"The way to my throne is paved by your sacrifice and I have waited too long to let it slip by once more," he snarled. His eyes shone red and the stone door to the hallway slammed shut along with closing the shaft above to leave us with only the soft light of the statues.

He easily overpowered me with his hand gripping the back of my neck so tight I thought it would snap. I was about to free myself again when a voice shouting my name rang out and then fell silent just as fast.

Set threw me across the room and into another wall with such an impact I was knocked out for a second. He was nowhere in the room when I got up, but I heard his voice speaking with someone from where I had heard the shout.

"Make this easier on me and tell me where the kid is. I know he's here and I already got in, so you know I can get out just as fast." *That was Noah! What is he doing here?! No, it can't really be him. It has to be a trap. But why would Set bother with something like that when he had me right where he wanted me?*

"The young god stays with me. There is nothing you can do for him or yourself now that you are in my world, but kneel and pray for my mercy," said Set. His voice was still being projected into my mind so he wanted me to hear this.

"Young god? I'm talking about Dorian, the little shit with the big mess of hair." *Nope, that's definitely Noah.* "I don't give a fuck whoever else you've got at your party. Gimme the kid and I'll give you this sword. I know it's gotta be worth something to you since you're all about souls and demons and magic."

"I have no use for that worthless relic, but if I did there is nothing to stop me from simply taking it after I kill you."

"Fine. If you don't wanna play nice I could also just stab the sword through your ugly dog head."

"Noah!" I yelled as close to the sound of their voices in the room that I could get. "You have to get out of here!" There wasn't any more talking. I started to wonder if it had just been Set messing with me when I felt someone come up from behind.

"Hey." Noah appeared from a cloud of mist that snuck in under the door.

"Noah, what are you doing here?!"

"Saving your ass? Now get on my back and don't let go for anything."

"We have to save Gianluca and Empress Kamakura and get Set's staff—"

"Priorities, kid."

"They're all a priority!"

"Not mine." The door to the hall opened with a ferocious, earthshaking gale of sand. Set appeared, staff in hand, but Noah was off like a lightning bolt before Set could act. He stumbled through the storm at first getting sliced by the cutting winds, but regrouped quickly and shot through the maze of corridors with me hanging on to him for dear life.

Noah was going faster than I could perceive. I shut my eyes and held on tight. His speed bent time around him and even though I had traveled with him like this before it seemed we were going for much longer than in the past. "Throw us straight up, as high as you can go. Outer space high. Don't ask questions, just hurry," he said.

We were outside now. The pyramids of Giza were far behind us. An aurora like the ones seen at the North and South Poles was covering most of the night sky and an unnaturally large blood moon hung in the distance along with a regular full moon overlapping it, all together creating a bizarre atmosphere not of this world. That was what the light from the ceiling shaft was from, not the sun.

The land around the pyramids was like the vision of ancient times that Isis had shown me only I doubted that this was just an illusion. Ahead of us was a raging wall of wind like the same storm that cut down Giza and sliced Cairo in half.

I followed Noah's orders and shot us straight into the air. He took over again before I could process what was happening, but from the split second glimpse I caught he was using the momentum to throw us over the storm to safety. On the other side where we stopped for a moment, everything was normal.

Noah sped off and didn't stop until we hit a large body of water near some city lights. "We should be good here," he said and let me hop off his back. "We're somewhere on the Mediterranean now. Dogface won't follow us this far out."

Chapter Twenty

"You all right?" he asked as I sat at the edge of the water to wash my face.

I hadn't said much since we got to the coast. My body was feeling fine and there wasn't a scratch on me after regenerating from total disintegration back in the pyramid, but my mind was going in eight different directions at once. The most troubling thought was the fact that my powers had no effect on Set, thereby making me unable to save Gianni and Kamakura.

"Yeah, I am now thanks to you, but we can't leave the others there. That guy is... he's... How'd you find me?" I changed the subject to avoid any emotion in my voice that would tip Noah off to what he had dropped in on. He'd probably blame me for letting Gianni get me involved.

"That temple you went to got blasted by Dogface, but your pilot survived by jumping in the Nile. It took him two days to contact your cop friend, who then told Rudgar. I was let out of the barn on a short leash because Aurelia wanted extra security while she was hosting all these world leaders and I overheard the message."

"Two days? She has the leaders of the human world at her place? And then she just let you go?"

"It's been three days now actually. She promised them she would handle Dogface, but yesterday he woke up again and wiped out most of Egypt. Rozalin said he broke the veil between the Earth and the dimension he came from, causing it to spill out like what happened when we fought Hell. He built that area pretty much overnight and was able to go around to other temples to wreck them. He won't leave his hideout where he's getting his power from and there's a hurricane that's cut it off from the rest of the world."

"How'd you get in by yourself then?"

"Mist. I rode the current until I got thrown high enough then turned back so I could land where it was clear." Noah sat down beside me on the beach. "What's with the loincloth? Why are you naked?"

"I don't want talk about it." I got up and waded into the sea to wash the rest of myself off. "You really would've given up the Muramasa for me?"

Noah shrugged without an answer. "What's with your aura?" he asked. "It's bigg...er."

"I met with another god named Isis that has been giving me these omens. She healed my soul from all those times I got hit with hellfire and supposedly I'm a god now too..."

"Yeah, right."

"I'm only telling you what I was told. Then Set came and I couldn't stop him," I sighed and sat back down on the beach. "We should head to PROJECT: UNITY's base. I'm sure Lyle is freaking out and I don't want him doing anything stupid."

"Give me a minute." Noah was sitting there staring down at the sand between his feet. He had some minor cuts and scrapes from running through the sand blast when we escaped. Most of his tattoos were gone or damaged from the multiple times he had recently been tortured.

"Do you need blood?"

"No." We sat there in silence listening to the sound of the sea rolling onto the shore. Noah didn't move and I wasn't sure what he was waiting for. "Love makes you do pretty stupid things, huh?"

"I... really don't want to talk about it." This wasn't the time for one of his lectures on how much of an idiot I was for my relationship with Gianni after all the warnings.

After another long pause Noah spoke again. "I was in love before, more than once." *Now he decides to open up to me? We've known each other for years and he's never brought up his past.*

"Sophie was the first. I met her in the early 1960s right after I returned from my training in Japan. I went back to Aurelia thinking I was gonna be her hero or something, but—that was stupid. She wanted nothing to do with me unless I was killing somebody for her, so she'd send me into Paris during her parties so I wouldn't embarrass her. That was how I met Sophie.

"She was gorgeous. And it was *real* beauty, not that fake Archios bullshit like all the porcelain dolls walking around the chateau. She was young, and with legs for days and these big beautiful brown eyes... Aurelia sent me to watch Sophie's parents, who ran a bunch of fine art and jewelry galleries for her. They were supposedly involved in a lot of thefts and smuggling activity that was drawing unwanted attention, but I spent most of the time watching their daughter from a tree outside her window instead.

"She'd always look out at me like she knew I was there even though I was invisible. One night she whispered to me, in French of course. I was actually nervous, so nervous that I said hello back in English. I couldn't believe how she wasn't afraid of me when I showed myself. She barely came up to my chest and had to have weighed ninety pounds, and here I am looking all massive and awesome with my *wakizashi* and tattoos and fangs.

"You know what she said to me when I asked her why she wasn't scared? She said, 'Well if you were here to hurt me wouldn't you have done it by now? And if you're going to, you aren't doing a very good job so far.' I'll never forget that line. Who says that? She was something else.

"When I asked her how she knew I was there she said it was because the branches of the tree I was on bent differently in the wind. This mortal girl who didn't know the world outside of her own street was able to spot me like that..."

That was similar to how Noah had taught me to be aware of my surroundings.

"I started visiting Sophie almost every night for months. I used to like holding her in my arms and looking out at the city from a chair on her balcony while she read. She made fun of my French all the damn time and said I spoke like a drunken retard, so she insisted on teaching me. She was so fiery...One time she slapped me for dropping in on her when she wasn't decent. She loved putting me in my place. It was so hot I almost proposed to her right there. I had just taken her virginity the night before, but she had to act all proper just to tease me."

"Uh, how did you have sex?" I broke in. "You're undead. I thought none of that worked down there."

"It works just fine like the rest of me, but it's not like anybody's getting pregnant."

"Okay, so... what happened to Sophie?" I already knew the vague details of the story from Vivi when she told me years ago, but if Noah was sharing all of this now after so long there must have been a reason and it had better not be to harp on my mistake falling for Gianni.

"She wanted me to marry her. She told me straight out one day when we were on a walk—"

"*You* went on walks?" I interrupted again. This was starting to be too much for me to picture.

"Are you gonna listen or be a brat?"

"Sorry," I coughed out to hold back from snickering.

"She said to me 'You know a real man would have asked a lady to marry him by now.' I told her I wasn't aware I was in the company of a lady, but if I'm being honest, I thought about it all the time.

"She wanted me to go to some formal event with her and said I'd have to wear a suit—"

Noah in a suit was the last straw. Castile would have an easier time changing Gianni's shadow armor with his reality-warping abilities than putting a suit on Noah. "Don't tell me you actually wore one."

"I was too big for anything of her father's so she went out and bought me one, which still didn't fit. I tried the jacket on, that was it. The little she-devil probably would've staked me if I hadn't.

"I think she got the wrong size on purpose though, so she could alter it herself. She wanted to sew for a living, but the family was loaded and said it wasn't a real career for someone with money. I told her to do whatever made her happy.

"I wound up never needing the suit though... The next night Aurelia summoned me before I went to head out to see Sophie. She wanted me to kill her... said the family had to be taught a lesson. I had started taking jewelry to give to Sophie as gifts throughout the year and since I was the only one sent to watch them I figured no one would find out. Her room looked like a diamond mine after a year. I liked to give her things and see her smile. I was addicted to it.

"I came clean and said I'd get the jewelry back and that the family wasn't responsible. Aurelia told me she knew and that the whole thing had been a set up to test my loyalty. She insisted I kill Sophie also on the grounds that no mortal was ever supposed to know what we were or have control over me.

"It was the only time in my life I've ever begged, I even promised I'd never see her again, I promised to take my own life to spare hers..." Noah went quiet. I hesitated to say something to console him, but then he continued. "Back then I still wasn't sure about most of Aurelia's power. I lied and agreed I'd do it as long as I didn't have to make her suffer. My plan was to help Sophie escape the country and send her to America where I felt Aurelia wouldn't know, but I was wrong.

"As soon as I entered Sophie's bedroom, Aurelia took over my body. Sophie ran to greet me as always and held up the dinner jacket that she had been working on for me to see..." Noah's voice kept getting softer to avoid being choked up. "I was forced to watch as I tore her limb from limb with my bare hands until there was nothing left of her... I tried to kill myself after by running east toward the daylight, but I was dragged back by Aurelia still in my head."

"...I'm sorry..." I didn't know what else to say. For the first time I felt this emotion in his voice that I never knew existed in him to this depth.

"I tried killing myself every night for a week after that until eventually Aurelia was in control of my body full-time. She said I was her property and until she no longer had a use for me, she didn't want her property damaged. That was when I started becoming a real asshole around the chateau. Any chance I got to act on my own I used it to lash out.

"I got savvy about it after a while and did what I could to stay off the radar so she'd loosen her grip. I also got real good at burying my thoughts as deep as possible. Most mind readers—including her—have to put effort into it if they want anything from me and by that time I usually know someone's in there. I was stupid to have ever fallen in love in the first place though...."

"I'm not in love with Gianni. I care about him and maybe I love him as a person, but I'm not *in* love with him. We're just too different and not in the right way," I said.

He hadn't looked up from the sand between his feet for more than a second the entire time he spoke. Now that he wasn't speaking, it created a sense of awkwardness, so I spoke again to fill the space. "I know you're telling me this as a final warning and I admit I was stupid too. I didn't want to believe in a world without a chance at love, but I see the bad it can cause in our lives. If I didn't open myself up to have feelings for him our split wouldn't have happened in the first place and he wouldn't have run off to face Set unprepared. None of this would've happened."

"It isn't your fault...this just wasn't how I pictured things," Noah said.

"How you pictured what?" I asked.

He brushed his hair back and tapped his foot in the sand. "Nothing. Forget it."

"Tell me what this is about," I insisted. "Why are you acting so nervous?"

"I'm not nervous," he sighed. "I'm pissed that I'm making the same stupid mistake all over again..."

"What are you saying? Who do you ever *talk* to besides me?" Noah didn't say anything in response. He glanced at me out of the corner of his eye and then put his head back down. "What?"

"Stop acting like you don't know," he said and gazed out at the water. "I know it's been obvious for a while, so stop pretending. You're just doing it on purpose to piss me off."

"What the heck are you talking about? *What's* been obvious?" I demanded.

"It's *you*, okay?" He sounded angry about it and got to his feet. "I have feelings for *you*."

I didn't know what to say. I expected him to come out with some sarcastic remark, but he kept his eyes forward without so much as a smirk. "Is this supposed to be some sort of joke? Because if you're setting me up to ridicule me on the dangers of love again—"

"I wish." He was almost never this serious and when he was, it was a big deal. I started to get nervous now myself. "But I'm a fucking slave that can't even control his own body let alone— forget it."

I sat there in shock not knowing what, if anything, I could say. I thought back at all our times together. I knew he respected me after I had saved his life from the Carpathians. I knew he cared about me after I showed my care for him when bargaining with Kamakura for the Muramasa. I knew he trusted me and only me when he wanted us to go to Thailand together after our fight in Hell. But, this? "You're not even into guys," I said.

"I'm *not* into guys, I'm into *you*."

"Uh, I *am* a guy."

"I mean it's because of who you are, not what you are. I've always been into women, but after you've been undead for as long as I have a lot of that shit starts to not matter. The bite feels good whoever it's with. You can't always be searching for your ideal match to feed from and they never have enough blood in them if you do happen to find somebody you're into.

"You start biting around out of necessity, whatever's available. Lines blur and before you know it, things happen..." He sat down a few feet away and ran his fingers through his hair again. "You're not the first guy I've had these feelings for."

"Is it only about the bite or—"

"No... I used to tuck you in sometimes when you'd fall asleep because you had this habit of sleeping on top of the covers wherever we'd go," he blurted out. I did remember a few times I had done that and woke up covered... I always thought it was Gianni. "You'd get these nightmares. I could tell by your face, it was like someone was stabbing you. I'd have to bite you so you'd calm down."

"What...? Since when?" I did used to get night terrors pretty much every time I slept, even for a nap. I thought I had gotten over them, except for the occasional nightmare. They were always about burning to death, or losing my parents again.

"Since that first time we were in Japan. It wasn't even cold out and you'd be shivering under a tree like a wounded animal. I couldn't leave you like that..."

"That's how I felt when I saw you in the cellar of that barn... Japan was a long time ago— but wait. How could you have done that? I learned pretty fast how to sense when you were coming to ambush me."

"No you didn't. I used to let you think you could to build your confidence. You still couldn't sense me coming if I didn't want you to. I wasn't more than fifty feet away the whole time." His smirk was back in all its aggravating entirety, but I welcomed it. "It wasn't until after that when I knew my feelings for you were getting serious. It pissed me off because I didn't wanna go through that again, but there was always part of me that still did."

Chapter Twenty-One

"So, who was this other guy, or guys?" I asked.

"The first and only was a French Archios, Jean-Luc. He was another little shit like you, only taller and actually combed his hair. I met him ten years after Sophie.

"He seemed like a typical Archios when he was with the crowd; stuck up, empty, miserable. Aurelia wanted me around, but out of sight during her parties to keep the guests safe in case of any trouble. I'd hang out on a balcony bored to death watching everyone.

"Jean was new and missed the memo to shun me, so the second night he comes upstairs and starts talking to me like we had already met. I didn't know if he was being sarcastic or stupid so I ignored him. Then he says 'You're not like the others. I don't hate you yet.', so I say, 'What can I do to change that?'

"We got to talking, but I wasn't buying any of it until he asked me to train him to use a sword. I said no and then he challenges me to a race through to the other side of the hedge maze. I laughed in his face thinking he was crazy. I won of course, but when he caught up to me by the fountain we started laughing for real because he got lost and cut through the bushes. I hadn't laughed like that since Sophie. I figured Aurelia would be pissed and that made me enjoy it even more.

"He added me to his rotation in the crowd to chat with during the next parties and I overheard him saying my name to one of the other guests when he excused himself to talk to me. I didn't feel like an outcast with him. It was casual between us and became a regular thing until I started to be the first person on his list he'd go to as soon as he arrived. He brought up the sword training again months later and I told him I'd consider it.

"That was around the time Vivi and I started to get closer. Up until then she was pretty cold. I knew she distanced herself from me because I didn't fit in and she probably thought I wouldn't last long, but we grew on each other like siblings at the time. She was Aurelia's right hand and the two of them were almost never apart so I asked her if she thought it'd be a problem for me to train Jean. She told me that she didn't think there would be an issue because it wasn't like he'd ever become a threat.

"I taught him a few basic moves and we practiced together more than once. It was actually fun to blow off steam and reminded me of what I enjoyed about training in Japan, only with me as the *sensei*. I stopped going easy on him after a while and made him bleed. He whined about it, but didn't give up and I respected him for that.

"Anyway, he claimed I owed him blood for making him bleed. I had never let anyone bite me before that and wasn't about to have him be the first, but I knew Aurelia *didn't* want me sharing my blood with others so that made me want to do it more. I let him bite my wrist and it still felt as good as...well you know, but when he started getting touchy with me I shoved him away and left.

"He tried apologizing to me a couple of times over the next nights, but I ignored him. Then one night when he had given up I overheard him talking to some other guests that were being assholes to him now that he had gone back to them instead of spending time with me. The whole party had turned on him and it was getting ugly so I dropped in, picked him up, and brought us outside.

"I couldn't help feeling bad for him, but I wasn't into that stuff with a guy. We talked about it and he explained it how I did with you. We put it behind us and got to know each other as friends at the parties throughout the year until I started visiting him.

"He lived in a poorer part of Paris. The one who had turned him was a regular in Aurelia's court. He had taken Jean out of poverty to polish him up, but something happened and he disappeared, leaving Jean back in the slums. I'd steal money from around the city for him to get somewhere better to live, but he always got insulted by it.

"He used to antagonize me when we were sword fighting since I couldn't read his mind. It reminded me of Sophie insisting I learn French. I actually bit him for the first time when I had him pinned because he kept projecting dirty thoughts into my mind to distract me. It escalated fast from there and we were together for three years after that. I guess you could say that we were in love. We never said the words, but we didn't really need to either.

"Aurelia never made any mention of it and I figured it was fine since Jean was also an Archios. She called me in one night at dusk and told me I didn't have to attend the party. My first thought jumped to spending it with Jean instead. Aurelia answered my thoughts out loud and agreed she wanted me to go to Jean. I knew something was up and told her I didn't want to anymore, but she insisted where I couldn't refuse.

"When I got there she forced my body to stab Jean through the shoulder with my *wakizashi*. I couldn't say anything when he screamed in pain and yelled at me. I... cut his arm off and he tried running away. I knew he didn't stand a chance. I struggled to get control of my body back so maybe he could use what I had taught him to stake me, but it didn't work.

"She made me cut off his leg and watch as he crawled away from me with this look of confusion and betrayal until the game finally ended the same as it had for Sophie. Except Jean stayed alive long enough to see me rip his spine out through his stomach.

"Aurelia said she didn't want anyone in my mind but her and demanded my undivided attention. I killed someone I cared about again and was powerless to stop it. After that was when the bleedings started to serve my blood to her guests. I didn't have it in me to do anything but follow orders and hope they'd cut deep enough one night to end it... It wasn't until I met you that I got back that drive and wanted to break free..."

"Noah..." I got up and moved closer to him. I wanted to put my hand on his shoulder in comfort, but I still had in my mind how touching him, unless he was gravely wounded, was usually a bad idea so I just stood there. "I thought you hated me when we first met."

"I did," he said with a laugh. "God, I hated you so much in the beginning. You were so annoying and useless."

"Okay, this isn't helping me believe you about your feelings."

"*But* you never gave up once you were pushed to your limit," he quickly added. "You had more thrown at you in your first week in the supernatural world than I had in a hundred years. You rolled with the punches and kept improving. I knew there was something special about you before anyone else, but I didn't want to say it because I knew the more appealing you were, the harder a life you'd have.

"You reminded me of myself when I saw you trying to hold in your feelings after you lost your family. I remember you running across the front lawn of the chateau toward me for help when you were being chased. Most people run away from me. I knew I had to keep you at arm's length for your own good, but you always saw past all that no matter how much of an asshole I tried to be.

"With what you said to me and Vivi about killing Aurelia to free ourselves, I knew you had no idea what you were saying at the time but it got to me. Nobody had ever dared to say something like that and here's this stupid, dirty kid that can't even throw a punch, ready to take down an Ancient for a couple of people he didn't know."

"Don't call me stupid, you big idiot."

"It's a good stupid. I'm even more stupid for falling for you. I know I am. That's why I trained you, so you'd be able to kill me when the time comes and take care of yourself when I'm gone."

"I'm not going to kill you, Noah... There were plenty of times when I would've liked to, but I'd never actually do it."

"You won't have a choice and she'll make sure you don't. I'm fine with it. I know you can't die and there's nothing I can do to keep you down, Aurelia knows too. She's pissed because I'm in love and she can't do anything about it to play her games. I buried it as deep as I could for a while, but you're all I think about lately. If there's anyone I'd die to and be at peace with, it would be you."

"Don't talk like that. It's not gonna happen."

"It wouldn't if things had gone like I was planning, but everything has been screwed up since the Italian got involved."

"I'm not in love with him," I reminded Noah, but also myself.

The longer Gianluca was gone, the more I missed him and the more I had to keep telling myself that we had only dated for less than a year and weren't compatible. He had taught me a lot about myself in that time and was caring and incredibly handsome. I had to be truthful and admit that I still held feelings for him, but I didn't want to remain together and ignore the problems between us until it was too late and I was wrapped up in something I regretted. It may have been a mistake to let our relationship go on for as long as it did, but I wanted to give us every chance to make it work.

Now all I wanted was to be able to put that in the past and move on so I didn't have to feel the pain of losing the good times we shared. I knew that once we saved him I'd be confronted with this all over again, but I'd have to keep a level head so that I didn't cave to my emotions. I was stronger than that. Right?

"It's not that," Noah said. "I've been fighting to be free, doing things I wouldn't normally do, just so that we could have a chance to be together... I was worried the Italian would hurt you and there wouldn't be anything I could do to stop it. I don't mean a broken heart, but *hurt* you... I knew he wouldn't turn you evil. That's what I love about you. Anyone who's been through what you have, especially with your power, in such a short amount of time would have, but you keep defying it and it's only changed you for the better."

"Thank you, Noah... That's really sweet."

"It's true. I was worried the Italian would do something to take you away from me forever while I ran around the world to get what I needed to free myself. But I came to the conclusion you might've been safer with him because Aurelia wouldn't do anything to you with him around."

"Doesn't Aurelia *know* why you have the Muramasa though?" I questioned. "I'd think she'd realize you were planning to kill her."

Noah had had his memory erased by Vance in the past to prevent some of his plans from being found out, but I was never sure what was going on in that head of his and tried not to bring anything up that might have triggered something he wanted to forget.

"She didn't bother reading my mind as often after she felt she broke me when Jean died. If she does, it's only on the surface and, like I said, I'm good at burying my real thoughts. She feels that she's untouchable and is probably waiting for me to make an idiot of myself. I just have to make sure that doesn't happen. And before you say it, no I don't want your help. Whenever I said 'Don't worry about it' was because I didn't want you getting any crazy ideas and putting yourself in danger."

"You still need to learn how to accept help from people who care about you," I reiterated one of the hardest lessons I had learned. "What got screwed up by Gianluca if I'm not in love with him and he kept me safe from Aurelia?"

I sat beside him. Noah still hadn't looked at me.

"When I found out you had been taken by Dogface I figured you had gone to save the Italian. I overheard a lot from Rozalin and Rudgar and it sounded like you could've actually died... If I had been free before all this and told you how I felt then you'd never have gone to save the Italian and been in trouble.

"I didn't want to lose you. I didn't want you to die thinking that I was really the jerk I tried to be when I was only doing it to keep you at a safe distance. I'm the fastest guy there is, but it always seems as if I'm too slow when it counts... like with Vivi."

"Vivi's death fighting the Carpathians wasn't your fault." I hesitated, then put my hand on his shoulder. "Sorry, I know you hate being touched."

"I like when it's you doing it." He removed my hand from his shoulder and placed it on his cheek with his eyes closed.

"Really? Anytime I did I always felt like I was petting a wild, angry tiger that was about to lash out."

"I can be your tiger." He let out a deep growl and nuzzled his scruff against my palm. Sharing in this affection reminded me of Gianni, but there was a very different chemistry with Noah. If it could be called that. "I'm not gonna wear another leash though."

"I don't want to tame you. I want to set you free." I pushed his face away to be playful.

"I wanna be sure you know that this isn't only about the biting shit. I'm not really good at this stuff, but I like the way you look too."

"Thanks," I laughed. "You're pretty okay yourself."

"I'm saying that even when you're dirty and tired and just finished crawling through some sewer to save the world, you still look good to me. I like the sound of your voice, and the way you care too much about everything and everybody... You probably know me better than anyone ever has before. I mean, you're perfect to me. You're a definite ten. I'm an eleven, but you're a solid ten."

I flicked him on the nose as payback for his ego. He laughed, bit my thumb with his fang and then kissed it. Although I understood a lot of his past behavior was an act, it was still surprising that he was being this affectionate. I could sense in his voice that he was relieved to be getting it off his chest.

"You think you could ever fall in love with a guy like me?" he asked. "I know I might not be the most romantic or have a stupid Italian accent, but I'll always treat you as an equal and I'll never stop fighting to keep us together."

"This is a lot for me to take in all at once... and things with Gianluca *just* fell apart... then there's everything with Set..." I had been pushing that whole unpleasant situation out of my mind. I was thankful Noah was able to distract me from it. "I need time to sort it out in my head."

I stood up to relax the situation between us so we weren't so close. I'd be lying if I said there wasn't some excitement to finding out someone's feelings for you. But this wasn't just anyone. This was *Noah*. I had never considered it in the realm of possibility or even in my wildest fantasy.

Maybe that wasn't true...

Despite all of his obnoxious personality flaws, he had grown on me. He made me feel safe while still pushing me to be strong and fight my own battles. He taught me instead of holding me back. He made me laugh even when I was angry and miss him when he wasn't around. Most of all, we had a similar philosophy on life. We dealt with our problems when they came up without compromising who we were, but in the end both of us wanted to be left in peace.

"Yeah... I can give you that," he whispered and pulled me back down to sit by him. "But first I'm gonna take care of whoever's been watching us from those dunes."

Chapter Twenty-Two

"Humans. Three of them." Noah got to his feet and stood between me and where he was gazing over to by the dunes. "I must've been pretty distracted by something to let them slip by unnoticed like that." He looked back and grinned at me. "And now they're gone."

"Good. Now you can stop human-watching so you can help me get back to base."

"I mean they're *gone*. Humans don't just disapp—" Noah drew one of the *wakizashi* from the sheath on his hip just as three curiously dressed individuals appeared from a distortion bubble in the air in front of him that resembled the effect of a heat wave.

The trio, made up of two men and a woman, immediately dropped to one knee with their heads bowed upon arrival. "Forgive us for any disrespect we may have caused by such an intrusion. We've come to present ourselves to the newborn god. Am I correct in assuming that you are his Chosen One?"

"Yup, I'm the guy he chose." Noah looked back at me again with a devilish smile.

"I haven't chosen you for anything yet," I said with a smirk of my own and stepped up next to him.

"What? Not enough time?" His smile didn't leave his face as he looked down at me.

"Who are you people?" I asked the trio who had been polite enough not to interrupt our banter. "And how did you sneak up on us like that?" The older man who had done all the speaking so far looked to be in about his mid-to-late forties. His hair and short beard had hints of gray, but other than that he appeared to be someone that took care very good of himself and was aging extremely well.

He and the younger, clean-cut man with the closely buzzed haircut shared many of the same robust facial features—high, pronounced cheekbones, strong chins with sharply defined jawlines.

The woman to their right, who had a pixie haircut and shimmering blue eyes, looked quite spritely compared to the stern faces of the other two. She was about my height—a tad shorter than her two companions—but her poised stature brought a level of dignified charm.

The group was dressed in an interesting and stylish take on medieval attire. Their predominantly black outfits fell somewhere in between a royal knight's armor and an aristocrat's casual wear. The clothing had an unmistakable authenticity to it that couldn't be replicated by just anyone who wanted to dress up for a reenactment. The older man and the woman had side swords at their waist while the younger man had two blades on his back.

Unlike the Blackbourne's demonskin hunting armor, there was some variation in color, but not much. It more closely resembled Kenneth's armor, with a blend of fine darkly colored fabrics and furs, leathers, and some exquisite metalwork. There were arcane etchings on some pieces and a single gemstone inlaid differently for each of them that swirled and shimmered under the surface like it was alive with power. The older man had a teardrop-shaped sapphire the size of a quarter affixed to his fitted breastplate. His younger counterpart had an oval-shaped emerald hanging from a silver brooch on his belt and the woman had a round sapphire in her gold circlet.

I envied all these outfits and armors. They were so impressive and heroic. In any other context they may have come across strange and eccentric, but in the world I lived in I took them as status symbols.

"We are theurgists of the Goetic Order of Man," said the older knight. "We traveled here from across the Mediterranean by use of ley lines."

I didn't understand a word of that and hoped Noah would say something first.

"Hey," he nodded and put away his sword. *Well it was something.*

"Nice to meet you, but we were about to leave...is there something you needed?" We didn't have time to be social and had already wasted the little we had by chatting for almost an hour. Then again, I was curious how they knew I was a "newborn god".

"Wait, please," the older man begged and went to stand up, but decided to stay kneeling. "You are here to seal the God of Chaos, are you not? We've come to pledge ourselves to you and offer our assistance."

"We were actually here for a picnic, but—"

"It's on the to-do list," I cut Noah off. "But you're humans. No offense; he'd stomp you into the sand.

"Perhaps, but we aren't afraid of death. We are here to serve you, if you'll let us."

"Because you think I'm a god?" I asked.

"We *know* you are," the older man replied and bowed his head with the rest. "With respect, we've been tracking you for years and waiting for your transcendence. There is much we'd be honored to share with you, but I know you must be eager to release your allies from the God of Chaos."

"How do you know they're my allies? Just how much have you been spying on me and why should I trust you?"

"Recently, we've seen you in the deserts with the shadow god. We've been keeping watch for sightings of you in the Middle East ever since you were seen sealing the portal to Hell in Iraq and undoing the evil in that village. We had first been made aware of your connection to each other when saving the tourists in the Roman Colosseum from the fire spirit. One of us witnessed the attack that felled the shadow god and the dragon god earlier this week. We were relieved to find that you weren't present and set out searching for you."

"Why do you care? We don't know each other," I said. "And you can stop kneeling..."

The three got to their feet and the older one continued to supply me with answers that led to more questions. They stood at attention with perfect posture; hands clasped behind their backs, chins up and facing forward, feet positioned evenly apart. "Our order has been around for centuries and each generation is tasked with the same duty: to usher in the new age of gods and serve the Ascended. Since the gods have abandoned the world we live in due to man's arrogance, the Earth has become hostile and chaotic, and spiritual energies are unstable. We know that you will play the most important role in restoring the balance."

"So why didn't you go kiss the Italian's ass when you had the chance?" Noah asked.

"The eternal void that the shadow god draws his powers from negates our own," the woman spoke. "Scriptures that have been passed down from the dawn of our order warned us of the Nether. It is the antithesis to everything we are and should be wielded by no single man at such great magnitude, Ascended or otherwise. There are legends of the horrors it can cause. Our worry was that the shadow god would interfere with your transcendence. You are one of many souls with potential that our order has watched. We've records of dozens that have perished, turned to evil, or simply failed on their journey."

"They don't like the Italian either," Noah turned to me. "I'm starting to like these guys."

"If you don't trust Gianni...the shadow god... then why offer to help save him?" I asked.

"The last time you were seen with him in the desert he had kneeled to you as a sign of servitude and so our fears were laid to rest," the older man answered. "You are the first to ascend in centuries and the only other one we know of on this Earth besides him. It speaks to the success of your reign that you are able to command such a powerful being even before your full ascension."

He wasn't kneeling to me in servitude... This was a lesson in perspective. Correcting them didn't matter much at the moment. It was nice to have a perspective in my favor though.

"We were under the impression that you had chosen him, but now I see that you've made a much better choice in this man," the older one continued and raised a hand to indicate Noah. Of course that only made Noah's ego ten times the size. He crossed his arms and puffed out his chest with a grin.

"What are you talking about 'chosen'?" I asked.

"To be your champion."

"Hear that? I'm a champion," Noah boasted. "They know I'm better than the Italian too. You should listen to them."

"Nobody is my champion of anything," I clarified.

"That is fortunate news," the older man said, seemingly pleased, although the younger one's face looked strained for a brief moment. I realized they were probably related. "Every generation of our order is groomed since birth to be that champion in hopes of being chosen when the Ascended return. We put our stock in the one we deem most worthy should the time come to make the choice easier, but it is of course always left up to Our Lord."

"But... you haven't had any Ascended in centuries and your order is only centuries old, so you've been waiting all this time and never had any proof it was real or would ever happen?" I questioned.

"Our proof, as with any religion, is in our faith and our scriptures, only we actually have verifiable insight into the alignment and progress of the spiritual nature of the world through our magic," the woman answered. "We've known since the beginning that it was only a matter of time. I'm grateful it happens to be now while I'm alive to see it, but also when the world needs you most."

"You guys have sat around for generations waiting for someone to serve?" Noah asked. "You know how stupid that sounds right? That's living hell."

"We keep busy with a strict daily training regimen to hone our bodies, minds, and spirits. We work as arbiters of the use of magic across the world to prevent magic from getting into the wrong hands. This allows us to put a stop to supernatural disturbances. We'd be honored if you would come and stay with us to see for yourselves who we are; our home is just across the Mediterranean."

"Look, I don't want anyone serving me," I said. "I respect what you're trying to do, but I'm not your god."

"I mean no disrespect, but I insist you are," said the older man. "We knew you were the one we had been waiting for when we saw your triumph over Hell. Should another Ascended have come first that was not of the Nether we would have served them.

"What I am about to say may be blasphemous, but it is from the heart and I believe you can appreciate that. I know we all secretly wished for when the Ascended should rise that they be on a path of balance to right the world, even though we are sworn to serve regardless of their alignment to chaos or order. You are the ideal to an already unfathomable situation."

I looked at Noah, not knowing what to do after hearing all that. "Can you give us a minute?" I asked them.

"Of course," the man said. He kneeled with the others again and they disappeared back into the same hazy bubble.

"Zip us out of here," I told Noah. "I don't trust that they aren't listening."

"Jeez some humans kneel to you and you start dishing out orders." Noah slung me over his shoulder and brought us to another sandy location that was almost exactly the same as the last. "We ditching these guys or what?"

"I was going to ask what you thought of them."

"I can't read their minds, but I can tell they haven't been lying. They really think I'm that awesome."

"I'm being serious, and you can put me down now." Noah still had me over his shoulder while we were talking. He put me down, but kept his arm around me and rested his chin on top of my head.

"So was I. They haven't been lying so far. Humans used to worship supernaturals like gods all the time—and these are just a bunch of old-school human mages. Their aura isn't anything special so it's not like they'd be a problem to get rid of, but it's up to you if you wanna bother with them. I'm surprised you weren't jumping at the chance to make more friends with humans involved in the supernatural like you always do."

Human mages. I had never met any of those before. Vance had told me about them in the past.

"I don't like the whole 'god' thing," I said as he put his other arm around me now too. "Noah, what are you doing?"

"Nothing much. What are you doing?"

"I mean you're hugging me."

"Yeah, so? I can't do that?"

"Now's not really the time..." *It did feel nice though...*

"I can talk and do this at the same time. I'm good like that. If you're looking for me to give you my approval on whether or not it's a good idea to get involved with these guys the only thing I have to say is that I don't see the harm in it, for now at least. The worst that happens is they die and that's on them. You've given them fair warning. Just don't be a pushover with them either way so that they don't get any funny ideas."

"You're not usually so willing to work with other people," I pointed out.

"Yeah, but you are and I've learned to deal with your shit. Don't get me wrong though, if they get in my way I'll kill them myself. It'd be a shame too. They have good taste."

"That's the real reason you're so okay with them. It's no secret that you like them driving in how bad Gianluca is and how good you are."

"Never said it was." I felt Noah flex one of his arms. "I didn't realized my biceps are the size of your head."

"I guess we'll see what they can do. Maybe they can help us get back to base faster."

"Hell, my thigh is bigger than your chest I think."

"Noah! Focus."

"I can't help it. I'm kind of hungry. Let me get a bite."

"Maybe later." I *knew* what that was going to lead to with him acting like this. We had to save Gianni and Kamakura and stop getting sidetracked before Set finished leeching their power or else we'd all be doomed.

"I don't like all these 'later's you're giving me. How about some 'now's?" He started rubbing his chin on top of my head.

"No— Ow! What are you doing?"

"I had an itch." He picked me up under his arm and bolted back to our rendezvous point with the Order. No more than five seconds passed when they teleported in on bended knee.

"I've made my decision," I said and tried to sound assertive. "We can work together for now assuming you can keep up and pull your own weight, but it's going to be dangerous. Anything more than that we'll have to see when we get to it. So, that leaves one last question: what are you guys bringing to the table?"

"Our magic works by channeling aether and invoking spirits across the veil between worlds," the older knight explained. "Spells are instantaneous active and passive effects such as conjuring fire, aura reading, or healing wounds. We start to learn these by rote in childhood until they become second nature. Rituals take preparation and usually, for more complex versions of spells that do things like raise or lower the ambient temperature over a large area or summon storms or spirits, a catalyst.

"Then there are hexes that debilitate and trap foes. There is a wide range of difficulty in casting them that starts at the level of a simple spell up to advanced rituals we use in containing formidable spirits and demons.

"Lastly, incantations are powerful beneficial spells that are used to ward against other forms of magic and mitigate damage with elemental barriers and manipulations of time and space around us. They require a great deal of aether and a spoken blessing in the Old Tongue, but we engrave our weapons and armor with common ones to bypass the need to recite them each time. Doing this allows us to trigger the incantation by only expending the necessary requirement of aether."

"What is aether again?" I asked. "And you can stop kneeling... again."

"It's the ambient spiritual energy of the planet, my lord," he explained. "Like most forms of energy it is invisible to the naked eye. Only certain souls are gifted with the ability to channel it."

"And the ley lines you mentioned before?"

"Those are currents of aether. Think of them as a network of blood vessels across Earth, but with aether instead of blood. Through meditation we can tap into these currents to restore our personal reserves and also use them to travel from one point in space to another. I'm greatly oversimplifying it, but for now that is the general gist of it."

"Simple is good because we're sort of in a hurry," I said, trying to emphasize the hurry part. This was all very interesting, but it couldn't have come at a worse time. "Do you think we can use those ley lines to help me get back to my friend?"

"Absolutely, my lord. Although it will take all three of us to transport you. With no small exaggeration, your soul is thousands of times greater than our own combined and will be difficult to traverse the ley lines with."

"That's fine and you can just call me Dorian. 'My lord' is weird. What are your names?"

"It... it wouldn't be proper to address our patron deity by his true name."

"I insist." The trio had been very well composed up until now. The three of them looked like they were about to start sweating in anxiety. I had thrown them into some perpetual loop in logic that it would be disrespectful to use my real name but also to disobey my request.

Noah, on the other hand, was chuckling to himself in amusement.

"Ah, yes... of course. As for introductions, I am Tobias Bennett, one of four on the council in the Order. Beside me are Helena Vaughn, another council member and leader of the Scribes, and my son Liam, the finest that the Order has to offer in all capacities."

"There are more than the three of you?" I asked. Noah also raised an eyebrow in question. We may have assessed the situation incorrectly... "I thought it was only you guys and you were a family or something."

"There are forty-six of us including the children, my lord," said Helena, ignoring my previous request. She was met with an immediate side stare from Tobias. "We live in an abbey on an island in Greece where we operate as a communal family. We all have a hand in raising and training future generations."

This wasn't just a few human mages, it was an army, an army that wanted to help me. It was like what Castile had said when showing me all the missing pieces on my side of the chessboard.

"You don't look or sound Greek," Noah said. "You speak in pretty generic English like you're trying *not* to have an accent."

"The abbey we live in has been with the Order long before the current nation was established," Helena explained. "Although we are exclusive, we don't discriminate based on anything except for magical potential. Most of us don't identify with any single race or ethnicity from generation after generation of blending."

"This is all really interesting, but we have to go," I said.

"You're not here to free your allies first?" Tobias asked.

"There's no way we can take Set on our own," I said. "I tried and my powers don't even affect him. He's physically *there*, but I can't get a hold of him. The only other time that's happened is... with Gianluca... Set's been draining his life away and I thought it was just for raw energy, but I think he's actually taking Gianluca's power over darkness too... and Kamakura's power over the elements. The storm that Set made when he first rose was nothing like the one that's still going on now around his new kingdom...

"Noah, you said that I was gone for three days. I spent two of these days petrified like Gianluca and Kamakura. In that time Set had rebuilt the ruins we saw during our escape. Set must have used *my* powers to do it! That prophecy having to do with Gianluca and the ancient darkness might still come true, but not directly caused by him."

"You're not still thinking about saving the Italian are you?" Noah asked and crossed his arms. "You *know* what trouble he's going to cause when you free him. Let Dogface finish him off, then take care of Dogface if you wanna."

"I'm *not* leaving him to die, Noah! I wouldn't leave you."

"Because you love me. Everybody loves me." He grinned. "I also don't want to take over the world."

"Can you teleport us into the pyramid to get the two of them out?" I asked the trio.

"Yes, my... I mean Dorian," Tobias caught himself. "Being that they are so weakened we should not have a problem carrying them with us across the ley lines, but we wouldn't be able to take both of you too."

"Noah, can you go into that city nearby to see—"

"The city is destroyed. Those lights you see are from abandoned rescue vehicles and spotlights to search for survivors. I'm going with you."

"You're going to help save Gianluca?"

"No. I'm going to save *you* when you get in trouble saving the Italian, *again*, because I know there's no talking you out of it," he said and then leaned in to whisper the rest in my ear. "I'll do whatever it takes to make this work between us, even if it means rescuing the Italian so you can get some closure. I also don't have anything else going on right now and I'm getting bored standing around talking."

"Thank you," I smiled up at him.

"Mm-hm. I'll need blood though."

"Okay, but we have to come up with a plan first."

"Remember that time in Germany when we fought the demon? The one we needed to keep busy until it was sent back to Hell?"

"You mean the time you stabbed me in the stomach to get my powers to react? Yeah, I remember."

"It was a love stab, like a love tap but more pointy. The reason I'm bringing it up—"

"Is because we can't defeat Set by force so we'll need to keep him distracted long enough while the others rescue Gianluca and Kamakura." I took the wind out of Noah's sails by finishing his sentence for him. I was proud of myself for knowing where he was going with that and it also made me smile that we were in sync. "We'll need to lure him far away from the pyramid so he doesn't notice."

"I'll do it," said Noah. "He's slow as shit and I'm pretty good at keeping people's attention."

"People love to hate you," I corrected. "But Set is more interested in me. I'll do it while you go in with the Order then. I'm pretty sure I can play keep away to buy you enough time."

"Don't tell me what to do." Noah put his finger in my face. "You're too slow and it won't be as fun having you around if you're a statue. We do it together or not at all."

"Fine," I agreed. "As long as you guys don't mind going into the pyramid yourselves." I turned to the trio. Under less dire circumstances I may not have been so trusting, but should they betray us it would be easier to take care of them than Set. Maybe that was cold and manipulative of me.

"There wasn't anybody else inside," said Noah. "He won't consider you three a threat to go back for while fighting us judging by your auras."

"It would be an honor to serve." Tobias bowed. "Our auras are cloaked for that exact reason while investigating the disturbance here. We will enter as soon as you are engaged and bring the others back here, where I'll conjure a flare to let you know we are clear." *Cloaked auras...? We already underestimated their numbers. Did Noah underestimate their strength too?*

"Thank you," I said. "This won't be won in a single battle and I can already tell the battles won't be won by brute force and anger. I'll understand if you don't want to get involved in it anymore after this."

"Spoken as a wise and true leader," said Helena. "I speak for all of us including our many ancestors when I say that we have trained tirelessly, studied endlessly, and prayed enthusiastically for this very moment to stand with you."

I caught Noah rolling his eyes, but the trio didn't seem to notice. They were enthusiastic all right. I felt the immediate pressure of responsibility I was worried about when Isis had mended my soul to help me transcend. I was beginning to worry what the Order would think of me once they found out I wasn't the high and mighty deity they were expecting.

"I hope I live up to that," I said. "I have to feed Noah, so give us a minute if you need to prepare."

"Finally," Noah grinned and approached.

"Just make it quick and keep it appropriate."

"Have we met? Since when am I ever appropriate?" Noah laughed and was at my throat in an instant. For once he didn't grab me and bite into me like he was eating corn on the cob. He had his hand on my lower back and the other tilting my head to the side. I tried to tune out my thoughts to something neutral but it wasn't as easy with him holding me like this and having the start of romantic feelings build up between us that I wasn't ready to deal with yet.

I put my hands on his arms to squeeze them as I started enjoying myself and braced for when he finished and threw me to the ground as he always did. This time was different though.

He began gasping for air as his chest heaved and he hugged me closer in a panic. "What the fuck is happening to me?" he choked. "What the hell did you do to your blood?" He let go and backed up until he fell over in the sand staring up at the stars in a daze.

"I didn't do anything!" I exclaimed as he started to smile unlike any smile I had seen on him before. It was a wide smile from ear to ear, the kind you only get from something of life changing importance. "Are you...breathing?" I sat next to him and put my hand on his chest.

His heart was beating.

"I've never tasted anything like it," he said and held my hand with the smile still plastered across his face and his eyes staring off into the distance a million miles away.

"Is this the first time he drank from you?" Tobias asked.

"No, he always has," I said. Noah's heartbeat slowed to a stop, as did his breathing. "He did just a few days ago."

"Before your transcendence, yes?" asked Helena. "He is imbibing the blood of a god... divine ichor."

"Holy shit it's true. You really did ascend or descend...transcend... It was the best thing I've ever tasted and felt before. I want more." Noah sat up and bit into my neck with a voracious hunger. He let out muffled moans of pleasure as he drank. I was glad the Order was too busy casting an array of colorful spells on themselves in preparation to hear. Once he finished he licked my neck clean and then collapsed in the sand again with the same dumb smile on his face.

"Am I going to have to carry you?" I asked and tried to nudge him to get up. I liked to see him smile, knowing that he was able to exhale and open up about his true feelings after all these years.

It wasn't easy to deny my own emotions were starting to be stirred in that direction as well. But should anything come of it, there was still the matter of what Gianluca would do when he found out. I wouldn't leave him to die to avoid it, I could never choose between the lives of two people I cared about, but his propensity to make rash decisions when he was sure he was right wasn't something to take lightly.

"It'd be a nice change." He hopped to his feet and put me on his shoulders. "Give us a minute once we get over the storm before you go in," he told the trio. I'll keep Dorian on my back so we aren't split up and he can launch us out of danger if it gets rough."

"You ready for this?" I asked him and slid down his back to put my arms around his neck before we zoomed away.

"Please. I'm always ready to show off."

Chapter Twenty-Three

"Remember not to get too close and don't let Set use the staff or we'll get petrified—" I warned as we descended into the eye of the storm. The ominous celestial sky and twin moons were so bright it could have been high noon.

"I know what I'm doing," said Noah. "Just relax and enjoy the ride like good bait. If we get split up for any reason, fly yourself as high up as you can first before leaving so Dogface can't catch you in the storm and I'll use the mist to meet you back on the other side where it's safe."

We went unnoticed upon landing, but I knew that we wouldn't be for long. My quick scan of the arena before the madness was to ensue revealed that there was about a mile in all directions we had to work with around the pyramids. Aside from high dunes and steep valleys that had been forged and excavated by the storm, there were many tall obelisks covered in hieroglyphics that had been erected by Set. They all had a glowing pale blue rock floating above them that illuminated the area further. For a dark and evil God of Chaos, this guy sure liked his light.

"Those look important," I said to Noah and pointed to the top of an obelisk. "They could have something to do with the storm or the weird sky."

"Let's break it and find out." He dashed us up to the top of the nearest obelisk and nabbed the stone, smashing it to pieces. Nothing changed anywhere that we could see. Noah tried two more, both without any discernable effect on the atmosphere but we did get Set's attention.

The imposing Egyptian god's ebony frame stood out against the sand with his staff in hand. "Giddy-up!" I put my arms back around Noah's neck as he narrowed his eyes at me over his shoulder. We raced to the opposite side of the clearing where we waited for Set to pursue us.

I thought he would turn into a sandstorm and charge, but instead he burst up from the ground beneath us. Noah was prepared and dodged effortlessly by zipping us up another obelisk.

"A wasted effort returning here," Set called out to us. "I would have come to capture you as easily as last time once I was ready, but if you are so willing to give yourself to me arrangements can be made." I tried to attack him with a blast of my powers to check if he was still unaffected outside of the pyramid. It did nothing, but I realized I that could manipulate the sand when I saw it splash back from the impact.

I molded and compressed the sand around Set in the same way I did the pillar in Isis's chamber to create fine points. When I tried to run him through with the spears of sand they crumbled before ever touching his skin.

"I am lord and master of this domain and none of it shall betray me!" he declared in triumph.

Noah leaped from the obelisk right in time as Set went to use his staff to petrify us. We evaded over and over again until he had enough and drove the staff into the ground. The earth shook and erupted into mountainous spires and crags, making it far more difficult to navigate the terrain. "Fly," Noah told me as the land kept shifting up and down violently.

We flew up and as far away as I could get us before seeing the bright light of Set's staff from behind. Noah used his speed the same way as when we vaulted over the storm to get us out of range at the last second. "Lost sight of him. Stay up here." Noah turned into a cloud of mist that was carried away by the wind, leaving me hovering in the air alone.

I spotted Set first down by the pyramids with the grounds of the clearing still in a tumultuous uproar. He was facing me and raised his staff to the sky. I thought he was going to turn me to stone so I flew up as high as possible like Noah and I had planned.

The sky darkened and thunderclouds rolled in with a deafening bang and a flash of lightning.

From this height I could see the clearing getting wider as the storm wall expanded outward at an alarming rate. Set's power was increasing and soon he'd be able to use that storm to cleave through any city or country in his way to growing his empire.

I had to fly back down or else I'd be struck by lightning, which played into Set's intent. I evaded a bolt that set my hair on end as I flew back to lure him further from the pyramids. A heavy rain started with enough force to push me off balance. It turned into a flash flood in a matter of seconds that washed down the peaks of the terrain and formed large pools of sandy water across the clearing.

I was getting concerned that I still couldn't see Noah and tried to reassure myself that he knew what he was doing until I saw him tackle Set from behind. I had to help, but also knew he told me to stay away for a reason.

Noah had both hands on the staff and one foot on Set's stomach in an attempt to twist and push off of him, but Set wasn't giving up. The two of them struggled as Noah popped in and out of mist form to avoid any counterattacks. I flew down to take shelter from the lightning near one of the upturned obelisks. Noah was going down the list of submission and striking moves on his repertoire trying to out maneuver and out muscle Set for the staff, even landing a flying roundhouse kick to the back of his head and putting him in a figure-four armlock, when the staff let out a brilliant flash.

When it cleared, Noah was nowhere in sight.

I went to fly in when I was grabbed out of the air around my waist.

"I told you to stay." Noah had his arm around me and dashed away again.

"Are you crazy?!" I shouted at him over the storm. "I told *you* not to get close to him!"

"Yeah, but I wanted to impress you." He grinned at me. "And I know you wanted that magic stick."

The water was rising past Noah's ankles from the heavy downpour even though we were on high ground. "This seems familiar doesn't it?"

"I was thinking the same thing."

Noah and I had encountered a similar situation together when we ventured into Yomi and fought Empress Kamakura's guardian spirits. They had flooded the land to trap us in water and be electrocuted by the lightning. Any attempt at escape had been thwarted by razor winds and more lightning to keep us grounded. "All that's missing is Rozalin coming to betray us."

As I said that, a large object streaked across the sky above the storm wall.

"It's your friends," said Noah. I held on to him tighter to keep from slipping as another of the same figure passed overhead. "The annoying ones."

"Lyle? He must have seen us on satellite. We can't let him join this."

"Not much we can do about it." Set hadn't reappeared and that wasn't a good sign. We were supposed to be keeping him distracted.

"Not good," Noah said and ran with me along the perimeter of the clearing. When he stopped I saw what he was referring to. A tsunami of sand that reached up into the storm was heading toward us from the center of the clearing.

"Mist yourself into the storm," I shouted over the roaring winds. "I'll be fine."

"I won't be able to get to you in time while you're healing though." Going too high up meant lightning that would disable me long enough to get caught if shocked. Trying to penetrate the storm wall would lead to the same result; getting crushed beneath the sand left me equally vulnerable.

"I've got an idea, stay behind me," I told Noah and dropped down. I couldn't turn the sand against Set, but I might be able to sap its momentum. I closed my eyes to block out the distracting rain and flashes of lightning. Pushing out with my powers, I could feel every particle of the sand tsunami almost upon us as my reach engulfed the wave. I let loose a pulse of telekinetic energy and then heard a calamity all around us.

"Nice one," Noah said into my ear over the noise before I opened my eyes to see what had happened. "It's so hot when you cause mass destruction."

Not only had I stopped the tsunami, sending millions of tons of sand crashing into the ground, the shockwave negated the strength of the storm behind us, causing it to drop the sand it carried.

Set emerged from the desert with his staff aimed at us. Noah went to pick me up, but I stopped him.

"Give me both of your *wakizashi*," I said.

"Not the time to spar," Noah argued but handed them over anyway. I sent them through the air toward Set. "That's not going to work—"

Set had dominion over everything in his land, but the swords weren't from here. When I had tried to stop Gianluca after he was taken over by the dark side of his soul in Hell, I used the metal in the facility we were in as a medium since I couldn't affect him directly.

I bent both *wakizashi* around each of Set's wrists and pushed back. Set may have tapped into Gianluca's darkness, but as long as Gianluca was still alive Set didn't have control over all of it and couldn't make himself the immovable living tank that Gianluca was. My plan worked, but instead of only holding Set in place to stall for more time I launched him over the horizon.

"Shit..." Noah put his arm over my shoulder. "You owe me a new pair of blades."

"Oh, shut up." I laughed and hit him in the stomach with the back of my hand.

"I'm adding it to the list along with those sunglasses you still owe me. Don't think I'm kidding either." He smiled down at me.

Our celebration was short lived as the winds began to churn again and Set came flying toward us in a rage. Unfortunately, I had lost the swords wherever Set had landed and he wasn't kind enough to return them. We didn't have anything left to use against him for a repeat performance.

Set commanded the wet sand to ensnare us as he drew closer with his staff readied. I freed us just as there was a bone-rattling explosion in the sky several miles away. "That's our cue," said Noah and picked me up under his arm. It sounded more like a missile attack than a flare if that was the Order's signal.

Noah stopped and put me down once we were a safe distance from Set's territory but not quite at the rendezvous point.

"Not good. Dogface's land is spreading," he said. "This was clear before."

We were at the edge of the strange celestial sky that was still creeping outward across the desert. "Just... remember what we talked about after tonight, all right? I don't know what's going to happen and... I want you to know that it was real."

"I'll never forget it. And thank you... for everything tonight and all the times before it."

"You're worth it." He poked my cheek.

"We make a great team," I smiled.

"Yeah... a *team*."

"That's not what I meant. I was just—" There was some commotion going on in the direction we were headed. Noah didn't give me a chance to explain. He picked me up one last time and dashed over to where the Order was in a standoff with Lyle and PROJECT: UNITY. "What's going on?!" I asked.

The Order was guarding Gianluca and Kamakura's statues with flaming swords drawn at PROJECT: UNITY, who had their rifles pointed at them. Behind UNITY was a military-grade dual propeller helicopter used for large transports and one of the two-seater jets.

"Dorian!" Lyle shouted. "Nuke these guys! They've got Gianluca and are trying to deliver him to another god."

"Stop it. All of you," I said. Immediately the trio sheathed their swords and kneeled in compliance. "Okay, that works. Still overdoing it a bit, but whatever."

Lyle and his troops put down their guns. He ran up to me while the Order kept a close eye on him like he could possibly do me harm. "What's going on?" he was frantic to spit out all his questions at once and looked like he wanted to hug me until he noticed Noah's arm over my shoulder. "What...what is, uh....?"

"It's mind your own fucking business or get your throat ripped out," Noah snarled. "That's what it is." He disappeared without another word.

"I thought you were a statue too," Lyle said to me. I could see in his face that he was still trying to figure out what was going on between me and Noah.

"I was, but I'm fine. I'll fill you in on all the details later." I walked over to the members of the Order, each one of whom was still kneeling. "You guys can get up."

"Who are they?" Lyle asked.

"Tobias, Helena, and Liam," I said. "Guys, this is my best friend Lyle."

"Our apologies," said Tobias. "We didn't know of your friendship to, our lord—"

"Ah, that's enough of that!" I stopped him.

"Our lord?" Lyle gave me the eyebrow of inquisition.

I sighed and spit it out, better now than later. "They're part of an order of human mages that consider me a god. Go ahead and laugh."

"God?" As expected he started to laugh but tried to hold in the really deep kind. "Is that why you're in a toga, or a loincloth, or a bikini or whatever this is?"

"It's a shirt, dumbass. It was that or totally nude." I started to shiver now that the adrenaline of battle had worn out and was still soaking wet.

"Here." Tobias removed his cloak and presented it to me. I wasn't going to refuse, especially after Lyle's comment.

"Soft and velvety," I announced after I put it on and wrapped myself up in it. "Jealous, Lyle?"

"Not really," he started to laugh again.

"Laugh all you want, but the Order went in and got Gianluca and Kamakura out of that pyramid while Noah and I kept Set busy."

"Again, our apologies," said Tobias. "It took longer than expected. There was resistance inside of the supernatural kind. Set had summoned Infernal guards and it appears that they are able to exist in the domain of the God of Chaos undeterred."

"Speaking of which, his influence is spreading." I pointed out the sky to everyone. No sooner did I say that than the storm wall returned along with an even bigger tsunami of sand headed straight for us.

"Everyone in the 'copter!" Lyle yelled. The sand at our feet was being sucked toward the storm so I lifted everyone at once—including the statues— into the nearby helicopter. We took off instantly, but it still wasn't fast enough to escape.

I didn't have to close my eyes this time when I flew out to face the sandstorm. All I had to do was stare it down and imagine.

"That was amazing!" Lyle exclaimed when I returned to the helicopter with the sand falling from the sky behind me.

"Of course it was," said Helena. The earth split open under us and traveled along gigantic cracks into the desert. There was nothing I could do to stop the further spread of destruction right now, but this war was far from over.

Chapter Twenty-Four

"You can fill us in on what you've been up to on the way back to base if it pleases Your Majesty," Lyle joked with me. "Then we have to plan our next move."

"May I suggest returning to the abbey instead?" asked Tobias. "We are nearby and you will have a place to rest comfortably."

"This isn't the time to get comfortable," Lyle said. "Close to eighty million people died or are still unaccounted for this week. We had a big victory, but that doesn't mean it's time to relax."

I had been looking out the window of the helicopter hoping that Noah would be okay. It wasn't Set I was worried about doing anything to him, but what would happen when he returned to Aurelia.

"We're not doing either," I said. "Have PARAGON find the next closest Temple of Isis outside Egypt."

If my research was correct, Isis was one of the longest worshipped Egyptian gods that became integrated into other ancient religions and assimilated with their deities. That means she would have temples free of Set's influence that I could use to contact her.

One of the troops was quick on the draw and found my answer in seconds. "There's one in Pompeii and one on the island of Delos in Greece, but it doesn't look like there's much left of that one."

"Delos is the closest. Our home is right outside the Cyclades archipelago where it's located," said Helena.

"We'll try there first then," I said. "I'll build her a new temple if I have to."

"You heard him. Get us to that temple in Delos, Greece," Lyle shouted to the pilot. "What is Isis about?" he turned back to me.

"She said she can restore Gianluca and Kamakura and I trust her. She healed my soul from all the hellfire damage that I had taken in the past and helped me... transcend. She'll need Set's staff to help these two, but maybe there's an alternative. Set is using the darkness that he stole from Gianluca and is in total control over the elements from Kamakura. If we can get them back on their feet hopefully they can take their powers back to weaken Set enough so I can get the staff."

"That works for me, man." Lyle shrugged in agreement. "Guess you already had a plan all along. Nice to have one for once and not always be doing things on the fly."

"True, but it's the players on the board that matter more than the plan itself and I couldn't have done it without everyone that's been involved so far." I nodded toward the trio. I thought they would be in awe of the high-tech helicopter, but they didn't seem fazed in the slightest. They always came across as being very serious, even when some level of excitement would have been appropriate.

"What was all that about with Noah?" Lyle asked. "Kinda weird to see him acting like your buddy. I know you two were friendly the last time he was with us, but I never thought I'd see him actually touch someone unless he was maiming them. I almost didn't think it was the same guy until he threatened me."

"I don't know," I lied to avoid getting into all the details. "He was in a good mood after our victory, I guess. You know Noah, always unpredictable."

"Got that right. Must've been a really good mood."

The flight to Delos was short but it gave me enough time to catch up with Lyle on the short version of everything that happened in the three days since I had seen him last. He had convinced Owen and Micah to take over guarding Castile so that he would be free to bring a small extraction team to Egypt. Owen had misplaced his hunting gear while on a drunken bender so that left us down a suit that could protect against hellfire, but Owen was crazy enough not to care.

According to Lyle, what Noah had said about Aurelia hosting the world leaders was true and still going on. Aurelia's influence on the human world was a slow burn compared to Set's catastrophic impact. Ever so slowly, she had expanded her guest list each night to include more and more high-ranking representatives. She had singlehandedly put a stop to most major wars in the current mortal world. Heads-of-state and diplomats that previously could not even be in the same room without hurling insults and threats over some international slight they had felt were now practically holding hands and singing campfire songs as best friends. More accurately, they were entranced into absolute compliance by their new queen and saw no other goal than working toward pleasing her.

On the other hand, Aurelia had forsaken the six billion other "peasants" that were rioting in panic over losing eighty million of their own by Set's tantrum. The world leaders and their subordinates that joined their queen's mindless collective pledged non-interference with the events in Egypt so that we could take care of things uninterrupted. This was a tremendous boon, as now we would not have to deal with every military in the world pointing weapons of mass destruction at us. However, at the same time the public was getting riled up and angry as they witnessed their elected officials and dictators do nothing to protect them or ensure their safety.

Lyle was hesitant to show me news clips from around the globe. It wasn't only major cities that were holding protests and riots, but even small towns that felt they might be able to appeal to their local government since the higher ups were unresponsive. One video Lyle had shown me was of Manhattan from last night, where the streets looked like a mosh pit at a concert venue that even the most reckless taxi driver couldn't navigate.

It didn't feel as if what I was watching was real. This was a different kind of chaos all together than what was going on out in the desert.

Had I already reached the point where I was okay with temporarily enslaving humanity just so they would calm down and let us do our job? No, I couldn't let myself think like that. That was exactly what had caused the rift between Gianni and I and what I feared would be the outcome from Aurelia's takeover. There weren't many other answers though, if any at all, and soon the balance would be tipped beyond salvation in chaos's favor if the state of mankind remained like this.

"We're here," Lyle announced and slid the door open as we landed. "Not much to look at." He wasn't kidding. It was worse than I thought. There was no real temple left, only the hollowed out shell of one with a few broken walls, a couple of columns, and the bottom half of a statue I could only assume was supposed to be of Isis. The statue was in Greco-Roman style from what I could tell and looked nothing like how she appeared to me.

I brought Gianluca and Kamakura and set them down on either side of Isis's statue. I had always said Gianluca was statuesque, but to actually see him in stone was upsetting.

"Stand back," I told everyone from the helicopter who had gathered around me now. "I'm going to try something."

I closed my eyes and felt out the broken statue with my powers. Starting at the feet and working my way up, I tried to mold the stone to match my memory of what Isis had looked like when she appeared to me.

I can feel the feet, the toes; they're all way too big and she didn't have these gladiatorial sandals. Her dress wasn't as heavy as the toga of the Greeks either; it was a thin linen without so many layers. Her hips are close to what I remember. She was petite, but still had modest curves that were appropriate for a goddess of motherhood and fertility.

Then there's the years of dirt caked into the cracks and crevasses. I can feel it all, but I have to go slow, one inch at a time to be sure I'm removing the right thing. The dirt is only slightly less dense than the stone after being exposed to the elements and baking in the sun for centuries.

"Damn, dude. That's amazing," Lyle said in fascination behind me. "You couldn't do stuff like this before, right? It isn't like the carvings you used to make."

"No, but I haven't opened my eyes yet so I don't know if it's accurate. I can feel the stone is hard and smooth, but any time I put pressure on it or pull pieces it feels pliable, like a really soft rubber that takes whatever shape I contort it into without actually losing its natural properties." I was surprised and proud of how close I had gotten the bottom half when I checked. That was the easy part though. *Now I have to do the rest from scratch.*

"What is making her a statue going to do?" Lyle asked.

"Spiritborn deities, or 'True Gods', are tied to their places and icons of worship," I explained like I was an expert on this. "It's a hub to direct prayers. Picture it like ringing God's doorbell and leaving a thank you card in the mailbox. The weaker the gods get from the lack of prayers, the closer they have to stay to their places of worship I imagine, which is probably why Set can't leave his front lawn.

"Since he's a 'God of Chaos', his influence grows the more chaos he causes or is in contact with. I'm assuming because he is Isis's brother and they're often in the same legends together, he was able to jump around to her places of worship too, which is how he got me once I returned some of the artifacts to a major temple of hers."

"Isn't this a really bad idea then? You're going to lead Set right to us."

"From what I know, other cultures only continued to worship Isis. Her relationship to Set wasn't mentioned later on when she assimilated with other deities...that I know of. Then again I didn't read much about that, so... Worst comes to worst I blow up this 'temple' and send him back to Egypt before he can cause any trouble."

"Man, why'd you have to say that," Lyle groaned. "All right everyone, lock and load. Pilot, keep the 'copter running and get ready for a fast exit."

"Silly human, guns aren't going to do anything." The futility of it was almost humorous in some sick way.

"Spiritborn deities are constructs of pure aether that have been tempered by mankind's collective consciousness," said Helena. "Mundane weapons won't have an effect since their corporeal form is only a projection."

I picked up a large chunk of a downed column and placed it on top of the bottom half of the statue to begin shaping like clay. The hardest part was connecting the two separate pieces. I kept mushing them together, but the molecules, or whatever I was manipulating, wouldn't attach. I decided to create grooves for the pieces to fit into and finished working my way up the rest of the statue.

Forming each individual feather of her wings was the next arduous task. I found that the less I concentrated and the more I let my imagination visualize the end result, the easier it was to make progress.

"You have returned, Young One." The statue of Isis came alive the moment I was done. Her voice rang in my head with the chorus of birds and jingling of the *sistrum*.

"Whoa," Lyle exclaimed as we watched the statue move as if it were real.

"You can manifest yourself that easily now?" I asked, expecting I'd have needed to remake the whole temple and gather artifacts all over again.

"I have attuned myself to your energy of infinite souls by your blessing." I would have rather she didn't say that. I didn't need everybody to hear the source of my power and judge how I used it.

"Isis, I wasn't able to get the staff from Set, but we were able to rescue our allies. Set is too strong for just us. Is there any other way you can undo the spell without the staff?"

"The staff itself holds no power, it is the Eye of Ra at its apex that I require. It is a source of limitless energy, but Ra placed an enchantment on it so that only those whom know his true name can unlock the Eye's full potential."

"I know, you told me," I said, trying to be patient. "What about my power? You're tapping into it right now."

"The energy it would take to reverse a spell cast by even the limited amount of power my brother has harnessed from the Eye would erase you from existence, Young One. Your young soul is a gateway to a dimension of near-infinite energy, but to draw too much power through would smash it to splinters."

Erase myself? That sounds a lot more permanent than dying. "The Spiritborn are beings of aether, right? What if we plug Isis into the ley lines around here? Is there any way you can direct them to her?" I asked the Order. "That should help supplement my power so I'm not... erased."

"Yes, my lord, but I would strongly advise against it," said Tobias.

"Why?"

"I'm afraid the explanation is not a short one and would be better told at the abbey."

"No time for that. Give me the short version."

"Over two thousand years ago when our Order was formed and up until the Dark Ages we worshipped a polytheistic pantheon of Spiritborn deities not associated with any single religion," Helena started. These guys really needed to work on their sense of urgency. "They are the ones that taught man how to use magic.

"Some of our ancestors had grown so powerful that they felt they rivaled the strength of their mentors and no longer needed to worship them. These were the first Soulborn, or 'Ascended Ones', on record. The vengeance of those Spiritborn, after having been betrayed, left the old Order broken. They stripped mankind of the ability to use magic and commanded the mortals to kill any remaining heretics or suffer divine punishment.

"The Order was reformed in secret by those who had escaped judgment along with a handful of pagan witches that sought protection in numbers from the witch hunters. Ever since then we have done whatever necessary to keep magic out of the hands of those who may wield it irresponsibly and draw the attention of the Spiritborn, for fear of their continued wrath that may return us to darkness."

"We can't limit ourselves to new alliances based on that," I said. "You've proven yourselves to be trustworthy when you helped me save Empress Kamakura, and she's another Spiritborn. Sometimes we have to do things we're uncomfortable with so that we can move forward in ways we never thought we could. Trust me, okay?"

"By your command." Tobias resigned with a bow.

The trio lined up and got down on one knee in front of Isis. They plunged their swords into the ground, drawing out a pale blue energy that they directed from their hand to Isis. The glow it gave off was the same as those floating rocks above the obelisks that Noah had busted. It seemed that Set had the same idea we did and found a way to do it himself.

The statue of Isis began to soften into skin and cloth, but was stopped half way. "Okay, now for my turn," I told her and went closer. *This had better work...*

Chapter Twenty-Five

The life drained from my body as a tide washing out to sea. It didn't hurt, but left me too exhausted to stand. The Order was quick to descend upon me in support.

My vision faded as a warm light shined from the living statue of Isis. She was reborn in all her glory, at least for the time being. The light stretched further as she unfurled her wings until it enveloped the statues of Gianluca and Kamakura. And then...

"That is all I have... Good fortune...smile...you..." Isis's voice left my mind on the tail end of a breeze, her statue returned to inanimate stone. With her gone from this world, the light went out with her and left behind Gianluca's unconscious body on the ground.

"Thank god, or goddess..." I mumbled in relief. Gianluca's armor hadn't disappeared like another time he was rendered unconscious. That was a good sign that he still had his strength. "Where did Kamakura go?" I asked and looked around for any signs of her glass prison.

"Returned to the aether," Helena answered. "She will most likely rest in her native dimension until she has the energy to manifest again..."

"Man, this guy weighs a ton!" Lyle exclaimed as he tried to lift Gianluca to get him in the helicopter.

"He's not easy to wake up either," I said, feeling nostalgic over our good memories now that we were together again. "I can't lift him when he's in his armor so you're on your own, Lyle. Better muscle up."

"You aren't in any shape to exert yourself, my lord—"

"*Dorian*," I cut Tobias off to correct him again.

"Apologies," he said. "It will take some getting used to, but in the meantime this may be a decent opportunity for us to escort you to the abbey where you can rest."

"I feel fine," I said and got to my feet with his assistance. "My power is already coming back." I may have been exaggerating.

"Dorian, you should really come back to base," Lyle added and looked at the trio with distrust. "*Especially* if you're weak."

"My, you are weak more often than not," a voice called from above. *Minerva!*

"Shoot her!" Lyle shouted to the troops. They opened fire, but the high-caliber bullets of their rifles ricocheted off her barrier and back at us. She raised her hand in a ball of hellfire and shot it at the statue of Isis. The statue exploded and scattered flaming rock everywhere.

"Liam," Tobias said calmly.

"You can't! She'll kill you all," I yelled, but Liam had vanished in that hazy bubble the Order used when teleporting. "Give me one of your swords and I'll fight her. She can't stick around for long."

"Trust us," Tobias encouraged and tried leading me away from the battle with my arm over his shoulder. "My son is more than capable of doing battle with a demon."

Minerva raised her other hand and blew up the helicopter, sending Lyle's troops flying. "What a pathetic excuse for a *god!*" she taunted and fired off a shot at me. "I come with a message—"

Helena drew her sword and stood her ground in front of me. Her blade let off a blue flash when she used the broad side to smack the incoming ball of hellfire back at Minerva. Liam appeared in the air with his swords rimmed in the same blue light and struck them against Minerva's barrier to shatter it. The ball of hellfire connected with Minerva, roasting her to a crisp and forcing her to retreat back into a portal to Hell.

Liam landed on his feet and walked back to us as serious as ever. There was no swagger or even a smile and none of the trio offered each other any word of praise. "That was awesome," I said to them, but the most I got in response was a slight nod.

"Is everyone all right?" Lyle shouted. Nobody had been seriously injured that I could tell. "Looks like we got some broken bones, but no casualties," he reported after surveying the area. "And Big G is still sleeping like a baby in a suit of armor."

"Liam..." Tobias spoke in the same commanding tone as last time. Liam walked back to where PROJECT: UNITY was assessing their wounds and began healing them with a touch of his palm and a faint glow.

"He can do that too?" I asked.

"We all can," said Tobias. "It's basic combat triage we learn around five or six years of age. We start introducing it as young as possible so it is ingrained in our nature. By two all members know their first spell to produce light. The same goes for combat training and survival tactics. At three years old all begin to learn the basics of the sword and how to hunt, gather, and farm for food."

"That's unbelievable that humans still live that way today," I said. "It sounds like the Spartans."

"Any of the Order could have bested an adult Spartan in solo combat by thirteen years of age and taken down a small army of them alone by eighteen. Anything less would be an inexcusable failure."

"Then what?" I asked and removed my arm from around Tobias's shoulder now that I felt my strength coming back for real this time. "If they fail, I mean."

"There is no failure," said Helena. "We don't allow it."

Liam started to walk back, again without any change in expression after having completed his task. Lyle was at his heels. "Hey, wait up, man," Lyle called to him.

Liam turned to acknowledge him and Lyle put out his hand. "Thanks for helping my men back there. That was pretty cool with the demon too."

Liam glanced down at Lyle's hand. I thought he was about to snub him, but they shook. "You're welcome." That was the first time I had heard Liam speak and it was so short I almost missed it.

"He doesn't talk much," I said to Tobias.

"There is strength in silence."

"I wonder what that message was Minerva had for you," Lyle said to me as he and Liam joined us.

"Typical demon bullshit. If I really am some sort of god now that my soul was healed then she was probably trying to weaken it again. That was a rather tame showing for her though..."

"Yeah, well, let's be glad she sucks at her job," said Lyle, rubbing the back of his neck anxiously. "I radioed for backup to come get us. I should be more upset about the helicopter, but the fact that everyone's alive and on their feet thanks to this guy has me counting my blessings. We'll keep a crew here to work on clearing the wreckage and see what can be salvaged while the rest of us head back to base."

"I, uh... I think I'm gonna go with the Order to check out the abbey," I said.

"By your leave, I will inform the others of your arrival," Helena bowed.

"Uh, sure." I wasn't certain if that was a request for permission or a statement, but she departed via the ley lines without another word.

"What about Gianluca?" Lyle asked.

"I'd...rather not be there when he wakes up. Not yet."

"Is this about your argument?" he prodded. "I'm not gonna tell you what to do, but I think you should move past that for the sake of everything that's going on in the world. You've both been through a lot these past few days and I'm sure he's gonna want to see you to talk things out."

"He can come find me when he's ready," I said. "Besides, I owe the Order my attention after what they've done for us today."

If I was to think rationally and logically (as any good leader should), then I didn't want to get caught up in an emotional tug of war with Gianluca when there was more at stake than whatever feelings we had for each other. It would be a waste of time for me to wait for him to wake up when I knew he was safe.

There were other avenues to explore so that we could eek out our next victory. The Order had proven themselves to be valuable allies, although I had initially written them off as nothing more than humans that knew a few magic tricks and wanted to play in the big leagues. Ignoring them any longer would be foolish and possibly detrimental to our cause.

"You're really leaving me again? Just like that?" Lyle joked.

"Want me to hold your hand until your ride comes to pick you up?"

"Maybe."

"Too bad," I grinned and then we both busted out into laughter. The Order must have already been regretting choosing me as their god. "I'll only be gone a day or two at most and then I'll come back to base whether Gianluca is awake or not. If anything happens to me I'll have one of the Order keep you in the loop so you don't do anything stupid like I would do."

"All right, man. Remember that we just lost eighty million lives and six billion more are at stake, so don't get too comfy."

"It's a business trip, Lyle, not a vacation."

"Go ahead. Shouldn't be long until evac gets here. Don't forget to bring me back a souvenir from the gift shop."

"Can you take me to the abbey with only the two of you?" I asked Tobias.

"Yes, it will be much easier while you're still weakened if we make haste. It isn't far and the islands here have a strong network of ley lines."

"Okay then. Let's go."

Chapter Twenty-Six

The journey across the ley lines was brief. There was the disorienting sensation of going cross-eyed when arriving on the other side, similar to opening your eyes after a vigorous rubbing. The transition itself was instant—the same as traveling through the shadows with Gianluca when he knew the destination, only with an initial feeling of the world falling out from under you.

I was relieved not to have been bombarded once we got to the abbey. I was expecting the Order to be gathered so that they could stand around and gawk at me like I was used to whenever meeting a new group of humans. Instead, Tobias and Liam had brought me to an empty bedroom.

"Bedchamber" might be a more fitting name for the room we were in. It sounded more impressive to me and matched the surroundings better in my mind, even if it meant the same thing. I had seen all levels of wealth and poverty during my adventures, and the abbey fit somewhere pleasantly in between.

The interior architecture was a medieval style that seamlessly blended together several types of buildings from that era into a unique final product. The row of floor-to-ceiling windows looking out over the coast resembled a gothic cathedral with arches and glass paneling.

The walls were comprised of crude stone masonry, as would be used in a fort or castle keep for defensive purposes. Along with the iron trimmings for things such as the door hinges and sconces, it was a glaring contradiction to the windows that added a touch of elegance and negated all protection from invaders.

There were no signs of electricity usage anywhere, only candles and old-fashioned lamps. An enormous fireplace that took up most of the far right wall could have supplied heat and light to every corner of a room this size on its own.

The finished hardwood floors and large area rugs, including one of fur by the fireplace, were the type seen more often in a noble or royal's living quarters than a cathedral or fort. It was touches of luxury like these, the mahogany furniture, and the woven banners hung about the room that made even the cold stone seem inviting, but not over-the-top extravagant.

"Do you like it?" asked Tobias as he and Liam stood at attention while I studied the room.

Two brown leather armchairs with ottomans sat opposite each other on either side of the rug by the fireplace and a leather sofa with a fur blanket folded at one end was placed by the corner of the window. A king-sized four poster bed was centered along the back wall with matching end tables on both sides. The bed was done up with a dark gray fur comforter and a collection of the fluffiest pillows I had ever seen. If I was alone I would be tempted to roll myself in all of it.

"Yes. I thought it would be something Greek considering where we are, but it's really nice."

"This abbey was originally located in England. It was transported here by the last Ascended before they fell in an attempt to flee the Church when we were deemed heretics."

"Wow that must have been startling for anyone nearby," I laughed. "Is this your room?" While the furniture was clearly newer based on its condition, nothing here had stood out as insincere to the authenticity of the Old World style. It was also worn in just enough to be cozy without jeopardizing its quality or integrity. The room was what I would call "readily livable", compared to that of Aurelia's furnishings, which were striking as museum pieces that one might admire but not ideal for curling up for the night.

"No, it's yours."

"Uh—"

"I apologize for being so forward." Tobias cleared his throat. "We had prepared this room in anticipation of the coming of Our Lord. I don't know how to say this any other way, so please forgive me in advance for any unintended offensive, but we were unsure of who exactly we would be receiving.

We did our best to transform what was once our sacrarium for meditation into a personal sanctuary for whomever would be gracing us."

"Okay, so you mean it wasn't set up specifically for me. That doesn't offend me, it makes me feel a little more comfortable. If you didn't notice, I'm probably not what you were expecting from a god. I'm not used to being the recipient of all these formalities."

"You have exceeded our expectations in almost every way. I admit that we were negligent in our duties to welcome the arrival of the first Ascended as we should have because we had our reservations. It was not our place to judge and for that I take full responsibility for our sins." Tobias got down on one knee and bowed his head. Liam just stood there, which made me smile at what must have been going through his head watching his father act like that. "Passing such judgment upon the divine is not the place for mortals. That same arrogance is what marred the Order of our ancestors and cast a darkness on the world the first time. It is a lesson we teach from birth, but one I had disregarded because I thought I knew better than the old teachings."

"Okay, you're losing me and you have to stop with the kneeling. It's embarrassing."

Tobias got to his feet and stood at attention. "The Dark One was the first Ascended of the New Age. It is he whom we were to swear allegiance to as the scriptures demand. We...I...was hesitant. I defied the others of the council because I believed it to be a sign that his dark powers did not resonate with our own. I felt that this would cause discord amongst the Order and decreed that we reserve our welcome until we could be sure."

"Judging is a part of human nature tied to free will, so it isn't a sin if it's with the best interest of your people in mind," I said. *That was a tremendous grey area and a constantly evolving conflict though, so maybe I shouldn't be so dismissive of his worry.*

"We watched his actions from a distance as they became more aggressive over the recent months. I used that to convince the Order that I was right in our hesitation. We had been watching you for years as a potential Ascended as I explained earlier. Your actions were always noble and just. You brought peace to the chaos around the world and balanced the Dark One's unmitigated wrath in the Middle East. I was sure that if you had succeeded in your transcendence you would be the one we were waiting for.

"We tell our young that the Ascended will be our saviors and a hope for mankind, but many wise to all angles of history know that not all of the Ascended were virtuous. I would be remiss if I did not admit the unspoken concerns we all have had at one time, praying silently that it was not an Ascended from the past that managed to return to us."

"I thought that they all died when they angered the Spiritborn gods?" I asked.

"Death is rarely a permanent solution—and certainly isn't for any form of god. There are scriptures stating that our Ascended ancestors whom doomed our Order and mankind with it would return and be the ones we are dictated to kneel before."

"Well, I'd rather you didn't kneel to me, but I'd be happy to work together and get to know each other more," I said and took a seat on the bed. "Thanks for not teleporting me into a crowd with everyone staring at me, by the way."

"We figured it would be best to let you get accustomed to us at your own pace. But it goes without say that the rest are all equally as excited to meet you."

"I'm looking forward to it too, but we need to stay focused on current events. Set's range is growing and this place is dangerously close."

"Yes, of course."

"What's this?" I asked and pointed to a neatly folded pile of black clothes at the foot of the bed.

"An offering, for you, of course," said Tobias. I was still in my ripped shirt for a loincloth and his cloak which I had grown fond of. "This I can say was made specifically for you by our very own."

"You guys make your own clothes too?"

"Yes, every member of the Order fabricates his or her own clothes for daily wear, as well as weapons and armor," he explained. "It is all part of learning self-sufficiency and discipline."

"So everything you're both wearing right now, you made that by yourselves?" That was almost more impressive than Liam and Helena's display against Minerva.

"Yes, that is correct. Tailoring and smithing are only two of many crafts we practice our entire lives. We make everything from candles to furniture."

"Who made these?" I asked and unfolded the shirt. *This is amazing!* The first thing I noticed was how soft and lightweight it was, just like the cloak. The texture was somewhere between velvet and silk. It was all black, with some ribbing and a deep V neck that had a thin silver chain across it at the collar with little silver swords hanging from it. The best part was the hood, seeing as I lived in hoodies for most of my life.

The ensemble had a very high fashion feel to it that I felt would look better on someone like Owen or Micah. I was just glad it wasn't a page boy's tunic or friar's robe. The black leather pants might have been a bit much for my more modest taste, but they went with the boots. I couldn't decide if I'd look like a medieval socialite or a fantasy fashion model.

There was such silence after my question while I inspected the clothes that I had almost forgotten what I asked until Tobias spoke up. "Liam did."

"Thank you," I said to Liam with a smile. "This kind of blows me away more than anything else so far." Even Gianluca had never done something like this for me. Sure, he had "acquired" clothing for me as a gift, but nobody had ever made something to give me. Of course, they could be lying but I would find out as soon as I tried it on.

Liam *almost* smiled back. I could see it on his lips trying to get out, but he managed to refrain and keep his title as most expressionless being on the planet. I knew dead bodies with more lively personalities. "How'd you know my size?" I directed my question at Liam.

"I had been watching you so often that it wasn't too much trouble to estimate, sir..." Liam closed his eyes for a moment in embarrassment after realizing how creepy that sounded once the words left his mouth. Tobias didn't flinch, but I couldn't hold in my laughter. This poor guy hasn't said more than two words all night and the first time he does, *that's* what he had to say. It was even funnier to me because Liam was quite attractive and somebody who I would expect to be well-spoken and confident like his father.

"It's okay, I understood what you meant. I'm a pretty easy size to match," I said, trying to console him as his face turned bright red. "The thing is, clothes have a very short life expectancy with me. I don't want these to get ruined."

"That is the best part," Tobias exclaimed and came over to take the shirt from me. "This fabric is called angel silk. It's woven from a rare fiber found only on the Astral Plane and takes a decade to grow to maturity. If picked and returned to the material realm in its native state, it will become brittle and unusable, so it must be saturated in aether by a theurgist with adequate power while it is spun into spools."

"That's making me want to not wear it even more," I said.

"A demonstration then." Tobias held the shirt up and set it on fire with a spell. My reaction seemed to amuse him when I cringed. The shirt wasn't burning. I put my hand over the flame to check if it was an illusion, but the heat radiating from it was hotter than any normal fire. "It is nearly impervious to both mundane and supernatural elements. It will hold its temperature too. Please, go ahead and feel it."

"Including hellfire?" I asked and took the shirt back once he extinguished the flames. He was right. Even after being exposed to such high levels of heat, the material was room temperature.

"Yes, although it does have its limits they will be almost impossible to reach and I've yet to witness any myself."

"Is it resistant to tearing too?"

"Give it a test," he encouraged. "Gently at first." I tugged at it using my powers with enough force to tear a person in half, yet it stayed intact without any sign of ripping. The cloth was definitely more resilient than any other material I knew. "Steel blades will not be able to penetrate it, but it doesn't offer much protection in the way of blunt force trauma since it is still cloth. We can have proper armor crafted for you if you wish."

"Can I try with your sword?" I asked.

"I'm afraid our weapons will be able to damage the fabric. They are made of an enchanted metal known as orichalcum. The chain and trimmings by the collar, along with any other metal you see such as the buckle on your boots, are also orichalcum.

"Orichalcum is naturally a copper color until infused with aether to unlock its mystical durability after being forged. You would be hard pressed to find another material in existence to match its invincibility. What you see on your clothes is only for prestige since it is quite rare and rationed sparingly for nothing more than primary weapons and vital armor pieces."

"This is too good to be true," I laughed. "You don't know how badly I've wanted something like this that wouldn't get ruined. What about the leather of the pants and boots? Is it demonskin?"

"A good eye, my lord. It is purified demon lord hide. A much higher grade than regular demonskin. The purification ritual removes the soul corrupting properties for your safety. It has similar attributes to angel silk in that it is nearly impervious to the elements and most weapons."

"How did you get the hide from a demon *lord*?" I asked.

"All the materials required were gathered by Liam and his cabal." Tobias went over to him and put his hand on Liam's back with fatherly pride. "Demon exorcisms and slayings are one of many tasks the Order undertakes to keep the world safe. For this particular set they first summoned a demon lord to the Astral Plane to lure it from its lair and then slew the beast."

"I... I don't know what to say. I'm blown away by all of this, your generosity, your hospitality, your strength and courage... all of it."

"It pleases me to hear that with no exaggeration of the term." Tobias bowed. "We will allow you some privacy so you can change and have a moment to relax. Would you like us to draw you a bath?" Tobias offered.

"Maybe a dumb question, but do you have running water here?" I asked.

"Yes. You have your own washroom back there." He pointed to what I had thought was a closet door. "Knowing that the Ascended have roots in the human form, unlike the Spiritborn, we thought it appropriate to include." *They had really put a lot of effort into planning this out. Not that it was so unheard of to have a bathroom attached to your bedroom, but the way they treated me like I was some divine being it would be an easy oversight to assume that I didn't just poof into magical energy like Isis or Kamakura.*

"How come you guys have running water, but not electricity?"

"We have no need for electricity because our magic is used in its stead, and should the need arise we can conjure it ourselves."

"Makes sense," I said. "I think I'll be fine managing the bath myself. I've lived in the wilderness." I was sort of joking, but recalling that tale wasn't as impressive anymore when the Order had toddlers that could do better.

"Very good. I will convene the Council to begin talk of wartime preparations. Liam will await your command from the hall should you need anything and escort you to the Council chambers when you are ready." Tobias and Liam bowed with a hand over their heart and left the room through a great arched wooden door.

I found myself happier than I thought I'd be from coming here. I also found myself happier than I thought someone could make me without all the confusing emotions of romance attached to it. Although I wasn't ready to trust them unquestioned, the Order seemed to have simple goals that I could respect. I just needed to keep my new team on track to defeating Set now that orientation was over.

Chapter Twenty-Seven

"—and you stood there like a dullard. He looks at you as if you were dim and if I didn't know better I would have to agree—"

No sooner did the door close behind Liam and Tobias than whispering started between them in the hall. I floated my way over to the door to listen so that they wouldn't hear my footsteps. If I had let my guard down entirely I probably would not have paid much attention, but I was still keeping an ear out for any hint of deceit. At the moment, I trusted the Order enough to be in their company and agree to work towards a common goal. Better for them to follow me than Gianluca, who would have had them conquering countries.

Noah had always taught me to draw out people's true colors by observing them under pressure. He did it by antagonizing them until they snapped. I decided to take a more benign approach by showing I had no suspicions at all to lull them into their comfort zone while I paid attention to how they handled the events unfolding around us. It was something I had learned from my relationship with Gianluca, only now I was doing it on purpose.

"It should be *you* explaining these things to him. You are the Order's Chosen; my time has passed," Tobias continued his hushed rant. "Instead you hide behind my coattails as a child. Your whole life has been for this moment and you get cold feet. What has the Order spent the last eighteen years training you for if you cannot even answer simple questions about who we are?" *Liam is eighteen? I thought he was into his twenties by the sound of his voice and how mature he looks. Did he go through puberty when he was ten or something?*

"Six hundred years our people have waited for this moment and you stand there silent awaiting my command for such simple tasks as slaying the demon sorceress in Delos and healing the Ascended's followers that had been wounded because you were slow to act. Not to mention you've made me a fool by not kneeling in repentance for our sins."

"But he doesn't like it when we kneel, sir."

"Have you considered that he is testing our devotion to see if we are worthy?"

"No, sir."

"How are you to become the Ascended's champion if you do not even speak and kneel when appropriate? We have been blessed to be in the presence of an Ascended so merciful. I have put myself and every member of this Order in mortal danger when I persuaded the Council to neglect the holiest of scriptures that directs us to welcome the *first* Ascended to rise.

"He is to be our salvation during the Great Reckoning and it will be you alone that ruins this if our worship is rejected. Should it have been Marianna we appointed as our Chosen in your place?"

"No, sir. I'm sorry, sir..."

"Spare your words of apologies for those better spent in the company of the Ascended. I am to convene the Council. Stay here and do all it takes to serve Our Lord at any cost. Should he request you sing him a song, you will sing him a song. Should he ask you walk to China and pick him flowers, what will you do?"

"I will walk to China to pick him flowers, sir."

"Helena should have already instructed the others that no one is to disturb the Ascended while he rests, but should any of the children come by it is your duty to enforce that. Do you understand?"

"Yes, sir. I understand."

Poor Liam...

The whispering stopped so I headed into the bathroom to wash up. There was no sink, mirror, or medicine cabinet in the small stone room, but there was a cast-iron clawfoot tub, towels on a rack, and a toilet. Most important was the bar of soap to help wash away all the sand stuck in places that sand should never be on a body. *I bet they make their own soap*, I thought as I filled the tub.

Being that it was the morning there was enough natural light from a window to allow me to see, but I got the feeling that it would get annoying after a while to light a slew of candles every night for every room. I wondered what the Order used their magic on in place of electricity because I didn't see any light bulbs or electronics to be activated anywhere.

I took a bath without giving myself much time to relax and enjoy it. The warm water and moment of solitude did feel tempting to indulge a while longer, but there was work to be done. I was also a little excited to try on my magical custom-made clothes, so I dried off and hurried back into the bedroom to get changed.

The shirt was a perfect fit and kept me warm despite feeling as lightweight as tissue paper. I couldn't say that I had ever considered wearing leather pants before, but once I put them on I regretted that I hadn't tried sooner. I knew that Lyle was really going to give me shit about it when he saw me, but I felt like a different, more confident person when wearing this as opposed to my typical sweatpants and T-shirt or tattered rags.

"What are you doing here? Did my father send you?" I heard Liam speaking with someone out in the hall while I was getting dressed. He wasn't exactly whispering this time.

"You can't be here," Liam asserted. "You need to leave before my father sees you." I assumed he was talking to someone who wanted to sneak a glimpse at me. Normally, I would have waited in the room until the new person left before I went out, but I wanted to get things moving and knew I'd wind up being gawked at sooner or later regardless.

Standing beside Liam in the narrow stone hallway was a taller knight dressed unlike the others of the Order I had met. His full suit of armor—which included a helmet—was of the same pseudo-gothic aesthetic as the rest but crafted with the need for a much stronger defense in mind. He carried a great rectangular shield on his back that could have covered me to my chin if stood upright on the floor. There was no exposed skin anywhere on his person and his joints were protected by chainmail, unlike the cloth and leather that made up the majority of the trio's set.

I hadn't been uneasy around any of the Order thus far—I found them quirky at worst and fascinating at best—but when the new knight rushed toward me, I recoiled.

Maybe it was the concerned expression on Liam's face as he failed to stop the knight from getting close, or maybe it was how the knight dropped to one knee at my feet with his head bowed low and never uttered a word. I couldn't see his face and it unnerved me that I had no way to get a read on him. His helmet was a cross between a kendo mask and a knight's helmet, but I couldn't see through the horizontal openings.

Liam scrambled to intercept the knight. He grabbed the man's pauldron and whispered a word under his breath that was so quiet I couldn't make out what it was. His hand glowed blue and the knight was sent away somewhere through one of their hazy teleport bubbles.

"Forgive me." Liam bowed his head and got on one knee.

"It's all right and you don't have to kneel. I'm not testing you."

"I'm sorry, my lord," Liam said and got back up.

"Just call me Dorian."

"But..."

"I'm serious. It's not a test. You've been watching me haven't you? You should know I'm just a regular person—as regular as a supernatural can be. I might be more powerful than some, but I'm not a divine being from a thousand years ago. I grew up in Boston, Massachusetts, I'm twenty-four-years-old, hell I only started getting involved in this supernatural stuff a few years ago by accident. I'm not someone worthy of all this formality and worship."

"Our formalities are a show of respect for *who* you are, more than *what* you are. My father taught me that and worked hard to make the others see so too. He did not want us to serve someone he felt would only bring more suffering to the world."

"What do you believe?" I asked. "You can stop standing at attention too."

Liam looked like he knew his answer immediately, but wasn't sure if he should share it. "I believe that my father made the right decision. When I was a child he brought me to witness the great battle in America where you fought the horde of undead and the same demon sorceress from earlier. Since then I've witnessed many of your victories and have been inspired to be like you."

This wasn't the first time someone admitted to seeing that battle. It was the first time anyone ever told me I inspired them. "That was four, maybe four-and-a-half, years ago. You're eighteen, right?"

"I will be in two weeks." *Oh god, he's seventeen... I was an introverted high school senior worrying about getting into college at his age and he's fighting demon lords.* "I was twelve back then. I stayed to fight the creatures that were attacking civilians."

"Twelve? You were fighting those things at twelve years old?" *I remembered having trouble with the infected humans he was talking about when I first encountered them. I was twenty. I did so poorly that I was bitten by one and the ritual to save me from the infection is what turned me immortal.*

"Yes, sir—I mean Dorian."

"Why would your father let you fight those when you were so young? That's crazy."

"They weren't difficult. We train in combat our whole lives for much worse. We must be able to defend the Ascended should they not be able to themselves."

"Well, your training paid off. I was seriously impressed seeing you in action. You're giving me a lot to live up to though."

"It's the Order that has so much to live up to. You've already set a high standard for more than just combat. This is why my father feels you would lead us down the best path of enlightenment and salvation. You are aware of the situation in the world today and act with empathy."

"I try to do my best and help out when I see something wrong. I still don't think that's worthy of so much praise, but I do appreciate being recognized for my actions and not just *what* I am." As self-sufficient as the Order was they seemed to suffer from being a flock without a shepherd. They could keep themselves alive like sheep grazing on an open plain, but once a storm comes they needed guidance to avoid getting blown away; otherwise, they would keep their heads down and stuck with what they knew. The same could be said for most religions.

It was a good thing for them then that Tobias strayed from the flock and played the role of the black sheep to find a better way. The more I found out about the Order, the more relieved I was that they came to me instead of Gianluca. Tobias and Liam had a desire to be more than mindless warriors blindly serving a god that sought glory. My role in this was becoming clearer, but I still needed to tread carefully.

"Who was the person with the helmet and the big shield before?" I asked.

"A guard. Again, I'm sorry he disturbed you. He wasn't supposed to be here." It struck me as a little odd that he was referred to so impersonally as "a guard" when I was told the Order lived as a communal family. Why would a family of magical knights need someone designated as a guard anyway?

"Oh, I almost forgot to tell you that I like the clothes. They fit great and feel even better. I'll have to find some way to repay you."

Liam smiled. It was subtle, but it was a smile. "It's an honor enough that you're wearing them. It's been an honor just to meet you."

"I do have one favor to ask."

"Yes, anything." I should have asked him to sing just to see if his expression would change, but that would be cruel.

"Try to treat me as a friend. I'm not comfortable with the whole god thing and I *want* friends, not followers." I also wanted someone on the inside to pull back the curtain and let me know about any skeletons in the closet around here.

"I'll do my best."

"Can I speak with your father and the other council members now? I want to start making plans to deal with Set."

"I'll take you to them. They should already be waiting for you in the conclave. There shouldn't be anyone on the way there, but I apologize in advance if we're disturbed again."

Liam led the way through the abbey. Most of the halls were narrow, but it was cozy and not claustrophobic. A burgundy carpet lined the middle of every hall, dampening the sound of walking on stone. Only the rooms had hardwood floors and even those were mostly covered in rugs. There was plenty of light due to all the candelabras and lanterns and braziers. Windows of various sizes from large decorative paneled glass to thin portholes lit the rest.

The mahogany and leather furniture around the abbey was the same as in my room; antique yet comfortable. Although the décor was dark and medieval it still felt welcoming. There were fireplaces in almost every room and banners with heraldry hanging from the walls. In most rooms, I could also see swords and shields on display along the walls.

The abbey was rather large, but individual rooms and junctions weren't overpowering despite the size of the building. It felt more like living in a typical house with a lot of rooms than an enormous palace like Aurelia's, where you could get lost in the bathroom for days.

"I like your swords," I said to Liam now that I could see them up close. "Did you design them yourself?"

"I did, yes. Thank you." The swords were gun-metal gray with a wide, curved blade like a modified cutlass. A short protrusion, both elegant and barbaric, came down halfway toward the hilt from the apex of the curve, which looked designed to hook and tear flesh after the initial penetration.

"Are they orichalcum? They aren't silver like what's on my clothes."

"We can change the color of almost anything with magic. It's something we learn as one of our first spells as children." I did remember Tobias saying that their armor and weapons were made of orichalcum, but none of it was as shiny as the embellishments on my outfit. They kept a rather dark, dull color scheme.

"Here we are," Liam said as we arrived at a door that looked like any other in the abbey. He opened it for me and stood back.

"You're not coming in?" I asked.

"No, it wouldn't be allowed since I'm not on the council."

This was my chance to push buttons of my own and see the reaction I'd get like Noah always did. I wanted to see how the leaders would react if they were thrown off their game a little. Surely they had been in there preparing exactly what to say, word for word. If they were as genuine as I felt Liam was so far then there shouldn't be much of a problem. "I'd prefer if you stayed," I said and walked into the small circular room.

Tobias, Helena, and two men shot up out of their chairs from around a table in the center to greet me by kneeling. "You can stand," I said and tried not to roll my eyes.

Tobias gave a sharp look to Liam, who was still standing by the door. "Dorian has requested I stay," said Liam. The four councilmembers, most notably Tobias, looked as if they were about to faint at hearing Liam's words. "He...has also requested that we address him by his first name."

Chapter Twenty-Eight

"Dorian, this is Rhys Ellis-Morgan and Pavel Levendakis," Liam introduced me to the two other councilmembers.

Both men appeared to be approximately Tobias's age and looked quite dignified in what I assumed was ceremonial wear. Their clothes were tailored to fit snugly along every inch of their bodies. There weren't any frills nor ruffles nor billowing sleeves that I associated with the medieval period that inspired their style. I could tell that at least some of it was made from angel silk so I suppose if they needed to they could have fought in these clothes without their movements being limited.

It must have been around eight in the morning and the original trio was still standing after our long night in Egypt. Helena and Tobias hadn't even changed from their armor during their absence when I was with Liam. That could be beneficial to getting more honest information out of them, but they showed no signs of exhaustion.

"Nice to meet you all," I said. "Let's get down to business."

Aside from the kneeling, none had gawked at me yet or made me feel out of place. I felt pangs from my conscience that I was looking to trip them up to get honest reactions and not be my usual open self, but the game had to be played. I had been through too much to ignore past mistakes.

The council assembled around the table behind their high-backed seats and waited for me to take mine first. Liam pulled out the chair out for me and I went to sit until I realized he was without a place.

"Do you want to sit?" I offered my chair to him. "I don't mind standing."

"No, please, go ahead. Thank you," he said while avoiding eye contact. The council was squirming in their skin and Liam sounded like he wished I hadn't offered.

We took our seats with Liam standing at attention behind me at a respectable distance. On the wall were banners that lined up with each of the councilmembers' positions around the table.

"Our family crests," Tobias explained upon seeing me examining them. Only Helena's made any sense to me. I could pick out two white owls in her crest on a powder-blue background. The others were fancy designs, but their symbolism was lost on me.

"We four are the heads of our households, all of which are the eldest in the Order. The purest blood lineage to the original survivors of the first Great Reckoning, you could say."

"The Levendakis house only dates back to *after* the previous Ascended brought the abbey to Greece," said Rhys. "They were not part of the pure-blood survivors if historical accuracy is to mean anything."

Pavel's expression didn't change, but he did give Rhys the eye from across the table. *That was easy. All I had to do was look at something and already they're going after each other. I thought there would be more unity among them.*

"Apologies, Ascended," Rhys said. "I only meant to be forthright so you would have no reason to doubt us when you inevitably find out."

"Don't be afraid to speak your mind. We're all in this together and I need your help," I encouraged. "With that said, my concern right now is Set." I was surprised that none of them had the same look of horror as when Liam was invited in and offered a chair. Maybe this was normal for them.

"Ours as well," Helena spoke up and pulled out a world map on a large piece of parchment. "I have already filled in the others on the events from last night. At the rate his influence spreads, and if keeping in the same circular pattern, he should be at Israel's door by tomorrow—a mere two hundred and fifty miles away.

"Israel is another eight million victims should the storm land, but bigger still is what comes after: Turkey, Saudi Arabia, Sudan, Iraq, and of course by then we will be consumed also for a rough total of two hundred and eighty million additional lives lost on top of those already deceased in Egypt."

"We need that staff of his," I said. "But he's unstoppable while he has it. He also has the dark powers of Gianluca the shadow god and the elemental powers of the dragon god, Kamakura. Rescuing them gives us hope that they can take back what Set stole, but there's no telling how long it will be before they're up for that. Not to mention that the more chaos he causes, the stronger he gets as the souls of his victims fuel the Infernal Kings in Hell he's working with."

"We have our answer to defeat an unstoppable foe; we must take him apart piece by piece, but the first piece must be removed before the rest will fall," said Pavel. "I suggest we focus on a plan to prevent more losses in the meantime. One godly foe is problematic enough, we do not need a chain reaction giving rise to more demons."

"We would need to evacuate entire countries," Tobias said. "Displacing three hundred million people in a day is out of the question."

"Would spurring them to run for their lives not cause *more* chaos to hinder our cause?" asked Rhys. "The focus should be on stalling the enemy until reinforcements arrive. Bait him in a direction where there will be less casualties. Here, into the heart of Africa." He pointed on the map.

"And what bait do we lay for this plan?" Pavel asked. "This is not a hungry lycanthrope. Tossing a deer carcass into the woods and waiting will not work."

"Me," I said. "He...wants me. We'll just leave it at that. I'm sure he'll come for me if I'm within reach."

"My lord—Dorian, the risk is far too great," said Rhys. "I implore you to rely on us to take the front line. We cannot chance losing the Ascended."

"I'm used to being bait. Trust me. Besides, you won't stand a chance against Set in direct combat. He's slow and you could probably teleport around for a while, but eventually you'll get tired, or he will and just end you. I've lost too many people in my life to willingly sacrifice more." Everyone in the room appeared surprised that I cared.

"Dying in your service is not something that any of us fear," said Tobias. "We are here to fight to the bitterest of ends. The Order's purpose is as your sword and your shield."

Gianni had said something like that to me once. He thought the prospect of dying in battle was as honorable and glorious as victory. Then when I almost lost him, even after breaking up I felt guilt and regret that I hadn't done more to help. I felt that way losing Vance, I felt it losing Vivi, and most of all I felt it losing my mom and dad.

"Swords and shields don't die," I said. "You're artisans, you're healers, you're *parents*. Your lives mean so much more than throwing them away to become another bloodstain on the sand."

The room fell quiet. I worried I may have shown my cards too soon by exposing my emotions toward loss.

"We like to say we live full and meaningful lives in the time we're given," said Helena. "We do what is in our power to keep the peace from major threats at any cost. I believe Tobias was so adamant we pledge ourselves to you because of your record doing the same."

"Then we need to find a compromise like our last encounter with Set," I said. All this talk about losing people was making me nervous. "I won't consider it a victory if one of our own dies. What do you think we should do, Liam? I've heard from everybody except you."

Tobias gave a subtle nod to Liam who was still behind me. It wasn't enough that the Ascended asked him directly, Liam still needed his father's coaxing to speak. When he was out of his father's shadow he spoke more openly, so it wasn't me that made him nervous.

"I think... we should focus on minimizing losses, but know that we won't be able to avoid them completely. Too much effort spent on preventing them could stop us from moving the battle forward."

"Well spoken," Tobias chimed in.

"I can't see you back there. Come to the table and tell us what you think we should do first," I said to encourage him. The council seemed to want to keep my ear for themselves, except for Tobias who wanted his son to get close to me outside of the conclave. Either the council had something to hide or there were a lot of differing opinions amongst the Order.

"We could use the Empyrean Jewels—"

"How do you know of the Jewels?" Helena asked him.

"I told him," said Tobias. "He will be on the council soon enough."

"Marianna and Alexandre will be too, but now is not that time," Helena said.

"What are the Empyrean Jewels?" I turned to address only Liam. He looked to his father again who nodded despite the scoffs and disapproving grunts from the rest.

"I've misspoken," he replied.

"They are—" Tobias went to explain, but I interrupted.

"No, I want to hear it from Liam since it seems he isn't trying to hide anything from me. Go ahead, Liam."

"The Empyrean Jewels are crystallized aether, imbued with elemental forces. They are some of the last remaining gift from the previous Ascended. We could use them to bring back the dragon god in the way we did the goddess at Delos."

"Have you gone absolutely mad?!" Rhys almost jumped out of his seat. "Those stones are meant—"

"They are meant to be passed on to the next Ascended, are they not?" asked Pavel.

"Yes!" exclaimed Rhys. "*Not* a Spiritborn that will turn against us the moment their prayers aren't to their suiting or leave us to take a nap. It has taken the Order *centuries* to reclaim the Empyrean Jewels after they were scattered about the world during the last Great Reckoning and you want to dissolve them as a temporary energy source?"

"It should be up to the current Ascended to decide," said Tobias.

"Liam, tell me more about these stones and don't leave anything out. I'll know if you're lying," I bluffed to keep them on their toes.

"Aether crystals are solid manifestations of raw aether. On Earth, only a theurgist tapping into a ley line can form them, and their formation is determined by the skill of their caster. The more-skilled the caster, the better-quality crystal," Liam said before showing me the silver brooch with the oval emerald hanging from his belt.

"Crystals can be refined into gems like this one," he continued. "Since the crystals are pure aether they can have a spell imprinted on them that will stay in effect without the need to cast it each time. We use them mostly for protection so that we don't have to worry about casting and maintaining defensive spells in battle or if we are ambushed."

"Any spell can be imprinted on an aether crystal, but it will only work for the closest soul it can resonate with and the strength of the spell depends on the quality of the crystal," said Tobias.

"Meaning that only the person wearing it will get the benefits?" I asked.

"Yes," Liam confirmed. "They can work with any soul, but only those that know how to channel aether can activate or deactivate the imprinted spell without having to take it off. We also use them in emergencies to replenish our aether supply if there aren't any ley lines to tap nearby. We like to use unrefined crystals that haven't been imprinted for that, as the process for making them is not easy."

"Those who are Spiritborn—like the dragon god—are made of aether, the same as the goddess in Delos. Even all of our best aether crystals wouldn't be enough to energize her, but the Empyrean Jewels were made by an Ascended and a lot more powerful."

"Why don't you guys use them?" I asked.

"The energy they contain would overload our souls and scatter every fiber of our existence across the universe," said Pavel. "They can rupture the delicate temporal and spatial balance, creating anomalies and atmospheric disturbances in reality itself.

"When the Empyrean Jewel of Lightning was found last century in the Atlantic Ocean, the search party handling it caused a magnetic disturbance covering over one hundred million square miles that remains there to this day."

"Are you talking about the Bermuda Triangle?"

"Exactly."

"The Eye of Ra on Set's staff has to be another aether crystal. It's causing some serious disturbances in the atmosphere and Isis told me that it has the power to grant omnipotence to those who know how to use it," I said. "If none of you can use the Empyrean Jewels and I can't use them because I don't use aether, then there's no point in keeping them locked away when they could be what we need to turn the war in our favor. I say we bring them to Kamakura while Gianluca rests. At least we will have one ally back in business."

"By your leave then," Rhys consented to my decision. I wasn't sold on his unquestioning loyalty like the rest, but I could appreciate someone who was outspoken. God or not, if I was to stay here for any length of time I wanted open conversation, not subordinates that would say anything they thought I'd want to hear.

"Do you still have scouts in the desert?" I asked.

"No, they had returned after you were located," said Pavel.

"We should send them near the border of Israel to keep an eye out for Set and help innocents escape when it comes to it. My friend Lyle that the others had met has troops there no doubt, but they're always shorthanded."

"People do not take well to magic and will have difficulty discerning us from the enemy," Tobias said.

"The age of hiding behind fairytales has passed," I told the table. "I know you're all probably worried because of what you've heard from the time of the witch hunts, but now is the time to build our public image.

"We're going to be revealed sooner or later. We want it to be on our terms."

"We are worried," Helena admitted. "Greatly so. There are children here, and when those children become of age and have their own children..."

"You're hoping the Order will go unnoticed through the apocatastasis, or the Great Reckoning—whichever you want to call it. Then what? Come out of hiding when the dust settles and the odds are more in your favor? That's exactly what the undead are plotting. Most of them." I couldn't believe it, but I was about to use Aurelia as a positive example.

The council looked caught off guard. So that was their plan. They wanted me to shield them through the transition, not from the monsters but the humans. That was why they picked me and not Gianluca. The dark god that swallowed cities into the shadows wouldn't be a friendly face for the public to accept and by association, the Order would be feared in the way they were back during the witch hunts. That must also be why they didn't seem in too much of a hurry to deal with Set when I kept bringing it up. Now their stalling by telling me more about themselves and how much they exalted me seemed like a strategy.

It was sad, but I could understand. There were plenty of times I wanted to bury my head in the sand and let the world crumble. If that was what their cards were in this game then I didn't have a problem playing as long as they held up their end when I needed them. It was possible they would even get through this with a new outlook on their place among mankind, but I wasn't about to make any promises. I did wish they would just drop the divine worship routine.

Chapter Twenty-Nine

"Before we end our meeting I have a favor to ask."

"We are at your service," Rhys said.

"The demon sorceress we encountered in Delos, her name is Minerva. She's doing the bidding of the Infernal Kings, if you've heard of them. They're major players in all that's been going on. Minerva was sent by them to collect one of the Ancient Undead's souls that was used to raise Set.

"There are still four more Ancients remaining and PROJECT: UNITY is guarding them under my friend Lyle's command. The problem is that they don't have what it takes to fight off Minerva during the day while the Ancients sleep. Do we have anyone who can watch after them?"

"Of course! It would be an honor," Rhys spoke with genuine enthusiasm for the group.

"I'd also like someone to watch out for Lyle and Noah specifically. They're very good friends. You'll have to stay at an extreme distance with Noah and especially the Ancients in France. I'd rather they not know you're there. Whoever we send to Lyle, I want no further than his shadow at all times and to act as a liaison since we have no way to communicate at the moment."

"We will send them right away," said Tobias.

"I'd actually like to pick them," I said. "I haven't had a chance to meet the rest of the Order and this would be a good opportunity."

"Absolutely," Helena agreed. "Liam and I will assemble everyone in the courtyard right away." She didn't move to get up until I realized that they were waiting for me to stand first.

I had a plan. One that kept with Noah's lesson on applying pressure to bring out true colors. I remembered the meeting with PROJECT: UNITY where everyone was in an uproar over how to handle guarding the Ancients and the public at the same time. Everyone was being spread thin and it weakened the group as a whole.

I wanted to scatter the Order across the globe with mundane but important tasks to test how trustworthy they were. My instincts were telling me that I could trust them, but there was no room for error and I did not want to be too trusting, too soon, adding another chaotic element to the already volatile mix of our alliance.

My reason for wanting to pick who goes where was simple. I had already seen a quick display of what Liam was capable of. Sending him to protect Lyle, only for him to turn on us, meant a dead Lyle. I could see Liam taking out most of PROJECT: UNITY on his own between his teleporting abilities and incredible gear if he caught them off guard.

Whether or not Liam was loyal there was also the possibility of the Ancients getting in his head and turning him on our allies. They could likely do that already with another of PROJECT: UNITY that was on guard duty, but it would be much easier to take down a rogue soldier than a member of the Order. The less tempting the bait, the less chance that someone like Aurelia would bother putting the effort into twisting them to her whims too. The weaker, the better for once.

"Don't you guys miss walking places?" I asked. The other three teleported us to a small courtyard somewhere within the abbey once Helena and Liam had left. I levitated an inch or so off the ground for effect...and to make myself appear taller.

"We prefer it, but were considering what would be most convenient for you," Tobias said. "Traversing the ley lines is fairly taxing. It is a higher level spell than most of the Order can handle."

"There are forty-something of you, right? And you're all from the same four families?"

"Heavens no," said Pavel. "There have never been more than two or three members of the same family in the Order at the same time. Most are individuals and it is exceedingly rare for any to marry within, seeing as each generation grows up as if they were siblings."

"Is your wife in the Order?" I asked Tobias, looking down at his gold and silver wedding band.

"No. She lives in the town at the bottom of the hill along with some of the Order's other family."

"Is that safe? I mean you were worried about people knowing..."

"She is also magically adept although she doesn't practice. Most of those we have children with are, with few exceptions. It increases the chances of attracting another gifted soul to the unborn child. However, only those who are born into the Order may be one of us."

"We go into town often, dressed more commonly of course," said Rhys. "The island is so small that there are barely a thousand residents and most never leave. They are used to the abbey being a fixture in the background like an old oak tree that they never question how or why it's there."

"So, you *can* feel comfortable around the public then," I pointed out.

"If we are the old oak tree, then the townsfolk are the grass at our roots," Rhys said. "They are as much a part of the same picture as any of us, so much that they are practically honorary members without even knowing it. They're not the ones where our concerns lie."

With that, the rest of the Order began filling the courtyard; some teleporting in, some walking, others peeking first before following closely beside a buddy. Some kneeled until another would whisper to stop them. It happened more than once and made me laugh to myself.

I noticed a variety of faint accents among the crowd. Noah was right when we met the first three that they sounded so proper it was as if they were trying to eliminate any trace of one and speak in a very generic tone. There was a definite blend of everything from British to Spanish to German and Russian.

The three men of the council remained the oldest out of them all that I could tell. The youngest were no more than four years old, but even they were dressed in impeccable formal attire. I had to hope that it was only for the "special occasion" of my arrival and that these kids weren't stuffed into prince and princess costumes year round. Some of the children came holding flowers and one of the grown-ups had to catch a little girl from running up to me with her offering.

The more members that filed in I started to think that I was being lied to about how many of them there were. Forty-something seemed an awful lot like one hundred-something by the time they were finished packing the courtyard. Suddenly I wasn't feeling so smug anymore about my master plan. I was getting nervous having to address them all.

Alongside the anxiety came another unforeseen emotion that stirred quietly at first but became more pronounced as I looked out at all the faces staring back at me. No one was gawking, but plenty didn't seem to know what to do with their eyes. They'd try to keep their heads bowed or maintain a respectful stoic expression, but would slip and crack a smile or shoot an excited nod to someone in the crowd.

They were acting like I was one of them that had gone missing and had just returned. It was a different look than what I was used to where even the friendliest faces had stared in curiosity and I'd know that they were trying to work out in their heads what I was. Those before me now weren't doing that. Even in my all-black outfit, with my hood up and my eyes inverted black and gray from using my powers to float, they seemed to know exactly what—*who*—I was and were bursting at the seams to welcome me.

I didn't have one word or phrase to describe the other feeling growing inside of me. "Territorial" sounded too aggressive. "Protective" sounded too much like pity. I thought of the council's fears for the future generations growing up in a world where they would be persecuted like their ancestors were. It was a fear almost every supernatural I had met shared, but seeing the children, the teenagers, and the adults side by side... these were mortals with finite lives. If things got unbearable in the world, they couldn't just sleep it off for a century or two. They'd suffer, they'd endure, they'd die.

As much as I wanted to defeat Set because he was the "bad guy" there was so much more that needed to be done once the battles were over. Peace wouldn't come as a result like flipping a switch after killing him, or Minerva, or the Infernal Kings. To think that Aurelia was the one and only political figure representing our corner on the road to peace made me realize that someone else needed to step up if these children could ever hope to lead a life without constant misery. I could see her snapping her fingers once the wars were over to outlaw any and all supernaturals that didn't swear undying servitude to her as "heretics".

"That's everyone," said Helena after returning to where I was standing with the rest of the council. "Would you like to say a few words?"

"I'm not really the public speaking type. Are you sure this is only forty people?"

"Forty-six," she affirmed.

"There's no need to be nervous, my lord," said Rhys. *Was it that obvious?* "We can work our way through the courtyard one cabal at a time, I suggest, with a wee one mixed in here and there."

"What's a cabal?" I asked. "I've heard it mentioned before."

"Forgive me. A cabal is what we call a small coterie of theurgic knights. Everyone is assigned a cabal once they complete the rite of passage to adulthood. Usually they group themselves together by who were the closest friends when growing up, but sometimes the council steps in to rearrange things if a cabal is unbalanced and in need of a particular skill set that they're lacking in times of war."

"Liam's cabal is rather outstanding. They have all passed their trials together this summer beyond expectations," said Tobias.

"It doesn't hurt that two of them have council members for guardians," Rhys added.

"Where is Liam?" Helena asked. "He came with me to gather everyone and left before I did."

"I'm sure he's just checking that no one was left behind," Tobias said an extended his arm to welcome me into the crowd. "Shall we?"

"Dorian, this is my niece, Marianna Vaughn." The young lady introduced to me by Helena looked like she could be her sister, or a younger clone of her. The only other difference was that Marianna's hair reached more than halfway down her back with a braid around her head. She was wearing leather pants too and a linen blouse opened enough to show the aether crystal amulet hanging from her neck.

Marianna smiled and gave a polite bow of her head with a hand over her heart. I was learning to accept the bow, it was far less awkward than the kneeling.

"The gentleman to her right is Rafael Mezzio," Helena continued the introductions. Rafael had mocha eyes and tanned skin, but most noticeable was his neon red hair that was so shocking it could be seen a mile away. "And to the left is Claudius Jorgensen."

Claudius had eyes like aether, a smattering of muted freckles, and snowy white hair spiked forward. His cinnamon eyebrows gave away his natural hair color. He was wearing a bandana tied around his neck to be pulled up over the lower half of his face like a bandit. Between the bandana and the hair colors I was getting a conflicting sense of how straight-laced this Order really was.

I went to return the greeting after they had all saluted when I saw one of the royal munchkins holding up a flower for me. "Thank you." I said with a smile and took the tulip that I saw him pick from the courtyard garden not more than thirty seconds ago after realizing he didn't have one to offer like the other kids. He ran off and wormed his way back into the crowd shouting, "I did it!" until one of the adults quieted him down.

"And that was Georgie," said Helena. "Except for him, these three make up the rest of Liam's cabal."

"Nice to meet you all," I said. "I like your hair. I take it you use color-changing magic for the red and white?"

"Raf did, but Claudius's was a mistake when he botched the spell as a child," Marianna shared. "Now he keeps it like that so people think it was on purpose."

"That's enough, Marianna," Helena warned.

"Faketh until thee maketh," Claudius retorted in good spirits. I liked them already. They were a lot more casual and talked to me in a way that I was used to.

"Was that a real dagger in Georgie's waistband?" I asked.

"Yes," Marianna answered first.

"Aren't you scared he'll hurt himself if he trips? He's what? Three? Four?"

"Then he will learn an important lesson that he will surely never forget to always watch his step and keep a sure footing," said Pavel. That was harsh. I wanted to round out the point and turn it into a butter knife next chance I saw him, but being that this was their lifestyle he'd just get his hands on another one. At least they had healing magic...

"What can all of you do?" I asked the cabal. "Please try to keep it simple though. I don't know much about your magic yet."

"We bend the natural laws of space and time," said Rafael.

"Why does everyone always have to mess around with those?"

"Because it's cool," Claudius answered.

"Claudius!" Tobias shouted. "Watch your tongue."

"It's okay," I said. Claudius slid his bandana up to hide his crafty grin.

"It's also two of the most difficult fields to master," Marianna interjected. "We mostly specialize in space though with a minor concentration in time."

"Then there's the basics like healing, conjuring elements, and aether crystallization and projection," added Rafael. "Space and aether studies are what's needed for teleportation using ley lines, but we can combine it with other elements to mess with gravity or magnetism and open spatial warps, create barriers, or turn invisible by partially phasing out of this dimension."

"That all sounds...dangerous, even from my perspective," I said.

"It is!" Claudius enthused. "Raf is horrible at archery, so he used to cheat his exams by opening spatial warps to correct the arrow's trajectory."

The council's faces were filled with restrained rage. I really wanted to laugh, but didn't want to make it worse for Claudius.

"It was a technique I was practicing, it wasn't cheating," Rafael argued.

"We'll discuss this later," said Rhys.

"We already completed the rite of passage though and that was years ago." Claudius didn't know when to quit while he was ahead, or at least not six feet under. "You can't un-pass us...can you?"

"Dorian, let me introduce you to my brother, Alexandre," Pavel ushered me away from the entertaining trio just as Liam returned. They were the best part of coming here so far aside from the clothes.

Alexandre was a tall young man with hair as black as coal and as long as Marianna's. He was close to Gianluca's height of around six-foot-four, but with a slimmer build with a small waist that exaggerated his broad shoulders. He wasn't as pale as his brother Pavel, but shared his brother's somber expression. He had a bit of an exotic look to him; I wasn't able to place his origin.

"Nice to meet you," I said in response to his salute.

"It is an honor, Ascended."

"Where are Anatole and Ruben?" Pavel asked his brother.

"Over on the other side." Alexandre's voice had such bass to it he sounded like he was hooked up to a subwoofer. He seemed resigned to the fact that these two other men Pavel had mentioned were off on their own. Perhaps they were part of his cabal, I thought.

"What can you do?" I asked to keep this moving.

"I'm a whisperer." His answer seemed ironic after my thoughts about his voice. Despite the solemn mannerisms and his large stature he wasn't imposing at all and had a warm way about him. "I commune and make pacts with spirits."

"That's very interesting especially since we're dealing with Spiritborn."

"It is...forbidden to commune with them, but there is a large spectrum of other spirits below the Spiritborn gods that I can make contact with. I've cataloged over two hundred individual spirits, from spirit animals and guardian spirits to elementals to abstracts."

"What exactly do these spirits do?" I asked.

"They all serve their own unique roles. A fire spirit can provide light and warmth, or burn down a forest. A nature or life spirit could help regrow the forest later. A hawk spirit could fly somewhere to spy for you and let you see through its eyes. Many also enjoy chatting and can give insight into things that humans can't sense on our own."

"That sounds complicated, but I can imagine the payoff is incredibly useful," I said.

"They can be fickle and it isn't always easy to get the desired result. Even though the spirits are only aether constructs, they take their desired forms very seriously and won't go against their natures. So, a hawk spirit will never dive underwater and swim around for you. You have to have patience and a high level of empathy to bond with them. I consider them part of my cabal, even if others don't."

"What particular traits are you looking for to assist you?" Pavel asked me. "It may be simpler to narrow it down that way and continue further introductions later."

"I'll know it when I see it." I didn't want to tell him I was looking for the weakest of the lot so they wouldn't pose a threat to my friend. I was starting to wonder if I was trying to be too guarded though. The more I interacted with the Order I felt at ease with them. I could split Liam's cabal and Alexandre among the Ancients to guard, but I couldn't shake the gnawing anxiety of putting PROJECT: UNITY in danger if things went south...

Chapter Thirty

"This is Connor Coetzee." Helena was on her thirtieth or so introduction, but I had checked out around twenty and was now holding a full bouquet of flowers from the children. There was no way I was remembering all these names in one sitting.

Connor was an eager, confident-looking teenager. I'd have guessed his age to be around fifteen, but then again I thought Liam was well into his twenties, so for all I knew Connor could be ten.

He stood at attention so stiffly, with head held high and chest out, that I didn't know if he was being serious or not. All of the Order members I had met that weren't covered up in armor were in remarkable physical condition—as someone would be who trained their entire lives to be a top in something that required discipline and coordination of the whole body. Connor was no slouch by any definition, but his stance made it seem like he was trying to compensate for something or keep up with the adults.

"What can you do?" I asked, trying not to sound too mechanical about it by this point.

"I know all of my basic elements—" I smiled at that because it sounded like when a little kid was proud of himself for knowing the whole alphabet or the numbers up to ten. "—and I can crystallize aether. I've also just finished memorizing my dispelling hexes. I can forge orichalcum and tailor clothing and I'm good at—"

Connor seemed non-threatening enough. "You're perfect. I have a job for you."

His eyes were huge with disbelief, as were everyone else's in the courtyard. The reactions were either aghast or excited, with not much in between.

"Really?!" he exclaimed.

"Yes, really."

The council was quick to swoop in and try to dissuade me from my decision. "Connor has not passed his rite of passage yet, my lord," Tobias said. "He is only fifteen and lacks any specialization. Surely Liam would be the best choice for what you have in mind."

"I submitted Liam in hand-to-hand training just last week—!" Connor shouted and broke his composure as his miracle was about to be taken from him.

"You beat Liam?" I questioned and was admittedly impressed. Size alone, Liam looked like he could pick Connor up and throw him across the courtyard, and Liam wasn't much bigger than me.

"On a technicality," explained Rhys. "It was a demonstration, not a real bout."

"My decision stands," I reassured Connor.

"Oh, thank you, sir, Lord Dorian, sir! You won't regret it! I'll do whatever it is and be the best at it!"

I had to come up with something to explain my judgment without the council becoming suspicious. "Have faith," I told them and then recited a lesson Noah had taught me when I wasn't feeling sure of myself. "For even a pebble can cause an avalanche."

"That *is* true," agreed Rhys. "I can see this being the perfect complement to your upcoming rite of passage if performed to the Ascended's satisfaction."

"I won't let anyone down," Connor saluted.

"You'll be going to Greenland to protect someone very important to me," I told him. "I'll point out the exact location on a map. If anyone has something to write with I'll send you with a letter to present to who you'll be guarding so you can teleport in without anyone bothering you."

"I, uh..." Connor hesitated.

"He does not know how to traverse the ley lines yet," said Helena who conjured a parchment and strange pen made from wood for me.

"Then someone else can send him there." I started to worry if I was doing the right thing.

Connor was so young. What if something happened to him because of me? He should be safe with Lyle though. I knew my best friend would look after him. Lyle would be less likely to do something reckless if it put someone else in danger. All I really needed Connor for was to be a messenger.

"If there are any signs of trouble, *any* at all, you are to retreat with who you are guarding and report back to me. These are your orders. They are *not* to charge into battle and risk either of your lives under any circumstance. Do you understand that?"

"Yes, sir, I do," Connor nodded.

"My friend's name is Lyle. He should have a radio or a communicator he can give to whoever is teleporting you to take back to the abbey so we can speak easier. I'll request it in the letter."

Lyle, I'm sending you a buddy. His name is Connor. Take good care of each other. I'm going to wake Kamakura, but I'll probably be back to base by tomorrow night. Give whoever brings Connor one of PARAGON's communicators so I can keep in touch from here. I'll be sending others to help guard the Ancients. Stay alert. –Dorian

The wood pen wrote in black ink despite being nothing more than a sharpened stick. I handed it back to Helena and folded the letter in four to give to Connor.

"Do what Lyle tells you to, but stay no more than ten feet from him. *Ten feet,*" I stressed. "Don't let him send you on an errand. That's how mistakes are made. If a battle happens, use your best judgment and drag him out if you have to. This isn't a trial by combat. Your success depends on his safety, not how many enemies you kill."

"Understood," Connor saluted again. "What will I be protecting him from?"

"It could be anything or nothing at all, so be prepared. Let's go back to the conclave," I told the council. "I'll show Connor where he's going on the map and explain the location to him along the way. I also want Alexandre, Claudius, and Anatole."

Anatole was a member of Alexandre's cabal that I had met separately. He seemed to be in his thirties, but I had given up trying to accurately guess ages with this bunch. "What *kind* of god are you, if I may be so bold?" he asked back inside. "All gods represent or stand for something."

"I don't know. I haven't had the chance to think about it," I admitted. "The whole 'god' thing is new to me and I don't feel that different, so I don't know if it's really clicked yet. You can be the first to know when it does though."

"I'd like that very much."

Anatole was erudite and polite, maybe even too polite. He was the only one who asked me questions back to strike up a flowing conversation when we were introduced. I swore he was being borderline flirtatious on occasion. He had slipped a couple of subtle compliments in so casually that it was hard to tell.

These weren't my reasons for choosing Anatole though. In fact, all of this might have worked against him because he talked himself into a job guarding Vyrlakalos. It took a certain level of testicular fortitude to flirt with "God" and he'd need it to not let Vyrlakalos get under his skin. The most I even remembered of what he could actually do—besides speak with a silver tongue—was something with alchemy and creating projectiles and temporary weapons of pure aether.

However, before shifting my focus in front of the council to Anatole, I needed to complete Connor's assignment; Greenland was a large country, and PROJECT: UNITY's base wasn't above-ground.

"This is where you'll be going, Connor," I indicated the southeast corner of Greenland on the map to him once we were all in the council chambers. "There's an underground base in the ice there full of the most advanced technology on the planet. It's a big culture shock coming from here, but if you ask me I like the ambiance here better."

"It pleases us to hear that," said Tobias. "I will send Connor when he is ready."

"I'll go get my stuff," Connor said. "Thank you again for giving me this chance, Ascended."

"You're welcome. Here, can you find something to put these in and bring them to my room before you go?" I handed Connor the wilting bouquet that I had been holding on to.

He went to leave and Tobias went with him. I started going over my plans with Anatole and Claudius, who were to respectively watch after Vyrlakalos and Castile. I informed them of what was at stake should the Ancients fall to the demons. I felt that Claudius would fit right in with the Blackbournes that were already at Castile's and that Castile wouldn't be as tempted to toy with his mind as he would be with Anatole.

Out in the hall I spotted Tobias speaking with Connor and slipping him something, but I couldn't see what it was. "You're going to France," I told Alexandre and pointed outside Paris to Aurelia's chateau. "You'll be watching someone else important to me. His name is Noah. Unlike Connor though, I want you as far away as possible. Heck, you'd probably be better off just staying here and sending a spirit to keep an eye on him if you can.

"He *will* notice you if you're anywhere on the grounds and that means so will the Ancients that reside there. I don't want that. One of them is a former undead necromancer turned powerful and evil phantom that will no doubt be able to spot your spirits, so you're really going to have to be smart about this."

"Ah, a blood wraith," Alexandre enthused. "Haven't seen one of those in a while."

"Make sure that Noah is okay and do what you have to so that the Ancients don't know you're watching. Noah doesn't play well with others, so if he is in danger make your assistance subtle. He may not even be at this location. He moves around a lot and is extremely fast, but this is the best place to start looking for him."

"I can scry for him using the map with the assistance of the spirits," said Alexandre.

"I don't know what that is."

"Scrying is a spell to locate a soul or spirit," he explained. "The ley lines are like a spider's web across the world. All it takes is an aether crystal, a map, and some knowledge of the target to sense where they are on the web. The stronger the connection with the target the easier it is find them, but the spirits can help gather information on him from his residence for me."

"Perfect. You should all do whatever you can to protect yourselves against the undead's mental powers in case they get bored or curious. Vyrlakalos isn't as bad with them, except she may try to eat you if you get too close. Castile is pretty benign but he does like to talk and mess around in there, which can distract you—he completely controls every element of the environment you'll be watching him in, and it can change on a dime. The one in France, Aurelia... she's the problem, which is why it'd be best to stay out of range."

"We don't deal with the undead often, but most of us have aether gems with wards against telepathic intrusion like the one in my circlet," Helena said. "If any of you need to borrow mine you can."

"I have an amulet I made years ago that I'll bring, thank you," said Alexandre.

I was proud of myself for taking charge and orchestrating this. It definitely didn't come naturally to me, but I covered as many bases as I could.

"Oh, don't let the Blackbournes talk you into any of their drunken sex parties," I warned Claudius.

"There will be no issue with that," Helena chimed in. "We practice *absolute* abstinence in the face of all carnal and worldly temptations, and we don't break that until ten years of adult service."

"Right." I looked Claudius straight in his crystal blue eyes that had grown as big as dinner plates at the warning. "I wouldn't mention that to them either. They get a thrill out of messing with those sort of people." It didn't take much to imagine Owen and Micah having whores airdropped outside Castile's property along with bottles of vodka and scotch.

We were swift about wrapping up any final details and concluded the debriefing with the three leaving to get their gear and head to their destinations.

Tobias rejoined the conclave a moment later. "Did you send Connor?" I asked him.

"Yes." He withdrew one of PROJECT: UNITY's pocket-sized tablets from a satchel and presented it to me. "The boy packed everything but the bed and still managed to almost forget his sword."

"I believe in him," I told the council. "Sometimes desire outweighs skill."

"The underground lair was intriguing, but too bright for my taste," Tobias said.

"I'll agree with you there. I'm not crazy about all the plastic and metal. Wood and stone like the abbey is much more my speed."

"Does that mean you will be staying with us?" asked Pavel who came to life after sitting quietly with Rhys throughout the debriefing.

"I...don't know. I never stay in one place for too long. I'd like to if everything works out. I'll put it that way." I was clicking around on the tablet and then realized I didn't get any reception here. PROJECT: UNITY did have satellite transmitters to communicate in situations like this, but Lyle probably hadn't thought of it and neither did I.

"Shall I take you to the reliquary to retrieve the Empyrean Jewels?" Tobias asked.

"Good idea. Then I'm off to Japan."

Chapter Thirty-One

"This is beautiful..." I said aloud, half to Tobias, half to myself.

I looked around the small room filled with stained glass windows that Tobias had brought me to. In an inconspicuous hallway, and behind a tapestry depicting a heavenly scene of winged beings descending from a light in the clouds, was an illusory stone wall that Tobias dispelled with a touch to grant us passage. "But we descended that long spiral staircase from the main floor. How is it...?"

"Sunny? This chamber is in a hollow shaft of mirrors that reflect sunlight in from behind the glass." Between each pair of windows around the room was a glass case that held shelves of aether gem amulets and brooches that sparkled in the light along with the specks of mica in the walls. The one exception was the case across from the entrance, which held six individual gemstones in the branches of a glass tree. These gems were not set in jewelry and emitted their own multi-colored light source.

"Are these them?" I investigated the special case from all sides.

"Yes." Tobias opened the case for me and stood back. "Procured with great sacrifice." Tobias actually showed a bit of emotion as his lips pursed and eyebrows raised in a fleeting display of sadness. "But that is a story for another time perhaps."

Of all the conversations that the Order dragged out, *now* Tobias decided he wanted to be tight-lipped. It may have been harsh, but I wasn't going to let it slide. If there was anyone in the Order that couldn't be trusted, it would probably turn out to be the council. Leaders of clandestine organizations always had the dirtiest secrets and schemes. It was the perfect time to apply pressure and see what true colors were revealed.

"I'd like to hear it now," I insisted. Tobias hesitated knowing that he couldn't refuse a request from me without either looking highly suspicious or insubordinate.

"Five of the Empyrean Jewels have been with us for longer than I have been alive. Aside from our duties to the Ascended and slaying those such as demons that disrupt the balance, it is our job to reclaim these treasures and any others that may fall into the wrong hands.

"Six years ago the council had located the sixth jewel buried hundreds of feet below the ice in

Antarctica, the last place anyone would ever look. There were five of us on the council at that time.

"The fifth was a theurgist beyond reproach. He was my mentor and a close personal friend. His name was Caylan and he set out with Helena to retrieve the gemstone. Helena was to stay at a lengthy distance to avoid being harmed if the situation became terminal, and had she not, we never would have known what had happened.

"Once unearthed and thawed by Caylan's fire magic, it let out a heat wave that vaporized him and nearly cost Helena her life from miles away. The heat also melted a great deal of ice in the area and raised the ambient temperature for thousands of miles that still linger to this day. The public speaks of things such as global warming and cite the results of that incident as proof, but we've known better for years."

"That's one take on it," I said. "I've heard it was because of Hell seeping through the veil between our dimensions."

"There are always many sides to the same story, even when you are there to witness it. The more desperate people are for an answer, the more sides there will be. I should have been there in Caylan's place, but he insisted he go in my stead. Liam was still under my care and Caylan had no children after the woman he chose was unable to conceive. Helena was also unable to after the accident. If Marianna had not been born to her brother, the long history of the Vaughn family would have ended there."

"How did you wind up getting the jewel then?" I asked.

"Against our code to ever involve those outside of the Order in our affairs, we paid a man in town a substantial sum to be our courier. Unlike our amulets with passive spells imprinted on them that anyone can receive the effects of, the Empyrean Jewels are a raw energy source that must be activated. The courier had no connection to the aether and no way to activate the stone, so the risk of a repeat disaster was significantly diminished. Helena is a master alchemist and so she concocted an elixir to wipe the courier's memory once the job was complete."

"There's one Empyrean Jewel missing," I pointed out an empty branch of the glass tree.

"That is still being debated by the Scribes."

"Who are they?"

"The Scribes do exactly what their name implies; they chronicle the history of the Order. There are five of them including Helena, who is the head librarian. She feels the seventh stone is a myth started by and further perpetrated by poor cataloging in the past and I tend to agree."

"Why would it be a myth? When we're talking magic, anything goes."

"There are still rules. The confirmed jewels represent the essences of fire, water, wind, earth, lightning, and light. The supposed seventh stone is claimed to represent oblivion, but knowing the way the Empyrean Jewels were made it wouldn't be possible.

"The scriptures read that the previous Ascended defeated a number of Spiritborn deities that were to carry out the punishment for his arrogance. He defeated them and used their essences to imprint aether crystals of divine quality. You cannot imprint the essence of oblivion, which is nothingness, onto something without also turning it into nothing in the process.

"Furthermore, we call each jewel by the name of the deity they were created from; Agni—fire, Varuna—water, Vāyu—wind, Bhūmi—earth, Vajra—lightning, and Surya—light. Many have tried to argue that there was no name recorded for oblivion because as the embodiment of true nothingness it had no name and was only an unseen force that erased what was unneeded from the universe."

"Oblivion sounds like a scary element."

"It can be in untrained hands. We use it all the time to dispel other spells and enchantments. That is how my son shattered the demon sorceress' barrier on Delos. To use it correctly, the caster must exert an equal counter-force and nothing more, or else the backlash of extra power can hurt them too."

"Empress Kamakura and her guardians represent all of these except..." I thought on it for a second. She didn't represent light, *but* supernatural light on this level *could* drive out any darkness I was guessing... I'd have to find a way to use it first though. "Actually, I'm better off taking all of them. You never know."

"Very good. I will give you my satchel to transport them," Tobias offered and handed it to me.

I floated the Empyrean Jewels into the bag, still wary about touching them.

"What makes these so unstable?" I asked.

"There is no higher tier in gem quality. However, the divine essences of these stones remain so powerful that their raw energies constantly test the limits. We can only assume that the Ascended did not put any further safeguards in place to be sure no one unworthy could ever use them."

"Hm."

"I meant no offense. I spoke only of mortals, my lord. You may not have a connection to the aether, but the spiritual energy you radiate in your aura is very pleasing to the senses."

"None taken and Anatole said something similar to me."

"We speak the truth. We can all feel it. Your aura is somehow a familiar and nurturing pervasive energy that we did not expect. I can't place it, but it seems to be a parallel to the aether in some way."

I thought of coming clean that the energy he was feeling was from other souls that were filtered through me. Isis had put my mind at ease about it, but other humans might not be so understanding. Then again, the Order was crazy about me; but I didn't want to give them a reason to stop being so.

"Can you tap into it in the same way you use aether for your spells? Like how the goddess Isis on Delos absorbed my power?"

"That would be—I could not imagine a greater blessing. The effects are unknown to us, but I can imagine them to be phenomenal."

"I'll keep that in mind."

"While we are on the subject, may I ask your thoughts on my son? Have you put any consideration into a choosing a herald?"

"A herald?" I looked at Tobias, confused.

"Or a champion. The wording can vary depending on the divine's wishes."

"I keep telling everyone I'm new to this godhood thing," I said, starting to get annoyed. The Order did a lot of talking, but not a lot of listening to someone that was so important to them. "I don't know what any of that means."

"Forgive me. There are still some lingering preconceived notions we all have," Tobias said, bowing before he continued. "Legends often tell of gods selecting a mortal to be their right hand; a champion to be their sword, a herald to be their voice, an avatar to be their vessel. Zeus had Perseus, Odin had Sigmund, and there are many more. In exchange for passing the trials set forth by the god, the hero would be bestowed with a fraction of their power to better serve them.

"The council chooses one person from the Order every generation against an exhaustive list of requirements that we feel would be most pleasing in narrowing down a candidate for the Ascended should they rise. It is one of the most deeply ingrained and respected customs we have."

"And Liam is this Chosen?" I asked.

"He is."

"This is about getting more power then? Is that it?" My annoyance was growing.

"No, not at all! Again, I ask your forgiveness. This is for the honor of being the right hand of God. Helena put it well when she said I was adamant we pursue you as our Lord for your past virtuous actions. Your ideology is something we feel strongly about."

"I'm not sure I have a need for a champion," I said. "I tend to keep people at a distance if I like them so they aren't hurt. It's why I move around a lot and am rarely with the people I care about during times of crisis."

"Ah, that sounds exactly why you would need one to act in your stead."

To be honest, that *was* exactly what I needed. I wouldn't tell Tobias that yet though. I was here on my own accord, but as my list of concerns grew about what was going on everywhere that I wasn't, I had to resort to taking risks in dispatching the Order to act for me. Now, it was also a test in its own right to see how loyal they really were and why I picked the weakest of the flock in case of betrayal, but when all of that was put aside and assuming I came out of this trusting them one hundred percent, my next concern would be that I was now putting *these* people in danger. Hell, I was already trying to tell myself that Connor would be all right. Having someone with my power that I could depend on, especially if it included my regeneration, to help me protect everyone I cared about would be tremendous.

"I'll have to think about it." I kept a good poker face for once. "I wouldn't even know how to start the process."

"Neither do we, unfortunately," Tobias confessed. "There is nothing in any of our records or scriptures. We've researched hundreds of legends and have come up with naught time and time again."

"We'll talk more on it later. Can you and the council send me to Kyoto, Japan? I want to restore one ally to power as soon as possible. I'll show you on the map exactly where the temple is that I need to go."

"Absolutely." Tobias closed the empty case and led the way back up the cramped circular staircase. "I will gather the council and meet at your chambers."

My room wasn't far and I made it there without getting lost. The halls were still clear as they had been when everyone was waiting in the courtyard for me. I passed a window on my way that looked out to a training ground where several of the Order were sword fighting. They weren't going easy on each other either. Blood was flying and I paused to watch a particularly tense moment when I thought a girl was going to put her blade right through her opponent's neck.

Back in my room I lied on my bed and started to feel the urge to sleep, having still been up since my escape from the pyramid the last night. I rolled over and put my hands under the pillow to relax when they brushed against something.

It was a note.

Not all of the council can be trusted. Please help me. Meet at the grotto down by the shore tonight. This is all I have to offer.

Folded in the note was a silver and gold ring on a thin chain. I had seen the ring before. It was Tobias's wedding band. The note was written on the same type of parchment with the same type of ink that Helena had given me to write mine on.

I looked around the room and saw the flowers from the children that I had given to Connor in a vase above the fireplace. *Did he...?*

"We are ready for you, my lord," Tobias appeared in the open doorway.

"Did you—?" I held up the note, but stopped short when the rest of the council entered with Liam. I shoved both the note and the ring in a separate flap of the satchel I was carrying. "Never mind."

"Is everything all right?" Helena asked and looked at the satchel as she opened the map for me.

"Yes." I spotted Tobias's wedding band still on his finger while I showed them the location of the temple. "I'm in a rush, so please hurry."

"Liam will escort you," Tobias said. "Long distances across the ley lines to unfamiliar places can sometimes not be entirely accurate, so he will guide the way once you are near."

We were almost ready when the tablet started streaming a video on its own, but it wasn't Lyle on the other end.

"Set?! How—?"

"Mortals. I address you with a simple message. You have seen my fury take form in the lands of Egypt which I hold dear. I have cleansed my kingdom of the blight brought upon it by the false religions that steal my rightful worship. I hold no such reverence for the lands beyond my kingdom and they will not know the mercy of a quick death. The storms will not stop until the Earth is picked clean of your remains.

"I offer only one hope: The first kingdom to unite and swear their allegiance to my sovereignty will be spared. If you do not wish to see the flesh stripped from your women and children by my sands, throw yourselves at my feet and pray, for I am the only god listening."

The transmission ended, but there was still no signal. "Send us," I told them. "If anyone else in the world heard that, we're in huge trouble. He's going to turn the public against itself in the biggest, bloodiest riot on Earth."

Chapter Thirty-Two

"I'm sorry. I think we overshot it," Liam apologized as we were thrust from the ley line. The final seconds before we arrived felt like we were strapped to the front of a speeding subway car about to go off the rails.

"Yeah, I'll say," I looked down at the familiar yellow river beside us after peeking carefully into the satchel to make sure the stones were okay and my tablet. I remembered the mysterious note and how Liam had disappeared for a while at the courtyard introductions. I took the ring and its chain, making sure he saw me now that we were alone, and casually put it on around my neck.

He didn't mention it or even flinch. Maybe he wasn't involved.

"That's never happened before," he said, still talking about our rough ride. "I don't know what went wrong."

"No, this is good. We're in Yomi. It's a lot more direct to reach Empress Kamakura than praying at the temple of one of her guardians. I didn't know you could get here so I didn't mention it."

"We can't. The only way would be if the veil between worlds was so thin that we leaped through a hole in the fabric of reality using the ley lines."

"What would cause—? Oh..." Across the far bank of the yellow river I could see Japan back on Earth—more specifically, the Kiyomizu Temple in Kyoto we were supposed to have been at. "That's normally shrouded in a much thicker fog."

"Demons," Liam stated.

"Maybe."

"No, I mean demons are *here*, sir—Dorian." Liam was standing by the gate into Yomi proper, a dreary and never ending feudal village of perpetual dusk that surrounded a great mountain where the gods slept at the peak.

"Oh, no. No, no, no, no!" I hadn't even *thought* about the consequences of Kamakura being incapacitated. Without her and the guardian spirits protecting here, there was *nothing* to stop Hell from marching its armies in to reap all the helpless souls of the dead. It had been days in the real world, but time flowed differently here and could have been minutes, seconds, or years for Yomi.

"We need to reach the temple at the base of the mountain," I told Liam.

"What about the demons?" Liam had already drawn his swords and lit them up with a blue rim across the blade. I looked in past the gate. It was bad. There were hundreds, if not thousands of them roaming the village. The streets were split open into giant chasms down to the fiery pits of Hell. The horned denizens were crawling up and snatching armfuls of villagers and dragging them down to the sulfurous void below. The modest shacks that lined the streets had been set on fire, forcing the residents to flee right into the demons' arms.

"We can't get distracted from our goal. We have to focus on...we can come back...Oh, fuck it. Let's take as many of these bastards down as we can!"

Liam clinked his blades together and then held one up into the air to cast a series of spells on himself. It was an impressive light show of dazzling prismatic colors and swirling projections of aether that looked like fireflies.

He took off for the nearest demon at a speed that almost matched Noah's, but slow enough for me to make out his figure moving about the sundered road with cat-like swiftness. His precision was stunning, beautiful, grotesque. Liam carved his way through the horde, not wasting a single inch of motion as he dismembered his targets with surgical refinement and deflected projectiles back into their ranks. Occasionally he would send a blast of his own in the form of lightning or raw aether to stun one demon while he worked on the next.

I should take this champion thing into more serious consideration. I flew high enough over the houses to get a view of the surrounding area. More time and space mumbo-jumbo prevented us from traveling in any direction at too great a velocity. The way I pictured it was that space folded in two here like the pages of a book so that more could fit in the same area than if it was spread out sequentially in a flowing landscape like on Earth.

The demons here weren't the same as the ones I had fought in the past. They spanned from roughly human size to triple that and were bolder, solid colors like turquoise, teal, and bright red, not the dark and leathery hides I was used to. Their horns weren't curved like a ram's; their faces resembled terrifying war masks with flared nostrils and tusks coming from their gaping mouths. Some had more than two arms with each one holding a weapon, such as a spear or spiked club.

I pummeled the Infernal horde with telekinetic pulses until there was nothing left of them but dust on any of the roads I could see from my vantage point. This was the easiest time I had fighting any Infernal, but squashing ants wasn't going to win the war. I sealed the chasms in the immediate area, but so much damage had already been done that there wasn't much point.

I landed by Liam ready to move on when he kneeled to me out of nowhere. "That was unbelievable," he said.

"I thought we were past the kneeling thing." I lifted him to his feet with my powers. "And they weren't all that strong, so don't be too impressed."

"I'm sorry. It's just that I've been wanting to fight by your side and see what you can do up close for years."

"Plenty more fighting coming up. I appreciate that you...appreciate...me, but give yourself the same credit. Your skills are incredible."

"Thank you. I will." He nodded. *Not even a smile after getting a compliment from "God" himself. Maybe I should have sent him to the Blackbournes instead of Claudius.*

"I don't know how you're still standing let alone fighting. It's been a long day for you, hasn't it?"

"I drank a decoction to ward off sleep while you were with my father in the reliquary."

"Coffee?" My ears perked up at the thought.

"No. It's something we learn to brew from our alchemical studies. I don't like the taste of coffee."

"Blasphemy!"

"I'm sorry. I didn't mean—"

"I was joking. Can you teleport us to the temple?" I floated him up with me to point it out in the distance, the golden doors glittering like a nugget in the mud. "I know we don't have the others with us, but it isn't far."

Liam disappeared into his hazy bubble and then reappeared two feet in front of where he was. He tried a couple more times until he gave up. "I can't. There aren't lines here. It's just a flat sheet of energy blanketing the area and it's very faint. I can go into it and it feels like I'm moving forward, but I end up not much further."

"Yeah, it's the same if you try to super speed a long distance," I told him. "I've been here with Noah. You can dash around in the general area, but never actually get anywhere faster."

It was painstaking to move through the village at the same slow pace no matter what we did when there was so much going on. Liam kept a few feet in front of me as if he was my bodyguard. It was a nice sentiment, but unnecessary when anything with horns that crossed our path was annihilated before it could act.

I held back at times to let Liam fight so I could watch him in action. There was something so entertaining about how casual he was firing off a stream of lightning to fry a demon off to the side, or dash up the body of one and cut it limb from limb on the way. He almost looked as if he wasn't paying attention and it was all reflex. I had seen mind-blowing speed and agility before and flashy magic spells plenty of times, but coming all from one human—and a teenager at that—was a first for me.

"Do you have to recast those spells on yourself after every fight?" I asked after noticing him pause to do so every time he killed something.

"Not usually. They normally last an hour, some like the Zephyr spell for faster movement only last five minutes, but everything is wearing off in seconds here. My amulet is enchanted with a time spell called Delay to slow down the decay of the other spells so they last longer, but it isn't working here."

"Don't waste your energy. I can handle anything we run into."

"I'll only use my swords if you like."

"That's your call. I'm just looking out for you."

"Thank you. I think the aether here is too thin to recover fast enough even if I meditate—"

"Hang back. There's a bigger one coming."

"It's a demon lord..." Liam almost sounded nervous.

"What's wrong?" I questioned. "Didn't you kill one to make the leather for my pants?"

"I was with my cabal and we had plenty of preparation time. We had also fought it on the Astral Plane where our magic is stronger."

"You'll have to tell me about the Astral Plane after. Leave this one to me." I put the satchel down and removed the necklace so I wouldn't lose it before I flew to meet the demon lord head on. Aside from being bigger than the rest of the demons here it had its own distinct look. For starters, its body didn't appear to be purely organic, but rather biomechanical. There were no tubes or wires attached to its body in a crude fashion, as if it had been jury-rigged to get it up and running again. It was a sleek and seamless composition of flesh and pliable metal made from technology centuries ahead of what even PROJECT: UNITY could dream up.

As I approached the demon lord it shrunk itself to a more human size and bowed to me. I was left stunned. "Are we sure this is a demon?" I shouted back to Liam. The others invading Yomi seemed primitive and barely more self-aware than a gorilla as they stomped around kidnapping souls and demolishing the village. Minerva and Lord Ma'al were the only two that had displayed higher intelligence, but they both lacked in the civility department.

"Yes, I'm sure," Liam called up to me. This demon lord didn't have much in the way of a face; just two pairs of ruby slits for eyes, no mouth, no nose, no ears. It was still able to speak to me, but in Japanese—not the Infernal language I had heard Minerva use. The demon gestured like a person in friendly conversation until it pulled a katana from a portal on the palm of its hand. Then it did the same with its other hand. Next it grew two additional arms and each of those summoned weapons too.

I flew down into the brimstone caldera to Hell knowing that an Infernal could only be vanquished for good in their native realm. On the other hand, they were also significantly more powerful there. The demon chased me, growing back to its original size on the way and attempting to slice me in two as I out- maneuvered it.

I blasted a hole through its core, exposing its semi-organic innards once we were far enough in and sending the demon reeling. A cloud of metallic insects was released from the compromised chest cavity and tried to swarm me. I only had to visualize crushing the bugs into a ball until they stopped moving for it to happen. No longer did I have to use my powers to feel out every object first before I could manipulate it. Destruction was my forte before I had learned to reshape matter and now both were similarly as natural to me.

I dropped the mangled mess of insects into the magma pits below and with one more strike to the main demon; its body was blown to pieces that fell with the rest.

"Damn. I should've gotten those swords for Noah," I said to myself. I hoped he was all right and pushed away thoughts about him so that I wouldn't be distracted, but it wasn't working. *Did he really have feelings for me? Did I have those feelings for him? And what if I did?*

I escaped the chasm and sealed it on my way back to Liam.

"Come on. We should be getting close to the temple," I told him and retrieved the satchel.

Slaying demons and liberating souls, we continued our trek through the village. I couldn't fathom what was going through Liam's head being here. Only seventeen and he fought with the skill and ferocity of an immortal ten times his age on top of being well-versed in non-combat abilities.

"Tell me about the Astral Plane."

"It's a dimension made from the collective conscience of all things, including spirits and the planet itself."

"That's it?" I prodded for more. His father would have given me a two-hour lecture.

"Yes. It's a land of dreams and memories. It isn't something that can be explained as much as experienced. All the other dimensions are connected to it through the mind. When you dream, your connection to it grows stronger and clearer. When you're awake your other senses cloud the connection. The stronger your will and imagination, the more powerful you are there. Even someone like me can defeat a demon lord if prepared."

"You're not being hard on yourself now, are you?"

"No, sir." He wasn't very convincing.

"Defeating a demon lord under any circumstance is amazing. You may be the most impressive person I've met throughout my adventures."

"Thank you. Anyone in the Order can do what I do though."

"Even Connor?" I smiled and tried to nudge him into taking some credit.

"In a year or two, yes."

"There's no difference who I pick to be my herald then?"

"That isn't for me to say. Only the Ascended knows who is right for them."

"You're very passive about the whole thing. Is it not something you're interested in?"

"I am. I have to be. It's why I was born." Liam dashed off to save two poor souls at the last second before they were captured and then returned to me.

"I'm sure that's not why. Your father and mother are married right? They must love each other and then you know...out came you."

"He chose her because she was a good candidate to give me the best chance at being strong enough for the Ascended. That's what he told me."

"Your father is very...proper. He probably wasn't comfortable getting into the details of his relationship with you."

"Anything is possible, but no one in the Order has a child for love. Not that I've heard."

"That can't be," I said, implicitly rebuking what Liam was saying. "I mean you're young, you have a lot of time until you think about that stuff. I only started to recently."

"When we reach puberty, we are supposed to abstain from all temptations until we are thirty. Then we have to find a mate with a gifted soul and have our first child." Liam hurled lightning from his fingertips and disintegrated a pair of demons chasing down a group of scared villagers.

"What if you don't want to have a kid when you're thirty or don't find someone to be with?" I was starting to feel sympathy for their lifestyle. They endured loveless lives in secrecy, all for the sake of tradition.

"It isn't a choice. I haven't known anyone like that, but I hear that the council will assign you someone."

"I don't remember meeting Pavel, Rhys, or Helena's spouses in the courtyard," I said while closing a fissure in our way, crushing the hellspawn between it.

"Helena couldn't bear children so there was no point," he said in such a matter-of-fact tone.

"Pavel's younger brother Alexandre was gifted so nobody questioned Pavel sponsoring him as his ward instead of having a child of his own. And Rhys's wife was Lynn."

"Who's Lynn?" We had finally reached the temple grounds where statues of samurai lay smashed to bits and claw marks were gouged into the golden door.

"Oh, she was a pagan witch that the Order had employed to watch you in Manhattan a few years ago. I think her last name was Sutherland. She died from the infection that had been mutating people there. Come to think of it, maybe Rhys loved her. He seemed upset about her passing, but it could have been because she was carrying his child."

Chapter Thirty-Three

The golden doors to the temple opened with ease. They shouldn't have. The doors were sealed so that only the guardian spirits could enter and exit, but they were gone or too weak to hold the seal. The braziers and lanterns were out, but there were no signs of demons within. The spirits must have used the last of their power to hold the door before we arrived.

"Start praying that this works," I said to Liam and walked up to the shrine of a dragon coiled around a mountain in the center of the room. Behind the shrine were four corridors with banners hanging from both sides of the entrances. On the left hung banners of animals that the spirits represented; on the right, the cardinal direction they were associated with in *kanji*.

"To you or the dragon?"

"Are you making a joke, Liam?"

"No."

"Too bad." I took out all of the Empyrean Jewels except for the one of light and floated them around the statue. "Fire for the Vermillion Bird of the South, Water for the Black Turtle of the North, Wind for the White Tiger of the West, Lightning for the Azure Dragon of the East, and Earth for the Great Yellow Dragon at the center, Empress Kamakura."

Nothing happened.

"Oh, come on! That sounded really official too." I had to try something else, so I levitated the four jewels that corresponded to each spirit into their respective hallway and left the earth jewel where it was on the shrine. "I'm out of ideas if this doesn't—"

The temple shook and a blinding explosion simultaneously occurring in each hallway ejected us back toward the village. I grabbed Liam mid-flight to stop him from crash-landing, but he snapped into action faster and teleported behind me. He swung us both around, behind cover as five colored lights matching the spirits streaked out of the temple and across the sky. The yellow light of Kamakura went up into the clouds above the mountain while the other four spread out through the village with a massive tremor upon impact with the ground.

The wind spirit appeared on the road that Liam and I were holed up on along the side. It wasn't the human form I had seen in our previous encounters, but a mammoth white tiger the size of an elephant with wind swirling and whipping about its fur. The tiger charged through the remaining demons tearing them apart with tooth and claw. Earthshaking roars called down tornados around it to clear the streets and batter those Infernals trying to climb up out of Hell.

I flew up so I could see over the buildings to the other roads. A scarlet bird of paradise with wings of flame and a sky-blue serpentine dragon that crackled with static electricity, both of which were the same size as the tiger, were decimating the Infernal horde with cataclysmic fire and lightning that left mushroom clouds in their wake. Water spouts flooded the village wherever a giant sable-shelled tortoise stomped its feet to wash away the evil. None of the devastation caused by the spirits caused any harm to the souls of the dead who carried on like they didn't exist.

The noise coming from the elemental rampage was too loud to shout over, so Liam and I waited and watched while the spirits cleaned house. I checked on Liam to see if he was doing okay, but he remained stone-faced as usual. Once the village was almost clear, the spirits returned to rays of light and shot up to the mountain. I took Liam and flew after them to a cliff high up on the mountainside where the empress stood.

Any time I had seen Kamakura she appeared in an almost featureless female form with skin that shifted in a multitude of lights and runes. Now what stood at the edge of the cliff was a regal woman in the silken garb of a true Asian empress and with the eyes of a dragon. She held out her hands and all of Yomi quaked as she closed the last fissures to Hell and extinguished the hellfires with a soothing rain.

"I like your new look," I said to her when Liam and I landed on the cliff.

"It has been centuries since I have had the power to manifest my full visage. I owe you my thanks," her voice tinkled in our heads with the sound of bells in the wind. I had always thought the glowing mannequin look *was* her real form.

"Glad I could help, but someone out there still has some of that power you need to get back."

"You speak truth, Young One. I feel as if this is the first we meet, yet somehow you are familiar."

"Uh, I've been here before…we've *met* several times and you usually ignore me."

"Forgive me, but I am bound by oath not to interfere with mortals and so they are banished from my gaze."

"I wasn't mortal when we've met in the past."

"Only those divine and infernal are true to the name immortal. All else appear as a distant dream that fades from sight."

"Are you able to see how many souls were lost to the demons?" I asked. "You had a demon lord here, but it didn't put up much of a fight."

"A great many souls were lost to the demons known as *oni* and now feed the fires of Hell. The lord acting as commander of the legion is known as a *rakshasa*. They have not been known to work together. Most troubling for our enemies to be forging alliances of their own."

"Do you think you have it in you to help us take down Set? We at least need you to take back the power he stole."

"So it will be. The Heavenly Ones Above have grown furious with the defiler and the desecration of our once great lands."

"We have to be more organized than last time. We have more allies of our own now. I found the voice that had been calling out to you and the Dark One. It was another goddess offering help in exchange for ours. I'll get everyone prepared and then we'll send for you."

"Very well." The empress bowed. "I will await your word, Young One." It amazed me how Isis putting my soul back together changed so many people's outlook on me, even though I felt like the same person but with some new tricks. I wondered how both goddesses came to calling me "Young One", as if it was written on a name tag. Perhaps any fresh from the oven deity was called that.

"Since you're already in my head can you send me and Liam here to a place in my memory?" I held onto Liam's arm in case Kamakura left him behind because she couldn't see him.

"Bring the memory forward and it shall be," she instructed. I thought of my room in the abbey and following a brief sensation of vertigo was back on Earth with Liam.

"Go get some rest," I told him and put the satchel down on my bed. "You did great."

"Thank you," he said with a bow and paused before leaving. "It was an honor and...it was fun."

Still no smile out of him, but at least he was opening up. That was, until his father came around and he clammed up again.

I retrieved the tablet from the satchel and planned to fly into town to find a signal I could connect to, but it was either broken or the battery was dead. I thought of asking someone in the Order if they could use their magic to power it so I'd know if it was broken or not.

Before anything else, I checked on the Empyrean Jewel of Light and took out the necklace with the ring to wear again. I put the ring down the front of my shirt so only the chain was showing around my neck and put the gemstone in my pocket. I needed to do something about that note I got with the ring. It was only dusk so I didn't miss my chance to meet with whomever sent it tonight.

I was about to leave my room when there was a chill in the air and everything went dark for a moment. "This room is very nice," came a voice from behind me.

"Gianni!" I exclaimed with a degree of unrestrained enthusiasm that I knew would complicate things once it slipped out.

"Ah, I am Gianni again. You are not so angry at me now?" He stood at the foot of the bed and walked over with his arms out. I caved in an emotional moment and hugged him. I was glad to see him on his feet in the flesh and... I had missed him. Being in his tight embrace brought back so many feelings I was trying to avoid. The moment his arms closed around me the weight of the world disappeared from my shoulders and I was lulled into blissful comfort.

"No." My response was met with a kiss to the top of my head. This wasn't what I wanted though. It was comfort in complacency. I had been feeling strong on my own. I was more independent and assertive than I had ever been in my life and felt respected, productive, and important. Now in Gianni's arms again I was a kitten; something cute and defenseless to him that wasn't taken seriously.

"But we need to talk," I added, even if it was the last thing I wanted to do. I had thought that diplomacy and politics were worse than being set on fire, but I managed to find something I dreaded more.

"First I thank you." He lifted my head to look up at him. "I know you come for me in the desert when I have a trouble." His face drew in closer to mine, but I pulled away.

"No, first we talk."

"Okay. We talk."

I took a deep breath and began to unload. "I care about you—a lot—but when I'm with you I don't feel like we're equals. I know you care about me too, but we want very different things from our relationship.

"You've taught me so much about myself. I'm strong—not only because of my powers, but also as a person. I can be a leader and I have ideas I want heard. You want someone to protect while you take on everything yourself."

"I want you to be happy," he said and held my hand. "The most happy in this world. I thought this will be when you make the building and create beautiful things so only I do the battles."

"That's another issue that has to do with this. I don't *like* to fight, but I will if it's important to me. I understand you enjoy the thrill of battle and I know that war is inevitable in most cases, but there's a difference between fighting to end a war and fighting to conquer for glory."

"You need war to stop the evil, little one. When we do not strike first is when the most good people die. I want to make a peace for the world. Yes, to conquer it so it can be like Roma. I am here to fix all the bad in my past.

"I think this is why I am so strong now. My purpose is to bring back the Roma I help destroy in my past. There was peace then. The empire goes to war, but only to add more land for the people. When all is under the Roman flag there is peace and a good fortune. I see this with my eyes."

"You were a soldier back then." I pointed out. "You fought what you were commanded to and told it was for the glory of Rome. I'm sure there were plenty of other places that were doing fine before Rome came and conquered them."

"Maybe. But they are better with Roma," Gianni argued. "There is no war if we all unite. No hate. A small war maybe for the leaders to make a decision, but it does not hurt the land. Today all is war in the world, people and the supernaturals. How is this better peace?"

"I can't agree with that. I'm sorry. I know you have good intentions, but it doesn't feel right to me. I don't think it's something I can be talked into without regretting it later."

"Come. I will show you so you see with your eyes." He put his arm around me and brought us into the shadows. What he had to show me was...terrifying.

"This can't be real," I gasped. "This is insane. There has to be thousands of people..."

"More, I think." We were observing the Giza pyramids where Set had set up shop. I couldn't even call it a crowd, it was more like an entire population that was gathered around. Set was kind enough to drop the storm wall so mortals could flock to him in prayer. It wasn't organized prayer though, it was a riot of everyone shouting over each other to claim themselves, or their nation, most worthy to be spared his wrath.

How much time could have passed while I was in Yomi? "When did this start?"

"Maybe two days? Many people still make the travel to come here and try to make a bigger war for their enemies. If this is Roma, all stand together and there is no enemy to hate."

"What is Aurelia doing about all this?" I doubted she could do much to take over all the mortals in the world when they kept coming to throw themselves at Set.

"She is with the leaders. She keep her promise like I say. I know what she want and I show her how to get this. The human leader are safe with her. She want them alive so when this is over they remember her as their ally and give her a respect like royalty."

"And what will happen to the countries about to be torn apart by Set after he's defeated?" I asked.

"We rebuild. Maybe, in the Roman way?" he smiled.

"I think the people should decide how they want their lands to be. We should give them back their homes. You need to take back the darkness he stole from you first."

"Yes, I will do this. The people will have the homes, but if we do not be the leader after then the same war will happen again. You see?"

"We should mediate then. Not rule. Nobody likes to be controlled. It's a false peace that will cause them to hate us and rise up."

"You will see with your eyes when it comes. They will like us if we are a good leader."

"I'm sorry, Gianni. I care about you so much and I want you to be in my life, but I can't be in love with someone that I disagree with so strongly. I can't stand by silent and pretend I'm okay with it. If you want to conquer and rule then you'll have to do it without me."

"I do not want to lose you, little one. You are mine. I know you will understand when you see, but now maybe you are too young."

"It isn't about understanding... I'll always be your friend as long as you fight for good, but I can't be in love with you. I'm sorry." *Why did I want to*

*cry when I said that? I was the one breaking up
with him, not the other way around.*

"Do not be sorry for your feeling. I know you
come back to me when you see the truth. But we
must stop Set so this can happen."

"Then we'll need to get all those people away
from the pyramids so we can attack him *together*
this time. Have Aurelia charm them."

"She will not like to be so close to danger."

"I didn't say to ask."

Chapter Thirty-Four

I lied in bed staring out the windows as the last touches of sunlight slipped down the horizon. Gianluca had left to deal with Aurelia when the sun finished setting in France. Once he was gone, I began having doubts if my final decision was the right choice. What if he was right about how to handle the world? Was I being ungrateful and selfish for not compromising more on my end?

Noah may have been putting up a wall to cope with his pain when he said that love was a weakness, but now I could empathize with it as I physically felt that weakness take over. I had to tell myself that I did the right thing in my time of strength rather than cave to that moment of weakness.

I stayed in bed for hours with only the moonlight keeping me company. I wished for sleep to take me, but I wasn't as tired as I should have been to justify letting so much time go to waste. If anyone needed me, let them come. I'd had enough of tracking people across the world for a while.

Another hour or so passed until I dragged myself into the bathroom to soak in the tub. I had to leave the door open since the small window didn't afford me much light and I had no way to light the candles without asking someone.

This would've been the perfect time for Noah to come slap me and tell me to get over it and stop feeling sorry for myself, I thought. Not while I was in the bath though...maybe. I never had all those doubts about him like I did Gianluca, not after I realized I could trust him early on. I used to tease him knowing he cared a lot more than he wanted to admit. I was surprised by how right I was.

Noah infuriated me sometimes, but I kind of liked it. We treated each other like equals regardless of age, powers, or status. In the beginning he was the one to drag me unwillingly up to his level when I knew nothing of the world or myself. As chaotic as his personality appeared on the outside, he was stable and a constant in my life—like Lyle. There were times I even considered him a closer friend than Lyle. But could that ever successfully translate into something more? You aren't supposed to date your friends—like how people said not to go into business with family members because it would complicate a relationship that already existed.

The concept of "dating" seemed wildly inappropriate for the lifestyle we lead. That word alone made me think of it in the most traditional sense; going to the movies and out to dinner, anticipating the first kiss. Not slaying demons. In the beginning, Gianluca had liked to be traditional by bearing gifts and flowers and taking time to visit exotic places together for a quick getaway.

I couldn't picture Noah doing anything of the sort. The stories he told me of his past romantic encounters were of a different Noah than he was today. He'd probably think sparring was romantic...which now cast some of those times grappling together in a different light. Still, I couldn't imagine him doing something more thoughtful than throwing a slice of pizza in a paper bag at my head and playing tag with his swords.

After my bath and back in my room I spotted something on the ground. It was a note that had been slid under my door.

Please come to the grotto I will wait for you until dawn.

I had almost forgotten about the first note with everything else going on. This was a good way to end my moping and get on with life. I couldn't let myself be held down by feeling sorry for myself when so much counted on me. If I wanted to be respected for being strong, I had to continue to show it. I liked being a leader. As long as it didn't require any public speaking.

I left my room without a clue of how to leave the abbey since I had always been teleported in and out. I knew how to get to the courtyard so I could fly straight up from there to look around. The halls were empty with everyone in bed, but it was cozy even late at night with only candles and torches lighting the stone interior. There was a part of me that was still on edge from sneaking around.

"Hello, Dorian!" Marianna's cheerful voice breaking the stillness nearly made me scream and jump out of my skin as I passed the kitchen.

"Oh, hi, Marianna."

"I'm sorry. Did I scare you?"

"No. I was just…surprised you called me by name."

"That's what you want isn't it?" she asked as if it were obvious.

"Yeah, but nobody's really listened. What are you doing up?"

"I couldn't sleep so I was making protein pancakes." She held up a mixing bowl to show me the batter.

"You should meet my friend Lyle. He loves midnight pancakes."

"I'd be honored. Are you hungry? They're healthy!"

"Not really, but thanks. I was just going to go down by the shore to do some thinking and relax."

"Okay, but watch out for sea monsters."

"…really?"

"No! That would be fun though, wouldn't it?"

"I'm not so sure about that." I laughed, but it was more at her jubilation than the idea of sea monsters. "You and Claudius—well a lot of you except for Liam—act very differently than the older generation. The Order seems to be frozen somewhere between two eras."

"Liam's always been too serious. I'm pretty sure he was born an old man. We know you're our age, I mean, we've been watching you forever. Some of us tried to tell the elders that we were going to scare you off if we kept treating you like you were from another time period, but they're afraid that if we don't you'll think we're being disrespectful."

"It's taking some getting used to, but I like it here."

"Oh, good! We're all worried, I guess. It isn't every day we get to meet the person our legends have told us about in vague detail since we were babies. Nobody really knows how to act. You're a mix of new and old yourself and the answer to a lot of prayers.

"We all know what cell phones and the Internet are and all that, but we never let anything new into our lifestyle. We keep up with everything so we aren't clueless when we're out in the world, but don't adapt to it. I don't mind too much. We're happy here and what we do keeps us busy.

"We must seem pretty strange to you coming in from the outside, but I bet it's nice to be someplace new and already be loved."

"Loved?"

"Yes, you're the Ascended. We were born to love you, like any religion does their god, I suppose. Loved just sounds better than worshipped. Worship always sounded creepy to me. Don't tell the council I said that...especially not my aunt. She'll have my head."

"I won't." Our conversation put a new spin on things and gave me a lot to think about. The fanatical side of the Order was what made me skeptical of them. "Thanks for the talk, Marianna. It definitely made me feel more comfortable staying here."

"No problem! Don't forget me next time you need help. I know Claudius will be rubbing it in for months that he got a mission and I didn't."

"I won't forget. I promise." I continued outside and flew up above the courtyard. The abbey was laid out in a two-story square with some areas that branched off going up to a third floor. Most of the immediate grounds were lit by lamps and torches. I wondered whose job it was to do that every night, but with magic I suppose it could be done with the snap of a finger.

There was a small farm that looked as if it existed more as a hobby than as a reliable source of food, along with a decent-sized orchard with a gazebo next to where I had seen some of the Order sword fighting the other day. The town was closer than I pictured; only about a mile down the hill. I could see clear across to the shore in the farthest direction marked by lights down by a dock.

I assumed my destination was somewhere still on the abbey grounds so I headed toward the opposite shore beyond the orchard. I wasn't seeing a grotto anywhere. The property ended in a steep cliff above the water. I floated down to be sure I wasn't missing anything. Sure enough there was a cave opening by the water with only a foot of sand that could be considered the shore. It was pitch black inside and I was starting to have doubts.

"Anybody here?" A torch was struck and a figure emerged from the mouth of the cave and immediately kneeled. "You? You're the guard from the other day. You weren't at the courtyard when I was supposed to meet everybody were you?"

He shook his head without a word. He was still dressed in his full armor including the helmet and was carrying a beat-up old book in one hand. "You don't have to kneel."

The guard remained on his knee and opened his book to write in with a magical ink pen that was inside the pages. "You can speak... it'd make this a lot easier. I don't think anyone can hear us here."

He shook his head and handed me the book to show me what he wrote, but another figure appeared and grabbed it from him.

"Hey!" I shouted. "Tobias, what are you doing?"

"I apologize, my lord. I never meant for him to bother you."

"He wasn't bothering me, but you are by interfering."

"Please, allow me to explain," Tobias coaxed while trying to walk me away from the mystery knight. "The boy's name is Nathaniel and he has brought nothing but shame and dishonor to our Order since the time he was born."

"That's harsh criticism for a baby. I'd still like to hear what he has to say for himself."

"I'm afraid that wouldn't be possible as the boy is mute." Tobias kept calling him a boy, but Nathaniel was bigger and taller than him although not by much. It could have been the armor though. "The curse of silence was the only way to stop the lies that came from his mouth at every attempt to manipulate us. He was commanded to stay away from you, but this would not be a first for him disobeying a direct order for his personal gain."

I looked over at him still down on one knee with his head bowed. I couldn't see his face and didn't know him from a stranger, but there was something about Nathaniel I couldn't explain that was telling me to hear him out. I also didn't want to search for reasons to distrust Tobias and the Order based purely on imaginary suspicions when Tobias could be the one telling the truth.

"He betrayed the Order as a child when he murdered his guardian with a dagger to the heart," Tobias continued. "It is a case of bad blood. His father had the same murderous intentions, but we gave the child a chance."

"And you keep someone like that around the children today?" I questioned. I'd also like to know how he pulled that off, assuming his guardian was older and stronger than him.

"We have a strict code against exile and execution. Drawing blood of our own for any reason harbors ill spirits, and we would not release such a person into the public with the secrets they know. We keep close watch on him and have stripped him of his spells, but cannot sever his connection to the aether. As an act of penance we resurrected an old tradition known as the Adamant Aegis.

"You asked what happened to those who fail. In centuries past, those of poor showing were not cast out nor punished, but given a newer, stronger connection to the aether as a chance at redemption. Their bodies became conduits of immense aetheric energy that made them physical powerhouses—and the perfect guards for the council in times of war. They carried only a shield and knew no spells, but used their bodies as the ultimate defense to help the Order stand strong."

Something didn't add up. Tobias was smarter than that to leave such a glaring hole in his explanation. "So, on top of keeping this guy around children, you gave him *more* power?"

"Our children are never without their guardian and our hands were tied between tradition and justice. He has become a fairly productive member ever since he became an Adamant Aegis until defying orders upon your arrival."

"Good. Then if he's on the path to redemption I'd like to speak with him and find out what it was about me that set him off so we can fix it."

"I—I must—"

"Do as I say, yes." I was really starting to get the hang of this Ascended thing, but it was more so because Tobias was pissing me off.

"By your leave." Tobias bowed and then waved a hand releasing Nathaniel from the curse.

"Is it done?" I asked.

"It is, my lord."

"Good. You can go. Make sure there aren't any more interruptions either." Tobias complied without another word leaving me and Nathaniel by ourselves on the shore. "Can you speak now?"

"Yes, thank you...thank you so much." The deep hollow voice echoed from within his helmet and into the mouth of the cave he was kneeling by.

"You're welcome. You can stand up and take off your helmet."

"I–I shouldn't...I'm not worthy."

"How old are you, Nathaniel?"

"Twenty, my lord."

"I'm twenty-four. Ascended or not, we're basically the same age. You can show me respect by telling me the truth, but do me a favor and treat me as anyone else our age."

"Is this a test?"

"No. Jeez...all right, if you won't stand then I'll sit." I took a seat by him at the cave opening. "Will you sit?"

There was a pause while he worked out my request, but he did decide it was acceptable to sit. "Can you take off your helmet so I can see your face?" I didn't like the secrecy and it was much easier to lie when I couldn't see him. I knew I was constantly trying to talk everyone down from considering me the high and mighty, but I also didn't want to admit I couldn't tell if they were lying by telepathy.

"I shouldn't..." he hesitated.

I sighed and leaned over to remove his helmet myself. I was expecting the face of some deranged psychopath by how Tobias vilified him, but Nathaniel was the exact opposite. He was handsome, clean shaven, and had long caramel blonde hair draped over his wide shoulders.

His face...his face was so sad. This wasn't a passing expression in response to something that had just happened and not one that could be faked. It was engrained after years of depression and so palpable that you didn't need telepathy to be able to share what he was feeling when you looked at him. He wouldn't make eye contact and kept his head low to hide behind his hair. The little I did catch of his eyes when he looked at me after removing his helmet was that they were dull and lifeless—the hopeless eyes of a person on the brink of no return.

"This thing is heavy." I flipped the helmet around to get a closer look at it. It weighed as much as a bowling ball. I couldn't imagine how uncomfortable the rest of his armor was. "How do you wear this all day?"

"I don't have a choice. It is my duty. The Order does not want to look upon the face of a traitor."

"Where is your accent from? I can't place it." I was trying to keep the conversation on the light side while we built rapport, but his face grew nervous at my words.

"It's...it's Dutch. I'm sorry...I haven't been able to practice my English accent without my voice." He spoke more slowly to try and enunciate in the same generic way the rest of the Order spoke. His accent was almost unnoticeable. If he didn't look so afraid I would have thought he was joking with me. "I hope... it doesn't offend you. I'll... work on it immediately."

"No! I didn't mean it like that at all. I like it. It's very subtle anyway and even if it wasn't, it's nothing to be ashamed of."

"Thank you. You're very kind just like everyone said."

"And is what Tobias said about you true? Did you kill one of your own?" I was eager to get straight to the point. My compassionate side told me not to push him like the others though.

"Yes..."

"Why?"

"I don't remember..."

"You're going to have to do better than that if you want me to stay," I told him.

"I can't. I try and I try, but... nothing. No matter how hard I try I can never remember what happened that night. All I know is that there was danger, but I can't remember why."

"Maybe because you don't really want to. You were young. You could have repressed it."

"But, I do want to remember. I want to know before I die if I'm the monster they say I am."

"You have a while before that happens. I'm sure it will come to you if you let it."

"No. My end is soon, a few more years at most. The connection to the aether it takes to be an Adamant Aegis is a death sentence. It's too much for our bodies to handle and we die young. It's something we call aether poisoning."

"That's...horrible." Tobias said they don't execute their own, but this was worse than a clean death. Make them serve by killing them slowly while telling them they're redeeming themselves.

"I'm not afraid to die. I only want to know the truth before I do so that my soul will be able to rest. There's so much clouded from my mind that the council says I'm lying about."

"Is that why you asked me to come? To help you find answers?"

"Yes. If I'm as bad as they say then I deserve the death they've given me, but I don't *feel* that I am. I don't want to hurt anyone. I don't even like to use a sword."

Nothing he could have done as a child deserved a slow and painful death sentence. It was suspicious enough that he was able to kill an adult of the Order as a kid to begin with. "I promise I will do everything I can to get answers."

"Thank you. I've prayed to you every day since I can remember. I knew you could help."

"What's this ring?" I pulled out the necklace tucked in my shirt that he had left for me. "It looks like Tobias's wedding ring. How'd you get it?"

"It isn't a wedding ring. It's one that the council leader wears. That one was my father's. It's all I had to give as an offering."

"Your father was on the council?"

"Yes. Before Tobias killed him..." Nathaniel's expression turned sadder still. "Please. It'd rather not talk about this."

"That's a pretty big deal though... I'm sure if he hasn't been quick to offer that information there's a good reason. I'd like to hear it from you. You can take your time. I'm not going anywhere."

Nathaniel was quiet for a while and then spoke with his voice wavering on the first couple of sentences. "I was five when it happened. I saw everything from where I was hiding behind a curtain. There was an argument between the council members and Tobias stabbed my father in the chest with his sword. When they heard me crying I fled to my room. That's when I was assigned a guardian since I had no other living family members in the Order. Everything changed after that and it's my only clear memory of my childhood except for fragments here and there."

"You're all raised in a violent atmosphere to begin with. It isn't like it's much of a stretch to see that you're taught how killing is the solution to your problems. Maybe you lashed out in anger one day and have been repressing it ever since."

"If that is it...then I do deserve my sentence. Forgetting my crime isn't an excuse."

"There still has to be more to it than that. You were a child, hurt and confused. You might have done something horrible, but punishing you this way without giving you the chance to change is just as bad. I don't think the Adamant Aegis sentence and taking your voice is real redemption. It's sweeping it under the carpet and pushing the odds against you so you'll die without the council having the blood on their hands as if they executed you directly."

"I find joy in duty though. Protecting others makes me feel better that I'm taking the pain instead of them. I don't feel very much anyway because of the aether."

"How would you like to come with me wherever I go next," I offered him. It was a snap decision, but I felt it might benefit us both. "You can find real redemption and maybe make peace with yourself instead of staying here waiting for the inevitable. You might even start to get your memories back so you can deal with them if you're exposed to new surroundings."

"But, Liam is the Chosen and I'm not the best with a sword—"

"I'm not choosing anyone for anything just yet. Come with me as a friend so you can find your way."

"I'd be honored to serve you, master. I'll do my best to protect you." His excitement was real, but still dampened by his crestfallen demeanor.

"You don't need to protect me. There are some ground rules though: no calling me by anything but Dorian and no kneeling. No helmet either, unless it's for combat."

"I understand."

I handed him back his helmet and removed the necklace to give him. "You should hang on to this."

"I'd like you to have it. It's all I can give to show my gratitude."

"Okay. I'll hang on to it."

Chapter Thirty-Five

"You admit to killing his father then." I had decided to confront Tobias on his side of the story since even if everything he said was true, there were still parts that bothered me.

"Yes, but it isn't so simple. It was in self-defense. Nathaniel is only telling you a half-truth. His father and I were to engage in a friendly duel for the right to lead the council. When he lost the duel he lunged at me with his sword when my back was turned. The only thing I could do in the moment was strike back. It all happened so fast.

"Granted, there was always some tension between us. I had been warned on numerous occasions, but never thought he would go through with an attempt on my life. I would *never* cut down one of my own with such disregard as Nathaniel tells it. He was a child and I understood his misinterpretation and did everything I could for him."

"But you still assigned a guardian to him immediately after instead of taking him yourself because you wanted *your* blood to be the next Chosen. Were there any witnesses to this duel?"

"Only Caylan was present."

"Who was your closest friend and happens to be dead now."

"I know it looks bad—"

"We're on the same page there. I'll be taking Nathaniel off your hands. Should he decide to forfeit the connection to the aether that's *killing* him, you *will* do him the honors by releasing him from his sentence."

"I'm afraid the process is irreversible."

"Then you'd better start finding a way around that."

"Yes, my lord. Please know that I never meant it to come to this."

"I'm sure you didn't. Yet you tried to keep him away from me so I wouldn't find out. He was a child that needed love and guidance. No child is born evil or with 'bad blood'. Evil is taught, so maybe look at those around him that set the example and start by looking in the mirror."

I left Tobias to return to where Nathaniel showed me he would be waiting in his room. It was down an isolated hallway, but at least his living conditions were comfortable. His room was just a modest down-scaled version of mine with a smaller bed, and no fireplace or personal bathroom.

"You will put your helmet back on this instant!" Rhys wasn't being too quite about berating Nathaniel as I came down the hall.

"Dorian told me not to..." I heard Nathaniel answer from inside his room.

"You speak?!" Rhys shouted in amazement. "And you dare address the Ascended by name like some commoner and include him in your lies? Does your lack of respect know no limits? This will be the end of you! You've had far too many chances."

"He isn't lying," I said and floated past Rhys to enter Nathaniel's room.

"My—my lord, I'm sorry! I didn't know—"

"No, you didn't. Now stop shouting. The sun isn't even up."

"My lord, you must be told; the Van Dalen family is nothing but traitors and—" I slammed the door in Rhys's face before he could finish.

"Are you okay?" I asked Nathaniel.

"Yes. Thank you." There was a timid smile that came and went as he stared down at his helmet resting on a desk. On the wall above it was a banner like the ones I had seen in the conclave. The black-and-white heraldic crest looked like the Order's amulets with a sword through it.

"Good. Don't get too relaxed though. I'm probably going to need your help in the near future."

"I'm ready to accept any challenge you have for me to prove myself, master."

"*Dorian.*" There were aether crystals of all sizes on the shelves in Nathaniel's room. I picked one up that was in a cluster that resembled the inside of a geode. "Any reason why you have so many of these?"

"It feels better to release the energy when too much of it builds up. I don't have any spells to imprint on them and I was never taught how to refine them into gems so I just keep them around because I like the way they look."

"Yeah, they're pretty."

"You can have them if you like. I could try to make you a nicer one, but everyone else in the Order can probably do it better than I can."

"That's all right. You've already given me something valuable to you. I didn't come here to clean you out." I put the crystal back after checking the rest. "Does it hurt all the time? To have the aether flowing into you like that?"

"Yes, but I'm used to it. It starts as a headache or a nose bleed but can become a fever or feeling like your bones are breaking if you don't find a release. The pain gets really bad when my organs start tearing. It can turn into a stroke or heart attack without much warning from there, but that hasn't happened to me yet."

"Hopefully it never will."

"I'd be useless without it and that's the last thing I want. Especially now. I'm prepared to deal with whatever consequences I'll have to face."

"You're a brave man knowing what's coming and being so calm about it." I would have demanded

Tobias free Nathaniel of this fate, but I wanted Nathaniel to make the choice on his own. I didn't want him to resent that I robbed him of his only strength until he realized he had more to offer as a person than that power. It was a lesson of self-worth I had learned myself, but unfortunately the Order seemed to place their martial and magical skills as top priority over all else.

"Thank you. No one's ever told me that before."

"Now that the other gods are back up everything should be in place to take down Set. I want to return to my friend Lyle's base in Greenland where I had sent Connor. I lost another friend of mine recently that used to be our magical advisor so I'm hoping you and the others I take can fill that hole. Do you have any issues with Liam, Marianna, or Rafael?"

"No. They've always been good to me." *Interesting. I'd have thought he'd not want anyone linked to the council to join.*

"Okay, good. Do you think you four can use the ley lines to bring us there? I don't feel like asking the council."

"I...don't know how. I'm sorry."

"Don't worry. We'll get it done. There are plenty of other options. You should take a nap or something. The sun will be up soon and you've been awake all night, haven't you?"

"I won't be able to sleep. I've gone longer without it though, it won't be a problem."

"All right then, you can help me round up the other three since I don't know my way around."

"Gladly."

Marianna was easy enough to find. She was reading by candlelight in a big comfy leather chair in the hall outside the kitchen, her empty plate of pancakes beside her.

"I'm keeping my promise," I told her as we walked up. "Sooner than later too." She looked up and stood to greet me with a bow, but her eyes went right for Nathaniel.

"Nathaniel...?" 'God' was right there telling her something yet all she saw was him.

"Hello," he said.

"You can talk?!" she gasped.

"Yes. No more helmet either, at least not out of battle." He sounded unsure or that he was trying to keep it quiet expecting the council to jump out and harass him.

"I can see that..." The way Marianna stared was making him uncomfortable. He cleared his throat and tried diverting his gaze.

"You've *never* seen him without it before?" I asked. "You've lived together your whole lives."

"Maybe when we were children. Does the council know?" she asked.

"Yes," I answered. "It was my decision."

"I think that's great," she smiled. "You shouldn't have to hide that face, or that voice."

"Thank you." Nathaniel cleared his throat and tried to play it cool, whether out of respect or just uncertainty how to react, but a meek smile of his own broke through.

"The two of you will have plenty of time to get reacquainted where we're going," I told them. "But first we need Liam and Rafael."

"I can get them for you," Marianna offered.

"Thanks. Meet at my room so I can get my stuff and then we're off to Greenland." I didn't want to leave the tablet behind, but more importantly was the Empyrean Jewel of Light.

Nathaniel got more stares of shock and bewilderment than I did as we headed to my room. They weren't unfriendly looks, but I was familiar with being on the receiving end of similar gawking. "This is almost making me want to put the helmet back on..." he said.

"Don't. You shouldn't have to hide *that* face," I repeated what Marianna had said to make him smile. "There have been so many times when I wanted to hide, but it was never the answer."

"Thank you. Thank you for everything." I caught him still smiling to himself on the way into my room. It felt good to be able to do something for someone just by being me—no big battles or life-threatening adventures required.

Nathaniel and I chatted for a minute until he started zoning out. I assumed his head was filled with thoughts of the future, but then he leaned against the wall clenching his fist and squeezing his eyes shut in pain.

"What's wrong? Are you okay?"

"Yes, I'll be fine. It'll pass in a moment. I'm sorry."

There was a knock at the door. Marianna showed up with Liam and Rafael just in time. "Help him," I told them.

"No," he protested, his fist shining blue with aether. "I can do this."

"What's wrong with him?" Rafael asked.

"You really know *nothing* about him? He's only a couple of years older than you and grew up living in the same building." I snapped in frustration that someone under their own roof had been suffering in silence for so long without anyone making an attempt to find out. "He's being overloaded with aether by the stupid Adamant Aegis thing. Can't you take some of the excess away and make it into a crystal or something?"

Liam surprised me when he went over and threw Nathaniel's arm over his shoulder to practically carry him to the bed. That was the most assertive I had seen Liam act off the battlefield. Rafael and Marianna joined in when Liam started draining the aether from Nathaniel's body and turned it into beautiful blue crystals in their hands.

"He's asleep," Marianna said. "I never knew he suffered like that..."

"Yeah, me either..." said Rafael. "I don't think any of us thought much about it after getting brushed off whenever we'd ask why he was always in his armor and never spoke. It's easier to ignore when you can't see the person face to face."

"I knew," Liam confessed. "I used to go to his room to help him until my father caught me. I went to check on him the other day while everyone was in the courtyard. He was on the floor in worse shape than this. I thought he was going to die, so I delivered a letter from him and put it under the Ascended's pillow hoping he could do something."

"That was you?" Liam surprised me again. "I never thought you'd go against your father. Why didn't you say anything when you saw me with the necklace in Yomi?"

"I knew Nathaniel wanted you to have it, but I was afraid if you questioned my father first or it was traced back to me Nathaniel would be in more trouble. My father is a good man. I know he cares about all of us including Nathaniel, but when the council gets together as a group... I don't know. I was always told he was dangerous, but Nathaniel's always watched out for us. When we were kids and would get hurt training outside he'd help bring us to get healed and the adults would shoo him away. He saved my life before."

"What happened?" I asked.

"It was in New York during that outbreak where I first saw you. My father usually brought Nathaniel along as a guard. I wanted to impress my father and got in over my head in an abandoned hospital that was swarming with undead and mutants. They had me trapped, but Nathaniel saved me. We both almost died, but if it wasn't for him I wouldn't have escaped. My father blamed him though, even after I said it was my fault. I think he was punished for it somehow. I never found out."

"Something like that happened with me too..." Rafael said. "I took him for granted...never really thought about the person behind the mask after being told not to for so many years."

"I've never made stupid mistakes like that because I'm a girl, but I know Georgie is pretty attached to him," Marianna added. "I see him trying to get Nathaniel to play fight with him in the halls all the time and my aunt tells me to keep him away. Nathaniel is always so gentle with all the children though."

"Nathaniel doesn't have that long until he dies," I said. "The aether overload is killing him. It's too much for his body to handle and he only has a few years left. He wants to keep it that way because it's the only way he feels useful and thinks he's making up for a crime he doesn't even remember committing when he was a child.

"He *needs* people to help him work out his memories. He says it's all cloudy and as long as he feels guilty he doesn't want to stop this death sentence. There's a lot that doesn't add up about his past that you could help unravel, but it'll mean digging into things that someone in the Order wants to remain hidden. If there's any chance of me staying it won't be with secrets like these around."

"We'll do it," all three agreed.

Chapter Thirty-Six

"This is Rafael and Marianna," I introduced Lyle once we got Nathaniel set up in the Medical Ward. We had arrived on base to the wonderful sound of blaring sirens alerting everyone about the unregistered presence of my new friends.

"That's a huge sword. Are you sure you can swing that?" Lyle asked Marianna, referring to the bastard sword on her back that was almost as big as her.

"I work out," she smiled. Her eyes went right to him like they had to Nathaniel earlier. I was afraid I just enlisted Owen's magical female counterpart. Something told me that the Order's strict vow of abstinence was their least appreciated tradition.

"She uses magnetism," Rafael interjected. "It doesn't give the fine control of telekinesis, but it helps with heavy lifting and broad movements."

"Where's Connor?" I asked Lyle. "You didn't lock him in a holding cell did you?"

"I thought about it. He's on a snack run so I could breathe for five seconds. Thanks for that by the way."

"You're welcome. Can we go down to your office or the conference room to start discussing battle plans for Set now that Gianluca and Kamakura are okay?"

"Yeah, but I need to talk to you alone first."

"Why are you wearing one of your old NYPD caps?" I asked as the two of us went into an unused lab across from Nathaniel's room.

"We gotta have a serious conversation," Lyle said without answering my question after he closed the door.

"Uh oh, a serious conversation? Am I in trouble?"

"I don't know. Are you?"

"What are you talking about?"

"What's been going on, man? Do you have any idea how freaked out I've been? I tried playing it cool after Egypt because your new crew was around, but again you've disappeared for days."

"Time flows different in Yomi. I didn't know how long I'd be gone…"

"Do you know where *I've* been the past two days?"

"No."

"Japan. Looking for *you*! While there's an apocalypse going on over on the other side of the globe and I'm trying to lead a team of frightened people through it."

"The tablet was out of battery or broken after a fight in Yomi and I thought Gianluca would tell you he talked to me yesterday," I explained. "You're safer when you're not around me anyway—"

"I thought we were past all that leaving each other behind stuff, man. Don't you get it? We're fighting this war for the people we care about; our family, our friends, and I consider you both of those things. I don't want to lose anyone else in my family to selfless sacrifices.

"I'm not giving you the choice this time. We're sticking together through this to the end. And I appreciate you sending a babysitter to watch after me, but it doesn't make it better when I don't know if *you're* okay."

"I still get freaked out myself thinking that I'm going to be the cause of you...you know. You're human and—"

"Oh, bullshit. Don't give me that because I'm human I gotta sit at the back of the bus crap. I earned my way here and we may be fine on our own, but we're fucking badasses when we're together."

"Have you ever thought anymore about maybe getting turned?"

"What? Undead? No way. That's the last type of supernatural I'd want to be if I even had a choice. I'm proud of doing things the way I am."

"Pride has toppled empires and gods, Lyle. I'd feel a lot better if you could take a hit without getting splattered. That's not a dig at you either, it's all that goes through my head when we are fighting side by side."

"We watch each other's six like we've always done. I wanna be living proof that humans can do things they never thought possible with what they were given."

"That's very noble, but..."

"There's no 'but'. We're in this together for who we are. I've never tried to change you. You're like a little brother to me... no, let me say, you *are* a little brother to me just the way you are and always have been. So either accept me for who I am too or... well there is no 'or' either. Just deal with it."

"All right, all right. I give up. We'll stick together, but only if you promise no more lectures."

"Deal. Now give your big bro a hug and let's get out there and kick some ass."

"You're such a dork it hurts sometimes."

"Funny. Nice clothes by the way. You thinking of ditching us to try the modeling thing one more time before the world ends?"

"Shut up."

Lyle bust out laughing at his own weak jab. "But seriously, I'll be glad to have you around again.

I feel like things are falling apart here real fast and people are noticing."

"I don't know how I can fix that."

"I really need you to talk things out with. You're the only person that I feel doesn't have his eyes on me expecting answers."

"What about Timmons?"

"She's just as overwhelmed, but she's more small military and I'm still trying to keep things NYPD," he said and adjusted his hat.

"I'll do what I can. I have my own little following to lead now too."

"So what happened with Set when you were gone for three days?"

"Nothing. I was a statue."

"Why am I getting the feeling you're not telling me something? You were un-stoned when Noah found you, weren't you? Why you and not the others? They were almost dead. If there's someone he wanted to gloat to it'd be the ones that were too weak to fight back."

"I don't know, Lyle. Dog-headed Egyptian gods are weird, what can I say?" Back in the Medical Ward corridor Connor was with the other three from the Order holding the bags of chips he had fetched for Lyle and wearing a PROJECT: UNITY T-shirt.

"Please, don't be angry!" Connor pleaded with me and handed over the snacks. "Commander Turner was hungry and I had to protect him, so I thought he needed food to live, right? I was only gone a minute!"

"It's fine," I said, trying not to laugh. Rafael and Marianna also seemed immensely amused by Connor's panic. "Go back to the abbey. You've done well and I'll pass along your success to the council when I get back." I nodded to the other three to send him away. He kneeled as he was being sent and Marianna kicked him in the behind for it.

Nathaniel stepped out from his room and stood in the doorway wearing only his tights after being examined by medical. It was the first time I had seen him out of his armor. I had never used the word 'strapping' to describe a person, but it seemed to fit him well.

"Feeling any better?" I asked.

"Yes, thank you. All of you. I'm sorry for this," he apologized while rubbing the side of his head with a bashful expression. "I'll be sure it doesn't happen again."

"It's nothing to be ashamed of. We were about to start discussing plans for Set. You can stay here and rest and we'll fill you in later."

"No, I'll be fine. I want to be there. I won't get in the way."

"It's your call. Just put a shirt on before Marianna hyperventilates." Even Liam cracked a grin at that one.

Lyle and I went down to the conference room with the Order. They didn't seem all too impressed by the drones buzzing through the air and the warm glowing plastic walls of the rest of the base or the high-tech medical equipment and PARAGON terminals along the way.

"Any idea where Big G is?" Lyle asked after we took our seats around the table.

"No, and stop calling him that. The last we spoke I suggested he get Aurelia to lure the crowds away from Set so we can put him down without collateral damage."

"Good idea. We've been lucky to have some time to regroup while he basks in the spotlight. There haven't been any storms, but people *are* rioting against each other for his favor. I assume you saw that transmission the other day?" It was still taking effort for me to wrap my head around the fact that we were sitting around discussing the fate of millions that were in imminent danger like it was nothing. I kept wanting to run in and get it over with, but I knew it couldn't be done that way this time until all of our pieces were in position on the board. In the end I was sure that it would come down to a slugfest between whoever was left standing, but getting to that point was slowly killing me.

"Yup. I didn't know Set was so tech savvy," I said.

"He's not. It was a curse he put on the other satellites above Egypt he didn't destroy to spread his message to the world. He probably thought it was some magic star. His reach has grown about a hundred miles in all directions and that blood moon... I thought it was just an illusion but it's caused the Nile and the Mediterranean along the coast to rise significantly."

"Let's just hope he doesn't figure out how to curse any weapons of mass destruction, not that he needs any. This ends tonight though. Kamakura is back in action so she and Gianluca can take back what power Set stole from them, making him much more vulnerable for me to snatch that staff away. Then we'll beat him to death until I get the staff to Isis so she can banish Set for good."

"It's still gonna be a hell of a fight, man."

"When isn't it? But we have a whole team of heavy-hitters in our corner this time and don't have to worry about keeping things secret. There's no holding back anymore."

"Scary stuff, but whatever it takes. Sounds like you have it all worked out, except for where I come in."

"Snack run?"

The lights in the room dimmed to nothing. I knew what was coming.

"Good day, my friends!" Gianni appeared from the shadows and took a seat next to Lyle across the table from me.

"Hey, G. Good timing, we were just discussing how to take down Set tonight."

"It is no problem. Aurelia agree to help bring the people to a safe place." He kept his eyes and friendly smile directed at me with every word.

"Make sure you don't go without us and get turned into a rock again," I said.

"Don't worry, little one. I don't leave you."

"You've learned contractions? Who's been teaching you English?" I was stunned.

"I practice for you," he replied with a proud grin.

"Oh, good, you two have kissed and made up," Lyle said with the worst possible phrasing ever.

"Yes, I will like to," said Gianni, focusing his attention to my lips without any concerns for modesty.

"*Commander Turner, our VIPs have started to arrive.*" Commander Timmons's voice interrupted over the intercom.

"Shit!" Lyle exclaimed and took off his hat to fix his hair. "I didn't get a chance to tell you."

"Tell me what?" I had a bad feeling about that.

"Okay, don't freak out, but we might be having a couple world leaders over to show them the base."

"That's pretty ballsy, but what's that got to do with me?" I asked. If he was going to ask me to give a speech I was glad the Order was there to teleport me out.

"Well, it's more like most of NATO for starters. We thought it'd be a good idea to show them what an international organization could achieve if they worked together with supernaturals. Most of these countries *were* original investors in secret until things got too political. It would really put a lot of minds at ease going forward on both sides. On the back end, we want to show that we can offer sanctuary to the officials that are sticking their necks out to go against the public's wishes to do something about Set."

"Let me guess, this was Aurelia's idea."

"...Yeah."

"Wait. *She's* not coming, is she?"

"I bring her before," said Gianni.

"What?! How could you let her in here?"

"It's a good idea either way, Dorian!" Lyle argued. "She does technically own ninety percent of PROJECT: UNITY and this is exactly what we stand for; to be an international police force that mediates the natural and supernatural worlds. Protection for all. It's not like I could tell her no. This is the perfect opportunity to build up our reputation with the international community now that things are out in the open. Rudgar thought it was a good idea too."

"Rudgar is a mouthpiece, Lyle! She's controlling him to play the human side of things. This is about her publicity to cement *herself* as a world leader; you know that, right?

"It's morning. Let's open a window or something and send her back under her rock. She's only doing this during the day to make an even bigger show of it that she doesn't hide in the dark."

"Don't stir up shit. This is huge for us. With or without her past reputation, we couldn't have done this so easily on our own."

"It will be okay, little one. I am here so there is no trouble," Gianni assured me as Lyle slipped out of the room.

"Why don't you check in on your people at Castile and Vyrlakalos's using the terminal in your room?" Lyle called in a ploy to keep me from making a scene in front of his guests.

"Yeah, maybe that's a good idea," I said to no one in particular. "Then we can get out of here until tonight when it's time to go for Set."

"I will take you," Gianni said and before I could refuse he whisked us away to our old room in the barracks.

"I know what you're trying to do and it won't work," I told him as my entourage teleported in after us to check on me.

"Please. Leave us," Gianni said to them. "We will like to be alone."

They didn't budge.

"They only take orders from me," I said. I was thankful they showed up to put the brakes on before he got too close, but then thought it may make things more awkward for me as I fumbled through trying to distance myself from him yet again.

"See, you are a very good leader so soon. I think maybe you want to make your own empire without a help to show me."

"You guys can wait outside the room," I told the four standing guard around me. "I'll be fine."

They left me to deal with Gianluca by myself. I knew he understood me, but I didn't think he *believed me* when I said I wanted to call it off. It further solidified my point that he didn't give much credit to what I had to say. Yet, the way in which he went about talking to me, even if not giving any credit to what I said or who I was, was so charismatic that I still felt guilty pushing him out of my life.

"I know you worry I will be evil if I am a leader in the new world. We can both be a good leader together. I see you want to have a place for yourself in the Greek lands."

"That's not what happened." I knew it would look bad saying the Order worshipped me as their god. "They're following me because they believe in what I'm trying to do. I don't think *you're* going to be evil, but I don't agree with how you want to handle things. Even with the best intentions, conquering and ruling people without giving them a say in their lives never works out. I don't have to physically see that to know that.

"I've got other reasons. You think things should be the way they were back when you were human, but they weren't that great. You're okay with people being considered slaves or that men can do whatever they want if it's for honor and glory. You treat me like my opinion matters less than yours because I'm younger, like I'm not as important a man as you are. It's not evil, or even wrong, but it's not for me."

"You are less, you are a little man, a very beautiful one." He stepped forward and put his hands on my arms. "And very important. But it is the Roman way, one is the leader, the strong one. Is the better way to know I am responsible. I give you the best life, the whole world if you like, or a little piece."

His smile turned serious as his face drew closer. "Gianni, you're making it hard to stay friends when you do this…"

He didn't listen, of course. His lips teased mine and he held me close with one arm around my waist and the other hand caressing my cheek. "I know you are for me," he whispered. "I know I will make you happy if you stay."

My body was screaming yes from being pressed up against him, but my mind was struggling to fight for control. The stalemate persisted until our lips finally met and my mind was silenced. We hadn't kissed in so long and I had missed being close like this with someone after having a taste of how good it was. I embraced him back and was quiet when he stopped.

"We do not make the mistake again to go to war without love first," he said and picked me up to go to the bed. I knew we had to stop before it went any further, but he was already kissing my neck where I was weakest. He dissolved his shirt into the shadows and placed me gently on the bed.

"I can't do this," I protested firmly and went to get up as he got in bed on top of me.

"Why? I know you like this," he continued to whisper in my ear and send chills of pleasure down my spine.

"Because he's with me now, you piece of shit," came Noah's voice from across the room.

Chapter Thirty-Seven

As if the situation with Gianluca could get any more uncomfortable, Noah had to come and make everything exponentially more complicated. There was the possibility that this was exactly what it might take to have Gianluca back off, but there was also the other possibility that it caused him to throw Noah into the Nether for eternity. Noah was recklessly showing his emotions now after hiding them for so long. He was either desperate or at the final stages of his plan to be free. Either way, I didn't want to see him fail.

Aurelia was more secure than ever because of her new position. Even I had to give pause when considering the vital role she now played. My hope was that she would be made obsolete quickly after Set's defeat.

"One moment. I take care of this." Gianluca stood to confront Noah.

"No!" I leaped from the bed to get between them. I knew Noah would wind up on the losing end of any conflict between them if it turned violent. "Don't hurt him, please!"

Noah put his arm around me to pull me away from Gianni. "You okay?"

"You don't have to do this," I said to him.

"I know you like the slave, but his master will not allow it and he will die if he try to be free from her," said Gianni. "A slave cannot take from a man what is his." Noah was tensed and started to narrow his eyes like he was getting ready to attack. I put my hand on his chest and whispered to him to calm down.

"Gianni, please just leave him alone. If you really care and want me to be happy you'll stop this so we can still be friends." As much as it filled me with rage to hear Noah being referred to as a slave, I had to defuse the situation before it got any worse rather than let my anger get the best of me.

"Is the slave that always cause the trouble, not me. I want to give you the world, he only give you trouble. He has no honor and he say he is a man. Is this what you love?"

"Yes. Maybe. I don't know! I'd like to find out though and I don't want it to start a war."

"There is no war, little one. He is nothing to me. I know you are young. When you see the world and how this one will treat you then I know you come back to me."

"Maybe. But if you make us enemies then I'll never have a reason to come back. Is that what you want?"

"No... I let you have fun and see your mistake with your eyes then."

"Thank you." Gianni left and yet I still felt like crying when I watched him go even after that volatile situation. I closed my eyes to hold myself together. "I'm sorry," I said to Noah.

"For what?"

"Everything he said and holding you back. I thought you were going to jump him."

"I wasn't about to watch him force himself on you."

"You shouldn't have been watching at all!"

"I worry, okay? Don't be a dick about it. I knew he wasn't gonna stop the more you pushed him away and I wanted you to know I had your back."

"Thank you, especially for letting me take care of it. The problem is I didn't know if I *did* want what he wanted."

"You didn't or you wouldn't have hesitated so much. You always let your stupid head get the best of you."

"My stupid head is what was telling me *not* to go through with it. It was my body that had doubts."

"My body's better than his, so you're not missing much."

"Don't start."

"You know it's true. That's why you picked me, and I'm okay with that." Noah's dumb smirk drove away some of the lingering sadness.

"I didn't pick you for anything *yet*."

"You said you wanted me to be your tiger."

"No, I didn't. *You* said that!"

"That's not how I remember it." I wasn't entirely sure he was joking, and knowing him he probably made himself believe it.

"I still need time," I said after unsuccessfully holding in a laugh.

"*More* time? It's been like four days. How much more time do you need? Have you *seen* me? Front *and* back? Come on." He couldn't say it with a straight face.

"I hate you." I removed his arm from around me and went over to the PARAGON terminal.

"That's not what you said in the desert."

I shook my head and sat down at the computer to check in on Claudius and Anatole. "You have a very different perception of reality," I said.

"Yeah, a better one." He took a seat on the desk next to where I was sitting and stayed quiet for a record-breaking ten seconds. "So, are you gonna be okay?"

"Yes. I'm fine." He knew me better than that and raised an eyebrow in disbelief to prove it. "I *will* be fine. I just need time. I want to be *sure* before I do anything like this again and so that I don't make another mistake."

"Any more time and you're gonna get old and then I won't want you."

"I'm immortal, jackass."

"Oh, yeah," he smirked. "Listen. You can't let yourself be frozen in fear of making a mistake. There's no way to know if someone's right for you until you give them a chance. That's like any decision. You won't know if something is right by sitting around worrying about it."

Maybe I'm so nervous because I know I do have those feelings for him and don't want it to get messed up.

"What happens to us if we don't work out though?"

"I don't know. You're kinda hard to kill, so..."

"I'm being serious."

"I know you are and that's the problem. Just relax." He rummaged around in his pocket and pulled something out that he kept hidden from me in his hand. "What are you wearing, by the way?"

"Like it?"

"Yeah, actually. I do. It shows off your tasty bits."

"Tasty bits?" I laughed.

"Let me see your hand."

"Why?"

"Just gimme your stupid hand." I complied and held out my hand for him. I thought he was going to bite my wrist, but he took what he was holding and put it on me. "Damn your wrist is small."

"Prayer beads?"

"Yeah. I made them during my first time in Japan at a Buddhist camp. These are supposed to purify the mind. I always used to wear them until my mind became someone else's playground and I lost any faith I had in them. They're probably the last thing I have left from that time in my life now that you lost my *wakizashi* in the desert and I have to use some shitty replacements. I figured you might want to break these too."

"Shut up! Don't say that..."

"I'm kidding!" He let out one of the most genuine laughs I had ever heard from him. "You like them?"

"I do. I don't want them to get ruined though."

"That's kinda the point. I know I'm not giving you the *world*, but it's one of the last things that means anything to me and I wanted you to have it so you'll take care of them and yourself."

"Thank you, Noah..." He took my hand again, this time just to hold it. The two of us examined each other's faces like we were meeting again for the first time. We looked each other in the eyes and his gaze, though steel sharp as always, became inviting and familiar. He leaned in and without notice put his other hand in my hood to bring me in for a kiss.

My mind went numb. The beads must have worked.

I couldn't believe he did that.

"You're a terrible kisser," he whispered.

"I wasn't kissing you back! I—"

"Well, there's your problem. I can't always be doing all the work for the both of us. We're just gonna need to keep practicing until you get it right."

"We'll see about that," I laughed and pushed him away. Noah vanished, but I knew it wouldn't be for long. With him gone for the moment I used PARAGON to try and contact Claudius. He was with the Blackbournes guarding Castile, but I assumed Lyle had given them a way to keep in touch with the base when the other troops were pulled out.

No one was answering.

It was daytime, but that didn't mean one or both of the Blackbourne brothers weren't passed out in a bush somewhere to sleep off their liquor from the night before. I decided not to panic yet and try Anatole next.

"Ascended," Anatole saluted. One of the PROJECT: UNITY troops picked up right away and called him over. I expected Anatole would find it easy to mingle with them. "How can I serve you?"

"How's it going there?"

"You'll be happy to know that everything has been quiet. There isn't much to look at here, but I'm fortunate to be in good company."

"Tonight should be the last time that anybody needs to spend there." I'd let Gianluca handle watching over the Ancients after this since he wanted to be a soldier again so badly.

"Have you given anymore thought into what kind of god you wish to be known as?"

"No, but you'll still be the first to know when I do. I haven't forgotten my promise." *I'd like to be a hermit god, but what are the chances of that lasting more than a day?*

I hung up with Anatole after saying goodbye and went to check on the Order waiting in the hall. They were all standing at attention like they were guarding Buckingham Palace and Alexandre was now among the other four.

"Did you chase Noah all the way here?" I asked him. That was impressive. Noah wasn't easy to keep track of in a single building.

"I did. More precisely, I anticipated him coming here after overhearing a conversation. The blood wraith and the undead queen of that palace are…much more powerful than I had expected even after your warning. They are near gods themselves. You were wise to suggest staying at long range, but it was troublesome coaxing small enough spirits that would go unnoticed to get near them."

"You got it done, so that's all that matters. Thank you. I really appreciate it."

"It was an honor," he bowed. "And quite a fortunate mission. An undead male there is in possession of an artifact the Order has been searching for: the Griffon Claw Gauntlet. The aether gem appeared to be corrupted though, so it would no longer be of any use to us. It's probably for the better. Attempting to get it back wouldn't be worth the risk I imagine."

"That must be Kenneth. What does it do?" I questioned.

"Originally, it was meant to negate all spells and incantations on whomever it came in contact with to strip them of their magical defenses. But now I haven't a clue with the gem like that."

"Where's your amulet?" Rafael pointed to Alexandre's belt.

"I... don't know...? I had it when I came here. I'm sure of it."

"Claudius has lost his plenty of times. I once saw Georgie running around with three of them, all Claudius's."

"Speaking of Claudius—Marianna, can I send you to check on him?" I asked. "I can't reach anyone where he's supposed to be. I'll show you where it is on the computer."

"Of course." She bowed.

I sent Marianna on her way and then had to decide whether to stay here until the assault on Set tonight, or return to the abbey. I at least had to let Lyle know that I would be leaving if I did. I was also a bit curious to see the VIPs.

"You guys can wait in my room. I'm going to check on my friend." I searched for Lyle's location on base using PARAGON. He was in the atrium on the floor above, so that's where I headed.

The atrium was dark when I arrived except for the glass elevator in the center that was stopped halfway between floors. Aurelia stood inside giving another speech in French to a large gathering that lined the circular staircase around her. PARAGON translated her every word on its screens along the walls of the atrium. She looked like a piece of jewelry in a display case the way the light shined down on her from above and sparkled off of her amethyst pendant and earrings. I'd much prefer she be a sunken treasure a hundred or so miles beneath the ocean.

I spotted Lyle watching from behind the guardrail above alongside Commander Timmons and Rudgar. Gianluca was on the opposite side of the floor along with Kenneth. There were Archios everywhere that Aurelia must have planted to give an artificial sense of camaraderie between her people and the humans of PROJECT: UNITY. Aside from the Vice President of the United States, the Prime Minister of the United Kingdom, the President of France, and the Chancellor of Germany, there were another two to three dozen faces of importance that I didn't immediately recognize.

I thought back to a time when I had seen the Prime Minister of the UK at a function the Blackbournes were hosting. Funny that I could say I ran in the same social circles as him, even if it was a stretch.

I snuck into the mesmerized crowd to see if I could find Noah. I knew he would be perched high up somewhere, but if he was, there wasn't any sign of him—at least, not until I felt someone grab my rear end. I spun around, but of course he was gone, unless that was the Chancellor of Germany getting frisky with me.

After I had my fill of bullshit I decided I was better off staying at the abbey until tonight. The air was too tense with all the high-powered figures on base and most of it was from one particularly vile woman. The upcoming battle with Set was the first I ever had the luxury of preparing for well in advance and being picky about where I rested the day before. It was a sign that I may have finally crawled out of the bleak day-to-day fight for survival and into loftier affairs that required critical thinking and meticulous planning. Millions—*billions*—of people's lives were on the line, yet I had to sit and wait patiently to make a move so that I didn't charge in and pull a proverbial "nuclear tripwire" that would doom an entire population.

I had finally met an opponent I couldn't smash with reckless abandon until I was victorious and it made me miss those simpler days. Slow and methodical tactics observing the enemy's moves to deduce a counter were not my specialty, nor what my instincts had been retrained to handle. It really was like I was playing chess.

Chapter Thirty-Eight

A long and drawn out round of applause from back in the atrium signaled the end of Aurelia's speech as I typed a message on a terminal in the hall for Lyle to read later that explained I would be going to the abbey until tonight.

"You leaving?" Noah came up behind me as I was about to send the message.

"Yeah, I haven't slept in a while and can't do it with what's going on here."

"Oh."

"Come with me," I offered.

"Can't." He held my hand that was wearing his prayer beads and then let go. "Stay and have your fan club make sure no one bothers you."

I thought on it and then deleted the message to Lyle. "Okay," I agreed.

"Thanks for sending me take out by the way, but I only like to bite you."

"You mean Alexandre? You knew?"

"Of course I did. Do you not know who I am? I figured he was one of yours when I saw the gear so I let him live." Noah hopped up on a guardrail and started to do one-armed handstand push-ups.

"Are you trying to show off?" For someone his size to have that level of agility was nothing short of phenomenal, but it *was* Noah after all.

"Not trying, *doing*. Bet the Italian couldn't do this."

"I've seen better." I rolled my eyes and pushed him off. He zipped back up to me so fast that I bumped into him face first on my way back to the room.

"Let's go back to our room and take a nap."

"Our room? You mean *my* room, and that's exactly where I was going."

"Yeah, *our* room. That's what I said. I'll meet you there in a few." There was always a healthy degree of annoyance that came from his persistence. It could be compared to Gianluca's stubbornness, except the difference was that Noah was doing it on purpose to get a rise out of me while Gianluca did it thinking no one else could know better than him. Knowing the difference made Noah seem more endearing in a comical sense. I never thought Noah could make me laugh as much as he did today, and during such an inappropriate time with the current state of the world.

God, this was a weird, but not unwelcome development.

Marianna was back and ready to report in when I made it to my room in the barracks. "Claudius is safe, as is the Ancient. Claudius had made contact with the Blackbournes and was playing a card game with them that he made up. The Blackbournes have been actively ignoring attempts to communicate because they said it was a bother."

"That sounds like them," I sighed. "What's this card game about?"

"Ah...it's just kid stuff based on the elements. You'd have to ask him."

"Really, Anna? You play with him all the time when it's supposed to be lights out," Rafael said. "Everyone knows you hide your deck in your armory chest."

"I might have humored him once or twice... Anyway, Claudius gave me this to deliver to you, Ascended. It's from the Ancient." Marianna handed over a parchment. It was the same one Vyrlakalos had given me to deliver to Castile, bloodstain and everything.

"It looks like a face," Nathaniel said, looking at the bloodstain over my shoulder.

"Oh yeah, kinda. I thought it was an ink blot test. He seemed to find it amusing when I saw it once before." Castile probably wanted me to visit him to muse over his ramblings, but it would have to wait. I had too much swimming around in my head for one of his cryptic therapy sessions. "Thanks for going. You can all relax and either go back to the abbey or take the spare rooms that are open down the hall until we regroup tonight. I'm going to get some sleep for the first time in days."

The five made the decision to stay with me on base in the spare rooms. I used PARAGON to look up a map of where we'd be fighting Set to see if there was any strategy I could come up with. To the east was Israel, a hundred miles away from the edge of Set's reach now, but still at risk if he decided to whip up another hurricane or terrorize a populated country to empower him with chaos. We could try to block him and hold the line or strike from the west to lure him to us in an area he already destroyed.

The safest option would be for Aurelia to draw the crowd south along the Nile in either scenario, but she'd have to travel quite a distance and fast. She'd only listen to Gianluca—if anyone at all—and he'd never take my advice on this. We would have to make her *want* to go in that direction on her own. Knowing Aurelia, she would only do it if there was a stage with the correct lighting.

That may not be such a bad idea...

"Hey." Noah reappeared with something that smelled great. "I got you slop."

"Why do you have to say it like that?" I laughed as he put down a closed cup of coffee and a PROJECT: UNITY knapsack full of bagels.

"It's all gross slop to me," he shrugged.

"Thanks, but you didn't have to get me every bagel in the place and is this...peanut butter?"

"I don't know. I guess so. It's for the bagels."

"You don't put peanut butter on bagels, you weirdo." I took a sip of the hot coffee without checking under the lid and almost spit it out, but turned so he wouldn't see. "This is black."

"Yeah. I know you like coffee. Is it good?" Normally, I would have loved to deflate his ego only I had never seen him trying so hard and couldn't bring myself to shoot him down.

"Yes. I'll let it cool off a bit though and have it later. I don't want it to keep me up." He had to know that I was lying, but didn't seem to acknowledge it. He was staring at the prayer beads on my wrist, or possibly lost in thought.

"Did you...want these back?" I wasn't sure if he was having doubts on giving up one of his last meaningful possessions.

"No. I like them on you." He went over and threw himself on the bed. "What are you doing with that map?"

"Trying to come up with some plan or at least awareness of the area to know where to strike from."

"Smart."

"Are you being sarcastic?"

"Not this time. Hit him from both sides, but give him an exit route in the most favorable direction. Trapped enemies always fight the hardest, so never let them get their backs against the wall."

"That's from *The Art of War* isn't it?"

"You remembered." One of my first interactions with Noah was his admission of praise for the Sun Tzu stratagems which he later used to teach me.

"How could I forget?"

There was silence and then he glanced over at me from where he was lying flat on his back. "Bring that warm little body over here."

I got a chill when he said that. It was nerves more than excitement. I still did it though and when he held out his hand, I took it. "Don't start this. I told you I need time..."

"I'm not gonna do anything. Just trust me." Then came the most ironic sentence from him as he looked up at me. "I can't believe you're the same person I met those years ago in New York."

"That's...exactly what I've been thinking about you."

"You changed me, or changed me back maybe."

"You've changed *me*," I said.

"Come take a nap."

"There's no room." I laughed again, a bit nervously, but also because he was sprawled out on the bed like a starfish. He budged less than an inch and patted the space next to him for me to take.

I sat down first, feeling relieved that he let me go at my own pace, then lied down and got comfortable next to him with his arm around me. I shut the lights and felt him throw the covers over us. "Glad I got to do this at least once," he said.

I woke up in a stupor, not knowing I had fallen asleep or how long it had been. I didn't think I'd be able to sleep next to Noah, but all those muscles were more comfortable than I would have thought.

"Hey."

"Sorry, I was trying to get up quietly so I wouldn't wake you."

"It's all right. I've been up a few minutes." Noah stretched and put his arms up with his hands behind his head on the pillow. I turned on the lights and fumbled for the clock while my eyes adjusted.

"It's after nine?!" I shouted.

"Yeah, something like that. What's the big deal? You were tired."

"I need to be in Egypt! Why didn't Lyle come get me? We were supposed to meet at sunset."

"Oh, he kept calling on the computer so I shut it." I looked down to see the wires to the terminal cut.

"Why would you do that?!"

"You were tired!" he shouted back. "Why are we yelling?!"

"Because there's a lot at stake! People are counting on me, the *world* is counting on me!" I went to run out the door when Noah grabbed me.

"*You* can't be responsible for the whole world, but to some people...important people, people like me," he grinned, "you are their whole world. Don't do anything stupid because you feel like you need to do more. You did your part. There are others that need to step up and do theirs."

"I'm not going to do anything stupid," I said and tried pulling away from him so I could go to find Lyle.

"Promise me. You have to accept failure if it comes to it and know to walk away."

"You don't think we can win?"

"I don't think this guy is gonna go down easy and I know that everybody thinks they're too special to follow one person's plan. I don't know what I'm gonna be forced to do out there and I don't want you to count on me if I can't control myself."

"I know." I hugged him and he hugged me back while I scanned the room quickly. "That's why you're going to stay here."

"Yeah, right. I'm not—" His body keeled over against me mid-sentence as I called one of his own swords from beside the bed to stake him through the heart from behind.

"You're right. You are important and that's why I can't take the chance. I don't trust that Aurelia wouldn't sacrifice you to save herself out there. I know you'll be pissed when you get up, but I'd rather deal with that than losing you." I placed him back on the bed and put the prayer beads in his hand. "Keep these safe for me until I come back."

I broke the door so no one could wander in and find him after I left and headed to get the Order from their rooms. They jumped up to salute when I entered. Somehow this time it felt more fitting. "It's time. I'm giving you all the option of not coming and I'll understand if you don't." They declined unanimously to sit this out so I brought them to the hangar where I already had a feeling everyone would be.

"Where've you been, man?" Lyle was angry. I could tell he was trying to hold it in. "I kept trying to call since I couldn't break away. We already finished the debriefing and it would've been nice to have you there."

"I'm here now. Where is everyone?" Most of the PROJECT: UNITY troops were there, but Aurelia, Kenneth, Rudgar and Gianluca were absent.

"Timmons took the first squads to the Israeli border to stop any more people from crossing into Egypt. The Israeli government and the armies of some of our guests pledged their aid. Gianluca went to get Kamakura. Hopefully four days don't pass while he's there."

"And Aurelia?"

"She left with Rudgar. They took our second armored transport helicopter that could've fit five squads. We wouldn't have to keep making round trips if we had it, but whatever... I also don't think it's too smart that they're heading out there without much backup."

"She's a big girl, I'm sure she can handle herself. All we need her is for one performance and then if accidents happen, they happen... I was going to suggest setting up some sort of staging area that she could lure the crowds to. We don't want them going east across the Nile to Israel where he could chase us to a large population. South might be best, so we can fight him to the west."

"What, like a concert stage? It's a little short notice for that and she's being tight-lipped about how far her reach extends.

"By the way, where's Noah? I haven't seen him."

"I'm sure he's around. Better to not bother him." I didn't want Lyle involved in that business. "Any chance I can talk you out of not going?"

I contemplated knocking him out and locking him in a closet. Lyle was extremely low priority for anyone like Aurelia to use as a human shield, so as long as he stayed at a reasonable distance he'd be fine.

"Nope. I won't be on the frontlines anyway, man. I'll be with these guys trying to keep some amount of peace escorting people to safety."

"And getting me snacks."

"What about the Knights of the Round back there?" Lyle ignored my snack request and motioned to the Order standing silently behind me. "Are there any more of them?"

"This is all we'll need. I don't want everyone tripping over each other." The real reason was that this was the group I trusted, but I wouldn't say that in front of them. I also didn't want to bring them all with me and leave the young children as orphans if something horrible happened that wiped out the rest in battle. I hated being responsible for people.

"Fine by me. You hitching a ride with us or what?"

"We'll teleport." I turned to check that it was possible and Liam nodded in agreement.

"Here. Take this so we can stay in touch." Lyle handed me an ear bud communicator.

"This is going to get broken before it's any use." I still had the Empyrean Jewel of Light with me because I was too afraid to leave it anywhere and let it fall into the wrong hands. I considered presenting it to Isis, but thought there might be another use for it in the future.

"Just take it so I can let you know when and where we arrive. A lot of it depends on hearing from Rudgar, who's gone rogue now that he's with Aurelia."

I walked up to him and spoke quietly so only he could hear. "Get out if things get too hot. There's no way I'm losing you or anyone else over this. You're no good to the world if you're dead. I'll come and cover you if you need to evacuate or I'll send the Order so I don't drag more danger with me."

"Hope it doesn't come to that, little bro."

Chapter Thirty-Nine

Why do I feel more unprepared now that I have a plan than all the times that I didn't?

"Nathaniel."

"Yes?" Nathaniel crouched beside where I was sitting in the sand. We were only a mile out to the west of Set's domain watching it creep toward us across the sky and land.

"How are you feeling?"

"Excited," his voice came from within his helmet.

"I meant your aether problem, but why are you excited?"

"Oh, I'm sorry. I'm feeling fine. Thank you. I'm just excited to be in your service."

"Yeah...about that." I stood to address him and the other four. "Listen, everybody. I'm not good at giving these speeches, but I'm going to give it my best shot.

"As much as I value what you're capable of, I can't have you in direct combat with Set. I like you guys a lot and I can't be responsible for any harm that may come to you. It's true that this is war, but I'm not one that has ever been comfortable with the idea of calculated risks and losses. We all have something we're good at and it doesn't mean there's any greater glory being on the front lines. I want you to stay with PROJECT: UNITY and do whatever it takes to assist them in saving lives."

The Order was quiet with disappointment, but I'd always rather have disappointment than death. I had sworn back when I lost my parents that I wouldn't be the cause of anyone else's demise.

I sat back down in the sand and continued to wait. "Those are aether crystals, right?" I asked, pointing to more of the obelisks with the shining blue stones on top that Noah and I had broken during our last fight with Set. There were several of the obelisks that had been erected this far out now that Set had claimed the area.

"Yes, large, but poor quality ones made by rapid crystallization," said Rafael. "Set must be using them as a source of stored energy to absorb later."

"He could plan to use them as homing beacons to travel to," Marianna added. "I've seen it done before. It makes it a lot easier to navigate the ley lines in a hurry."

"And breaking them doesn't do anything except return the aether back into the atmosphere?"

"Correct," Alexandre confirmed.

"Can we divert it away from him somehow, like what we did with Isis only in reverse?"

"Not that amount of aether and not very far," he explained. "Ley lines are fairly permanent, unless you're a god that can use them. They are a river of power."

"What if we pollute the river?"

"I...uh." Alexandre and the rest looked like I asked them to commit some atrocity. "That would kill any magic user that tried to tap into it later and throw off the delicate spiritual ecosystem, sending ripples of destruction through the other dimensions."

"How about only booby-trapping the crystals for when he goes for them? After his followers and powers are taken from him he's going to look for the next source of energy to keep up the fight."

"It's extremely dangerous," said Marianna. "None of us are strong enough to make any difference against a being on that level either."

"The blood wraith could," Alexandre suggested. "Is she on our side?"

"Rozalin? She's on her own side, but...that's...not out of the question actually." She would be with Aurelia, but Gianluca could convince her to help and that would keep her away from the humans for when she inevitably betrayed everyone. Aurelia also wouldn't want her spotlight ruined by her sister. The problem would be dealing with Gianluca.

"A spirit," Alexandre indicated the tiny sparrow flying overhead toward the pyramids before it disappeared.

"Isis," I said. "I hope that's an omen of good luck."

An hour passed until I heard from Lyle that he and his team were gathered to the south of Set's perimeter. "Rudgar's a good ten miles north of us," he said over my earpiece. "Aurelia shared your idea of bringing the crowd south so we're off to a solid start." Normally, I wouldn't consider an idea that Aurelia and I shared to be a positive thing, but under the circumstances I'd take what I could get. "Still no sign of Big G and the dragon though."

The celestial night sky began to grow dark after ten minutes had passed. "He's here," Lyle informed me. I was hurt that Gianluca didn't come to me, but I was more concerned that I could see the darkness of his from this distance.

"Take us south," I told the Order and after a quick skate across the ley lines we were at the rendezvous point. The PROJECT: UNITY jets were arranged in a semicircle around Aurelia with the helicopter in the rear.

Gianluca had fashioned himself an updated version of his armor, or maybe it was a throwback. His helmet and some of the styling of the torso were now closer to those typically seen on the armor of a Roman soldier than on a knight.

Rudgar was the first to approach me. "Our Lady has requested you to be front and center to intercept any opposition expected from this, since one of her guardians seems to be indisposed."

"*Your* Lady can kiss my ass."

"I am enough." Gianluca came over at the sound of my retort.

"Gianni, I need to talk with you before we start," I said to him with my back turned to Rudgar. I was glad that if there were any bad feelings between us they didn't show when he walked with me away from the rest and removed his helmet. "Those towers Set has with the blue rocks on top can be, um, sabotaged by powerful magic to weaken him. Only Rozalin would be strong enough to do this, so maybe you can talk to her."

"I see. And...this is all you have to say?"

"Yes...?" His new Roman helmet came from the shadows around his head and he started to leave. It was spooky that I couldn't see him through the holes in it, like with Nathaniel's mask, only Gianni's had smoky shadows that spilled out from within.

"Why the new look?" I asked.

"Tonight I return the glory to Roma. Tomorrow there is a new Roma."

Shit.

If there was one thing I never wanted to do, it was fight Gianni over his vision for the world.

"Can we talk about this?" I called after him.

"We talk enough."

"Gianni—" I wanted to stop him, but he kept on walking to start a discussion with Aurelia.

"Are you all right?" Nathaniel came over separate from the Order.

"Yes, just... pre-game jitters." My face probably told another story. "Thanks for asking."

"Do you want me to stay with you during the battle?" he asked and took off his helmet. "You said we're all good at something, but the only thing I'm good at is standing in the way so important people don't get hurt."

I wanted to tell him to stop being depressing. "The innocent people in the crowd are important. Everyone is important, including you, and everyone has their own story that deserves to be told."

"Are they really that innocent if they came here under their own free will to pray for the death and destruction of others?"

Lyle came running up suited with all the gear and guns he could wear. "Showtime! Come on!"

"Just listen to what your heart tells you and do what feels right," I shared with Nathaniel on my way back to the staging area, which was probably the most clichéd piece of advice to ever slip out of my mouth. I was surprised to see Empress Kamakura and her four guardian spirits come down from the sky as balls of light and then appear in their human form. They spoke with Gianluca briefly and then left the same as they arrived. I was anticipating that she would show up as the dragon once the fighting was underway.

A perfectly timed breeze swept Aurelia's hair back to mark the beginning of her coup. I thought she would be leading her flock like the Pied Piper, but it was now apparent she had no interest in moving a step in any direction, nor did she have any need. Her hazel eyes emitted a faint luminescence as she gazed into the distance toward her targets to call them to her.

"Beneath us!" came a shout from the troops, and then everything descended into madness. The earth burst into geysers of sand and the ground split open, swallowing people and vehicles into the depths below.

I was able to rescue everyone by lifting them to safety along with most of the aircraft. Aurelia and Kenneth saved themselves by vanishing from the area, only to reappear a moment later on top of a high dune to watch the battle. I looked frantically for Lyle and shouted his name over the roar of the quaking sands until Liam got my attention to show me he was safe.

"You have to get out of here *now!*" I told Lyle.

"We need to get around this to the people while they're clear!" he replied. The troops scrambled to regroup under Lyle's command. I closed the pit, but not soon enough. Set flew upward from between the cracks with staff and sword in hand.

"The humans have made their choice and they have chosen wisely," his voice boomed with snarls and growls in our heads. "Who are you fighting for but yourselves? Heroes you are not. Selfish dogmas of the impure and independent crusades for fame and glory are what brought this world to its knees.

"There will be no more men who walk as gods or false idols to take what should be mine! I will not grant you the mercy of stone's cold, unfeeling embrace this time. Your suffering will quench my land's thirst for vengeance after ages of ruin."

Gianluca unleashed a fearsome war cry and tackled Set out of the air and through a portal of shadow. Off to the east where they reemerged the sky began to rain fire that cut through the darkness and torched the desert. I flew after them to help keep the battle away from the humans. It looked like Gianluca was already reclaiming the shadows from Set, but Set wasn't giving up without a fight.

Set raised his staff to attack as the darkness was drawn from his body. The white tiger spirit leaped from a gust of wind and smacked Set away with its giant paw before he could use the staff. The other three guardian spirits appeared and pursued Set with the same ferocity they showed against the demons in Yomi.

I called broken parts of one of the jets that had been damaged by the eruptions of sand to me so I could use them to bind Set. We were making one mistake—surrounding him so he had no way to escape. At the moment he was too busy being juggled between the four spirits and Gianluca, but at first opportunity I feared he would retaliate tenfold.

Gianluca was more relentless than any of the spirits in his pursuit of Set. He had run Set through with his sword and grabbed him by the throat as the darkness within roiled from his mouth and into Gianluca's armor. Set's sword did little but clang against the dark forged suit, but the staff was the real problem. I couldn't navigate the swirling bits of metal through the air fast enough to bind Set with how they kept tumbling through the desert beneath the firestorm.

Set let loose a blinding flash from the staff. I panicked, thinking we were all about to become stone, but it was only light. Supernatural light. A supernatural light of such intensity that Gianluca's shadow armor was driven back to the realm from where it came. He was left exposed long enough for Set to pierce his side with the previously useless sword that now plunged through his abdomen.

Gianluca didn't have any supernatural healing ability like the undead or I did. Once damage was inflicted it meant the same for him as it did any mortal human, sometimes worse being that it was near impossible to suture an injury with skin as tough as his. Gianluca's one and only method of survival was his godly defenses. But it seemed that all it took was a godly blade to penetrate them when stripped of his armor.

Gianluca flinched, but didn't back down as his blood poured out onto the sand. He reformed his armor and slugged Set in the face with such force that Set's body created a shallow crater when he hit the ground. I flew to Gianluca with my chunks of scrap metal orbiting me to block the rain of fire from above. As the spirits chased Set, Gianluca rested on the hilt of his sword, clearly in terrible pain from the wound under his armor.

"Gianni, are you all right?" I asked and tried to comfort him, but he refused my help. "Let me take you somewhere safe so PROJECT: UNITY or the Order can take you out of here."

"This is not bad. I live." He refused another attempt I made at putting his arm over my shoulder to help him up.

"Let me at least see. I can bandage it with my shirt."

"No. The shadow does it for me. I take almost all the dark back from Set. When I finish then we can have a victory." He stood and held his side. From what I had seen, Set had to have pierced at least one vital organ. "I will show him a true darkness."

Gianluca sank down into his shadow that kept growing across the sand until everywhere they eye could see was covered in blackness. The sky darkened again and snuffed out the firestorm. Though the desert was transformed into a version of the Nether where all was dark, objects could still be seen. I had no idea what that meant for humans, who couldn't survive in the real Nether.

Massive tentacles of biblical proportions rose from the abyss and descended from the sky, causing violent earthquakes as they smashed into Set. The divine light from his staff blasted the shadow constructs away with ease, but more kept coming until he was overwhelmed. They bound and crushed him, yet he wouldn't break and neither would his grip on the staff.

The spirits and I tried to assist. Set took his chance and transformed into the cyclone of sand I had dealt with before, but faster than I could react to stop it. All four guardian spirits were defeated in an instant by the cutting gale and although my clothes only sustained minor tears at worst, the shrapnel orbiting me as well as the unprotected parts of my body were shredded down to nothing. The pain was fleeting and not as bad as it could have been due to how fast the nerves were severed. The brief period of regeneration was more agonizing than the damage itself.

When my senses were restored, Gianluca was back in person and engaged in combat with Set again. He created a shield from the shadows this time to use in conjunction with his sword. Empress Kamakura also appeared in her human form— a much smaller target than the dragon—and drained her elemental powers from him to throw right back. The lightning strikes conjured from her finger punched a hole through Set's shoulder, leaving a red-hot smoldering wound in its place.

Set dropped the staff.

I called it to me, but before it was in my grasp Kenneth jumped in and grabbed it out of mid-air. All hell broke loose once more as the staff kept exchanging hands. Set turned back into a whirlwind of sand and sliced into Kenneth, retrieving the staff when he flinched. Kenneth's resilience was still astounding. The razor winds did little but scratch his skin to draw blood and cut pieces of his armor that regenerated along with him. It was demon leather armor, as I had thought when I first saw him.

Empress Kamakura summoned a pillar of water to douse Set and throw him from his cyclone, then zapped him with lightning from above and immolated him in a ball of brilliant flames. I crushed him with all the force I could muster and felt his body snap like dry twigs.

Gianluca went to stab his sword down into the mangled remains of Set, the fallen God of Chaos, but the body disintegrated into a series of flickering lights that floated upward and disappeared.

I thought it was over, but I was wrong.

Set reappeared without a nick of damage where he had fallen and that's when the battlefield became even more crowded. Rozalin came forth from the amethyst pendant of Aurelia's that Kenneth was holding, hurling crackling bolts of black lightning only roughly aimed at Set until Gianluca shouted at her in Latin, presumably to be careful. She might have the power to sabotage the obelisks around the desert, but I also hoped that Set would do away with her and her sister for good. I would rather deal with the repercussions of their souls getting into the hands of the Infernal Kings than have the sisters torment us anymore.

The staff continued to swap hands until I lost count of how many times it had been passed.

"This will only end in your failure," Set bellowed with the staff back in his possession. "I am a *god!* None of you are able to destroy me, but with the exception of the goddess who I have already defeated once, you can all be destroyed! The people of the New World have spoken and pray to *me* as their ruler."

"Their prayers are in fear of you," said Kamakura. "Fear does not last forever. Once shown your weakness they will have naught to fear and you will starve."

"All there is to fear is death itself. Chaos has no precedence over the absolute order of its sweet embrace!" Rozalin released a stream of dark lightning that chained from one obelisk to the next forming a ring around us. As Set tried to draw power from it to continue the fight his body grew brittle. She let out a high-pitched banshee's wail that shook the ground and sky and shattered pieces of Set's body. I lost my hearing from the sound and felt my head about to explode. Empress Kamakura and Kenneth were both forced to retreat a significant distance to avoid sustaining fatal damage.

Set's skull and ribs were partially exposed from the sonic scream that blew off his crumbling countenance. He raised his staff to the sky and called down a beam of intense light that purged Rozalin from this world and all the darkness summoned by Gianluca up to now, returning the sky to the celestial vision of his wishes. Kenneth was burned down to his skeleton in places by the searing beam and left the arena before he could be vanquished for good.

There was no stopping Set. Not this way. The three of us that remained would eventually be worn down as he said.

"We've got trouble!" Lyle shouted to me over the earpiece. I thought it had been broken during one of the attacks, but must have been far enough in to be protected by my hood. "The people we're trying to help are attacking us!" I heard him shouting and the sounds of gunfire when the transmission cut out.

If Set's main source of power now was the people, then he wouldn't put them at risk. I had to get to Lyle and let Set chase me. Once there, Set wouldn't dare do anything that would kill them and I could use that to bargain a stalemate...for now.

I grabbed the staff from Set with enough rage that it tore half of his now-vulnerable body off with it. Gianluca swung his sword through Set's torso as it was pulled forward and cleaved him in another two pieces. I sped through the air toward the blood moon over the pyramids where Lyle and the others would be. Set was already back and in better shape now that he had left the ring of corrupted aether crystals.

"He is a manifestation of the faith his followers have in him," Kamakura's voice projected into my head. "It is no lie that he cannot be defeated in his realm. But erase all symbols of that faith and he will cease to be."

Storm clouds circled above as we all raced across the desert to where this waking nightmare had begun. Gianluca and I clashed with Set at points but never stopped moving forward. I could see the crowd ahead and it was larger than anything I could have ever imagined. An ocean of millions of people packed together shoulder to shoulder were rioting amongst each other with gunfire and torches. Men, women, and children all moshed together in uncontrollable mayhem.

These were not locals; they had perished as a display of power at the hands of Set prior. These people came from all over the globe to vent their fears and anger in the most violent ways they were capable of. And somewhere in the mix, my friends were trying in vain to make a difference.

"I just saw you overhead!" Lyle shouted in my ear. I was able to breathe a bit easier knowing he was at least alive. "This has to end and fast! People are killing each other down here and we've got injuries on our team!"

Where was Aurelia? Rozalin and Kenneth had joined in but she remained noticeably absent.

We were almost at the pyramids when the storm clouds broke and the head of Empress Kamakura's dragon form peaked through. Her titanic serpentine body coiled through the air and with a lash of her tail she struck down one of the three bigger pyramids, reducing it to rubble and sending tons of rock showering across the sands.

Set had reached the apex of his anger upon seeing the crown jewel of his empire struck down in a single blow. I blasted him to pieces when he grappled with me for the staff, but he got the drop on me when he returned. He drove his sword through my chest and managed to reclaim his prized possession from my grip. Gianluca leaped onto Set from the shadows and pulled him away from me, but was getting weak from the wound he had sustained earlier.

Then in a flash of light, Gianluca was turned to stone and fell into the riot below.

"Gianni!" I cried out and wanted to go for him, but there was nothing I could do and knew my priority had to be the staff. Isis could restore him after. At least now he wouldn't suffer from his injury.

"I had smote greater serpents than you in my youth!" Set roared at Kamakura as the dragon melted another pyramid into slag under her molten breath. He pointed his staff at her, but I intercepted and blew him apart. The staff went flying, and he got the drop on me again when I went for it. This time his sword struck through the back of my skull.

Everything went red and then black. I was dazed and momentarily paralyzed. When I came to in the clearing that the people created around us, Set and I were not alone.

Even though he did not stand a chance against Set, Nathaniel had come to my aid and was struggling to hold the God of Chaos back from using the staff on me until I could heal. Set stabbed his sword right through Nathaniel's midsection and twisted it before shoving him to the ground. The rioters swarmed Nathaniel, kicking and beating him to please their god.

"NO!" I screamed. "GET AWAY FROM HIM!" I lost control for a split second and wasn't thinking when I threw away everyone around us like ants. I ripped Set apart once more and snatched the staff away as Kamakura demolished another pyramid in the background.

"Nathaniel!" I crouched down next to him and removed his helmet. "Why did you do that?!" He was still moving. I yelled for the Order to come and heal him, but it was impossible to hear any one voice in the crowd. When Set came back this time I caught him before he ambushed me and dragged him away from Nathaniel.

Set had gotten wise enough to turn to sand before I could obliterate him, making this all the more infuriating. We both had our hands on the staff and just as he was about to use it to turn me to stone, Nathaniel grabbed him in a chokehold with the last of his strength. "Nathaniel, no!" I shouted.

"Go, Dorian! Get out of here!" he shouted back.

Set turned to sand and reappeared behind Nathaniel, his sword through the young knight's heart. Nathaniel bled out instantly. The sight of his lifeless body in a pool of his own blood brought tears to my eyes that I couldn't stop.

"I will kill every single person here until I erase you from even the most obscure memory on Earth!" I shouted at Set through the tears. Angry tears. Vengeful tears. Tears of *rage* and dark thoughts.

"You have not what it takes to see through such threats," Set sneered. "Barely could you handle witnessing the death of *one* worthless human. To compare you to young Horus may have been a gross overestimate. Perhaps because his power was always in his mother, a luxury you are lacking—"

"You killed a friend of mine. Your followers mean *nothing* to me." I lifted one of the men from the crowd that had a knife to Nathaniel's throat and was about to claim a trophy for Set. "You are nothing but a pawn to the ones who dreamt of having me at their side! It has been by *choice* that

I've shown this world any mercy at all and now I HAVE CHANGED MY MIND!"

Set's follower popped like a bloated tick in my grasp and showered the crowd with blood. "I WAS *MADE* FOR PURPOSES GREATER THAN YOU! I AM DESTRUCTION INCARNATE!"

Chapter Forty

"You know not what you do, petty fool. These souls—all of my followers—are promised to Hell upon death. *That* was the deal; the throne of my empire returned to me with the souls of my followers repaying the debt one at a time upon their death. Do you not see your error? The Kings of Hell will never let me fall. I am their Reaper of Souls, the Chaosbringer Reborn."

Set was rattled. He couldn't stop me without his trump card and I just showed that I had no issue murdering those he needed to exist. The ebony frame of the anthropomorphic God of Chaos wasn't as imposing anymore as I floated there looking down my nose at him.

"The Kings will rise," I said. "It's inevitable, or so I keep hearing. Why should I care about trying to prevent it then? I'll let them have these souls.

Either way, you'll be gone and all I'll have to deal with is them."

I disintegrated him in one blow and waited for him to return to continue.

"Did you really think they would keep you around once they rose? They call themselves *kings* for a reason and you are not one of them. You are no king. You're here to serve a purpose, one I was meant for and chose not to fulfill. Now I've changed my mind thanks to you, and with that, you made yourself meaningless."

He attempted an ambush, but I erased every particle of sand he transformed into and waited once more for him to reappear before going on.

"You were a backup plan; the best of a bad situation. I don't need *prayers* or temples. I don't tire and there isn't anywhere I can't go." I levitated a group out of the crowd I had seen taking part in the violence, some of whom had beaten on Nathaniel when he was down. I directed my question toward them and spoke with authority. "Do you truly want to serve a god knowing your fate with him ends in Hell?"

The group cheered Set's name, but he didn't look too happy about it as his eyes darted between their faces. "Then let's cut to the chase." I closed my fist and with another shower of blood, ended their story on Earth so they could start their next one in Hell.

These people weren't from one ethnic background or a particular class level. They were businessmen, clergy, gardeners, and more coming from countries at all levels of economic and social development to spew their hatred and wait for Set to answer.

I could hear it now that I was in control and could pay attention; across the crowd, the shouts you'd never hear in public, rarely if you did: racist chants, ethnic slurs, homophobic remarks. Nathaniel was right. They weren't so innocent if they came here of their own free will with these intentions.

My time in Hell in the depths of Lord Ma'al's lair had shown me some of his "finest" acolytes that fit the same variety of descriptions to perfection. They were the people with the smiling faces on the street or in the stores we shop that hold the darkest secrets in their shadows. All it took was the opportunity to wish misery on the targets of their hatred and they were thrown into fits of excitement at the promise like a pack of wild dogs fighting over fresh meat.

"What do you want?" Set snarled. "The world is changed forever. There is no going back."

"I know," I agreed. "I came here wanting peace, but now I want your empire. Once the good empress is done trampling the land for me so I'll have a clean slate to work with." Kamakura was still wreaking havoc on the few structures that remained in the cluster of pyramids.

"Do you feel yourself getting weaker? I can speed it up if you want." I snapped my fingers and another group of the crowd exploded, hitting Set with their entrails. "It's so much easier this way. They will fear *me* now and there is nothing you can do to save them."

I had shown him the monster I was made to be and was now a formidable rival with no limits, not a righteous hero bound by morals.

"No more!" he demanded. "If you wish your ally back from stone I need the staff. You are not from here. We can divide the world in three for you, I, and the serpent goddess."

"I don't need you to break the spell."

"My sister cannot help should you banish all knowledge of us."

"Then I guess I'll have a new statue to decorate my new empire," I said. "Leave now and I'll spare you any further indignity. Stay, and I'll make you even more of a mockery in the company of your followers before sending them all to their final reward."

Set growled and without a verbal answer he faded from sight. I made sure he was gone for real first and then flew down to Liam and the rest that were around Nathaniel's body. The crowd had begun to disperse rapidly after the second group of people I killed when they saw Set wasn't going to save them.

"Time to go," I told the Order. "Is there anything you can do for him?"

"No," Liam said, more somber than usual. "He's gone."

"We have to get Gianluca and round up the others, then meet back at the abbey. Take Nathaniel first, then come back for Gianluca and get me last while I help PROJECT: UNITY evac." The Order did as I said. Lyle wasn't hard to find as he was the only one running toward me and not away.

I knew a long lecture filled with yelling for how I handled that was coming.

"You did it," was all he said as he stared at the staff. He looked awful, physically and emotionally.

"We lost Nathaniel though..." I had been trying not to let it get to me and show weakness, but now all I wanted was to cry. I had to hold it in until we were away from here.

"I'm sorry, man. We just...I...I saw people dying right in front of me and I couldn't do anything. Fights were breaking out. I shot someone in the leg to save another person and then that person started beating on the one I shot.

"It wasn't like the other times. They weren't possessed or being controlled. It was like they were aware and just didn't give a shit. Like this was some big playground without anyone monitoring. But we're supposed to be the law, we're supposed to keep order and make sure people are safe...I couldn't do *anything*."

"But you need to do something right now," I said. "You're still in charge and you need to get your people out of here." I decided to make it easier on him by picking up every member of the team I spotted and deposited them next to him.

"All of our jets except one were busted between the mob and the earthquake."

"I'll get more of the Order to come and teleport you guys. Then, I think I should go with them...for Nathaniel." I took out the necklace with his father's ring to make sure it was still safe. I also checked the Empyrean Jewel. These clothes were amazing—if only I had more to cover my hands and face.

With Set defeated for now and abandoning the ruins of his land, Empress Kamakura returned to Yomi. "Three thousand year old architecture crushed into pebbles overnight," I mumbled to myself. It didn't feel real.

Reinforcements from the Order arrived to evacuate Lyle and his troops to their base. I promised Lyle I would come see him tomorrow, but I had also promised Nathaniel I would help him clear his name too. I had promised myself no one else would ever die because of me again.

"Liam, do me a favor." I floated him up to me while I supervised the evacuation. "Go to my room on base and get Noah for me. Bring him back to my room in the abbey as he is."

When all was finished I was in the abbey again, staff in hand, Noah staked on my bed, and Gianluca frozen in stone beside it. Liam and the rest I had brought with me were exhausted from the drain of traveling such long distances more than the actual melee in the sands.

"I assume you have some custom to honor the passing of one of your own?" I asked.

"We lay them out for the day to say our farewells and then cremate and return them to our ancestors in the Earth through the soil of the garden courtyard," Rafael explained. "Unless there's something...you do?"

"I can't bring him back." Noah's poisoned blood couldn't turn him either.

"We were victorious all thanks to your strength though, so that's a positive," said Marianna.

"This wasn't a victory and I wasn't the only reason we had any sort of progress," I said. "I don't consider it a victory if we lose any of our own."

"You're right..."

"I can mend your clothes for you," Liam offered. I didn't know if he was trying to change the subject to elevate the mood or just that socially awkward.

"Later. Go rest. You guys did well. I need to take care of things here and clear my head. You can call Claudius and Anatole back to say their goodbyes too."

I was left to deal with the angry tiger in my bed.

I removed the blade from Noah's back and as I thought he bit down hard into my neck. It wasn't a pleasant bite. He took what he needed to heal and backed off, nostrils flared and squinted eyes: his usual warning signs.

"I had to," I defended my decision. I stood by what I did more than ever. He cracked the stone wall with a punch, and then another. "I didn't want to lose you. I *couldn't.*"

I almost started to cry as I let it all out. "It all went wrong. We lost one of the good ones and I couldn't handle it...I said I'd never let that happen again and when it did I just lost it. I don't know what I would've done if it had been you or Lyle."

"Why do you think I'm pissed?" he asked. "Because you *had* to, because I *couldn't* be there for you, because I'M SOMEBODY'S SLAVE!" He punched the wall twice more. "You did what I would've done and I'm pissed that's how it had to be. I knew it was coming and I let you stake me because there wasn't another way."

We were quiet as he paced the room until he calmed down and spoke again. "I'm glad you came back safe."

We hugged and it was the most welcomed and needed expression of comfort in years. "We didn't all come back though."

"You did everything you could."

"How do you know?" I asked. "You weren't there."

"I didn't need to be. I know you. You fought yourself down to the bone and kept running into the fire no matter how bad it hurt until there was nothing left for anybody to do. I *know* you."

"I don't know myself, or maybe I do and that's what has me so much more upset. I've seen so much death, but seeing someone die right in front of me that I liked and felt responsible for... it brought out this dark personality. I wanted to say it was an act to seem tough, but it really wasn't."

Noah picked me up in his usual crass manner and dove onto the bed with me. "Go on."

"I've felt that anger before. It wasn't a burning sense of conviction. It was cold and unfeeling. Something was switched *off*, not on, inside me. When we escaped Lord Ma'al's lair and I saved that village from the terrorists I was motivated with positive feelings by the good and innocent when I rebuilt their homes. Today I justified murdering unarmed people because I didn't like them and their opinions. They weren't innocent, but it scared me how much I just didn't care during the act of killing them. I made Set back off by outdoing him, not in numbers but in intent."

"You don't need a sword or a gun to be armed. The mind is a dangerous thing," he said and poked my forehead.

"They weren't supernatural."

"That's not what I'm saying. It's those people that create the demons and the evil gods by their thoughts and actions. They're having others do their dirty work even though they're on the bottom of the food chain. It all comes back around." Noah put the prayer beads back on my wrist that I had given him to hold on to.

"My fear of becoming the monster that *I* was created to be is back."

"So you killed a bunch of people that had it coming. You saved another billion that would've been at their mercy if they had their way. You did the right thing, like you always do."

"It wasn't so easy to tell this time. I've learned as much from my enemies as I have from my friends."

"Learning is good. We're all playing one big game and you have to change as it changes. That's why I'm always interested in knowing people's true colors to see where they really stand." That reminded me to meet with Castile. I hoped that by neglecting to see him before the battle I didn't give up something that could've helped the outcome. "Now can we get this statue of your ex out of our room? It kinda ruins the mood."

I raised an eyebrow at him. "You need a time out."

"You can't cage this beast," he said and flexed his biceps with a grin.

"Go to bed, beast. The sun is coming up." I got up and pulled the heavy curtains closed.

"You joining me? Go throw that statue in the ocean and let's do more of that cuddling stuff."

"Noah."

"I'm kidding…about the first part. Sort of."

"I'm going to try and summon Isis outside so I can give her the staff." Her remaining temples were no doubt being watched by our enemies waiting for me to come. I lifted Gianni and headed out. "Oh, and take off your boots in bed."

"*Suneate*, not boots. I never take them off when I sleep in case I need to get up fast in an ambush. Same reason I always leave a blade under my pillow. I taught you that."

"Yeah, but I don't want you getting my sheets dirty."

"*Our* sheets!" he yelled back after I closed the door. I don't know how he did it, but once again that big idiot was able to make me feel better in the worst situation so that I could keep on going until the next.

Chapter Forty-One

Down by the grotto I erected a statue of Isis from the sand and rock as close to her true form as I could and placed the staff in her hands. The response was immediate. The goddess sprung to life and brushed off the debris coating her.

"You are victorious, Young One, and in only a single decisive battle."

"You could say that... There were losses of assorted types on both sides."

Without asking she released Gianluca from the stone. He was still swinging his sword and I had to get in his way to stop him and let him know it was over.

"What is this?" he asked. "How? Who is this?"

"This is Isis, Set's sister, and the one who broke his spell on you the first time," I explained.

He removed his helmet, dissolved his weapons and kneeled to her in thanks. When stood he reached for his side where he had been stabbed and dissipated the armor, but the wound had also been healed.

"My thanks for all you do for me," he said to Isis. "I am Gianluca Belisardi, a soldier."

"You are a humble man, Dark One," said Isis. "We had spoken before when I tried to request your help."

"This is the voice? You are this woman?" he asked.

"Yes, Gianni. Only you became so interested in conquering the area that Isis couldn't reach out to you anymore so she came to me. I would have told you the *last* time we saved you, but any time we try to talk…"

"I make a mistake." He gave me a remorseful look. "How do we stop this evil in the desert? Tell me."

"The Young One has been quite clever. As myself and my son had learned, Set cannot ever truly defeated by force. War is chaos and he is the embodiment of that result. But Set is prideful and has been shamed by the Young One's cunning display of dominance. Set did not expect one of the other side to take such actions and it has bought us time until he considers striking again."

"What action?" Gianluca asked. "What did my little—what did Dorian do?"

"I killed some of his followers and Empress Kamakura destroyed his home in the pyramids...sorry about that by the way," I apologized to Isis.

"It is only stone," she replied. "The tombs were not meant to endure war of this nature and not meant as places of direct worship to him. It was sacrilege against his own people to claim them for his purpose."

"You kill the people in the desert we try to save?" Gianluca wasn't happy. "I kill the bad soldier and you are angry with me. Why is this better? Explain."

"I did it to *stop* the energy that was fueling Set and scare him, and the other humans off that were praying to him. They wanted him to commit evil and make others suffer. You just wanted to conquer the whole Middle East for the glory of Rome."

"It would bring peace."

"You would also ruin the home of good deities like Isis. Would you also conquer Asia where Kamakura lives?"

"No. I do not hurt my ally and you know this. I do not know of Isis until now."

"Because you wouldn't *listen*!"

"My head is clear now and I listen!" he shouted back, but I had heard him say that at least twice before and was done believing it. "I am only a soldier. War is how I know to fix these problem. Why do you save me if you do not like this?"

"I *care* about you, that's why! But you never want to admit you made mistakes and kept treating me like I was blind to everything and you knew better. I don't know how many times I have to prove it to you. You refused to let us be equals and that's *not* what I wanted from a relationship."

"The Roman way work once to tame the sands and make it better. This is why I try again."

"Our land was tame and prosperous before the Romans invaded and pillaged our great temples," Isis declared. "You did drive out most of my fellow pantheon and although I endured, the Roman people only replaced one evil with another."

This was going nowhere good fast. I had to get us back on track before *another* rivalry started. "Where do we stand with Set, Isis?"

"He is weakened and humiliated from battle, but not enough to drive him to quiescence. His followers have scattered thanks to your well-played strategy. While most will not return, the mere belief in him has spread worldwide and will keep him active until a future dark age that drives the gods to slumber."

"We can never get rid of him then?" I questioned. "Not until *everyone* in the world stops believing he's real? Even if they aren't openly praying?"

"You are correct, Young One. The next age of the gods has begun."

Well shit…Now my immortality will be spent locked in a constant stalemate until the Infernal Kings decide to end everyone. "Does that mean you and Empress Kamakura are here to stay too?"

"I have not been made known to the people yet, but soon I may be. The dragon goddess has already begun to draw a following after her appearance. I can hear those in the East speak of her in elated whispers."

"What about the staff? Can you use it to banish Set for good?" I asked.

"The staff has lost a great deal of its power due to misuse in my brother's hands. It was meant only for those whom speak the true name of Ra, one he does not know. It may have enough left to seal the breach between our worlds in Egypt, but it will not stop him from returning when he desires.

"He grew mad with the promise of power from the Kings of Hell and what he stole from the dragon and you, Dark One. With that lost to him now we will surely have a moment of respite as he licks the wounds to his ego."

"Then we prepare," said Gianluca. "I will conquer no land that is claim by our ally. I promise this. But I still make Roma great again to protect the people. I have Aurelia talk to the human leaders. This is okay?"

"Aurelia was useless with the humans in the desert, although I guess she would have had to enslave them for the rest of their lives so they wouldn't return to worshiping him...Do whatever you want, just don't wake up any *more* gods we'll have to deal with. If you want to go stand in the middle of the Colosseum and wave a flag then knock yourself out."

"Why me? Is the enemy I knock out," he smiled.

"Cute, but not what I meant and you know it."

"Yes." He turned and bowed to Isis, excited to leave at the prospect of possibly seeing the empire of his past returned to him. I still sympathized with him when I remembered how he had been displaced from his time period, unlike the other immortals I knew that at least were able to watch the world progress.

"I wish you good fortune on your journey," Isis bid him farewell.

He kissed my hand and looked me in the eyes to say goodbye. "Thank you, all these time you save me. I make no mistake again. Then maybe when you see my Roma you come back to me."

Gianluca left through the shadows. The feelings for him were all still there. I would always have a weakness for him, but the mountain of evidence to stick with my better judgment kept growing.

"Isis, you healed his wound and restored him from stone, I read that you had brought your husband Osiris back to life. Can you bring back someone who was killed by Set while trying to help me?"

"There is no sure answer that I can give. True resurrection is a curious thing. The soul must not be claimed by a higher power and must also desire to return to its earthly vessel."

As odd as it was to say, I guessed that I was the closest thing to being Nathaniel's "higher power".

"I imagine he'd want to come back," I said. "I don't know anyone who wouldn't. I promised to help him clear his name so he has unfinished business."

"There is but one more matter to address. The soul must be bound by a deep connection to the one returning it to life. For this reason, even the highest beings do not often resurrect their followers whenever they fall. Many pray for the wrong reasons, even the devout, and they never know a deep spiritual connection. For this, some gods may return those souls to the cycle to be reborn anew in a different vessel so they may try again. Others may keep their followers' souls in the Underworld to draw out what prayers they can from them there, but when body and soul are not connected there is no mind and they risk going numb and becoming faithless."

That must be what Kamakura does in Yomi, I thought. I had always noticed that the souls of the dead there wandered aimlessly about the village and carried on like machines that didn't know their time was over. That's got to be why I've seen the fire spirit sing to them in the past. They were being roused into worship to keep Kamakura awake so she could protect them from demons.

"I guess it won't work then," I sighed. "I don't really know him. I wanted to though. I could tell there was a rare goodness in him and he only proved that more by sacrificing himself for me."

"There is another way, one to benefit you both. As your chosen disciple he would share a fraction of your strength for as long as you exist."

"Is that like an avatar or champion?"

"Yes—an extension of you. It would be wise to choose a mortal that represents your strengths and virtues to serve you. The Ennead would choose one mortal to serve us all and rule our followers in Egypt as pharaoh. We imparted these pharaohs with the wisdom to guide our faith and construct such wonders as the pyramids, sphinx, and temples."

"Can I still do it if I'm not a spirit that relies on faith?"

"You can and I will show you how, but you must be absolutely sure in your decision. It requires you to grant the one of your choosing a fragment of your soul to fuse with theirs. This process is permanent and may only be done once unless the fragment is returned to you upon his death. The recipient gains a portion of the might of the god they serve. You must be sure they are prepared to handle such power. The Ennead only granted divine wisdom to the pharaohs, but as a Soulborn you will not be able to choose what is passed on."

"What would this do to me if I'm missing a fragment of my soul? I'm guessing it would make me weaker."

"No, it will not be missing. Your soul—as long as it remains healthy—will still provide you the same strength at a distance. To you, the fragment is so small you will notice its absence no more than a fingernail."

"You looked into my soul to know everything about me when you put it back together. Is there any way we can do the same with the man that died to be sure I want to do this?" I would have liked to do this with Lyle to resolve the issue of his mortality, but he'd never go for it.

"Go to him and I will follow to show you what there is to see. Know that the shared bond between deity and disciple is a unique one unknown to man. Emotions and thoughts trickle between both souls and when apart, they will yearn to be reunited because of the piece of yourself given to the other. It is not romantic, platonic, or familial, but all and none of these at once."

I didn't know what to make of all that. I already had enough problems with my emotions getting in the way. I appreciated the crash course in godhood I was getting, but it still felt like I was "playing" at being a god and not actually one.

The courtyard where Nathaniel was laid out was empty when I flew down into it. He was still in his armor and had his helmet back on, which I removed. Someone had cleaned up the blood, but it seemed lazy and haphazard to me for an Order so rooted in culture and tradition that they didn't take an extra step to prepare the body in any extra way, even if he was to be cremated.

Marianna walked in with her head down. "Oh! I'm sorry. I didn't think anyone would be here..." she said when she saw me.

"Why?" I asked. "Everyone couldn't have said their goodbyes already."

"No. I'm sure they'll come later..."

"What are they doing?" I was starting to get angry again, but would give them the benefit of the doubt if there was some sacred ritual to be performed in private.

"Training...and...the usual." She put her head back down. It wasn't like her to be so timid.

"Are you kidding me?" I raised my voice. "One of your own dies and nobody cares enough to pay their respects in *any* way? Was he really that shunned?"

"I care...I think they're just shocked because he was always such a fixture here."

"I think you're lying."

"No, well, not lying, but...I heard my aunt talking with the rest of the council. They're planning on cremating him tonight instead of waiting the full twenty-four hours because they don't think anyone will bother coming."

Now I was angry. *Maybe I should stay on with them just to turn this place upside down.*

"Why did you bother?" I asked.

"I liked what I knew of him and...I felt guilty. We had split up in the crowd to cover more area. I should have known he wasn't trained like the rest of us when I overheard him telling you he was only good at standing there so important people don't get hurt."

"I'm just as guilty of brushing him off. I get the feeling people have been doing that to him his entire life and even now in death. Are you the one that cleaned him up?"

"Yes," Marianna said under her breath. "He said I was pretty... when we were alone in that plastic military building. It must sound terribly shallow of me to fawn over idle compliments, but I had never heard it before. The only boys I have contact with are those that I've known my whole life and look at me like a sister or a warrior.

"We're out in the world often enough to know how others act...I always see happy couples and think to myself that I'll never have that. All that matters is having a child by the time we're thirty so we can raise it before we inevitably die in battle... or from aether poisoning. It doesn't matter who we're with as long as they give the best chance at producing gifted offspring. My biggest fear is that I won't find someone in time and will be assigned a mate.

"The boys at least get to stay with who they're with for the nine months and then some after their child is born before they bring them here. But if you're a girl, you're encouraged to abandon the father and return to the abbey through the pregnancy. My aunt told me in secret that she was relieved when she couldn't bear children because then she wasn't expected to find a mate that she'd have to leave if she did like him.

"I don't want to be a machine used to give birth. I see the love that goes along with it and I want that. My aunt and Liam's father already have arrangements in place for us to have a child with each other by thirty if there aren't better candidates. They're pushing for Liam and I because we're both of a pure blood lineage traced back to the original order. Liam is like my brother though and he's...well, he's boring. I don't want to have a child with him. It would be too weird."

"Yikes...I'd have to agree. I know there are still arranged marriages in the world and I know what it's like to see others in love knowing that you're forbidden from it. You should be free to love whomever you want and be able to choose what you do with your body and when. But I thought Liam's mom and dad were married?" I questioned.

"He's not supposed to be, but he bends rules where he can and the elders resent him for it. I'd like to think that by doing that it would help break that part of the tradition, but it only made it worse. All the elders, not only the council, always say he's going to bring our end."

"That's odd. I would have figured him to be the strictest one by how he treats Liam."

"I'm not saying that he loves Liam's mother. The only reason he went out of his way to marry her was to show that he could. He says he visits her, but he doesn't. Liam does all the time though. If you're ever looking for him and can't find him, he's in town with her. We tease him because he's a real mommy's boy but tries to act like he's not...I'm sorry for telling you all this. We don't get to talk much about our feelings here and I can tell that you're approachable."

No less than six hours ago I made the God of Chaos back down by shouting threats of death and destruction after murdering groups of unarmed people. Marianna had an interesting interpretation of the word "approachable".

"That's all right. You've given me a lot of insight into your lives here and how I can help." I noticed the sparrow land by where Nathaniel's body laid. "Give me a moment alone with Nathaniel."

Chapter Forty-Two

"Place your hand upon him and we shall begin." Isis instructed. I did as I was told and following a sparkling glare we were brought to one of the many similar hallways within the abbey.

"Stay here, Mousekin. Papa will return soon." The voice came from within an open bedroom to my right. The owner of the voice was a man that looked remarkably like Nathaniel, or at the very least they shared the same long locks. I noticed the ring on his finger that matched the one on my necklace. He was talking to a small child that must have been Nathaniel himself. Young Nathaniel was so scrawny, it was as if he were made of toothpicks; hard to believe what he had grown up to become.

"Where are you going?" he asked his father as he swung his legs off the side of the bed, too short to reach the floor.

"Just to discuss matters with the council. I shant be long."

"Can I come?"

"Not this time, Mousekin. Stay here and be a good lad for me."

The vision faded out to bring me to another area of the abbey that I hadn't been to yet. It was a large, boring stone square of a room that appeared to be set up for indoor sparring by the racks of weapons along the walls. Nathaniel's father, a younger Tobias, and a third, older man off to the side were there.

Nathaniel's father was in a duel with Tobias, the one that must have ended his life. That would mean the third man was Caylan—Tobias's friend and fellow council member. But where was Nathaniel?

The duel ended with Nathaniel's father flat on his back. Tobias offered his hand, but when it was refused he turned away to replace his sword in the rack. I was watching what would happen between the two of them with such intent that I almost missed a ripple in the air from Caylan's hand before he shouted to Tobias to watch out.

Nathaniel's father lunged at Tobias, but it seemed as if his sword was acting on its own. Tobias swung around in time to see the attack and went to raise his sword to defend himself, but was too close and plunged it into Nathaniel's father's chest dropping him instantly.

Was Caylan using telekinesis? That was a rather sloppy application of it. Or was it magnetism, like how Marianna wields her sword?

There was a tiny cry from behind a curtain by the door. It was Nathaniel.

"I knew he couldn't be trusted," Caylan said as inspected the body. "I had found evidence that he was plotting an assassination against you during the duel to make it look like an accident."

"What? What evidence?" Tobias asked. He attempted to use his magic to heal Nathaniel's father, but it was sudden death. "Why did you never say anything to me before?"

"You're soft," said Caylan. "You would have denied it like all the other times and tried to talk it out while he had his sword in you. Don't fret over it now. It's finished and you are the new leader of the council. The Van Dalen bloodline has always been full of traitors it should come as little surprise to the rest."

"How could this have gone so wrong?"

"Wear it as a badge of honor to show your strength in doing what our ancestors have failed to do."

The crying from behind the curtain grew loud enough that the two men heard it now. Tobias went to walk over, but Nathaniel bolted from the room.

"Get the boy!" Caylan shouted.

"Why? Haven't we done enough to not let him see his father like this?"

"Their bloodline must end here."

"Have you gone mad, Caylan? I won't kill a child! The scriptures—"

"Then you risk the repeat of events here tonight when the bastard grows to avenge his slain father and it is your child's blood on the floor!"

"I will raise him as my own then. He still has a credible claim to become the Chosen and I will honor what good his father did for the Order with that."

"You would honor a traitor, Tobias? How will you raise both him and Liam? You put the fate of your own lineage into question over a runt that no one will miss. The Van Dalens are savages and never should have been in power, pure blood or not. Is this not proof enough?"

"Then I will assign him as ward to someone. Someone young with no claim to the council that will not be so worried with heirs and bloodlines. I will make it their rite of passage to adulthood to raise the boy."

The scene finished. Caylan was a snake and Tobias at that time was young, naïve, and inexperienced as a leader. Perfect to be manipulated by someone who wanted power without being known for it. It was too bad that Caylan was already dead or I would've enjoyed killing him myself.

I watched a vision of Nathaniel witnessing his father's cremation. I thought it was done more privately than just lighting the body on fire in the middle of the courtyard, but I suppose a modern crematorium wasn't something the abbey was equipped with.

"His howls have kept us awake for a week, sir. He won't stop crying no matter what we do." Another vision began, this one with little Nathaniel sobbing on his bed. The voices were coming from outside the room.

"Then if kindness won't work, try something else," said Caylan. "This is your duty, a simpler task than any known rite of passage in our history. Our leader has spoken and the traitor's bastard must be raised, but never said it had to be easy on him. Do whatever it takes and make sure to keep him from the other children so they are not brought down and distracted by him."

There were footsteps leaving and then a lot of hushed cursing about Nathaniel between three people left outside the door.

The next vision started. It was a short one. Young Nathaniel was asleep in his bed with tears still coming down his cheeks. Tobias entered and placed the ring on his pillow. Several more of these same scenes played out showing Tobias leaving toys for Nathaniel in the dead of night. I wondered if Nathaniel ever knew who it was that gave him them.

I watched another scene where three teenage boys were trying to get little Nathaniel to use a short sword in the orchard. Two of the boys I recognized, they were Anatole and his cabal member Ruben. Nathaniel looked terrified of just touching the sword. He was traumatized from what he saw one do to his father.

"What is wrong with you?" the third boy snapped at him. "You're five years old! Everyone knows how to swing a sword by your age! It's my future on the line if you don't."

"I don't want to hurt anyone," Nathaniel sobbed. The boy forced the sword into his hand and stood back.

"If you don't at least hold it you won't be able to defend yourself when someone wants to hurt you." The boy swung his own sword and knocked Nathaniel's right out of his hand. The tip of the sword sliced Nathaniel across the cheek and caused him to cry harder.

"Shut up! It's just a scratch!" The boy grabbed Nathaniel and shook him, but when he wouldn't stop he used his magic to heal the cut. "You won't learn magic, you won't learn how to use a sword. It's been almost a *year*! Crying isn't going to bring your father back, so get over it! If you don't learn this you're going to be the next one they kill and nobody will care."

"You're on your own, Elijah," Anatole told the boy and started to walk away with Ruben. "We've had enough of this. It's a waste of time."

"Yeah, so have I." Elijah punched Nathaniel in the stomach and left him crying on the ground to follow the other two back to the abbey.

Every vision that passed kept getting worse and was harder to watch than the last. "Can we see a good memory?" I asked Isis.

She showed me Nathaniel hiding under his bed on the cold stone floor. He was a year or so older and his hair had grown out, whether he was trying to be like his father or just because no one bothered to give him a haircut.

It wasn't easy to see what he was doing under the bed, but I could hear him talking. "Hi, Mouseykins. I brought you bread from my dinner because I wasn't hungry." I looked closely and could see him petting and feeding a little brown field mouse. "Maybe one day we'll get to meet the Ascended and we'll get picked to go on an adventure away from here! Would you like that, Mouseykins?"

For the moment I was relieved until the door swung open.

"What are you doing under the bed again?" It was Elijah. Nathaniel didn't answer. He squeezed his eyes shut and curled up in a ball holding the mouse in his hands to hide him. "Answer me!"

"What's his problem now?" Anatole walked in.

"The bastard doesn't even talk anymore when asked a question. He just hides under there all day." Elijah grabbed Nathaniel by his hair and dragged him out. "What's in your hands?"

Nathaniel kept his head down and wouldn't answer. He was trembling. Elijah pulled his hands apart and the mouse dropped to the floor. It went to scurry off, but Elijah set it on fire with a conjured flame after letting out a string of expletives. Nathaniel was hysterical and tried to help the mouse as it made it a few more feet until it died.

"Maybe if you learned how to conjure water you could've saved it," Elijah jeered.

"He cries enough, does that count?" Anatole joked.

"What is going on? What is that smell?" It was Helena who walked in next. She looked down at Nathaniel huddled back under his bed with the tiny corpse of the mouse.

"He was keeping a rat as a pet *again*," said Elijah. "I took care of it though."

"And now the room stinks of it," Helena said in a disapproving tone. "What have *you* been told about using fire indoors? Nathaniel will have to stay in your room tonight."

"What?!" Elijah shouted. "That's not fair!"

"You've made no progress raising this boy in the past year. It's a wonder he can dress himself. He will share a room with you from now on until you can bring him up to a satisfactory level. This is *your* failure, not his, but since you would rather spend your time training with Anatole and Ruben I'll assign them to help you."

"You can't do that," Anatole seethed. "That bastard is going to bring us all down and I have a perfect record!"

Helena left and once she was gone things only got worse. The two boys took to beating Nathaniel until he blacked out and then covered it up by healing his wounds. I was shocked to see mild-mannered Anatole partaking in this. It sickened me to the core.

The next scene showed Nathaniel trying to talk to Pavel and Rhys on another day. He could barely speak and was trying to verbalize what the boys had done to him.

"Hit you? You look fine," said Rhys. "We all sustain injury during training. If Elijah *hadn't* healed your wounds then that would be an issue. Granted, training should not be taking place in the bedrooms, so that is a matter to discuss."

Nathaniel was confused and didn't know how to explain. There was no doubt it was confusing enough for a child, but throw in a concussion and the use of magic as a cover up while he was unconscious on top of it. "Helena was there," he said.

"Helena was striking you too?" asked Pavel.

"No, no. She was there. She told them to take me to Elijah's room."

Pavel and Rhys called Helena over from an adjacent room. "Yes, I was there," she said. "There was no disturbance that I witnessed other than when Elijah had killed a rat Nathaniel was keeping."

"It wasn't a rat..." Nathaniel's chest heaved as he held back tears.

"Ah, so this is because you got caught keeping a rodent," said Pavel. "Do not lie to us to get other people in trouble in place of you, Nathaniel. This isn't the first time we've told you that."

"I'm not..."

"Every week it is something new and there's never any evidence to back it up," Rhys said. "If you spent that time training and studying instead of coming up with lies, there wouldn't be so much friction between you and Elijah. He is one of the most promising members of the Order and it's you who is bringing him down when all he is trying to do is prepare you for the road ahead. If you think your life is tough here wait until you see the outside world."

"I don't want to stay in Elijah's room...Please, sir."

"I think it will be good for you both to get to know each other better away from studying and training," Rhys insisted.

The vision ended. I hoped it was over. I couldn't take much more, but another started. Nathaniel was around nine or ten. Elijah, Ruben, and Anatole were all mocking him as he hid under the covers pretending to sleep so they'd leave him alone.

"Look what Anatole and I took from the alchemy lab." Ruben held up a bottle of pink liquid.

"What is it?" asked Elijah.

"It's a memory erase decoction, but I swapped some of the ingredients to give it a kick. All you need is a sip; otherwise, you'll probably forget your name."

After some debate, the three began drinking the liquid and spiraled into a drunken stupor. They remembered Nathaniel was still there and pulled him out to taunt him. They made fun of his long hair, called him a girl, and ripped his clothes as he tried to get away. Anatole gagged him so his shouts wouldn't wake anyone up after hitting him didn't work and then the final act of evil was committed that pushed me over the edge.

The boys vented their years of pent-up frustration and hormones on poor Nathaniel. I couldn't stop crying along with him and had to look away. I could escape the scene, but Nathaniel couldn't and he was only a child. When they had finished and realized what they had done they poured what was left of the decoction down his throat until he was unconscious.

The same events played out multiple times over different nights for years. Nathaniel tried to ask for help from the elders, but without being able to remember any of the details or even if it was only a nightmare, they didn't believe him and branded him a foul-mouthed liar. He was then afraid for his life because the three boys threatened to kill him if he continued trying to seek help. It wasn't until a dozen or so more of the horrendous visions that something changed.

Nathaniel was a preteen now. Elijah was alone with him one night and kept his dagger at Nathaniel's throat to keep him down without the help of Anatole and Ruben there. Eventually the dagger slipped from his hands as a result of his inebriation. Nathaniel reached for it and before Elijah knew what his victim was doing, Nathaniel shoved the blade into Elijah's heart as he had seen his father die. He pulled up his underwear and ran from the room covered in blood.

Anatole and Ruben heard him and came out to see what had happened. They grabbed Nathaniel and dragged him back to Elijah's room, in horror of what they saw. They drugged Nathaniel with what remained of the decoction left on the desk just in time for Tobias to arrive.

"He killed him!" Anatole cried. He picked the bottle back up to show Tobias and add to Nathaniel's crimes. "Nathaniel killed Elijah! Caylan always said something like this would happen!"

"I can't watch anymore," I said to Isis, but there was another vision already going with Nathaniel sitting in a chair before the council as they discussed his future.

"I told you the bastard would be trouble," said Caylan. "What if it had been you he attacked? Or Liam? To cut a man down in his own bed is the lowest form of treachery."

"I don't believe Nathaniel did this unprovoked," Tobias said. "The boy won't even hold a sword."

"He was under the influence of a weighty decoction that was tampered with," said Rhys. "That much alcohol in anyone's system would drive them mad. It was no secret there were already ill feelings between the two."

"Helena did agreed the mixture was altered in such an amateurish way that no one who knows the first thing about alchemy would do," added Pavel.

"Please, put this wretch out of our misery," Caylan goaded. "Your guilt over his father's death is no excuse for poor leadership and the endangerment of your own son."

"Nathaniel, you remember nothing at all that could help us see your side of this?" Tobias asked, but Nathaniel didn't speak.

"It was never easy to get the truth from him before this, do you think it will be that easy now?" Rhys asked. "Helena said that he'll probably never get his memory back and could continue to lose it for days to come. If I didn't know better I'd say he was trying to take his own life."

"Or forget his father so he could move on," Tobias suggested with a sigh. "What do the scriptures say as punishment for liars?"

"To cut the tongue from the mouth," Pavel answered. "But isn't murder the more pressing crime?"

"I'm not going to mutilate a child."

"Again you defy common sense and the written word," Caylan argued. "To what degree will this madness continue over a nobody?"

"I have to agree, Tobias. Why even ask what a law is if you never follow it?" Pavel questioned.

"When I feel it applies justly then I will follow it," Tobias barked back and sat in pensive contemplation. "As punishment for a dishonest tongue we will take his voice, not his tongue. Should we find him worthy of redemption as an adult the process can be reversed. Since he has made no headway in neither martial nor magical fields we will bring back the tradition of the Adamant Aegis to which he will be appointed to upon reaching maturity."

"*That* old thing you give credence to?" Rhys rolled his eyes and got up to leave. "I'll have no part in *that*, thank you."

"All he has to do is stand there so the actual contributing members of the Order aren't harmed," said Pavel. "Caylan may get his wish in one trip to the Astral Plane when a greater demon takes off they boy's head."

"I do not need a bastard to protect me, especially not this one," Caylan spat. "I would be better off with rabid dogs in his stead. You can keep your new pet all to yourself, Tobias."

And then Caylan got blown up by the Empyrean Jewel of Fire. Now that's karma. But I've always said that karma doesn't work fast enough in some cases and I've just run out of patience for some of those on its list that are still alive.

"I've made my decision, Isis. I want to give him the chance he never had if he'll accept it."

Back in the courtyard she appeared before me holding his soul in her hands over his body. It was so small compared to when she showed me mine.

"What are all those marks?" I asked her in reference to the lines on his soul.

"Scars from a trauma that cut deeper than flesh and bone." She handed me his soul and at once I felt the stifling depression he had suffered for years. "Once revived these wounds may open and the memories will flood back so that he may truly heal."

I held the soul to my chest to comfort it in the only way I could think of. "What do I do now?"

"Speak," Isis commanded and disappeared. I thought she was talking to me, but then I heard Nathaniel's voice coming from his soul.

"Where am I?" he asked.

"I don't know how else to say this, but you *died*, Nathaniel. I can bring you back. I want to give you the chance nobody else ever did."

"You already have. I was happy in the end."

"I mean a *real* chance at life. You aren't guilty of anything, Nathaniel. I read your soul all the way back to when you lost your father. The memories will return to you if you decide to come back. The decision is yours. I've already made mine. You're a good man with a lot to offer the world and it has a lot to offer you in return."

"You see more in me than I do myself."

"Isn't that what a god does?"

"You're right."

"I can give you all the power in the world, well close to it, but I can't change the heart of the man that wields it. What you've been through made you who you are today. Even if you don't remember all of it, your soul does and it never forgets. I grew up with far more privilege than you, then I lost everything, including my family. I started over from nothing. Someone saved my life when I was your age and gave me a second chance. Now I'm offering you the same."

I found I was no longer the one in need of convincing. I sincerely wanted him back as if the bond had already formed. I also wanted to set quite a few things straight in the Order for posterity.

"I never thought this could happen to someone like me... I'm ready."

Chapter Forty-Three

"Return his soul to his body," Isis's voice rang in my mind. "I take my leave to mend the veil in my land, Young One, and I welcome your herald back to this world."

I did as she said and pushed Nathaniel's soul into his chest. My hands glowed and I felt a rush of warm and cool. When the light dwindled, his body had healed and his eyes opened.

He sat up and I gave him a hug to let him know that all the misery of his past was behind him now, but he began to cry. "I remember...I remember everything," he sobbed. "Why? Why did they do that to me?"

"It was an act of pure evil and none of it was your fault. Anyone that twisted looks for the weakest victim they can prey on." I disintegrated his armor and hopefully some of the negative emotions that went with it. "No one will *ever* hurt you like that again. I promise."

We were still hugging each other as he cried to let out years of pain. I could feel all his sorrow, and also this indescribable call to nurture him as if he was my child, but also a friend and a soulmate. The bond between our souls was the strangest feeling yet, more than when I transcended and hardly noticed any change at all. It felt as if I was touching my own skin when I came into contact with his. I didn't think what Isis described would be so literal.

"Thank you," Nathaniel said as he calmed down.

"How do you feel?"

"Better...less confused. It feels nice, like you're a part of me, or I'm a part of you. Does this make me your champion like in the scriptures?"

"Yeah, I suppose it does. Is that okay with you?"

"Yes, wow...this is more than a second chance. But what about Liam? He's the Chosen."

"Liam doesn't want to be a champion, herald, whatever, any more than if I asked a random person on the street. He's only doing what his dad tells him to do. Liam needs to find something that makes him happy and I'll support it even if his father doesn't."

"I'm honored to be in your service and I swear to do everything in my power to please you and follow orders."

"But what will you do if I'm not around to give orders? You have to live your own life too—" I didn't finish getting the words out and Nathaniel already had his answer.

"I want to help children," he said with a burst of conviction. "I want to help as many as I can so that they don't have their innocence stolen from them like mine was."

"I can't think of anything more noble and appropriate. Children also always have the most to lose during war, and it's how they're treated that defines the future. If this war is going to continue as badly as I think it's going to, the world will need someone to look out for its tiniest voices that are often ignored.

"Just one more thing. You have every right to do what you want to with Anatole and Ruben, but I'd like it if you left them for me. There's a difference between justice and revenge. It's easy to get revenge when you have power. The hard part is letting go when you're done. Revenge is never as satisfying as you think it will be. It's a short-lived victory that leaves you feeling empty after and sets you on a hateful and self-destructive path. You'll only know how to resolve your problems through violence until one day you hit a brick wall that you can't knock down."

"I'm not looking for revenge. I don't care what happens to them, as long as they can never hurt another child."

"Oh...they won't." They wouldn't be doing much of anything once I finished with them. "Does the aether still bother you?"

"No, actually I don't feel it anymore. I wonder if I lost my connection." He made a fist and created a crystal in his palm. "I guess not."

"Good. That could be useful. I wonder what else you can do now. Did you get my telekinesis? Try moving that crystal with your mind. Picture it moving like you're dragging it with an invisible hand."

His concentration was visible across his face as he stared down at the crystal. "Nothing," he sighed and gave up.

"Maybe my regeneration then?"

Another voice in the courtyard interrupted our testing. "Oy! What's this now?"

I heard Claudius, but couldn't see nor feel him anywhere. "Why do you sound like a drunken Englishman?" I asked the air off to the side where I could sense it thicker than normal. "Why are you talking like Owen?"

"Blimey! Been there so bloody long the ol' chap must 'ave rubbed off on me." Claudius popped into view and dropped the terrible attempt at an English accent. "Hey, aren't you supposed to be dead, Nathaniel? I came back to see a dead body."

"I got over it," Nathaniel answered with a shrug.

"Ha!" I laughed. "And you have a sense of humor. This is great."

"Oh, yeah. Look at that, and you can talk now too," Claudius said. "I thought Marianna was pulling a trick."

"Claudius, let me have your dagger." He handed it to me and I passed it to Nathaniel. "Try to cut yourself and see if you have my regeneration."

"I can't do that either," he said after sliding the blade across his open palm. "Maybe my new power is to do absolutely nothing."

"Orichalcum can't cut you?" Claudius raised an eyebrow from behind his bandit mask. "You've got yourself a nice coating of aether and something else on—no—in your skin. I can see it with Aura Sight. Also: your aura is huge. Almost as big as the Ascended. What's going on?"

"Another energy?" I pondered. "Must be where I get mine from if we're connected now. Claudius, you can't say anything until we announce it to the whole Order, but Nathaniel is my herald-er-other."

"But Liam...? Okay. You got it, boss. But, it's going to be hard to hide. He's a big glowbug for anyone that can see auras."

Nathaniel was trying to stab himself with the dagger until finally it snapped against his skin.

"My dagger!" Claudius exclaimed. "My baby! She had so much stabbing left to do."

"I'm sorry," Nathaniel apologized and handed it back. "I didn't think that would happen..."

"That's all right, I suppose... Never seen orichalcum broken like that after it's been enchanted. Only seen it chipped once against a demon lord's horn. Guess it was worth the sight to be the first to see what the Champion of the Ascended can do."

"So, I suppose I'm still only good at standing in the way so important people don't get hurt." Nathaniel almost sounded like he was joking this time— actually I could tell he was.

"Defenses like that might rival a certain dark knight." I tried to push him with my powers and felt it ripple over him and push back. "You do have telekinesis. I can feel it. It feels like when I use my powers to sense the area around me or block something from hitting me. Yours is just, I don't know, infused into your skin instead of projected outward."

"Do you think I can fly?" he asked.

"People coming," Claudius said and vanished. "Don't tell anyone I'm here or they'll put me to work, boss."

In walked the council.

"Nathaniel, you're—alive," Tobias said.

"Praise be to the Ascended." Rhys dug deep to find a modicum of enthusiasm.

"You've chosen...Nathaniel as your..." Helena could barely get the words out.

"Assemble everyone *except* the children here in the courtyard," I instructed. Nathaniel was trying to hold back a smile as they left. "You're smiling! Let it out." I nudged him.

"Thank you. It's good to see them being humbled."

"We need to get you new armor. You're not part of that Adamant Aegis crap anymore. Maybe something white. You can be a symbol of hope."

"I like that."

I disintegrated his old helmet that was still sitting where he was laid out into a pile of metal dust. "Orichalcum isn't that strong. I don't know what the big deal is."

"That was impressive, but we could have reforged it into something else."

I floated the dust around and then smushed it into a ball. "We still can."

The Order began to arrive in the courtyard. This time it was Nathaniel getting all the inquiring stares, not me. "I normally hate public speaking, but for the first time I'm actually looking forward to it. If you don't want to be here for this I'll understand. It won't be pretty."

"Thank you, but I'm done hiding my face," Nathaniel said, his confidence growing before my eyes. I was glad to be there to witness it.

Anatole and Ruben were two of the last to enter. Anatole was brazen enough to approach me directly while I stood before everyone with Nathaniel at my side. "Nathaniel you're—alive."

"I noticed," he quipped.

"That's good to hear. Ascended, I'm pleased to report that everything has been going smoothly in the Carpathian Mountains."

"And I am just as pleased to hear it and have you back safe. Why don't you take a spot right up front by me," I offered.

"It would be an honor." He bowed. I saw him keep an eye on Nathaniel as he returned to the crowd.

"Is that everyone, Tobias?" I asked.

"It is, Ascended."

"Everyone," I addressed the crowd and floated high enough to see all the way to the back. It was pure emotion at the wheel now. "I think we can all agree it's been an interesting past few days. I know I've told some of you before that I hate giving speeches, but I'm making an exception in this case.

"You've been kind enough to trust me, take me in, and share your culture all without really knowing me. I admit it's all happened so fast that sometimes I can't believe it's real. You look at me as a god as others have looked upon powerful supernaturals in the past.

"Godhood to me means little about the power or the worship. I honestly felt no different after I supposedly transcended and I've always preferred being alone to being in a crowd.

"There were some new quirks in my abilities, but no great enlightenment. I don't have all the answers for you and I'm not all-powerful. Everything I know and how I act is from my experiences in this world. The only thing I claim to know is the difference between right and wrong.

"With that said, I have made my decision on whether or not I will be staying." I looked out at all the anxious faces. So many of them were smiling, but some wouldn't be for long. "I've decided to stay."

My announcement was met with applause and cheers from all, including Liam who nodded to Rafael as if he already knew the outcome.

"I know this is probably the worst kept secret in the past hour," I raised my voice to talk over everyone as they settled down, "but yes Nathaniel is alive and will live on as my...herald?" I looked over at him for confirmation.

"I liked champion," he whispered.

"Champion!" I corrected. "It was an impulsive decision, I know, and not one based on anyone else's performance. My decision came from the heart and was an opportunity I seized before it could slip away. Nathaniel died giving his life to earn me a few critical seconds in a battle against the hardest enemy I've fought to date. Without that sacrifice, I may not be here today.

"Nathaniel gave me a second chance, so I returned the favor. I would never ask nor expect any of you to give your lives for me. I will respect you as you do me, and together we can fight to protect each other and the world."

That gained me more smiles as faces continued to brighten and tensions eased.

"There are a couple of rules I'd like to tweak, if I can?" I directed my question to the council standing front row.

"We are at your service, Ascended. The Order is yours to rule as you see fit," Tobias answered. I didn't get any gnarled frowns or grimaces as I thought I might from some of the older members.

"Perfect. Please, for the love of Me, *stop* kneeling and calling me by anything but my name or I'll have you write it a hundred times. Ascended is okay sometimes, I guess.

"Also, and this is a big one, the whole rule about getting married and having a child by thirty; I've heard more than one version of this rule floating around and none of them sit well with me. You're all *mortal.* You more than anyone else on this Earth should enjoy every second you have and love or pursue whoever you want, whenever you want."

"How will we breed only the best for your Order without careful selection and a regimented process?" Rhys asked in a snide tone.

"First, it's not *my* Order. It's ours. Second, are you kidding me? You're not livestock. You're people. People aren't supposed to 'breed'. I'm not looking for perfection, nor am I looking to populate a small country. As long as it's between consenting adults I don't care what you do. This was like a eugenics program gone wrong…as usual.

"I've already chosen a champion. There's no need to try and produce the perfect specimen. There is no such thing as perfect to begin with. You've been chasing shadows for centuries. We're all going to have flaws and traits that make us different. Embrace them and embrace the love you seek. Your lives aren't something you put together on an assembly line in a factory. Everyone is unique. Discipline is good, but don't take it so far that life has no meaning."

The council was more bewildered that ornery in the wake of their traditions being uprooted. I had a feeling that I struck a chord with some of them that may have thought their chance at fulfilling the emptiness in their own hearts was gone.

"The children we welcome into our Order should be treated with love and not thought of as commodities for the future. We should respect them for who they are because we never know what they will grow up to be. Isn't that right, Anatole?"

Anatole was stunned, but still savvy enough to answer without showing it. "Absolutely. There is nothing more important to the future of our Order than the children we bring into it."

"Then why did you rape one?"

The gasps among the crowd were staggered as everyone took a second to process what was said. Anatole's silver tongue must have melted in his mouth because he had nothing to say in response. The sweat collecting on his brow spoke volumes though.

"You seem confused," I continued. "Maybe your friend Ruben can help you answer." Heads turned to Ruben in the back of the crowd. The stares were now divided between the two.

I continued pressing my case. "No? Nothing from either of you? Tobias can you answer for them? It seems someone took their voice."

"I...think this would be best discussed in private," he sighed. I checked with Nathaniel who was still standing strong and nodded for me to go on.

"There shouldn't be secrets among family," I said. "And historically, keeping secrets between members of a clandestine order never goes well for everyone involved once the secret gets out."

"I can only...surmise...what the accusations against them mean," said Tobias.

"Try harder."

"There were claims of misconduct against a group of boys when they were young, one of whom is now long deceased. There was never any evidence to substantiate the claims, however."

"Misconduct is playing ball indoors," I corrected. "Beating, restraining, drugging, and raping a child as a form of recreation is an act so disgusting there hasn't been a word created for it yet and there may never be."

Everyone in the courtyard was trying their best to hold back from causing an uproar. I hoped that Nathaniel was able to feed off my strength to see him through this so the chapter could be closed.

"We were only children at the time ourselves!" Anatole finally spoke in his defense. "You don't understand! It wasn't something we planned or even realized we were doing at the time—"

"I saw everything. I saw how the decoction was stolen from the alchemy lab, and I saw who stole it. I know who did what and every detail. I *watched*. You can't lie to me."

"P-please. I'll pay for my sins. Just tell me what you want me to do to be forgiven! Be merciful!"

"Oh, Anatole. I would, but...I'm not that kind of god."

Chapter Forty-Four

I blew Anatole's body into pieces so miniscule there wasn't a speck of blood where he once stood. Ruben tried to teleport away before I could get him, but I anticipated that. It only made his demise...messier.

"Consider that merciful because if I ever find out another child is treated like that again, so help me I will turn you inside out one body part at a time." I spoke calmly to restore peace after several screams went up in the crowd. Marianna was the first to state that she never liked Anatole anyway and then others joined in to share her sentiment. There was a part of me that worried the Order would turn against me, but it had to be done. There was no redemption for people like that in my mind.

"I'm not finished. There are still those who remain that allowed such horrible acts to take place.

Unfortunately, I'm not able to deal with Elijah, who abused a child in every way possible. He was already put down so that no one else would have to suffer the same cruel experience.

"Then there was Caylan, a former council member that prodded others into mistreating a child because of his lineage. He died to what I suspect was greed when seeking an Empyrean Jewel's power, not an accident. It was the same greed that caused him to manipulate Tobias into killing Nathaniel's father while distracted during the finish of a fateful duel. Let the false account of the treachery by the Van Dalens be stricken from the Order's history.

"Now to deal with the remaining councilmembers that had a hand in an innocent child's downward spiral; Pavel what's the punishment for incompetence, gross negligence, and a stupidity so thick that it allowed three teenagers to fool a group of grown men?"

"I...I don't know off the top of my head, sir."

"Well, I'll tell you and you can write it down after you're done copying my name a hundred times for calling me sir. In my eyes, the council has failed their most important duty and that was to look out for the welfare of all the members it rules. Whether you're all really that stupid, or you just wanted to ignore a poor child's pleas for help because it was easier not to investigate, you've made your positions worthless.

"I am hereby disbanding the council and sparing your lives so that maybe you can get your heads out of your asses and do some good. I don't think any of you were motivated by evil. Tobias, more than the rest showed, traces of wanting to do the right thing, but caved under pressure to uphold archaic standards and back a corrupt friend. The Order will now be led with me by those I choose based on merit and not inheritance. You have every right to leave if you don't find this fair. It's a big world and there are plenty of opportunities out there for you."

"I will gladly stay, Ascended," Tobias said in relief.

"Will I be allowed to stay on as head scribe to chronicle your glories and gospel?" Helena asked.

"That's fine," I agreed. "Just get a lock for your alchemy lab."

"I never liked being in charge anyway," said Rhys. "Now I can go back to demon hunting instead of this political bullshit."

"That's the first thing out of your mouth I've liked since I met you," I said. "Pavel?"

"It will take some getting used to, but we were prepared for much to change upon the Ascended's arrival, regardless of who that was. I would rather remain here where I can be myself than out in the world. May I stay and tend the gardens?" he asked.

"Sure. You can start by cleaning up what's left of Ruben. I won't even make you write my name a hundred times if you do."

"Very good, sir."

I rolled my eyes at him. He was in his late-forties and had the trouble of an eighty year old with learning new things. "One last thing. As I understand it, The Goetic Order of Man is the name given to the new Order after the last Ascended died and your ancestors were in hiding.

"I'd like to change that since we're not hiding anymore.

"There's plenty of evil out there in the world and we need to lead the charge against it. People won't know that we're the good guys unless we show them. We have nothing to be afraid of if we stick together. I don't intend to stop here, after our debut in the desert repelling Set. We won't all be fighting gods, but we all have something to offer the future of our world.

"That's why I'd like to change our name to something that better represents our message of hope to humanity and our pure intentions. The name I've come up with is The Alabaster Order."

I didn't expect such a reaction, but the cheers of "Glory to the Ascended!" were deafening and reached into my soul. I wanted to think it was all about the name, but I knew from youngest to oldest one of the biggest concerns within the Order was the fear of how the outside world would treat them once everything was exposed. It was a fear I had shared for so long, but I knew they looked up to me from my adventures and wanted me to be the buffer between worlds that shielded them from inevitable animosity. It was a job that only I could do and that made me feel unshakable.

"Thanks for listening, everyone, but I'm done with speeches for a while." I landed back on my feet by Nathaniel. I could tell he was happy.

The crowd was quick to disperse upon being dismissed. I knew they would be going to gossip behind closed doors about all that had happened and that was fine with me. I needed a nap.

"That was really moving," said Nathaniel. "You're a lot better at that than you think. I like the new name too and the way Anatole and Ruben don't exist anymore."

"Thanks," I laughed. "I tried not to think about it and just spoke from experience and emotion. As soon as I start thinking about what to say, I get nervous. I thought there would be more of a reaction at the death of those two, but I think I got my message across."

"We've seen death too often to be shocked by it anymore. Earlier this year we lost ten people to the possessed that were cropping up everywhere from that demon invasion you stopped."

"Ten? That's a lot. I'm sorry. Lesser demons that possess people aren't that strong, not compared to what I've seen the Order is capable of. How did so many die?"

"They fought them on the Astral Plane to avoid casualties on Earth since the possessed were blending in with normal people. Magic is stronger there, but so are the demons. Or so I've heard. I've never been there."

"The most important thing to me is that we don't throw away lives to solve a problem. Not good lives at least. Fuck the bad guys."

"I feel the same way," he agreed. "If you have time, do you think you could show me how you fly?"

"I never thought this day would come. *Me* teaching someone else. Okay, since your telekinesis acts like a field close to your body all you have to do is picture yourself lifting your body up and drag it where you want to go.

"Eventually it becomes second nature and you don't have to think about it anymore than walking. It'll take a while to get used to. I know I couldn't figure out how at first no matter what I tired until—"

"I think I'm doing it!" Nathaniel shouted as he floated upward, then gracefully glided to the left and right.

"So you are. Good job, you already showed me up."

"I'm sorry! This is amazing though! I've always wanted to fly. It's the ultimate sense of freedom." Nathaniel was as natural in the air as a fish in water. "This is exactly like in my dreams. Do you want to race to the other side of the island?"

"I think you're getting ahead of yourself. You've gotta walk before you run."

"You're right. Maybe tomorrow. I wouldn't want to show you up twice in one day." His grin when he said that reminded me of Noah when he was being playful. I was taken back, but wanted to encourage that behavior over subservience.

"You're on." I darted past him up out of the courtyard and toward the town. It was great to not worry about being seen.

Nathaniel was catching up fast. I could tell he wasn't finding it easy to keep his balance at this speed by how he was wobbling in the air. We were half way across town when he overtook me at double my max speed. I called for him to slow down, afraid he would crash and hurt himself or somebody else.

He made it across the docks on the far side of the island with me coming in right behind him. He was trying to stop himself and made the mistake of pulling back too hard and went tumbling toward the sea. I caught him and brought him back up.

"I'm sorry," he apologized sheepishly.

"You have to take it slow to practice your handling first before you jet around. Without question, when you get it down you're going to be faster than me."

We took our time heading back to the abbey. "We should start building good relations with the townspeople," I said. "The former council members told me how the town is already pretty neutral toward us."

"It would help to stop kidnapping their children."

"What?" I stopped short in the air and pulled Nathaniel back with me.

"They left that part out? I guess I'm not surprised. It's been tradition for forever. There's no way to keep the ranks replenished when those already in the Order only live long enough to raise one child. They don't believe in having more than one because all attention should be on that single child's training so it's perfect.

"When our ranks are low they 'recruit' by searching for magically gifted children too young to remember their lives before the Order. Only the young ones are allowed in because it's easier to train a child from birth than start with an adult, I guess."

"I have a feeling I already know, but I have to ask. What happens to the parents?"

"It depends. They call it 'liberating the child' by taking them from the mundane and bringing them into a life of magic where they can explore their full potential. Sometimes they kill the parents, other times they pay them off. They never leave loose ends in either case."

"And I'm assuming they don't recruit adults and give them that memory wipe potion because of all the loose ends that would need tying?"

"Yes. It's also not foolproof…unless you're forced to drink a whole bottle at once. They don't take from only this town, but all over the world."

"It stops immediately. We'll recruit adults if they're found to be trustworthy and gifted. I don't care about the façade of perfection."

"It isn't *all* bad. I've seen them save children who would have died of hunger or lived in war-torn countries. They take in orphans and abandoned babies as long as they have the gift. Georgie was found in his dead mother's arms in Cambodia. I think the village he was from was being seized by insurgents. The council went in and killed them all to rescue Georgie. I was there."

"You have a very level head to view them with any respect after how they treated you. I'm fine with them saving children to recruit them; in fact I encourage it. But when we get back, spread the word that we're not taking any by underhanded means. I can't imagine what that would do to our public image if it ever got out."

"Right away, Ascended, and...thank you again."

"Nathaniel, out of everyone in the Order, you're the last one I'll tolerate calling me anything but Dorian. You have a piece of my soul!"

"I know. I'm sorry. I only mean it to show you respect as my master."

"I'm not your master! Saying it like that makes it weird." I could only imagine the problems it would cause if Gianluca heard him calling me that...

I went straight to my room to take a nap once we had returned. England was two hours behind and I wanted to stop by and see what Castile had to say when he was up. After that I had to visit Lyle to discuss plans now that things with the Order were settled.

Set's defeat wouldn't last much longer. It was more of an intermission than a finale according to Isis. She seemed fine with the fact that he would keep returning to cause problems because of the nature of the true gods that prevented them from ever really "dying". It wasn't okay with me though. Set either needed to go down for good, or go down hard enough that he wouldn't return for centuries.

What we did have in our favor was the Infernal Kings' total lack of tolerance for failure. I had seen them send Minerva to finish off one of their own minions that had failed them. Chances are they wouldn't continue to support Set after he was made to cower by me. It wasn't out of the question that they would even help finish him off, though that was probably being too hopeful.

Back in my room, Noah was sprawled out across the bed, his legs hanging off the side with his boots still on. It was a decent compromise.

I took one of the fur blankets and settled into a comfy leather chair by the unlit fireplace to rest until sunset. I dozed off for who knows how long, but I was groggy and incoherent when I woke in the dark room and couldn't hold my eyes open. I felt that I was moving and being carried in someone's arms, blanket and all. My first thought was that it was Gianluca, but then I remembered Noah when I was placed on the empty bed.

He wrapped me snugly in the blanket and I was too comfortable to argue until he leaned in for my neck.

"It'll help you sleep," he said with his lips at my neck.

"I don't want to," I spoke half into my pillow. "I have things to do."

He bit down and my mind began to unravel as I drifted off into rapturous bliss. He took his time finishing, but when he was done I could feel him still standing over me. I heard his voice one last time as I lost myself to sleep.

"Thanks, babe...for everything."

Chapter Forty-Five

Later that evening I woke up feeling as refreshed as I had ever been.

I bathed and then inspected the tears in my shirt that I needed to get fixed. Two holes were a lot better than tattered scraps. I needed a shield I could hide behind, like that big one Nathaniel used to carry around. If I had the metal with me, I could make one on the fly instead of scrambling for materials in the area when I was already under fire.

I left to go find someone to send me to England. The hallway leading up to my room was lined with sparkling aether crystals, clothes, orichalcum rings and necklaces, flowers, and fresh fruit. Alexandre was walking up as I looked over everything. "What is all this?" I asked him.

"These are offerings from your faithful as a show of gratitude and worship, Ascended. I thought you might have retired for the evening. I was coming by to leave mine." He held out a crystal in the shape of three cubic spires for me. "I know you are uncomfortable with kneeling, so please don't take my presentation as disrespectful."

"That's all right and thank you." I took the crystal and peered deep into it. Inside, the crystal twinkled in a brilliant display of colors that reminded me of the celestial sky above Egypt, only not so...apocalyptic. "How did you get it to look like this inside?"

"A little Space magic, astronomy, and ingenuity. Space magic deals with volumes, and vortexes, and vertices that we manipulate with aether to bend the rules of reality. Part of that magic is Scrying—feeling a distant location—then there's teleporting—moving to a location, but we can also *see* through space to another location with Spatial Sight. I imprinted the Spatial Sight spell into the aether crystal like we would for an amulet. This one is looking out at a part of the Crab Nebula."

"This is really looking at *real* outer space?"

"Yes."

"That's so cool. I'm going to put it by my bed." There was something in the pit of my stomach bothering me when I said that and I couldn't figure out what was causing it. "I wasn't expecting to be given gifts after killing two people."

"Swift and fair justice is the crowning achievement of any great leader. We grow up fast in the Order. We see and experience hardships most of the civilized world only reads about in history books. We live our lives the same as our ancestors did with very little deviation. We aren't sitting on bloated coffers, and do not have control over the social schema outside these walls like many other supernaturals.

"When we are hungry, we make, hunt, or trade for our food as our forefathers did. When we're cold, we harvest and gather materials to fashion clothes. When our shelter crumbles, we all do our part to patch the cracks.

"Magic is no replacement for hard work. It takes our entire lives to study and train to become a complete person and a functioning member of the Order. We each stand on the shoulders of our predecessors and when one of us goes bad, the last thing we want is for that wound to fester and bring down the rest of what we've worked so hard to achieve together.

"Crimes against children and other such unspeakable acts have always been punishable by death on paper. Weakness comes from leadership that hesitates to act, not from the leader that takes a stand and says no more. Everyone here stands by your decision to strengthen us without question; not in fear of retaliation, but respect for having the courage to do what others didn't.

"It's a travesty what happened to Nathaniel, but it only proves that so many of us don't know the struggles of what goes on in our brothers' and sisters' lives. The message we are taught from birth to shun pain has grown diluted to become more about hiding it than dealing with it head on. The failure falls on the council as much as the criminals and I think even they recognize that and are happy to step aside with their remaining dignity so that we can continue to grow.

"I knew Anatole and Ruben perhaps better than some, but not well by any means. We were placed in a cabal together despite the age gap because our skills were supposed to have worked well with one another. In my adult years I found the two to be reserved and secretive among themselves, when a cabal should work as the closest unit in the Order. It troubles me to think that all that saved me from enduring a similar fate as Nathaniel was sharing my last name with a current council member."

"I appreciate hearing all of that and the support for bringing down the hammer of justice. Maybe you can join Liam's cabal. I'm closest with them from our time together this week."

"Thank you." Alexandre went on to say something else, but my mind wandered. That feeling in my stomach was gnawing at me. It reminded me of waking up after having a nightmare, but I didn't have any that I could remember. I slept fine. The only thing that happened was Noah biting me, but that wasn't anything strange. Was it what he said?

"Thanks for everything, babe."

That didn't sound like him. It was such an odd thing to say too.

Could I have dreamt that?

The feeling in my stomach worsened still.

"Sorry," I interrupted Alexandre. "But do you still have spirits watching Noah? I'm...I feel like something is wrong."

"No, but he returned to France earlier in the night."

"How long ago?" I started to panic.

"About three hours now. I overheard him asking Liam to send him to Paris."

"I need to get to the chateau. Grab whoever you can to take me there."

"Right away," Alexandre bowed and teleported out. He returned in a short time with Liam, Rafael, and Claudius as I paced back and forth in the hall. "I'll lead. I know where our destination is by heart."

"Hurry," I pleaded. The four took their positions around me and we were off in a blaze of aether across the ley lines.

My intuition was proven right as we arrived in Aurelia's ballroom.

Noah was locked in bloody melee against Kenneth and it was not going in Noah's favor. The Muramasa sat against the throne where Aurelia watched on from outside a ring of blue fire that separated her from the two combatants. Beside her, a more presentable human-looking (or should I say Archios-looking) Rozalin. The pale, raven-haired beauty stood chin held high and shoulders back as she reveled in the carnage with a glimmer of pleasure in her chilling eyes.

Owen's missing hunter armor was in shreds hanging from Noah's body. Alexandre's lost amulet that shielded against telepathy was clipped to the belt. One of Noah's own *wakizashi* lay in pieces and out of reach, the other remained intact in his hand.

There was enough blood on the floor to make even the most surefooted ninja lose his balance and I could tell most of it came from that ninja by his injuries. Lacerations covered his exposed skin and leaked blood like waterfalls. His nose was broken as were several ribs that protruded unnaturally from within his torso, limiting his range of motion. His right leg must have also been fractured from how he was limping. There was no speed and grace to his movements like usual. He had to be low on blood that he needed to fuel his supernatural abilities.

Kenneth wasn't in great shape either, but nowhere near Noah's condition; nothing that a human his size couldn't endure to carry on a brawl.

"Something's wrong," said Claudius as we hung in the air forced only to watch the battle in a sort of spectral form. "We're stuck between dimensional spaces."

"This is high-level dark magic," Alexandre explained. "It's the blood wraith."

"What does that mean? Get me down there!" I shouted in panic. Noah was keeping his distance from Kenneth. I knew he was trying to come up with another plan as Kenneth pursued him around the ring.

"We can't. We're trapped. Can't go forward, can't go back," said Claudius. "This was planned. They knew we'd be coming."

"I don't care what you have to do to get me in there. *Do it!*"

Noah wiped his poisoned blood on the blade of the *wakizashi* and managed to get behind Kenneth to thrust the sword into his back. The poison reacted instantaneously, turning Kenneth's skin anemic and withering his strength.

Kenneth swung around, but Noah dodged and struck again in an attempt to get at his heart. Even gravely wounded, Noah's movements made Kenneth seem like a lumbering oaf.

Unable to stake the heart, Noah skewered Kenneth through the back of the head and out his mouth. He climbed up on Kenneth's back to grip the other end of the blade and use leverage to rotate it in an attempt to rip Kenneth's head off. Still Kenneth was too strong. This was the undead that survived a direct blow from Set.

"We're only burning out our energy forcing our way through," Liam said. "If we can tap into the Ascended's power we may be able to bypass the spell."

"Yes! Do it! Go!" I demanded. I was still hopeful that Noah would walk away from this. That was until Kenneth got hold of him.

Seemingly unconcerned with the sword through his skull, Kenneth grabbed Noah's bad leg and fractured the ankle. Noah was tough even if he didn't have the blood required to heal himself. He didn't make a sound that he was in pain and still hung on to the blade, although his grip weakened. Kenneth put both hands on the part of the sword coming out of his mouth and rammed it back out the other end so that the hilt hit Noah in his already broken nose.

When Noah tried to get away Kenneth reacted faster than he had the entire time and caught Noah by the wrist after tossing the *wakizashi* out of the ring. Noah dropped down and swept Kenneth's legs out from under him, grabbing one leg and trapping him in an ankle lock.

Kenneth's ankle snapped under the pressure and gave Noah an opening to move into a calf crusher; a hold using Noah's good leg as a nutcracker to apply enough torque that crushed Kenneth's shin right through his armored boot.

This was looking up. Noah was regaining control of the fight which bought us more time until I could help.

Kenneth's strength was barely enough to free him this time, but not before Noah could take advantage of another opening. When Kenneth rolled onto his side to get up Noah used his knee to pin Kenneth's face. Noah clasped his hands together when Kenneth reached up to grab him and pulled in to break the elbow with a reverse arm-bar.

I thought Noah would be able to finish him, but instead it was Kenneth that became the dominant one again. He overpowered Noah and broke free at the cost of the use of his arm and chugged something from a flask on his belt that cured him of the poison. Now that Kenneth was crippled, Noah changed techniques to striking him with brutal left and right hooks, chambered punches, and palm strikes. It might have seemed like desperation, but Noah was pushing Kenneth back toward the ring of fire while keeping him from healing for a time now that the poison had worn off.

He landed a flying kick that almost staggered Kenneth into the flames, but that was where Noah's supremacy ended. Kenneth took the hit and then caught Noah by his waistband and put him in a spine-breaking bear hug.

Noah still refused to make a noise, but the agonizing sound of his bones popping and cracking in his torso as they ruptured his organs was enough. He began dribbling blood from his mouth and then full on vomiting it as Kenneth squeezed harder.

"Why isn't he turning into mist?!" I yelled. "He has to have *some* blood left in him! Just bite Kenneth!"

"The Griffon Claw Gauntlet's corrupted gem must be what is preventing use of his vampiric powers," Alexandre said.

There was no escape for Noah in sight. He spit blood in Aurelia's direction, which I wanted to believe was on purpose, but it was going everywhere. "Remove his tongue," she commanded Kenneth. "I have had quite enough of what comes from it."

"Make haste and end this, sister," Rozalin said to her. "I want that pretty soul for myself like you promised."

"NO!" I screamed and then directed my frustration at the Order. "Why aren't you doing anything?!"

"We're trying!" Rafael tried to sound apologetic through gritted teeth as the four were still straining to get through the trap Rozalin had set up. I wasn't feeling anything as they drew from my power, but I was also blind with rage that was dwindling into sorrow.

Noah was thrown to the floor with such force that his skull cracked on the marble. It was pathetic watching as he tried to crawl away in a daze. He got Kenneth to the ground one more time with a Heel Hook that twisted the knee around at the foot to snap the ligaments.

Kenneth was in pain, but had been healing steadily throughout the fight and regained the use of his arm and other leg. Noah knew what he had to do and bent away the metal collar that stuck up from Kenneth's armor to protect his neck. This was no ordinary metal by how much effort it took Noah to bend it. I wouldn't have been surprised if it was some form of orichalcum.

With Kenneth's neck partially exposed, Noah snared him in a modified Judo move known as *Kata Gatame*. In this move, his arm went behind Kenneth's head from the front to bring him in close while disabling the use of his gauntlet.

Noah only got his fangs into Kenneth's neck for a moment. Kenneth punched Noah in his broken ribs to make him let go and then slammed him to the ground. He lifted Noah back to his feet by shoving two fingers of his clawed gauntlet up Noah's nostrils, then forced the his hand into Noah's mouth and pried his jaws apart until there was a snap. I screamed with tears welling up in my eyes as Kenneth put him in a headlock and tore out his tongue that turned to ash.

Noah couldn't hold back anymore and began wailing and holding his jaw until Kenneth smashed his head repeatedly into the floor. Noah was still struggling to fight Kenneth off and wouldn't give up as they wrestled like snarling animals. Kenneth had a tremendous advantage in unarmed combat due to his strength and durability, even against someone as skilled as Noah if he was in perfect condition.

The two continued to maul each other as the one-sided fight turned even more unbalanced and the last of my anger changed to morbid depression. I couldn't shout at the Order anymore as tears ran down my face. Kenneth ripped a chunk of Noah's scalp off when he almost escaped Kenneth's grasp and was yanked back by his hair. Noah had been trying to crawl into the fire to end his life on his own terms.

Aurelia and Rozalin whispered to one another and then Rozalin faded away. "She's gone," I sobbed. "Can you get us in?"

"The spell remains even with the caster gone," Liam said. I tried using my powers, but there was nothing for me to use them on. We were ghost-like beings trapped in empty space.

Noah wasn't moving anymore. Kenneth sat on top of him, beating his face in until he was unrecognizable and then digging into his mouth to pull out his fangs. The red gem of Kenneth's gauntlet glowed any time it came into contact with Noah.

Aurelia looked bored, but that was nothing new. Kenneth didn't seem to be enjoying himself either, but wouldn't stop. I knew he couldn't if he wanted to anyway. I was praying that Aurelia wouldn't want to destroy her own property by going through with killing Noah, but with Kenneth in her service she didn't need him any longer.

I didn't know how much more punishment Noah could take. Kenneth stood and bent down to pick up him again, this time grabbing him by what was left of his face. He stuck the thumb of his gauntlet into Noah's left eye socket and gouged out his eye as he lifted him up.

Noah's screams gurgled up past the blood in his throat and rang throughout the ballroom to bring the first smile to Aurelia's face for the night. He grasped desperately at Kenneth in a final attempt to get free. Kenneth kicked him to the floor and stomped down on his forearm, shattering the bones with ease.

Rozalin returned in a dark fog along with a guest.

"What is this?" It was Gianluca. He looked on in confusion at Noah being tortured.

"Thank you for coming," said Aurelia. "I thought you should bear witness to this. An attempt was made on my life. It comes as no surprise to any of us present. I have been forgiving for too long and tolerated far too much disrespect. I cannot have these actions when such sensitive members of the human world are now common visitors at my residence. I'm sure you can agree it would be of great detriment to our alliance.

"It was to my understanding that *you* would deal with my protection as I handled matters with the humans, my dear. But so far it seems you are only interested in losing duels in the sands. I have taken this into my own hands to our mutual benefit. You are also aware that this man is the one responsible for turning your lover against you, are you not?"

Gianluca grunted in disapproval and crossed his arms. I was losing my mind being stuck between dimensions. I started shouting for Gianluca hoping he would hear me and bring me to him.

"Kill him and let it be done," said Gianluca. "There is no point for this mess."

"NO!" I screamed at the top of my lungs.

Aurelia nodded to Kenneth, who was crushing Noah's throat under foot. I was hysterical knowing what was coming next. Kenneth put one foot on Noah's side to hold him down while he pulled up on one of Noah's arms and twisted it. There was a pop, then a series of cracks followed by the sound of ripping flesh as Kenneth tore Noah's arm off.

The arm turned to ash. Noah couldn't stop howling and whimpering now as he flailed on the ground. His skin and remaining hair started to crumble into ashes and then his extremities.

"If he dies…" I cried. Everything was in slow motion to me as Noah fell apart.

Chapter Forty-Six

"It's down!" Liam shouted. We tumbled out of the dimensional void and into the ballroom proper. Kenneth was twisting Noah's head off with a finger jammed in his right eye as his body hung limp. I threw Kenneth out of the ring of flames in a ball of Underworld fire and right through Rozalin, causing her to vanish.

I caught what was left of Noah's body as it was turning to ash before it hit the floor and hovered over him protectively. "YOU WILL DIE!" I pointed at Aurelia ready to attack.

Gianluca stood in the way before I could disintegrate her, but my shot still went off. The wave of telekinetic energy slammed against Gianluca, staggering him, and let out a shockwave that reverberated through the ballroom. The walls shattered as easily as the windows and the ceiling began to collapse.

"I thought we were past all of this unpleasantness," I heard Aurelia say from behind Gianluca.

"Stop!" Gianluca yelled at me. I heard other screams from the far corners of the ballroom and looked around. Humans. The heads of state were all here mixed in with the Archios watching from the balconies.

"And I had just lauded your heroic exploits to them," said Aurelia. "You always were so ungrateful. Not one of the finer things Noah had taught you."

"I don't give a fuck what you say about me, you bitch."

"No? I think you will care once I reveal the *entire* story to our guests. I have some very telling evidence that our friends at PROJECT: UNITY were able to collect from their satellites. I wonder how the world will react to seeing the slaughter of the innocent people we were sent to rescue and your claims of being...what was it? Destruction incarnate? Even I may find that trying to erase from so many memories."

"It won't matter once I kill you," I snarled. I went to attack again, but Gianluca contained the blast in the shadows.

"Yes, murder me in cold blood in the presence of all these high profile witnesses. So *savage*. I dare say you enjoy letting out the monster that's inside you. You always did. However, your new family may not appreciate being hunted like dogs for their association with the one who assassinated Earth's cherished ambassador to the supernatural world. I can see the riots and witch hunts now! The sheer terror that will spread from the ruthless menace abounds—"

"Enough!" Gianluca yelled. "How much for the slave?"

"What?!" I screamed.

"He is not for sale. I believe you are familiar with the punishment for an attempt on an owner's life—especially one of royalty—being death. Even if I were to sell you what little remained of him, what guarantee would I have that you could handle him?"

"You have my word," said Gianluca. I grabbed Rafael's dagger from him and cut my wrist to start feeding Noah my blood. There was almost nothing left of him; an incomplete skeleton with shreds of muscles, sinews, and skin hanging off of it from head to toe. His heart was still in his broken ribcage though. I kept telling myself that that was enough to keep him alive, but the slightest movements from me to lift his head onto my lap caused more of him to crumble into ashes.

I looked at the floor where he had been lying face down. The pattern left in his pool of blood—it matched the stain on the parchment Castile had sent to me.

"Your word means little, Gaius. I have put my faith in your honor and upheld my end of our treaty to the letter, yet you were unable to prevent this attempt on my life and have done little to help our cause. What makes you think you can control this wild animal to any greater degree in the future? You have nothing to offer me for his ownership that I would be interested in regardless. I am afraid he has already passed."

"Get us out of here," I told Liam and the rest.

"That soul was promised to me." Rozalin reappeared just as we teleported away. "He has died. His soul clings to scraps held together by your former lover, Gaius. How embarrassing it must be for you that he chooses the ashen remains of a slave over your embrace."

Back in my room at the abbey I was as gentle as I could be at placing Noah on our bed. "Is there anything your magic can do to heal him?" I asked.

"He's...gone, Ascended," said Claudius. "Like the blood wraith said, the tiny flame of his soul is clinging to what you're holding, but there's no actual connection and he isn't even strong enough to manifest as a ghost himself."

"Our magic can't heal the undead either way," Liam said. "Could the goddess Isis?"

"I'll summon her. I need to be alone with Noah for a minute though first. Do everything you can to protect the abbey from anyone or anything that will come after him."

The four bowed and left us.

"Hang in there, you big idiot," I whispered to him between sobs. I went to hold his hand but as soon as I did it started to fall apart. My blood was having no effect. "I don't know if you can hear me...I never wanted to admit it to myself because I was always afraid something like this would happen once I did, but...I love you."

I sliced deeper into my forearm to let the blood flow freer. I was numb to the pain. Our blood soaked the sheets as it pooled in his mouth and ran out the sides. I used my powers to hold him together so no more would turn to ash.

Finally, I collected myself enough to create a statue of Isis out of the stone floor to summon her. "Isis! Come to me, please!"

She appeared at once like all the other times and approached the bed. "Help him, heal him, please."

"I cannot. The undead, the curse upon their soul prevents it. Light is the source of my magic and the bane of these tragic creatures."

"Then give him a fragment of my soul," I cried and wiped my nose on my sleeve. "Help me make him my champion."

"Only one fragment may be taken or else your soul will shatter and all will be lost. The undead curse prevents their souls from harmonizing with the living. He could not be your champion in any case."

"You can't do anything for him? Why did you show me omens of the birds that led me to him in that barn?"

"I had shown you the way to be each other's strength when his soul cried out for yours, even if his words did not. I knew the love you had for one another was deep enough to see you through the conflict with Set. I had shown him the way to rescue you when my brother had you imprisoned, but there is nothing more that can be done here. I will guide his soul to the afterlife. He holds on to this world for you, but he grows so very tired. Let him rest, Young One."

"But the undead go to *Hell* when they die!"

"He will, yes, but let him go with some strength. He is slipping, struggling in the dark to stay close to you. The last spark of his life wanes."

"No! I won't let him go!" I returned the statue back into the floor to dismiss the goddess before she could take Noah from me, but it wasn't long until another visitor came. Gianluca stepped out of the shadows beside me.

"Not now," I demanded.

"I did not let you kill her. I am sorry for this, but is on my honor to protect you both. You know it will bring a great trouble to you and these new friend if she die. I buy this one from her though and I return the sword to the empress. If he live he will be safe with me."

"I had hoped you were pretending," I said, anger now mixing back in with sadness. "I thought you were only saying that to call her off."

"No. He deserve the punishment of death for what he does to his master, but if he is a property for me then she will not touch him. He is safe with me and I teach him respect and a discipline. He is a fine warrior, but to be a man is much more."

"YOU HAVE NO RIGHT! He's a *person!* He didn't grow up in your time, just like I didn't! We aren't your or anyone else's slaves!"

"If he live, I will come to take him. I let you be with him when you want. I know you love him and he love you. I always know since I meet you."

"If you think I'm going to let you make him your slave..." I grasped the Empyrean Jewel of Light still in my pocket.

"Is already done, Dorian. Think what is best for him, not what you want."

"I'll buy him from you," I said and removed my hand from the stone.

"You cannot. Aurelia will know I give him to you. She only give to me because I promise he will not be a trouble."

"Then I pledge the Alabaster Order to the alliance."

"Alabaster Order? What is this?"

"The ones who fought with us in the desert. I'm their leader now and Noah was to join when he was free." I pointed to Alexandre's amulet still clasped to the shredded remains of Noah's pants as show of 'proof'. "They are the ones that helped save you from Set when you were turned to stone *twice*. If you have any honor you'll recognize them in the treaty. With me as their leader there will be no fear from our side of attacking Aurelia, as she should then have no reason to come after us, including Noah."

"This is a wise answer. I always know you will be a good leader. Okay. On my honor I keep both side happy and welcome the new allies. Noah will be yours if he live, but must not make trouble."

"Agreed."

Days passed. I didn't know how many with the curtains closed, but it was at least three. I sat on the bed next to him, never closing my eyes for more than a second or two at most, and recalled stories of our times together out loud.

I had changed the bedsheets twice already. I wasn't sure if my blood was being absorbed more by them or by Noah. I swore I saw progress when I thought his hair started to grow back, but it turned out to be my mind playing tricks on me.

"Ascended...Dorian." Nathaniel's voice startled me. "Sorry."

Nathaniel had checked in several times and was a much needed shoulder to lean on. It was good to see him in more casual clothing for a change; a linen tunic with leather pants and boots seemed to be the mainstay of his new wardrobe. Our bond was causing him to be affected by my sorrow, but he handled it well. I had him send some of the Order to Lyle to explain what had happened and keep an eye on him for me.

"Did you learn to teleport?"

"No. You fell asleep... Dorian, I think—I think it's time. You have to let go."

"Just a couple more days. He's starting to get better."

"He's gone, Dorian. You're holding together an empty shell. Let him pass. He wants to rest."

"You don't know what he wants! You don't know him like I do! If he were here he'd say...he'd say…" I started to cry again for the first time since this happened. "He'd tell me to…"

"I'm sorry…I can make the arrangements for you if you tell me what you want—"

"I want to be left alone."

"Look at what you're doing." Nathaniel brought over a candle to light up the room where the ones by the bed didn't reach. "These are your memories right? I can feel them like I've been there."

Areas of the room had been warped…transformed into other rooms I had been with Noah. Places I recalled with him over the past few days.

"Did I really do this?" The fireplace and the furniture around it had been reconfigured into his room back in the chateau, the swords on the wall turned into katana like he had in his mounted collection, the heraldic banners were now the Asian scrolls he had hanging, the mantle was the Buddhist shrine where he later kept Vivi's ashes. All the details down to the molecule.

"The first time I was in that room was after my parents had died. He told me they were better off dead than suffering. He told me… I had to mourn and get it over with so I could move on. God, I hated him so much for that."

"He knew what was best for you even though it hurt at the time," Nathaniel said and came to sit by me. "He deserves the same thing from you."

"All right…just…give me another minute with him to say goodbye."

I wished Vance were here. If light magic and aether magic couldn't affect the undead, the Strigoi's blood magic surely could.

That was it!

"Nathaniel!" I called him back as he was about to leave.

"Yes?"

"Get me Liam and his cabal."

Chapter Forty-Seven

"The Strigoi...*made* me. Their Ancient is dead and most of their coven wiped out, but they left behind libraries full of magic in their sanctuary. It's hidden in Munich and to get there you have to go *between* dimensions like when we got trapped in the chateau. They must have something to heal their own kind and I'm sure it's got to be pretty basic. They don't like getting hurt and I can't imagine them interrupting their studies to wait around for their wounds to heal normally."

"But, they use blood magic, Ascended," said Rafael. "Not only have we never done it before because it's considered dirty—er—forbidden magic, but we can't use our blood like the undead or we'll die."

"I can." Nathaniel stepped up. "If you can teach it to me. I can't die, right? And I don't think blood magic will ruin my reputation any more than it already was."

"Thank you," I said. "I was thinking we could use my blood, but if yours is as potent as mine now that we're linked that could work. You'll need to take as many of the Order as there are available. That demon sorceress we met in Delos, she used to be Strigoi. She's the one that came up with the idea to create me as her living weapon and she killed the Ancient there. I don't know if she'll show up or if she's already there pillaging whatever is left."

"Everyone is available to you," said Marianna. "We'll leave only those watching the children."

"Blood magic is in that weird language," Claudius said to her. "Tell your aunt to bring a codex to help us translate."

"Good idea. I forgot about that," I said and watched as Liam eyed the katana on the wall by where my fireplace used to be. "You can take a look if you want, Liam."

"Thank you. It's beautiful craftsmanship. I didn't know you knew how to forge swords or work orichalcum after it had been enchanted. I didn't think that was possible."

"You saw him turn Anatole and Ruben into nothing, armor and all. What did you expect?" Marianna asked.

"Breaking it is different than forging it," Liam retorted and picked up the katana to inspect it against one of his swords. "This takes a lot more precision and skill. It's an even finer blade than mine..."

"I did it in my sleep." I had never seen Liam so expressive. My subconscious was more creatively articulate with my powers than my conscious mind. The first time my telekinesis manifested was while I was sleeping so it made sense that there was a correlation. "Take it, if it'll help, but I want it back for Noah."

"There's, ah, more than one there, boss. Do you think I could borrow one too?" Claudius asked. "Someone has to get Liam's back if there's a demon bugger about."

Liam raised an eyebrow at him over his shoulder at the suggestion that he needed someone to watch his back.

"Yes, but stop calling me boss...and saying bugger," I sighed.

"I need one to protect Liam too," Marianna declared and swiped the last sword that Rafael was reaching for.

"You have more swords than all of us combined," he barked.

She winked at him over her shoulder after giving it a twirl. "A girl can never have too many swords."

I returned to tending to Noah after they had left. I knew I was pretending to see something that wasn't there when I checked for signs of progress, but it was all I could do to convince myself that everything would be all right.

"I have to get these guys to help me make you new gear," I said to him. I sat there for a while until I was visited by an unexpected guest.

"Hey! What are you doing here?" I asked Lyle after his escorts from the Order I had sent to guard him dropped him off.

"Came to check up on you. I heard what happened."

"I'm fine. Better now than I have been in days, actually. We came up with a plan to save Noah."

"Is this him?" Lyle looked at him on the bed beside me.

"Yeah. He doesn't look *that* bad. You can still tell who he is."

"Uh...sure. How are you doing? Are you...*okay?*" He took a seat on the couch by the window where some light streamed in from the side of the curtain and glanced over at the recreation of Noah's room from the chateau.

"I said I'm fine."

"You don't seem fine. I know you two were close, but I think it's time to move on. You know that Noah of all people would be the first to want you to get over him."

"I'm prepared to get over him *after* I'm sure I've done everything I can."

"Uh huh. And what is this about giving your soul to some other guy that died? The babysitters you sent me were talking about it like you're Jesus or something."

"I gave a tiny piece to bring back Nathaniel. He died against Set remember?"

"Yeah, yeah... I remember."

"What? Spit it out. I knew you wouldn't have wanted to be the one I gave it to."

"You're damn right I wouldn't, man. What were you thinking giving that to anybody? I know more than anyone how you don't want to lose people. I'm right there with you. I was there when you lost your family and saw it take its toll on you, but people *die*. It's something we all have to accept and come to terms with or life won't have any meaning."

"If I have the power to save lives, I'm going to use it."

"Saving lives and cheating death once it's already happened are two totally different things, man. I know you don't have a god complex that you want to take over the world, but it's a slippery slope to start hitting the reset button on people's biological clock."

"The undead do it all the time."

"The undead *can* die though." Lyle held his hand out to indicate Noah. "They're working on extended time yeah, but once they're finished that's it. I just don't want you to make crazy sacrifices. One day you won't have anything left to give."

"Nathaniel was a hasty decision, I agree, but it was completely justified. He was abused his entire childhood, given a death sentence he didn't deserve, and died to help me without being asked. He's already proven himself a good friend and valuable ally. Giving him that fragment of my soul doesn't make me any weaker so there's really no downside except for not being able to give it to someone else."

"You're still crazy."

"Eh, that's nothing new."

"Nice room, by the way. You got some good people in this Order from what I can tell. Looks like they made a pretty decent leader out of you too. I knew you had it in you, but always thought it'd be PROJECT: UNITY you'd open up to."

"They made it hard to say no. There were a few bad eggs, but they're gone now. I renamed us to the Alabaster Order."

"Homage to your time with Gianluca?"

"No," I snapped. "Well, maybe partially. I liked what it stood for; purity and hope. It was that ray of sunshine in all the gloominess that we deal with daily."

"Yeah, I get it. It's very 'white knight'... You know he's been talking to Aurelia about buying Rome to bring back the empire? Just Rome. Gotta start small. I don't think he gets that you can't just buy cities."

"I don't think he gets that you can't just buy *people*. I know what I'm about to say is going to sound messed up, but I *wish* he was evil. It would have been so much simpler. Instead, I'm constantly torn between staying with him because of what a good guy he is and then keeping my distance when I see these glaring warning signs that cause us to clash.

"He wanted to buy Noah from Aurelia. I know he was doing it to help me, but it's the fact that he sees absolutely nothing wrong with the concept of slavery. He said he'd teach Noah discipline. I could imagine how that would go."

"Shit. I don't want to imagine," Lyle chuckled. "What if Gianluca comes around though?"

"He won't. He wants to change the world back to how it was and I'm concerned because he's one of the few people that can actually do it. I should be glad that he's not trying to take Rome by force though."

"We don't need any more publicity scares. Which leads me to the other reason I came. You know I saw the whole encounter between you and Set."

"Here we go," I sighed.

"Hold it a minute. I stand by what you did, man. We all do on base. I erased the videos from the server, but I'm sure Aurelia had Rudgar make backups somewhere. Gianluca told me about the incident at the chateau the other day and her attempt to blackmail you, and how you almost killed about eighty world leaders when you brought the ballroom down."

"I'm innocent until proven guilty."

"That's funny. You'll be happy to know Aurelia claims to have wiped the whole thing from their memories. I guess it's the easier route for her to save face too. Either way, you're a leader now, a powerful one, and I don't mean because of your special abilities. I mean politically.

"All eyes are on us and Aurelia is going to be sure to twist everything her way. She can hypnotize the UN or NATO, but she can't take over the entire world...I think. She's going to be playing the politics game to get everyone else to love her and you know she's gonna be good at it, so watch every move you make out there. The days of crawling around in sewers and darting between buildings in the shadows to avoid getting noticed are over. If I were you I'd ride the whole white knight thing with the Order to Hell and back. Really get everyone to see how good you are and what you stand for."

"That's what I was planning," I agreed. "Join us. Aurelia has her hands around PROJECT: UNITY's throat. You're safe here with us. I can make an exception because you don't know magic. You can be court jester or something."

"Wow, that's really tempting."

"Really?"

"No. I'm not going to bail on my people because of Aurelia," Lyle affirmed. "I'm small potatoes to her, which could work to our benefit. Sometimes it pays to be the little guy. She only wants to deal with Rudgar and is only interested in us to gain the people's confidence that she works well with others. She won't have us do anything to ruin that reputation, but if she does you'll be the first I go to for help."

"And you can keep a closer eye on her than anyone now that Noah is free," I added. "Maybe it's better that we aren't tripping over each other."

"Two separate entities is a lot harder to bring down than one if we keep watch of each other's backs."

"I should probably dismiss your babysitters then."

"Yeah, I appreciate it, but if anything is gonna antagonize Aurelia it'll be that. They put a big spotlight on me too." I was happy to have Lyle here with me. It was always comforting to have an old friend close by during the darkest hours. I hated the word 'ally' that had been thrown around frequently as of late. There was such an emptiness to it; your bond was based on what you could do for each other and nothing more.

"Here, take this." I tossed Lyle the amulet that Noah had stolen from Alexandre. "It'll keep unwanted guests out of your head in case that PARAGON implant fails you."

"Nice. Thanks, man. So...what was going on between you two?" Lyle motioned to Noah. "I heard some things..."

I sat there quiet. I was reluctant to say anything to him that might jinx Noah's recovery. Everything was balancing on a hair. I also knew how much he would disapprove. "If you're asking, then you already know."

"I would have liked to have heard it from you is my point."

I spilled all the details of the bizarre turn that my friendship took with Noah. As I thought, Lyle was against the idea of me having a relationship with him. "You're out of your mind.

Assuming you even *can* bring him back, you're better off trying to teach Gianluca human rights. Noah might not be as bad as I thought when we met, but he's still...Noah."

"My heart isn't in it with Gianluca in that way. We don't want the same thing. It never felt quite right after the initial burst of passion."

"Your choice, man, but I know who I'd pick if I were you."

"You can date him and be his princess if you want. I won't get jealous."

"Oh, thanks," he laughed. "A little too much facial hair from what I'm used to though. Saving the world can be lonely. I look at Rudgar and think how much I *don't* want to be like him now. Career soldier and lifelong bachelor."

"What happened to Rebecca?"

"She told me she just wants to be friends. I thought we were holding off getting serious because of the war, but it turns out she wasn't feeling it. I think she couldn't get over me being her superior, even though I tried to never treat her like I was."

"I have no doubt that you'll find the one," I told him.

"Hope it's before I have one foot in the grave. I don't have all the time in the world like *some* people."

"You could if you wanted."

"What's the word with Set?" he asked to avoid my offer. "Sky is back to normal in Egypt and he lost his magic wand. Did we actually win a fight without killing the big baddie?"

"He'll come back, but not as strong. Unless the Infernal Kings that had him on their payroll do something about it first. Gianluca can have fun slugging it out with him if he pops up."

"That means no one can ever live in Egypt again if he could return at any time. We need to do something to make sure he doesn't come back. Something that sends a message to anyone else thinking of pulling the same shit and says 'Don't fuck with Earth'. Something *big*."

Chapter Forty-Eight

The Order returned to me in dribs and drabs with their findings over the next two days. Everyone, except Liam of course, was borderline hyperventilating in excitement over all the ancient arcane secrets they were uncovering in the Strigoi's old haven.

I was beginning to tire from holding Noah together for so long, but letting go was not an option. Not when we were so close.

"I found something you should see," Claudius said to me during one of his trips back to the abbey. He handed me an old leather-bound journal covered in scribbled notes on every page. I couldn't read any of it. The writing was a mixture of German and the Strigoi's unique gibberish. "Here. This page."

Claudius flipped a quarter of the way through for me and pointed to a page with my name. There was a rough sketch of my side profile matched to an old photograph of me stuck between the pages. On the next pages were scientific notes and arcane scrawlings that detailed pencil drawings depicting cross sections of body parts.

"Do you know any of them?" Claudius asked in reference to a long list of names on another page. Some were crossed out, others circled.

"No..."

"It says 'donations' here in German. Do you think this could be a list of those that the Strudel took from when making you?"

"*Strigoi*...and if they took anything from these people, it wasn't their money." It was most likely a list of all the people that the Strigoi used for their DNA samples.

Vance was on two lists, but one of them also had his brother Tristan and Minerva. That must have been the names of the Strigoi that worked on me. It would also mean that Vance was a donor. Gianluca did used to think that we had the same eyes.

There was another name I recognized on both lists. Octavio Jules.

"No, it can't be..." *Grampy? It has to be a different Octavio Jules, but how many people out there have that name and are also undead? That would mean he's a Strigoi, or that he was one before whatever happened to him to make him lose his mind. Was our meeting on the NYC subway that very first day during the Carpathian's invasion not really a random occurrence then?*

"Someone you know?"

"Yes. Good find, Claudius. Thank you."

"My pleasure, Ascended. Alex and Raf think they found a spell like the one you described. The Scribes are translating it now. We've got a massive haul over the last two days and aren't even half way done clearing the place out. We didn't have to kill anyone for their stuff either."

"How often do you kill people to take their stuff? Or do I not want to know?"

"More often than you think. Whenever some druid or new age Wiccan gets their hands on a real magical artifact and not some plastic piece of crap bought at a novelty store, we swoop in and procure it. Can't have real magic getting into the hands of amateurs."

"Yeah, they might turn their hair white on accident."

"Ouch."

"Why do you have to kill them though? Can't you just... I don't know intimidate them or something? Give them that mind wipe potion?"

"It's not always about the artifacts," Claudius explained. "Sometimes they dabble into real dangerous stuff; demon possessions, necromancy, blood magic... It's a 'better safe than sorry approach' to put them down. We'd need to have *millions* in the Order to keep checking up on the same people to make sure they never did anything stupid again.

"The memory decoction is only meant to erase short-term memories. I think it's more cruel to give someone permanent brain damage with an overdose than kill them. It won't erase the gift of magic anyway, so even at the correct dose it's pretty worthless."

"This was before we could recruit them," I said. "We could be killing potential allies and good people because they were curious. Let the rest know that we're not killing Wiccans, druids, and whatever else is out there that we can recruit and train properly instead. We have more important things to focus on with an impending apocalypse than someone with a Ouija board in their basement."

"Those things are the devil!"

I laughed for the first time in days. "You really cheer me up sometimes."

"It's because I'm a ginger. Everybody loves a ginger."

"Your hair is white, so I don't know about that. You do represent the alabaster part of the Alabaster Order well though."

"I knew that was the real reason why you renamed us."

"Sure, we can go with that," I laughed again.

"If I can be serious a moment...I'm glad you chose Nathaniel."

"Oh? Why is that?" I was as surprised to hear that as I was to see him being serious. I knew that Claudius was good friends with Liam who was anticipated to be the champion.

"He deserves it more than any of us. You don't survive what he did by training and studying. We can teach him all that stuff and he has all the time in the world now, but to survive to get to that point, it was all him."

"That's good of you to say. He's been through something no child—no person—should ever have to. I'm happy to hear he's finally being accepted."

"He's working harder than any of us, except me of course. He hasn't slept a wink, or maybe he doesn't have to anymore? Either way I think he's taking it personal to come out of the gate at his best."

"He doesn't need to prove anything to anybody," I said. "Especially not me."

"You're a good one. Most high and mighty beings don't give two shits about the little guys under their feet holding them up. I'm *real* glad Tobias insisted you be the one we follow more than ever. I only see good things ahead for us."

"Me too."

"I should get back to looting those ruins. The others probably thought I fell asleep under a stack of books somewhere and are trying to flush me out with fire."

"That would be...counterproductive to say the least. I'll see you soon I'm sure."

Claudius saluted and then he was gone, but I wasn't alone for long. Marianna entered with Helena and Alexandre.

"We've come to begin the preparations if that's all right, Ascended," said Helena.

"You finished the translations already?"

"It was very simple like you thought," Marianna said. "The Strigoi language is a bastardized mess from multiple other mystic languages. None of it is original, so it was easy for us to translate by flipping through the codex we brought. Only thing is that it's a rejuvenation *ritual* not a spell, so we need to make preparations. It isn't something we can have Nathaniel recite the words and cut his wrists to activate...or whatever those freaks do."

"We'll be using aether crystals around the arcane circle to work as a stabilizing agent," Helena explained. "Nathaniel will need all the help he can get keeping the proper balance and since adding more people to the ritual only makes it more difficult we found this to be the better alternative."

"I get training wheels," Nathaniel said as he walked in. Judging by his dry delivery you'd think he was bitter, but I could tell he meant it as a self-deprecating joke.

He handed me a cup of tea to help keep me awake and a piece of honeycomb from the apiary in the orchard. The Order wasn't big on candy and junk food—they followed a stricter diet than the most regimented professional athletes and even the pancakes Marianna made were healthy—but natural honey seemed to be the one vice they allowed. I was told that Rafael has been their resident head beekeeper since he was twelve.

"Right, well. Nathaniel, all you need to do for the first part is bleed into this bowl enough for us to paint the arcane circle on the floor around the bed," Helena instructed.

"I can't. My skin won't cut after Dorian brought me back."

"That complicates things. The blood needs to be the same as the person performing the ritual."

"Use mine," I said. "I've bled plenty this week and Nathaniel and I are connected. Mine gave Noah back his heartbeat and ability to breathe when he drank from me after I transcended. It's got to be better for the ritual than anything the Strigoi had."

"Very well, Ascended." Helena bowed and handed me a bowl and dagger. Each time the bowl was filled, Helena and Marianna used the blood to paint the floor around the bed with the runes they copied from the ritual scroll. Alexandre created and placed aether crystals imbued with the stabilizing spell at equal intervals around the circle while whispering a word of mystic origin to each. I sat with Nathaniel on the other side of the room and watched them work. It wouldn't be long now. I'd have Noah and his stupid cocky grin back soon.

"We're almost ready," Marianna said after I refilled the bowl for the third time. "Then I'll show you what you have to do, Nathaniel."

"I'm nervous," I said under my breath to him.

"I'll do my best."

"I know. It's not you I'm nervous about. I just hope this works. I don't have a plan B." I spent the last minutes before the ritual dictating the new rule of not killing other practitioners of magic in the world to Helena so she could put it in the records.

Nathaniel was in complete support, but out of all the changes I had made to the Order so far this was the one that seemed to draw the most negative response from the others.

Helena, Alexandre, and Marianna couldn't fathom the reasoning behind letting others be free to use magic. To them, unless trained by the Order, all outsiders were incompetent buffoons that would eventually doom everyone around them if any exceptions were allowed. What would be worse was if any of those practicing magic became proficient enough to become a credible threat. I was open to reconsidering my thoughts, but for the time being it had to be on a case-by-case basis since I couldn't have them running around cutting people's heads off; we were trying to project a friendlier image to those who were not part of the Order.

"Okay, we're ready." Marianna signaled for Nathaniel to go to the circle.

"Wait. What are the chances this doesn't work?" I asked. I had been holding Noah together for quite a long time with my powers, and was feeling my mind lose its ability to concentrate with each passing day. "And what happens if it doesn't?"

"There is nothing stated for conditions of failure," Helena answered. "The Strigoi kept meticulous records down to the last detail, making the translation as simple as being handed a crossword puzzle with the answer key. All that is left is for Nathaniel to activate the ritual. We have even taken out the step to recite the words by enchanting them into each aether crystal."

"All right...go ahead." I clutched Noah's prayer beads in both hands and closed my eyes.

"Okay, Nathaniel, activate each of the seven aether crystals starting at the north position and go counter-clockwise around the circle," Alexandre directed. "Each one that is activated should drain blood from your body. I imagine it will be unpleasant, but there is no other way."

"I can handle it, but how do I activate them?" I squeezed the prayer beads tighter after hearing him ask that.

"Just like you would an amulet."

"I've never had one...I'm sorry."

"I'll teach you," Marianna offered. Another twenty minutes later and Nathaniel had been given a rundown on the basics. My confidence in our success was plummeting. I didn't want to say anything, but I'm sure Nathaniel knew how I felt.

"Here we go," he said and took his spot at the southern position of the circle again.

"Please work," I whispered to myself and kept my eyes closed. The first crystal rang like a bell as Nathaniel started. Marianna gave him words of encouragement that I couldn't pay attention to; something about the blood being taken from him. By the fourth crystal I opened one eye to peek. Blood was in fact being drained from Nathaniel through his pores and into Noah's body. I had given Noah gallons of my own that did nothing, but if this was what it took...

I focused on the prayer beads to keep myself sane.

Five.

Something else caught my eye. My pocket was glowing and getting brighter.

Six.

"No!" I shouted as the Empyrean Jewel flew out from my pocket towards Nathaniel.

Seven.

Chapter Forty-Nine

The Empyrean Jewel of Light shot across the room, turning into a beam of pure energy that I couldn't grab a hold of. Helena recognized what it was instantly and yelled for everyone to get out as she teleported herself away with Marianna.

The light pierced Nathaniel's heart and flooded the room with its afterglow. I felt the pain in my own chest, but struggled through it to throw Nathaniel from the room and cover Noah's body.

I was too late.

Only ashes remained as a silhouette against the sheets where Noah had lain. I couldn't stop myself from screaming.

I almost didn't care what was happening outside when the abbey shook.

"Come quickly, Ascended," Alexandre prompted and tried to get me up from the bedside.

I flew out the broken window I had ejected Nathaniel through. At first thought I had been locked away in that dark room for too long. The sun seemed brighter than normal, but when my eyes adjusted I saw what was really causing the glare from above: Nathaniel.

I went up after him and immediately saw the effect the jewel had left on his body. As my veins were once blackened by the stain of the parasite, Nathaniel's were highlighted in blinding white light that converged at his heart. His eyes were now beacons in the clouds, in the opposite (yet same) way that mine had been turned dark by the transformation.

He held his head and clenched his jaw in agony. I could feel every bit of what he felt and reached out to him as he trembled.

"Please! Help me! It's—going to tear me apart!" he yelled. I held on to his head as if it were my own that I was bracing from the pain. "The aether—it's the aether poisoning. Worse than ever—I don't want to die!"

"I won't let anything happen to you, but you have to release it!" My own body was starting to glow now as the light overtook us both. "Now!"

My ears rang and vision was blinded by light. My heart pushed against the inside of my chest toward Nathaniel and then repelled us both away from each other in a detonation of raw energy.

I was the first to recover and darted after Nathaniel to catch him as he sailed through the air. The glowing veins and light from his eyes had diminished, but the unnatural brightness in the sky persisted. "We have to get back to the abbey," I told him once I was sure he was all right.

Nathaniel flew down ahead of me in a beam of light like the one from the Empyrean Jewel that shot into his chest. He was tens or even hundreds of times faster than me now. The power from it still lingered inside of him.

He returned to me before I made it halfway down to the abbey and took me the rest of the way. It was *not* an enjoyable ride, however. He wasn't nearly as fast as Noah, who moved outside of time and where there wasn't wind resistance, but was still fast enough to make me feel like my skin was getting torn off and limbs dislocated. He didn't seem affected which could have been because of his telekinetic coating.

He set me down in my room where I doubled over trying not to vomit.

"I'm sorry," he apologized and put his hand on my back.

Noah's ashes had been scattered by the strong gust upon our reentry. I sat on the floor in the smeared blood circle scooping what I could together and trying not to cry.

"Can I be alone with him for a moment?" I asked. He went to leave right as Helena and the other ex-councilmembers followed by Liam's cabal all came in to see what had happened. Nathaniel did what I was hoping and chased them off to answer their questions outside.

"I never got to tell you how much I love you. You looked out for me and made me who I am today more than anyone I know," I spoke to the bloody pile of ash that represented all that was left of Noah. "If I have to go to Hell to protect you until the end of time I'll do it."

The Order was making so much noise outside my broken window that it was hard to mourn. They weren't exactly a rowdy group so I had to wonder what the commotion was about. I placed Noah's ashes in the bowl we had used for the ritual and looked outside.

The sky was draped in a majestic aurora of glittering gold and silver that spanned the whole island. It was ironic that something so beautiful could come from so much misery. "You probably would have hated this and said it was dumb," I laughed through the tears to speak to Noah like he could hear me.

I picked the bowl back up and looked inside at the remains. I thought my eyes were playing tricks on me again. The ashes were gone and in their place sat a shriveled human heart.

I had to take the chance that it was real. I summoned the dagger from earlier to my hand and stuck it in my forearm after a deep breath. The heart soaked up the blood and turned a healthy red as it filled. Blood vessels sprouted like webbing and then muscle fibers that lead to ligaments and tendons. I took the heart out of the bowl and put it on the bed to give more room to grow as I kept feeding it.

Bones formed into a ribcage and spine then sprouted the hips, shoulder blades, and collar bones. From there everything went too fast to see what order it was happening in until the process was about finished. Skin grew out in layers across the body and then finally hair and nails returned last.

"Noah!" I shouted and held him in my arms as his eyes opened. "Please tell me this is real. Tell me it's really you."

He groaned and writhed in pain as the last of his insides regrew and his muscles pumped back up. "It's okay," I soothed. "I'm here. I've got you."

His body was warm and his chest rose and fell as he drew breath. When placing my hand above his heart I could feel it beating strong. "Too bright," he moaned.

I panicked, realizing a sliver of sunlight was coming through from between the curtains and shone directly on his face. "It doesn't hurt?" I asked and turned his head to the side to get the light out of his eyes.

"No." His voice was heavy with sleep, but he put an arm around me and brought me in closer with his eyes closed again. "Where am I?"

"You're safe. We're in the abbey, in Greece. My fan club, remember?"

"I...What happened?" He opened his eyes and looked around this time. "Why am I naked?"

"You...died. I brought you back with the Order's help."

"You mean I failed."

"No, no! You're free now."

"She's dead?" he asked. "I don't feel her in my head anymore."

"No, but I worked it out—"

"Then I failed."

"You didn't fail. You got the help from me you should have accepted from the start."

He was quiet. I thought he fell asleep, but he started rubbing my back and squeezed me closer. "How'd I die? She make me fight you and you killed me?"

"No. It was Kenneth."

"Fuck that guy and his magic glove...I feel weird. What did you do to me to bring me back?" I explained everything to him up to now, including my barter with Gianluca that won Noah his freedom. We kept direct eye contact the entire time, only a few inches apart from each other's face. I was scared that he would disappear if I looked away and that none of it would be real anymore.

"It had to be my blood used in the ritual that's given you back your ability to breathe and have a heartbeat. It's lasting longer than the other time you drank from me. The Empyrean Jewel that interfered might be what's keeping you from getting hurt by the light. We might've broken the curse!"

Noah felt his teeth with his tongue. "Nope. Still got fangs and craving your blood pretty bad. I can see your aura too so I'm guessing I still have my powers."

"That could be the best of both worlds then."

"I got the best part of my world right here."
He squeezed me tighter against him again. Our
faces were dangerously close now. "Did you cry?"

"Yes. More than I want to admit."

"That means you really do love me," he
smirked. "I knew it."

"I do love you, you big idiot," I said with each
word getting softer until our lips touched. It was by
far the best kiss I had experienced and neither one
of us would let it end.

When I kissed Gianluca it was electrifying,
arousing, and at times humbling by the sheer
perfection of both the act and the man on the other
end.

Kissing Noah was warm and passionate.
Although it was our *real* first time there was a sense
of familiarity that silenced any self-consciousness
and doubt. Someone that was so known for being
intimidating was now anything but that. We
matched each other's pace with every subtle move
and neither of us took the lead from the other for too
long. It was relaxing and more enjoyable than any
Archios bite.

"Damn, I love kissing you. You've been
practicing without me, haven't you?" he said during
a pause to catch his breath and pull me on top of
him. "Remind me to thank whoever it was with
before I kill 'em."

"I haven't," I laughed and pushed his face
down on the pillow. He smiled up at me and grabbed

me by the back of the neck to bring me back down to resume.

"I hope you know I was kidding when I said that you're a ten and I'm an eleven," he told me during another break. "You're definitely my better half. You're the total sexy package of brave, smart, strong, and gorgeous."

I started to blush and hit him jokingly on the chest. "Shut up! You're just trying to make me squirm."

"I can do a lot of other things to make that happen. I mean it though. Kissing you feels like this is how it should be between us."

"I actually feel the same way," I smiled. Intimacy with Gianluca was great and I could never say that it wasn't. But with Noah there was something so much more comfortable and solid.

I know many people get a rush from starting something new for how fresh it is, but this was the exact opposite. It wasn't the unknown, it was an established bond that was continuously being made stronger and just reached the next level. I didn't have to put on airs or worry about what he thought of me, or where this was going. It all felt... *right*.

"Hey." He stopped after another long bout and nuzzled his scruff against my cheek. "This place is disgusting."

He wasn't wrong. The room was covered in blood and ashes that were drying and getting tacky, not to mention my hands that were smearing it on the both of us.

"I should bathe really quick," I said and kissed him one more time.

"Yeah, we should," he agreed and picked me up off the bed in his arms. "But it doesn't need to be quick."

Chapter Fifty

"You've done that before. Don't lie."

"I already told you three times that I haven't!" I laughed.

"Yeah, but I thought you and the Italian were always doing it. How'd you get so good then? That was incredible."

"Yes it was. I never would have thought you'd be so...I don't know. Loving?"

"You kidding? I love that shit. You know what they say: big guy, big heart." Noah held on to my waist from behind as I went to leave the bathroom and started kissing the back of my neck. "Sorry if I got a little too rough, I was kinda in the moment."

"I'm used to a lot worse from you—Can you put a towel on?" I started laughing again as he walked out from the bathroom naked. "The Order is always dropping in."

"I like to air dry." He threw himself down on the couch by the broken window with a self-satisfied smirk. "So, I'm the best you've ever been with."

"By default, yes."

"Good, I wanna keep it that way." He held out his arms for me to settle in next to him. "Come take a nap."

"I'd love to, but I've got work to do," I said as I got dressed in one of my new outfits from the Order.

"Work? What the hell did you do, get a day job while I was dead? Get over here and love me."

"Aren't you the least bit interested in how and what the ritual did to you?"

"Not really. I'm here, you're here, and that's all that matters." Noah leaned back across the armrest and stretched with his hands in the sunlight coming in from around the curtain. "You know what I *am* interested in after that ritual though? Sunglasses."

I rolled my eyes at him and finished getting dressed.

"Why are you putting clothes on?"

"I'm going to see how Nathaniel is doing," I said.

"Who?"

"The guy from the Order I started to tell you about in the bath…"

"I wasn't listening to any of that!" Noah burst out laughing. "I was a *little* distracted."

"You're a dick."

"You weren't complaining about it then!" he shouted as I left, but then ran up from behind and picked me up. "I'm kidding. Just gimme a minute to clear my head? And some clothes?"

"Okay," I turned and kissed him with my hands on his face to feel his scruff.

"You like my whiskers, huh?"

"I do," I laughed when he rubbed his cheek against mine. He growled and bared his fangs with a big smile.

"You know, being with you just now... it really proved to me how right I was about you. It's better than I thought, actually. I've never felt this complete with anybody before. I don't even understand some of these feelings, but I like it. I want more of it..."

"Ascend—" Liam dropped in and made me jump out of Noah's arms right as our lips were inching closer. "Oh, I'm sorry. I didn't—"

I threw my towel around Noah's waist. "It's fine, Liam. What is it?"

"We wanted to know if you wished us to begin the repairs on your chambers. It will only take a short while with magic."

I looked to Noah, knowing he wanted a moment, but he nodded for me to allow them. "That'll be fine. Noah will need clothes and I need some of that enchanted orichalcum to make swords for him. You and the others can keep the ones I loaned you if you like. Please let them know."

"Absolutely, and thank you," Liam bowed with almost a smile.

"Where's Nathaniel?"

"He retired to his room about three hours ago."

He must have been worn out after everything that had happened. "Noah is undead, as you know, but after the ritual he seems immune to sunlight. Could it be from the Empyrean Jewel? Some of his life functions have been restored too, but I'm assuming that was a permanent side-effect from my blood being godly now."

"My father knows more about the jewels than I do, but a blessing of light to purge some of the undead curse seems the least they could do along with your blood."

"Any word on what exactly happened with Nathaniel? Why did the jewel react to a blood magic ritual?"

"Helena explained that since Nathaniel's soul is linked to yours, and you had the Empyrean Jewel on you, it created a chain reaction when he activated the stabilizing crystals. Since he never severed his connection to the aether as an Adamant Aegis, he absorbed the stone into himself as if it were raw aether. If he wasn't immortal from his link to you he would've died instantly and the stone's power would have gone out of control instead of being absorbed into him."

"Instead we just got that neat aurora."

"That's stupid," said Noah from the window, just as I had thought. "Draws attention to us."

"Thanks, Liam." I nodded to let him leave and went over by Noah. "Us, huh? I didn't think you'd take to being here so quickly."

"It's my new cage, isn't it? Better to get used to it now."

"What? I'd never put you in a cage and you know that. It's a home, with four walls to protect us and an open door to come and go as you please. We're finally home."

"I haven't had a home since I was human and even then it was never for long. The door's open, but if I walk out it's not free unless I wear a collar that says who I belong to."

I put my hand on his. "She can't hurt you anymore. You're free, but I didn't say we were finished."

He raised an eyebrow at me. "What are you talking about?"

"Don't worry about it. I let you do things your way, now let me do them mine."

"The secrets between us are over. If you think I'm going to let you do something dumb..."

"I wasn't carrying around that Empyrean Jewel of *Light* in my pocket by accident."

"...You telling me you planned this?" he stared down at himself in the sunlight.

"I can't take credit for the details of how it worked out, but I knew I needed it for something like this. I didn't get the chance to figure everything out before you ran off."

"I did it because I knew I couldn't wait anymore. I had to either be free so I could be with you, or die trying."

"Like I said: we did things your way, now we do them mine. Aurelia is at the height of her game right now, but the higher up you are, the harder it is to see the ground. I don't doubt she knows that I was able to save you. She's thinking we'll be too busy playing house and living happily ever after to risk that by attacking her.

"We have to look at the bigger picture; we need her to do her part in saving the world from total annihilation so our lives will be easier in the long run. After that, she's done and will have no reason for anyone to keep her around. We aren't the only ones that want her out of the picture, we just need to wait until they act and then make sure that they don't fail."

"It's really hot to hear you talk like that. When did you get so conniving and how long is it gonna take to change the bedsheets? I've got an itch that needs scratching."

"Patience, tiger." I played with his scruff some more while he rested his head on my shoulder.

"What are you hiding in here?" He stuck his nose in the hood of my shirt that I had up. "I smell something good."

He made me laugh and squirm in his arms as he tickled up and down my neck with kisses and nipped at my ear. "I love you," he said with his face still wedged in my hood. "I know I'm never gonna remember to say it at all the right times, so I'm just getting it out there now."

"I love you too." I pulled back so I could look him in the eyes as I said it.

"And you better not tell anybody that I'm saying this stuff or I'll have to kill them. I got a reputation to uphold, you know."

"Ah, Dorian?" Marianna was at my door with her gaze honed right in on Noah's body.

"Come back later," Noah said without even glancing over. "I'm about to defile your god all over the couch, and maybe the bathroom again."

"Noah!" I pushed him away and tried not to laugh. "You can come in, Marianna."

"We have the orichalcum you requested and we need Noah's measurements."

"About eight inches in the right direction," Noah grinned as I covered his mouth.

"Ignore him. He's just a little excited to be alive. I'll take the metal and we'll get out of here so you can 'magic' this place back into shape. When Noah calms down we'll come get him fitted."

I left to go outside with Noah and took the stack of orichalcum ingots with me that were waiting by my door. It was cute to watch him hesitate before stepping out into the sun, but after the first step he was fearless. "How does it feel?"

"Warm."

We went down by the shore where there was more privacy and sat together while I shaped the metal into a blade for him.

"It's called the *hi*, or as some idiots like to call it, the 'blood groove'." Noah ran his finger along the horizontal indentation of the blade that I created. Up to now, whenever I had made something with my powers I drew from a subconscious recollection that filled in the details. I didn't necessarily know what or why those details were what they were. "It's meant to make the blade lighter while retaining its durability. People say it's there to make the sword easier to remove after stabbing someone. If you hear anyone say that, you have to punch them right in the face to get the stupid out. That kind of stupid runs deep so it could take more than one punch."

Noah went over every part of the katana with me, but insisted I make the hilt and scabbard from real wood. "Never thought you'd be making my swords. This blade is unreal too."

"I never thought any of what's happening between us would be. It's a new chapter in our lives." I touched along his forearm where he was tattooed previous to having a whole new body. "You need to get all your tattoos inked again."

"I was thinking of doing something different. New chapter, new ink. Don't wanna be reminded of the past anymore."

Guess I'll change our room back from the recreation of his in the chateau. "Any ideas?"

"Some. Thinking about getting a sleeve. You can help me decide when it's time." He squeezed my nose and threw an arm around me with a kiss to the side of my head. "Think our room is ready yet?"

"If it is, we're not staying. I need to see Castile and it's long overdue. The sun is setting here so we've got two hours until it does by him."

"There's plenty we can do in those two hours," he smirked and gave me a roguish look out of the corner of his eye.

"Yes, like get you measured."

"No one's touching my inseam but you, and I'm not wearing a shirt. And I'll only wear black, none of that alabaster bullshit."

"My god, you're worse than a kid."

We spent a little while longer down by the shore before heading back in with our collection of orichalcum blades. The blood had been cleaned up in the room and the window fixed, only leaving me to return the fireplace area back to its original state. On the bed were a pair of shorts and boots for Noah resembling his old ones but with a medieval flair to the Asian style. There were armbands and a strap to wear over his chest that he could use to carry his swords on his back.

"This will never fit," he said, holding up the sword strap. "You see how big my chest is?"

"It's adjustable."

"Still...oh, it does fit." He dropped his towel and tried on the newly designed shorts and boots after he got the sword strap on without incident. "Not bad. How'd that weird chick know my size?"

"They probably took what was left of the hunter armor you had stolen from Owen as a guide."

"*These* definitely won't fit." Next he put on the armbands around his biceps and tried breaking them by flexing. He could tell I was amused by his failure. "They're a little tight. They make my arms look even bigger though and I know you like that so I'll keep 'em."

"What about these?" I held up a pair of bracers.

"What do I need those for? My wrists don't need protection." He was enjoying his new outfit more than he wanted to admit as he checked himself out flexing and stretching in it.

"I saw the fight between you and Kenneth," I reminded him. He stopped putting on a show and stood there silent.

"So what? You think I need to be babied now? I was fighting uphill on a handicap—"

"Stop." I went over to him and put my hands on his chest. "All I'm saying is that I never want to see you hurt like that again. Why not take every advantage possible? Isn't that what you were doing by collecting that gear before your fight with him?"

He didn't respond, but did put on the bracers. "They fit. I'll keep them around for the future just in case."

"Put this on *before* the sword strap." I handed him a hooded leather vest. I knew I was really pushing it.

"You know I'm not putting that on, so I don't know why you even bothered trying."

"Same reason as the bracers."

"We going to war now or something?"

"We should always be prepared in our lifestyle. You taught me that."

"I can't wear this." He started to smile. "It looks itchy and you know I have sensitive nipples."

"Oh, please."

He growled, narrowed his eyes, flared his nostrils, and puffed out his chest while I just stood there until he finally gave in. "Fine. I'll try it on, but if you tell anyone I'll kill them. *And* you owe me."

He put on the vest with a grimace and left it opened. I pulled his hood on and tugged it in place. "You look cute."

"*Cute*? I'm a beast. Beasts aren't cute."

"This is made of better quality leather than the Blackbournes' armor. It'll protect my beast's body from all types of fire and elements. It's sleeveless too, so you can still show off those arms."

"Playing to my ego *and* my sense of combat practicality. Smart. I like it. This isn't about vanity though. I was trained without armor and always felt it a show of weakness to need to rely on it. If I can't fight unprotected, I shouldn't be fighting at all. Look at where it got me with that douchebag. I died. A warrior's strength is in his skill, not in what he takes with him to battle. Anything else is a crutch. I'm as deadly barehanded as I am with a sword. The only reason I use one is for cleaner kills."

"I didn't think your reasoning behind it was so deep."

"It's mostly because I have an amazing body."

"Of course. I don't think you're any less of a warrior for using everything available to you to survive. I kind of want you to stick around a while, and maybe I like having that amazing body all to myself."

"Seduction now too? You're really asking for it. You don't poke the tiger unless you're prepared to get what's coming to you."

"Well, we do have another hour until sundown in England…" I said and poked him in the stomach.

"Damn, I love this side of you."

Chapter Fifty-One

"Precisely on time as always," Castile said, greeting Noah and I upon our arrival at his manor several hours after our planned time.

"I'm sure that's sarcasm," I said. "I'm sorry I didn't come as soon as I got your invitation—"

"Not at all. You are here exactly when you are supposed to be." He motioned for us to take a seat on the sofa in his parlor. "I see true love has finally blossomed."

"What's it to you?" Noah put his arm around me in his new outfit, top included. He didn't trust Castile or any other Ancient, even if Castile was the better of the bunch. I tugged on his vest as a warning to behave.

"Quite a bit, actually," Castile remained calm. "I see you are a changed man, manners withstanding. Your condition is of no concern though, only that which you both hold dear."

"What is this about?" I asked.

"He wants to use us against Aurelia," said Noah.

"I'm afraid you are mistaken. I have invited you both here to extend my congratulations and gratitude on your success. Your parts in all of this are finished."

"That's what thank you cards are for. Can we go?" Noah asked me.

"Wait. I came here for my own reasons too. If there's anyone who wants to see Aurelia fall as much as us, it'd be Castile."

"Maybe more so," Castile nodded. "Indulge me in a bit of conversation. It isn't every century that I may speak with a *god*."

"Just be forward about it. Noah doesn't have much patience and neither do I now that there are other things we could be doing together."

"You already know I was aware he would die, the message in the blood should have confirmed that. I've known how madly in love he was with you since that first night I had the pleasure of making your acquaintance. Of course, he might not remember our encounter. His memories were later erased in an attempt to keep his former master from knowing he came to me, but he still knows who I am."

I looked to Noah who showed no sign of whether he knew what Castile was talking about.

"To make this brief: I knew what he was fighting for and that he would not stop until he was dead. That forced our dear Aurelia's hand. She could have chosen to take over his mind indefinitely, even if it is not normally her way, however you already had feelings growing for him deep inside you. Your interference, even if it led to failure, would produce the same result: Noah would be taken from her one way or another. This would force her to replace him."

"Kenneth," I said. "He's strong, but what's the big deal about him when she has Gianluca?"

"She can't control the Italian forever," said Noah. "She doesn't like what she can't control even if she's pretending to play nice with him for now."

"Precisely. Do you know, by any chance, just who Sir Flannigan is?" Castile asked us.

"Another guy she suckered into slavery," Noah answered.

"In the basest terms, yes. A fallen noble of House Blackbourne during their eve some several hundred years past."

"He's a Blackbourne?" I questioned.

"A founding member before they became what they are today. He was set to hunt her, or so I hear. An ordeal that went terribly wrong as you can imagine. His party was led into the woods by her home, which at one time were thick with werewolves. He was the last to crawl out, clinging to the meager remains of his life. She offered him immortality. I'm sure you know how the rest of the story goes from there. He is, however, the keeper of her heart and since that time she has kept her fangs at the hunters' throats to guide them without their knowing."

"There's no way she's in love or ever has been," I said.

"He means literally," said Noah.

"Yes, Kenneth Flannigan, the Scottish nobleman, was the most recent of her children that was chosen to keep her heart in his care. For thousands of years she has turned those she deemed worthy into her undying slaves, with never more than three in existence at once. One for her strength, one for her speed, and one for her grace.

"You may ask why she allows a slave to hold her most precious possession in their chest. The keeper's own heart is turned to stone that strips them of desire and will. They retain conscious thought so as not to become exploitable drones, but lack any ability to betray her or be manipulated through emotion. Before one is chosen, her progeny are set to prey on one another and the survivor is awarded this 'great boon'."

It wasn't hard to figure out the rest. "She was down to only Noah, who she knew would betray her to be with me—or that I would kill her if he died, so she had to wake Kenneth from his torpor."

"Exposing her heart in the process," he confirmed. "Without you to interfere, had Mr. Burckhardt won his battle with Kenneth, she would have had her sister turn his heart to stone and take up the role as keeper. It is why I test each new generation of Blackbourne. I wish to see if they ever have any notion of being under her foot, and over the years of these tests have hoped to learn where her keeper is sleeping. She rarely utilizes them to hunt her enemies as she used to, but a tainted commodity is no longer a commodity in truth, so I continue to toy with them."

That meant she had ties to both the Blackbournes *and* PROJECT: UNITY.

"Why remove her heart in the first place?" I asked. "Just so she can't be staked?"

"It is a necromantic spell that keeps her true essence with her heart. No matter what harm may come to the body, she can never fall as long as the heart remains intact. Her powers may be diminished as a result of being separated from it, but in return she gains true invincibility. It has been the sisters' plan for centuries that Aurelia would rule the material world and Rozalin would hold dominion over the dead. They have accomplished much due to their patience and feigning rivalry."

"We kill Kenneth, we kill her then too."

"No, the heart has been removed from him temporarily while he serves her in place of Noah. She must find others worthy of being at her side first before returning it to him so he may once again slumber in hiding."

"Where's the heart now?" Noah asked.

"Somewhere far south from here in the ice and snow, but I'm afraid you cannot do anything about it just yet."

"Yeah, why's that?"

"I won't let you. You see, for the moment at least she is required to continue her charade with the humans. It is no lie that I wish for a peaceful transition into the new world with a population plentiful enough for all to feast upon. As of now she is playing her part splendidly, and I have been closely watching."

An image of Rudgar that was so lifelike I did a double take appeared in the room.

"What does he have to do with this? Is he spying for you?" I asked.

"You could say that," said the fake Rudgar in his German accent. "You and I are a lot alike, you see."

"Cut the bullshit," Noah exclaimed and took my hand. "Come on, let's go."

"No, wait. What does he mean?" I asked Castile.

"The good commander by Our Lady's side is a doppelgänger," Rudgar stated. "The Commander Lars Rudgar you were first familiar with perished quite some time ago."

"Then who, or what, is the doppelgänger?"

"A marvelous construct of flesh like you, Benoit, only I was made by The Old One of Boundless Flesh. We are one."

"Does Aurelia know?"

"No," Castile answered. "It's of no concern if she does, and eventually she will. You see, the commander at her side is a mindless flesh puppet created by Vyrlakalos after assimilating him. While *unpleasant* for the victim, the process granted Vyrlakalos total knowledge of his past life and gave us our ticket to walk through those chateau doors."

"It all started during a fateful mission invading the base of PROJECT: UNITY's old nemesis—Gestalt Industries," the image of Rudgar said. "The original Commander Rudgar was infected by Vyrlakalos. The Old One of Boundless Flesh lied in wait as not more than a single cell inside the human vessel to avoid detection. But what a cell it was. The Old One could direct the commander, learn from his memories. Once it was found that Commander Rudgar had ties to the Archios queen, a plan was made to infiltrate."

"Before your voyage to Hell, Commander Rudgar was summoned to Aurelia's side," Castile explained. "She did not want her pet lost to the Pit. Vyrlakalos decided it time to act, knowing that it would be more difficult to assimilate the commander undetected in Aurelia's presence. Vyrlakalos devoured the poor man from the inside out once he departed for Scotland to meet Aurelia. From that point forward, Vyrlakalos assumed his form as a perfect copy."

"I remember thinking how him bailing on us right before the big fight with Lord Ma'al was a little out-of-character," I said. "He had also acted pretty strange during that mission at Gestalt Industries now that you mention it. He tried splitting us and later denied it...I guess this explains why. However, Aurelia can read minds. How does she not know that this clone is Vyrlakalos?"

"Ah, that is where I join the show!" Castile gushed with a frightening smile and dispelled the image of Rudgar. "You see, Vyrlakalos and I have quite the history together, as most Ancient Ones do. In my case, only after my dissociation from the Archios did Vyrlakalos and I become rather well acquainted."

He pulled out a parchment from his jacket pocket and held it up. It was like the one with the bloodstain I had been given, only this one was clearly the silhouette of a man's head with three dots in a triangle on the neck. "Vyrlakalos knew only I could come up with a believable facsimile of the late commander's mind if given the proper background. She allowed me entry into the mind of the doppelgänger to read his memories and from there I remained in control of our puppet to do what I always do: watch."

"All this time you and Vyrlakalos have been walking around with Aurelia as a perfect copy of one of her servants and she had no idea..."

"I don't buy that she doesn't know," Noah said. "She's probably coming up with a way to turn this against the both of you and I don't want to be there when it goes down."

"No one ever truly knows who Vyrlakalos is inside or when," said Castile. "It's beautiful really. There is a good chance she is within the both of you right now. All creatures she comes across become one with her collective at some point."

"How can this help us get rid of her though?" I asked. "I doubt she's going to share any deep dark secrets with Rudgar whether she knows the truth about him or not and we can't let her stay in power once things have settled down. She needs to be dethroned *shortly* after she'd done her job and we'll need someone to step in ready to take her place."

"And you propose I be this person? I am flattered, but respectfully decline. The public eye is not where I belong. You would fare better than I. You've carved out quite an interesting little niche as of late. I must thank you for sending the spymaster to watch over me. I admit his talents are worthy of recognition. I can see the grass grow on the plains of Africa, yet the young rogue almost evaded my sight from right under my nose more than once."

"Yes, Claudius is very talented, but how can I convince you to help us bring down Aurelia before she's cemented herself into human history? I don't have telepathy—as the both of you do—to steer things in the right direction when they go off. Killing her after the war does nothing but leave the connection between humans and supernaturals severed and leaderless."

"Vyrlakalos may be interested if you appeal to her hunger," Castile mused. "Your answer is on your person as we speak."

"My clothes? The Order?"

"In a matter of speaking, yes. If you wish for order and balance then do it yourself. There is no reason you cannot be liaison to our worlds. Mortals are easily shepherded, but it was to my understanding that you were against one sole ruler having sway over the minds of many. Why do you seek someone of my particular skills?"

"My views have evolved since then for things like emergencies, making the bad eggs change their minds without killing them, undoing other brainwashing, being a comforting face to the public."

"All indeed admirable in their own right, but unnecessary. The point I was trying to make is that the gods will once again take over leading their people as you have your order. An ambassador between gods would be something of greater importance as the ones between the human nations. Such a position would find my talents underutilized."

"I guess Gianluca would be perfect for that if he can keep himself from getting turned to stone for five minutes."

Castile began chuckling to himself in a rather unsettling manner. "I'm afraid he won't be around much longer to take up the task."

"Why is that...?" I asked.

"The poor simpleton has been nothing more than a dupe from the start. He will fall under his own weight when the world pins all its evils on him and drives him from its lands in guilt like once before."

I didn't like the sound of any of this. I looked to Noah for support but his eyes were fixated in an icy stare of distrust on Castile. "Why would he be blamed if he isn't the one doing anything wrong?" I asked with certain reservations from wanting to know what came next.

"He is nothing more than a target for the Ancients to throw their poisoned daggers at in place of ourselves while we do the real work, and you of course. He thinks he is the one who came up with this plan to make us cooperate when in truth it was all whispered to him through the shadows while he slept by none other than Rozalin."

"That bat-shit bitch couldn't string together two solid ideas," said Noah.

Castile's chuckle turned into an even more haunting laugh. "That is quite amusing, however incorrect. She is a rather adept tactician, although not to the magnitude of her sister. The two are working in tandem though.

"His role was simple. We needed our own liaison to keep us from foiling one another as we worked toward a common goal so we would make it through this apocatastasis. We knew each of our skills were needed from previous catastrophes, but had no way to keep the civility without a mediator.

"The poor fool's pride was played upon to make him think it was his idea, but in the end he will take the blame for all of it with none of the credit. The destruction wrought by the God of Chaos, the rise of these Infernal Kings, it will all be placed on him and he will believe it. Once he feels his honor has been irrevocably ruined he will return to the shadows and take all of our problems with him."

"That's...horrible." I couldn't overstate how much I disapproved of using him like that.

"Is it? You have played your part in his downfall as well. You had *almost* spoiled it, but in the end the true love I see before me bloomed, leaving his heart broken and more easily manipulated.

"There is always a scapegoat in war. Had he been anything more than a simple-minded soldier lost in time, it never would have worked. He does not belong in this world nor the next. One whom does not grow has no place in the land of giants. Propaganda will put his anachronistic views and actions in the spotlight for the humans to revolt against as they seek the sanctuary of their gods in the new world and he will be driven out in shame. It will prevent much bloodshed and infighting amongst the thinned crowd to shun that which is different and foreign, a tactic not unfamiliar to mankind."

"I think we should be leaving," I excused us with a terrible pain in my stomach and headed for the door.

"Telling him will do nothing, but cause the loss of billions of lives," Castile called after me. "You saw what happened when Set asked the people to point a finger toward their hatred. Do you think the world will be so easily understanding after so many are inevitably lost once the Infernal Kings rise? They will seek answers to how it came to pass and turn on themselves, turn their gods on each other and destroy us all. The soldier, the 'ancient darkness' we are foretold of, was meant for this very purpose. Even the Infernal Kings that gave him his power used him to shirk responsibility for their evil."

"Why are you telling me this if you know I'm going to stop him?" I asked.

"Only because you can't. You never could. He would not listen to you then and he will not now. I had thought you would be more accepting of a plan to save the lives of billions and bring peace without enslavement to the world. The cost is one man's sorrow, a pittance really."

"Yeah...maybe you're right."

"As we speak, our sacrificial lamb is scrounging through the shadows to find a way to seal Set forever. A fool's errand; it cannot be done. But alas, his honor blinds him to sounder reasoning. If there is anything you should concern yourself with it is the humans that crawled their way from the desert. They gather in greater numbers in secret around the world and have begun more devoted forms of worship to bring him and his gift of chaos back to the world.

"Vyrlakalos has already created a plague to exterminate the worshippers of this false god and will be releasing it shortly. It will be tempered to run its course before reaching uncontainable levels; a flame that burns brightest burns least of all."

"And what happens when Set finds out?"

"Our knight will come to attack the moment Set shows himself, of course, and the plague will be blamed on him as his revenge against those who devoutly worshipped the God of Chaos. I hear the humans are most averse to biological warfare and will not look kindly upon our dark savior, no matter how he tries to communicate otherwise. He binds himself by duty to protect those of the alliance and since he still believes it was his idea for Vyrlakalos to do such a thing he will not deny the accusations."

      "Thank you," I said to Castile over my shoulder on my way out. "This has all been very...enlightening."

Chapter Fifty-Two

Back in the abbey I stood at my window, looking more in than out. I pondered my next course of action, with no choice any better than the rest. Should I disrupt the Ancients' plan to spare Gianluca's honor that he holds so dear? Individually they weren't to be trusted, but together the Ancients had survived better than even the gods for all these years because of similar schemes. It meant saving lives, including my people here in the Order. Although the logical choice seemed clear it still didn't sit right with me.

"I don't feel well."

"Come here," Noah beckoned from the bed. I went to him and was dragged under the covers to snuggle. "You already know you're gonna tell him, so just get it over with."

"How do I know that I should? Screwing with the Ancients puts everyone here in danger and retaliating against them only makes things worse for us."

"What would you do if it was me and not the Italian?"

"Of course I'd tell you."

"You'd do more than that. You'd stake me too."

"Because I love you."

"You love him too, only in a different way. I know you too well, so don't try to bullshit me and tell me you don't. If you didn't, you wouldn't even care. You'd be all excited to save stupid mankind."

"I guess...I do love him in a way. You aren't bothered by that?"

"I'm not the jealous type. I'm pretty secure in my abilities to keep you mine and I trust you more than anyone or I wouldn't be here. You don't need my consent." The overwhelming sense of relief having him understand me and be in my corner was too much to express with words.

"I'm so damn proud of what you've become," he said between kisses.

"I couldn't have done it without you. I really want to continue this, but I should get in touch with Gianluca..."

"He can wait a few more minutes...or hours..."

"Noah...! Stop! Down!" I couldn't help but laugh at his attempts to keep being frisky as they spiraled into him just rubbing his face on me. "What are you doing?"

"I'm marking you with my scent so he knows you're mine."

"Get off me, you weirdo." I put a pillow over his face and wriggled free. "I'm going to need to keep a spray bottle by the side of the bed."

"Tigers aren't afraid of water," he said, muffled from under the pillow, then sighed. "Fine. Go ahead and call him, but I'm staying. I might not be jealous, but I still don't want him getting handsy with you."

"*Please* be good and don't antagonize him."

"I hate the douchebag, so no promises. And don't even say that if I love you I'll do it because—I don't know. It doesn't sound fair."

I threw another pillow at his head and called to Gianluca so many times I thought he wouldn't come. When I was about to give up and send someone to see if Lyle knew anything, the candles in the room dimmed and out stepped Gianluca from the shadows.

"Yes?" He was clad in full armor sans helmet.

"Were you fighting something?" I asked.

"No. Why do you call me?" He looked over me to Noah on the bed.

"We need to talk about this alliance."

"There is nothing to say."

"Just listen to him, you douchebag," said Noah. "He's trying to help your stupid ass."

"Noah!" I shouted. Gianluca went to leave, but I grabbed his arm. "Wait."

"I only stay if he is not here."

"No deal," Noah refused.

"Gianni, just listen to me. The alliance is a fake. The Ancients are using you—"

He pulled his arm away. "They trust me. They trust my sword. Why do you try to say this? You already take away my heart, now you want my pride?"

"He still loves you, idiot, or he wouldn't be trying to help you," Noah said as he appeared beside me. "I might not like you, but *I'm* man enough to respect his decisions. You only have yourself to blame for pushing him away with all this honor and pride bullshit.

"You're selfish. Admit it. You want to save the world because it makes *you* look good, no better than Aurelia. You want to be the 'man' and make the decisions and control the one you say you love because *you* want the glory. You want Rome back because you can't deal with the world today, because you *don't* feel in control and that makes you *not* feel like a man. Well, here's some news: that's exactly what all the Ancients are using against you."

Gianni and I were quiet. "I'm sorry," Noah apologized to me. "But I had to say something. This guy won't listen to you. Castile was right."

"Why do you talk to him?" Gianluca asked.

"He sent for me to discuss these plans," I explained. "They're counting on you not listening to me, especially now that Noah and I...Anyway, he told us that all of the Ancients have been aware that they needed to work together since before you proposed the treaty. You're right, they do trust your sword and are using you to keep the peace while they go about their plans. I know that the idea for the treaty wasn't yours. You heard it in the shadows."

"It was like a dream. It is still from me." He didn't want to let go of his one claim to fame and I could understand.

"It was Rozalin, Gianni. She and Aurelia came up with most of this and used you as the middleman. It happened around the same time Isis was calling for your help. The two voices are what were confusing you until Rozalin's drowned out Isis. I'm right, aren't I?"

He refused to acknowledge it even in his body language. "What does this matter? Why do you call me here for this? If the people are safe I do my job the same."

"It matters because they are about to pin all of this on you, including the war with the Infernal Kings. Vyrlakalos has already come up with a plague to wipe out the rest of Set's worshippers. The Ancients are going to blame it on you and they are counting on *your* pride to make you take the credit.

"The humans will fear and hate you. After the transition into the new world *you'll* be blamed as the one who woke the Infernal Kings in the first place since your powers came from them. The Ancients want to give the humans something to focus their hate on and are counting on you retreating back into the shadows again. You will *never* see Rome rebuilt."

Gianluca didn't know what to do as he stood there trying to process everything I told him. "And you tell me this for love? I want to hear this from you if it is true."

"I do love you. We have very different ways of thinking and what we want out of a relationship, but it doesn't change how I feel about you as a person. We are going to clash in the future on some very important issues, but I'd rather that, than not have you around at all or in danger knowing that I could have saved you."

He smiled and reached out to take my hand, but Noah blocked him. "Hands off," Noah warned. I eased Noah back and took Gianni's hand and then hugged him. I could tell he didn't want to let go. I couldn't blame him. It was nice to set aside the recent animosity.

"It is good to feel this again," he said and let me go back to Noah. "Maybe I make a bad judgment on this one."

He motioned to Noah and took my hand one more time.

"I listen too much to my past and I envy what he have."

"I'm used to it," Noah said and wrapped his arms around my neck. "Everybody envies me, especially now that I got my better half."

"You are a lucky man, but I am lucky too. Dorian is my light in the darkness again."

"Yeah, well just like light; you can look, but not touch," said Noah.

"What will you do now?" I asked Gianni.

"I go to stop the Ancients' plan."

"I think you shouldn't. Let them do everything to help and then at the last minute turn on them."

Gianni raised his brow in surprise. "This is...not a very good way to have honor. I do not think to hear you say this."

"It's a good way to be *smart*," Noah said. "Dorian's starting to catch on to this stuff thanks to me." I bit his forearm for that.

"Start by taking PROJECT: UNITY from Aurelia. Offer to lead her army for her. You're a soldier, it's what you know best. You can protect them from her sacrificing them to danger. They already know you and will trust you. I know Lyle would rather follow you than her and so would I. They can help teach you more about the current world too."

"You want me to have this army? You do not like me to conquer."

"You have a lot to learn about human rights and civil liberties, but this isn't about declaring war. It's about taking away one of Aurelia's playing pieces from the board without needing to use force. They can help you *protect* humans and get others to trust you so you aren't as easily blamed in the end. I know you get along with Lyle, so rely on his advice and look after him for me."

"Yes, he is a good man, another strong leader with honor. I will do this with pleasure."

"Good. Now get out. We have a bed to break," said Noah, making me elbow him in the ribs.

"Keep an eye on the plague that Vyrlakalos is about to release. It's supposed to only stay in a small area, but I don't trust that and Set will be lured out because of it. You can't be locked in endless battle with him. The chaos from the fighting will make him stronger and you'll be blamed. In the meantime I'll think of a solution."

"Okay...Is a good plan. I will go to do this. You have many thanks from me, both of you." I can't believe I was so casual about a plague now. I wasn't sure if that was an evolved or degenerated point of view, but it was a low priority and I saw the purpose of it being a "contained" plague; I knew that Vyrlakalos wouldn't want it being too obvious so that it could be traced back to her.

I smiled and Noah grunted as Gianni left on a remarkably positive note. It was too bad that it took so much to get him to respect what I had to say, but I didn't want to look back when there was so much to enjoy going forward. In fact, it was the best outcome possible. We were able to remain friends and come out of all of our tribulations with a better understanding of one another.

"I was pretty good, right?"

"You weren't too bad," I said and turned to kiss Noah.

"I was awesome and you know it." He threw me over his shoulder and headed for the bed. "Time to feed the tiger."

After Noah had his fill we lied in bed together as we both fought to stay awake. "You hungry?" he asked.

"Eh, more sleepy. It's been about a week since I last slept."

"So, go to sleep. I'll chase the bad dreams away." He got up and walked around the room, putting out the candles before returning to me in bed. The light of the aurora through the window lit the room enough to make him out in the dark. I smiled and held his hand.

"Why haven't you been zipping around everywhere like usual?" I asked.

"No good reason."

"What's the bad reason then?"

"Just been enjoying taking things slow. Nice to feel relaxed for the first time in my life."

"That's not a bad reason at all."

He took my hand and put it on his chest. I noticed he liked that and when I played with his scruff. "You're the first person I'm able to sleep next to with both eyes closed. First time I've ever slept with both eyes closed, actually."

"You said you didn't have a home for long when you were human. What was that like?"

"I don't wanna talk about it."

"Hey, you said no more secrets," I reminded him.

"It's not a secret, it's just not important." I kept quiet and began to fall asleep when he changed his mind. "I can't even remember their faces."

"Who?"

"Family. We moved all the time when I was a kid, sometimes it was a big town, or a shitty tent in a settlement with others moving west, or just living out of an even shittier stagecoach."

"Were you and your family close?"

"I guess. No other options really...I had a younger sister. Grace. She was always sick. I never knew with what though, just that she was born that way. I don't think I ever saw her out of bed or heard her talk without coughing."

Noah's voice started to trail off. "Don't even remember what she sounded like, anyway..."

"You okay?"

"They never let me go near her," he continued without answering. "Like it was my fault she was sick. My folks would always tell me I'd bring in disease from outside and make her worse."

"It was probably for the best. I can't picture it being very sanitary back then. Did you used to take baths in a wash basin?" The thought of that was amusing, especially picturing Noah as an adult trying to fit into one.

"We spent all our money on medicine for her." Noah kept talking like he didn't hear me, but it wasn't arrogance. There was something in the way he spoke like he was reaching for the memories. Or maybe pushing them away. "Then the rest went to the farm we had for under a year once we got out west. One bad winter sank us...Pa had to take any job he could get to keep food on the table."

Pa?

"He started to build us a cabin on some ranch we rented land from. I slept outside on the ground with him most nights while Ma and Gracie got the stupid stagecoach."

Ma and Gracie? This isn't how Noah speaks, not anymore.

"That was until Pa got bucked off a horse he was trying to tame for the ranch owner and got his leg trampled. It never set right and was always getting infected. Stupid old man...I had to take over building the cabin before the next winter came. I must've been twelve, no, thirteen."

"That's a lot for a thirteen-year-old to take on," I tried to add to the conversation, but Noah was lost in his memory.

"Ma would clean the ranch owner's place during the day and patch up his clothes and cook while Pa watched Gracie. He'd shout at me from the stagecoach 'No, that don't go there! Put that there, secure this here' while I worked on the cabin. It was a piece of shit when it was done anyway. Like I was supposed to know how to build a fucking house. He didn't know any better either. He just acted like he did because he already got his balls cut off having to have his kid do his work."

"You were the man of the house." I put my hand under my pillow to change positions, but Noah took it back and put it on his chest again without stopping his story.

"First day of spring that year was the first time I killed someone. Got our place robbed at night and went for Pa's gun. We had fucking shit to our name and no one ever saw us in town before. Should've known it was the rancher's son.

"I cried like a sissy when I saw his brains all over the wall above Gracie's bed. Nobody said nothin'." Noah started to slip into a drawl I had never heard out of him. "Jus' packed up and moved on overnight. Left the cabin behind without a word before anyone found out. I ain't never—I've never told anyone that. Always said my first kill was in Japan."

I patted him on the chest to let him know I was still listening. I didn't know what I *could* say to any of this except that it was nice he was opening up to me.

"That's when we finally made it to California. The old man sold both our horses and the stagecoach to rent a place because Ma said I wouldn't last through building another cabin on my own. Instead they sent me to wait outside saloons for people looking to hire farmhands so I could earn our keep.

"I was a scrawny nobody punk that no one would even bother looking at. No one wanted some kid that couldn't even lift a bale of hay. I was fucking smart though. Used leverage to get the job done like I learned back on the cabin."

"That's what you taught me about martial arts too," I chimed in. He kissed the palm of my hand in acknowledgement and put it back on his chest.

"Didn't help back then when I'd get the piss beat outta me from the men in town angry that I was takin' their jobs 'cuz I'd do it for less pay than an adult." It was interesting that he'd started to slip back into this drawl whenever his mind would meander deeper into thought of that time in his life. I wanted to call him on it to see if he noticed, but also didn't want to interrupt.

"Pa was too much of a pussy to go to the sheriff. 'fraid word spread by then and there was a bounty out for killing the rancher's boy, so I just took the beatings and worked through it until I was older and big enough to fight back. Seemed like that day would never come and now it seems like everything before it never happened..."

I couldn't imagine Noah as a scrawny preteen. It was shocking to see Nathaniel's younger self, but by the sound of it Noah made an even more dramatic transformation.

"Had my first time with a prairie dove when I was seventeen."

"A what?"

"I used to take my time going home after work because it was miserable there and no one talked... I'd stay where it was light to avoid trouble, but didn't go into the saloons at that age 'cuz I was afraid I'd never come back out if I got jumped. She approached me thinking I was older while sitting outside one night.

"Had no idea what I was doing, but I was eager and lonely. I knew it was her job, but she made me feel special. I even brought her flowers the next day thinkin' it was the right thing to do. She just laughed in my face and said I had a lot to learn about the world. Guess I still do since I never got any better at that romance stuff.

"Pa whooped the taste outta my mouth when he found out I spent some of my pay meant for the family on a pro. Might've cured what ailed him by the way he leapt from that chair for the first time in months, or maybe it was the cheap gin he tried to pretend he wasn't drinking when we were all asleep.

"I left after that. Slept outside at the edge of the land I'd work at night, but would return home to slip money under the door for Ma to find before everyone got up. Took me three years to save up enough to get a room for myself on top of paying for them. Saw Ma in town a few times on her way to buy supplies at the general store. She begged me to come back and said that Pa wasn't angry no more. But I still was.

"Then I..." Noah stopped. His voice struggled on those last words. "Then I got turned. Left them...left them all behind.

"They would've died of starvation, or the cold once winter came back 'round and they couldn't afford rent no more...Ma started gettin' sick and didn't make enough for groceries, let alone rent and medicine. A town that size didn't need an old lady going too blind in one eye to sew. Not much to clean either in those dumps and no one had the kind of money to afford live-in help when they could get it done free from a wife or an illegal slave. She was too old to turn pro for extra cash and Gracie was too sickly. Gracie probably went first, unless Pa shot himself..."

Noah sounded like he had a lump in his throat. I put my hand to his face to feel if he was crying in the dark, but he grabbed my wrist hard before I could. "Sorry," he said when I flinched, and placed my hand back on his chest and held it there over his heart.

"I told myself for years that they cursed me with their dying breath for leaving them and that's why everything went to shit. I wanted a reason to hate them and forget so I wouldn't blame myself. I couldn't...I couldn't stop seeing their faces when I closed my eyes to sleep."

Chapter Fifty-Three

Noah didn't want to talk anymore after he finished sharing his oldest memories. He only gave one-word answers until we fell asleep, even when I changed the subject. When I woke the next morning he was gone.

I hurried and washed up in the bathroom while thinking about our next move against Set. Lyle was right; we had to do something *big*. We had to think outside the box more than usual. Killing him did nothing. Killing his followers only made things worse one way or another. Aurelia brainwashing them wasn't much different either, since it wasn't sustainable and he would move on to new populations.

Intimidation tactics were only temporary since I wasn't willing to outdo Set by being more evil. There had to be some way to bring order to the chaos. Chaos couldn't be stopped in its entirety, but it could be brought back into balance. That left the question: How is balance achieved?

The other issue to keep in mind was doing this without letting the Ancients use Gianni as a scapegoat.

I had finished in the bathroom when I heard a loud banging outside in the direction of the orchard and felt the room shake with it. I headed out to investigate the source of the noise and found Noah and Nathaniel fighting.

"Stop it!" I yelled at Noah who had performed a Judo takedown to a side arm-bar on Nathaniel. The earth was split in mini-fissures and holes around them from their fighting. "What are you doing?!"

Noah escaped my telekinetic grasp in a cloud of mist when I went to get him off of Nathaniel. "Dorian! I'm sorry," Nathaniel called to me as Noah reemerged from the mist to offer him a hand. "Noah was training me in unarmed combat."

Noah flipped him over his shoulder upon helping him up, but Nathaniel zoomed into the air before hitting the ground which forced Noah to let go.

"Practice your quick turns for a while, kid," Noah shouted up to him and sauntered over to me to plant a kiss on my lips. "Hey."

"You're teaching him?" I asked in disbelief.

"Someone's gotta do it while you're in bed all day," he grinned and messed with my hair. "You sleep good?"

"Yes, but why are you being so nice to someone...well someone that isn't me?"

"He's a good kid. Fists hit like a ton of dynamite. Last person I fought who was someone like that I wound up dead from. I remembered what you told me about him the other day. Figured there's work to be done to get him up to speed and somebody's gotta do it, so who better than me?"

"That's really sweet of you. I wish I wasn't so surprised about it, but thank you for doing this."

"Don't thank me until you see what I made for you."

"Oh, no... What is it?"

He raised one arm and flexed his bicep. "This muscle."

I snorted in laughter as he stood there smirking at me like a goofy idiot on purpose. "Just one?"

"I've got a package deal you might be interested in." He flexed the other arm with an even wider grin then put both arms around my head to hug me to his chest. "You eat yet?"

"No, I just washed and heard this happening so I came out. Can we talk about last night?"

"Nothing else to say. I think I told you pretty much everything. Let's get you breakfast. I wanna show you something."

"I'm trying to ask if you're okay. I know how good you are at hiding your emotions, but you're hiding them a little *too* much right now after everything you said last night."

"I'm not hiding anything," he reassured me. "I'm just not good at talking about this stuff, but I swear I'm being straight with you. There are a lot of things coming back to me now that I can relax and I have my thoughts to myself, but I'm dealing with them as they come. It's unbelievable how happy you make me and how good it feels to be free again. I didn't think it'd be this intense after so many years of trying to forget, so I'm as surprised as you are."

"That's all I wanted to know. All I care about is if you're happy and that you know you can tell me when you're not so we can fix it," I told him.

"I do. C'mon, let's get you breakfast," he said after another quick kiss.

Noah zipped us into the kitchen where there were fresh-baked breads and fruit from the orchard left out on the counter in baskets. The Order didn't have any modern appliances like stoves or refrigerators, so everything was cooked and baked daily with very little stored except for things like nuts and cheeses that wouldn't go bad. They did have ice chests to keep meat and bottles of milk that I was assuming stayed cold by magic.

He sat me on the counter and stood between my legs with his hands resting on either side of me. "What?" I asked with an uneasy smile from him looking at me without saying anything.

"Nothing." He smiled back and broke off a piece from a loaf of bread for me.

"Thanks," I said and started to get suspicious of his good mood again. It was sad—I was so used to him being such a dick all the time that when he was finally able to exhale and open up I then felt more on edge. "So, I've been trying to come up with a way to balance the chaos that feeds Set."

Noah leaned on an adjacent counter to listen while he tossed a peach in the air and caught it. "Give his goons something else to worship," he suggested and took a bite out of the peach.

"What—what did you just do? You can eat now?"

"Sure can, but now I remembered I don't like peaches."

"Don't waste it. I'll eat it," I said and took it from him. "When did you find this out?"

"This morning. I thought about how my insides are working again and I can be in sunlight, so I swiped a pancake from that weird chick." He tried an apple and made a disapproving face. "Don't like apples either."

"Are you actually digesting that though or is it just sitting in there? Like, what's going to happen...later?" I asked and took the apple from him before he threw it away.

"No clue, but guess we're gonna find out soon enough." We both laughed like a couple of immature kids and then he started throwing blueberries for me to catch in my mouth. "It doesn't fill me the same as blood does, so it's really only for taste."

"You only ate one pancake. You should eat more to test it."

"I'm gonna eat *you* later."

"Please don't," I laughed.

"Mhm. I'm gonna hunt you down like a tiger does and drag you back to my den." He ripped into a loaf of bread and swallowed without any complaints. "I like bread," he said with his mouth full.

"You might lose those abs if you keep stuffing your face with it though." I leaned over and patted his stomach. "Don't worry, I'd still love you."

"Careful with the tummy rubs. I bite," he growled at me with another mouthful of bread.

Tobias entered the kitchen with a group that bowed to us and offered congratulatory comments on Noah's recovery. They didn't seem well themselves. They looked about five days into a bad flu. "Are you all feeling okay?" I asked.

"We're suffering a bit of aether poisoning," said Tobias. "We finished our morning training session and were coming to eat to keep our energy up before meditation at noon."

"Why do you have aether poisoning?"

"We've been in contact with the ley lines more often than usual as of late. Traversing them so frequently and at such great distances has the same negative effects as that of the Adamant Aegis."

"Is this because of me?" I asked.

"Don't blame yourself, Ascended. We must identify weakness and drive it out from our bodies. This has been an important trial and we are grateful for it."

"Don't give me that, Tobias. You need to rest or purge the aether. Do *something* besides training. Don't get hung up on what you think makes you weak. I used to be like that."

"It isn't a problem, really. Liam and his cabal are suffering a bit more, but they'll pull through after some rest. It is an honor to serve you to the best of our abilities."

"Take some time off and relax. That's an order. You can all go back to training when you're feeling better."

"Thank you, Ascended. Dorian." Tobias seemed pleased, as did the rest of the group. "Meditation helps to disperse the aether in small amounts. We will have an extended session and retire early today."

"Nathaniel used to create crystals to release the build-up when it got bad."

"I've heard. We should try that," Tobias agreed whole-heartedly. He was looking wobbly on his feet and the Order always stood strong.

"We'll leave you guys to let you get food."

Noah was too busy stuffing the rest of the loaf of bread down his throat along with some cured meats, cheeses, and nuts to be bothered with the conversation, so I just lead him out of the kitchen by the waistband.

We almost made it to our room when Rhys came after us in a rush. "Ascended! Come quickly. It's Nathaniel."

Noah took off in a flash with me under his arm until he found Nathaniel out on the lawn surrounded by people. Pavel was watching from the side.

"What's going on?" I asked him and Rhys made his way over after us. "Who are all these people?"

"The townsfolk," Pavel answered. "They scaled the perimeter wall down the hill for the first time in history. They seem to think Nathaniel is an angel sent by the Judeo-Christian god and that he has blessed the island because of the aurora. He must have told them a hundred times that he isn't, but no one will listen. I admit it must be rather hard to convince them otherwise after seeing him fly around all morning, letting off light, and what not."

"He doesn't have wings or a halo though."

"Dumbasses will believe whatever they want when there's a chance it might benefit them," Noah scoffed and threw the end of the bread loaf into the crowd, which for some reason brought cheers.

"This is why we have rules against such negligent displays of magic," Rhys complained. "This very reason. I knew that boy—"

I stared at him to stop him from finishing that sentence. The townsfolk were all reaching over each other to touch Nathaniel and shouting in Greek and English for him to perform miracles. They were requesting to be absolved of sin, have their cars blessed, their sprains healed, to be made rich. One couple was even trying to give him their baby. It was a mess of bullshit gone rampant. Nathaniel kept trying to tell everyone to return home when convincing them he wasn't an angel didn't work, but the people only wanted their selfish requests fulfilled and weren't interested in what he had to say.

"This isn't necessarily a bad thing," said Noah. "If you're gonna do this whole god routine you should go all the way with it. Better they worship either of you than Dogface."

"I don't think Nathaniel is prepared for this, or wants it, and neither do I. Giving people hope is one thing, but we're not a miracle vending machine here to serve every stupid demand when there are bigger things happening."

"Gotta get the kid out of there before someone pushes him too far and he pushes back. Meet me down by the shore." Noah was gone and then Nathaniel vanished from the mob. I left Pavel and Rhys to deal with the townspeople while I went after Noah and Nathaniel.

"I told you to calm down, kid!"

"But those people need my help!"

I arrived as Noah had Nathaniel by the throat in an attempt to keep him from returning to the mob scene. Noah let him go when he gave up, but kept him blocked in the grotto.

"He's right, Nathaniel. Those people didn't need help, they needed a reality check. They're star struck by you and want whatever they can get."

"I know that, but some of them had information on a riot happening in Paris. They think I'm here to be their savior because some of them were praying for family they have there."

"How bad a riot are we talking about? I asked.

"It sounded pretty bad. People are upset with the government for not doing anything during the crisis in Egypt. They want to overthrow the European leaders and know they've been having parties while citizens died. I want to go help."

"If it was bad enough that it needed our help Lyle or Gianluca would've come to get me."

"The kid's presence might make everyone shut up though before it gets that bad if they think he's some angel here to protect them," Noah said.

"I'm not a kid."

"Take it as a compliment coming from him," I told Nathaniel, although I did agree that he was far from it, being almost Noah's size. "Maybe we should go then, but you're going to have a *lot* of eyes on you and not all of them will be friendly. Are you really ready for that?"

"I'm used to dirty looks, so yes," he responded with confidence. "This is what I want to do with my second chance. You wanted us to not be afraid of becoming part of the outside world and I'm not. Please, Dorian. I want to show everyone that there's always hope tomorrow will be better."

Chapter Fifty-Four

"Are you sure you want to be here?" I asked Noah.

"Yeah. Most romantic fucking place on Earth, right?"

We sat on the roof of a restaurant looking out at the park surrounding the Eiffel Tower. Unfortunately, romance was the last thing I was feeling here and it wasn't Noah's fault.

Paris was burning.

"I meant being so close to Aurelia," I said as we waited for Nathaniel.

"Are you kidding? I plan on chugging a gallon of water after this and taking a piss in her fountain. Vive la anarchy, baby."

Rhys, Helena, Pavel and a handful of others that were in better shape than most of the Order were able to send Noah and me there. Nathaniel insisted he didn't want their help and would fly there on his own. Noah had suited up in full gear without much argument before we left. We were already expecting the worst, but this went further than what either of us had in mind.

"I wouldn't feel right not being here for you or the kid, anyway. He's got a piece of your soul, and you're sort of important to me."

"So Nathaniel is the kid now?"

"I'm training him aren't I? The name comes with it."

Buses were overturned in the streets; cars were on fire, storefront windows smashed, and buildings being looted. People were shouting and spray painting profanities everywhere they went in two or three different languages. Gunshots went off around us so often it wasn't alarming anymore after a few minutes. Local police presence was minimal, but some of the national police force had started to arrive to take a crack at restoring order with tear gas before being swept up in the madness themselves.

This wasn't the Paris I knew.

"You've really taken to him," I said.

"He's a fighter. I see a little of both of us in him. I respect anybody who's been through shit like we have and doesn't give up."

"Just go easy on him. He's been through enough."

"No way. What did I just say? He's a fighter. If he hasn't been broken by now, nothing's gonna break him. Pulling punches would be the worst insult we could give him. It means we don't think he's capable of more. The kid has to learn restraint more than you did. He's used to releasing energy when in pain and has emotions like a ball of yarn. If he doesn't keep that in check it won't be pretty."

"You're right."

"I'm always right." Noah inched his fingers closer to where my hand was on the roof so he could hold it. "I ever tell you I like the sound of your voice? Especially when you laugh."

"Once, yes."

"Oh. Well I meant it. I like all your tasty bits too of course, but everyone says shit like that." With all of the mess enveloping us, Noah still found a way to keep the chaos out of our space. It wasn't just the compliment. Even on the battlefield, if he was there I always felt more at peace. It wasn't like that with anybody else.

"You can be pretty sweet sometimes." I squeezed his hand and put my head on his shoulder. "We should take that trip to Thailand after this."

"Yeah. I'd like that," Noah agreed. "Just the two of us though."

Neither of us seemed to know what to do with the city as it burned in more ways than one. Intimidating an already riled mob would only add panic to the anger. I doubted my trick of reconstructing buildings would do anything but give the rioters more to ruin. Not even Noah was fast enough to put out the fires before twice as many were started elsewhere. We were relying on Nathaniel to show us all a better way.

"This is pretty much Aurelia's backyard," I said. "Why isn't she doing anything?"

"The sun is still up, dummy."

"Barely."

"Something's going on." Noah hopped to his feet. "The crowd is moving. Wait here."

He was gone and back in under a minute holding a cellphone. "This isn't just some angry Europeans. Same thing is happening in New York and Taiwan." Noah sat next to me so we could both watch the news report covering similar incidents around the world that was streaming on the phone.

"Taiwan?" I questioned. "That seems random."

"We need a TV in our room, by the way. A big one."

A woman's voice was shouting hello from the ground. I ignored it at first until I heard my name. "Commander Timmons? What are you doing here?" I floated her up to us.

"The same as you, I imagine. It is good to see you again."

"You too. Is Lyle with you?" I asked.

"No, he is in New York. I came from a relief mission in Uganda with some of the troops once we heard what was happening through PARAGON. I thought Rudgar would be here, but PARAGON says he hasn't moved from the chateau of Lady Saint-Pierre."

"He's jumped ship. We don't need him. What about Gianluca?"

"I have not heard from him in some time."

"Good," Noah said under his breath.

"I'm getting a transmission," Timmons announced. "PARAGON is picking up more widespread riots in Tokyo."

"What do they have to be upset about?" Noah asked.

"New York and Paris? Okay, I can see that," I said. "They are two of the biggest Western cities with a lot of different cultures and activists defending them. But, Taiwan and Tokyo? Riots like that don't fit their behavior, not over something half the world away."

"Dragon lady is gonna be pretty pissed."

"The gods weep," another woman's voice said along with the familiar chirping of birds.

"Isis? What are you doing here?" I asked as the goddess took form before us on the roof with staff in hand.

"I come with grim tidings, Young One. My brother is no more. The Infernal Kings have claimed his spirit as due penance for his failure."

"That's not entirely bad. I know he was your brother, but he was also going to destroy the civilized world."

"Set only wanted to return our lands to glory. Although troublesome, he fought for Egypt."

"Sounds like somebody else we know, but Set killed millions of Egyptians," I reminded her.

"The unfaithful, yes it is true. The Ennead admonished him for those vile actions, but his purpose was a misguided rebirth, not destruction. It was the sacrifice of those souls that gave an Infernal King the strength to invade our pantheon directly and claim his being. His annihilation at their claws, I fear will bring only pure destruction in the rawest sense. They have subjugated his essence to fuel their ambitions."

"Spiritborn gods can't die though. If he's prayed to with enough energy he'll return. There's tons of chaos going on around us here now and in other cities as a result of him. Then maybe you can reason with him to help us after seeing the Infernal Kings were never his allies in the first place."

"I am afraid this is not possible. With essence divided and taken unto themselves, the Fallen Kings feed from him directly as would a parasite."

"These people acting like idiots aren't bringing him back then," said Noah. "Looks like these kings found a way to get what they wanted from him either way."

"Set both causes and is empowered by chaos in a perpetual loop," I said. "It must be nice for the Infernal Kings to have an endless source of energy now without needing to lift a finger. It doesn't even need to be *evil* chaos, right?"

"You do indeed speak true, Young One. The aether is what also grants us our life and it now can be twisted to the kings' desires. The very lifeblood of the planet, once untouchable by their kind, is now free to feast upon."

"What can we do to stop them?" I asked and looked to Noah if he had any ideas. His arms were crossed and brow furrowed as he thought.

"Sorry to interrupt," Timmons excused herself. "More reports of riots are coming in. This time they're in Dubai and London."

"Is Lyle okay?" I asked.

"I haven't heard from him, but PARAGON reports his vitals are normal."

"I sense a light, a surging vibrant light," Isis announced.

"It's Nathaniel," I said. "He's close. I can feel him." Just then there was a flash from over the horizon followed by a shooting star that was none other than Nathaniel.

"He's coming in hot," Timmons said while she watched him through the computerized visor of her helmet. "MACH 3 hot—!"

Timmons couldn't have been more accurate. Nathaniel's impact upon landing could be felt two blocks away. The sonic boom he caused scattered cars, trees, and people down the street and put a hole in the ground down to the sewer.

"Goddamn kid," Noah swore. "I *told* him to watch his landings. Stay here. I'll get him before he tears the city down to find us."

"He did make it here from Greece in only an hour," I said. When Noah returned with him he immediately dropped to one knee to apologize.

"Stop kneeling," I told him. "You got the people's attention, now disperse the crowd. Promise them candy or something, anything. Just get them to stop *fast*."

"Chicago was added to the list," Timmons informed us. "That makes seven."

"Seven. The same as the number of kings," said Isis.

"Obviously this isn't about the humans being pissed at the government, but how long until shit gets serious?" Noah asked.

"Lord Ma'al opened portals on Earth when he invaded and their presence alone drove people into a frenzy. We haven't noticed any, but there's no way we'd be ready to take on an Infernal King."

"I'm ready," Nathaniel stepped up. "Demons fear the light. I can hold them off."

"*No*," Noah and I both told him.

"But—"

"Just no, kid. Don't be stupid," said Noah. I could feel frustration and embarrassment starting to fester inside of Nathaniel. I floated over to him and led him into the trees to talk in private.

"You aren't the little boy looking in from the outside anymore."

"I don't understand." He was trying to keep his cool, but I knew what was really going on under the calm exterior.

"You're part of the group. You have friends now, and family. You aren't here to sacrifice yourself so others can live. There are no more others, we're one team.

"Look at everyone that was on the roof. We're all different levels of power, coming from different walks of life, some of us aren't even human. But we're all bringing something to the table for a cause and that includes you.

"Thinking in terms of sacrifice does nothing but weaken the group. Isis just explained that Set was butchered and divided among the Infernal Kings for his power. It isn't the first time I've seen them off someone that used to be on their side. We're the good guys. We don't do that."

"I want to prove to you—"

"There's *nothing* left to prove, Nathaniel, especially not to me. I've told you that. You're chasing something that isn't there because you've already got it."

"I see...It feels good when everyone is surprised at what I can do after being ignored for so long. The townspeople back home were all looking up to me. I *mattered* for the first time in my life."

"Nathaniel, you've always mattered, it just took being out in the world for people to see it. You're going to be getting *a lot* of attention now and that's why I asked if you were ready for it, not because I didn't think you were capable of following through.

"Noah and I were here waiting for you because you may be the only one that can stop these riots and slow the spread of chaos feeding the kings. People usually run the other way when they see me in action and as charming and eloquent as Noah is, they won't be drawn to him the same as they are to you. Having the undead control people's minds isn't going to cut it as a long-term solution. We need *you*."

"I'm ready. *Really* ready." He made a fist with both hands and emitted a brilliant light from them.

"Noah and I will cover you, but it's best if we aren't seen so people don't get confused. I'm also dressed the like Grim Reaper without realizing, so that's sure to freak people out if I get spotted. We'll handle the fighting to disarm people—"

"I can fight too. I'll come guard you—"

"*Nathaniel!*"

"Right, sorry. No fighting. I'll just be the big nightlight in the sky to calm everyone down. I should start with an aurora. It's sure to get people's attention."

"Now you're thinking. Go make yourself proud." I couldn't hold back from giving the poor guy a hug. He was so damaged he didn't know if he was coming or going. Noah was right about his emotions being a ball of yarn. He wasn't hopeless, though, and *that's* what mattered.

Nathaniel set off like a rocket into the sky as the sun finished setting and I returned to the roof where the others waited.

"We good?" Noah asked.

"Yes. I forgot to tell him not to punch a hole through the Earth when he comes back down, but hopefully it goes without say by now."

"What are our chances of these Infernal Kings appearing any time soon?" Commander Timmons asked.

"They will not chance an appearance until all is in place," Isis answered. "They have waited centuries and predate time itself. Recklessness will not be their undoing."

"The world hasn't gone to hell enough yet for the atmosphere to not be caustic to them too," I added. "That's exactly why Nathaniel is going to try his best to calm people down by making them flock to him. Noah and I already saw it happen by our home. The people in town thought he was an angel."

"That gives us time of our own to prepare as best we can then," Timmons said. "Forgive me for saying so, but with your brother out of the way, goddess, it will be easier to bring the nations onboard. People won't be so intrigued at the idea of fighting each other when there is a universal threat against them. It will be nice to see a unified population toward progress for a change."

"War brings out the best and worst in people," said Noah.

The sky above Paris exploded into a majestic aurora like the one over our island and down came the streak of light that was Nathaniel. I cringed waiting for the impact as he drew closer to the ground a block away, but he remembered to put the brakes on early this time. Isis seemed impressed by the display and raised her hands to the sky in admiration for a fellow being of light.

"Magnificent!" she exclaimed and flew up into the aurora as a sparrow.

"Commander, can you get Lyle and any troops with him to come here?" I asked. "I know he has ties to New York, but we can't spread ourselves thin. In case anything happens I want us all together."

"I'll regroup with my team waiting outside the city and get in contact with him at once," she agreed.

"Thanks." I climbed up on Noah's back. "Come on, tiger. We've got a show to catch."

Chapter Fifty-Five

Nathaniel captivated the crowd without hesitation. He seemed to flourish when being depended on and took on an assertive, stalwart persona like he had been practicing the role for years. I didn't know how he did it coming from the life he had lead up through now, but he wasn't soft-spoken in the slightest. The little boy that never got the chance to be heard had a lot built up inside of him that was waiting to get out.

"Kid's not doing too bad," Noah said as we both watched on from up in a tree. "They're already eating out of his hand. Imagine if he knew a lick of French. You'd think he was Archios."

"I don't like the way they're staring at him."

I could hear Nathaniel telling people to go home and be with their families. They didn't. The crowd kept their eyes on him, those closest reached out to touch the glowing man. It creeped me out, but he didn't seem to mind.

"Ascended." Liam appeared from one of the hazy bubbles coming out of the ley lines at the foot of our tree. Marianna, Rafael, Alexandre, and Claudius all followed in their armor ready for battle.

"What are you doing here?" I asked. "You should be resting."

"You're in danger," said Rafael. The cabal looked healthier than Tobias and the others did in the kitchen, but still fatigued. "Ley lines are being twisted toward focal points in cities like this one around the world. We almost got stuck between dimensions again trying to get here."

"We're talking huge knots of aether," Claudius said. "It'd take something crazy strong to do this. *Nothing* we've dealt with is that powerful. The whole continent is being blacked out of aether as the ley lines retract into the focal point here."

"Whatever needs that much aether will level the city when it's released," Alexander said. "The spirits have fled in fear as animals do a forest fire. We need to get you out of here before you're harmed."

"You don't know Dorian if you think that's going to motivate him to leave," Noah told them. "Now he's gonna want to stay and carry every last pigeon to safety."

The Order had fright painted all over their faces and nothing except being back in the abbey would help that. "I appreciate that you came, but

I'm sending you all back," I said. "Set has been split up and absorbed by the Infernal Kings he was working with so they can use him as a source of power since they both feed off chaos. Nathaniel is stopping the riots here to prevent the chaos from growing, but I'll get him to make the people flee the city."

"No, Ascended, please. You don't understand," Marianna implored me. "That much aether is only used for two reasons: opening a *giant* summoning gate like nobody's ever seen before or rewriting the current laws of reality on a global scale. It's already too late for the cities this is happening in. We *have* to get out of here."

I looked to Noah. "Do you want to—"

He put his hand over my mouth and a finger over his to keep the Order quiet. "Listen," he whispered. I didn't hear anything though. No shouting, no voices at all, no gunshots or glass being broken. It was quiet enough to hear the fires crackling. The crowd was still there though, staring with vacant expressions at Nathaniel.

"This is bad," said Liam. "We need to go."

When Noah started staring into the sky I knew I should be worried. "What is it?" I asked him.

"Yeah, this is…bad."

"Tell me!"

"Aura vision. I can see the souls of the crowd leaving their bodies. Thousands, maybe more. No, definitely more. They're all going up to the tower."

"If their souls are gone..." I turned my attention back to the street. "What's left standing there?"

"The Abhorrent Ones." Isis returned to us. "Soulless beasts. They are always the first of the Fallen Army to set foot upon Earth and draw out the breath of the living into the void of their empty husk. We must not let them escape the city, for every one that does ten more will spawn."

"Sword. Now." Noah demanded and caught one that Liam tossed him. "Prepare your sparkle magic, kids. We're in for a fight."

"Go ahead." I nodded as Noah disappeared going toward the direction Nathaniel was in. "And turn our clothes white. No doubt we're going to be seen by others around the world, I want them to know who we are and what side we're on."

They did as I asked with a wave of their hands over each article of clothing. "Now we really look the part," I said. The five of them continued casting magic barriers and enchantments on themselves in preparation.

"Many innocent souls remain within the city," Isis informed us. "We must spare them so at least they may have a chance to return to the cosmic cycle."

"Do you have enough aether left in you to fight?" I asked the group.

"Plenty," said Liam. "Nobody should attempt to use the ley lines. You could get sucked into the focal point at the top of the tower where all the souls are going or be lost between dimensions. The current is too strong to channel from either. It would cause instant aether poisoning."

"The Rift is between dimensions, isn't it?" I asked. "How come we didn't go there when we were stuck in the chateau?"

"The Rift is deep in. We were at the surface."

"Can you still fight without your spirits?" Claudius asked Alexandre.

"The bravest will come if I call."

Noah came back with Nathaniel flying in after him. "Everyone is standing around unresponsive," Nathaniel said. "They don't blink and I don't think they're breathing either. When the crowd stopped rioting at first I thought I had gotten through to them..."

"There's nothing we could've done," I consoled him. "But there are still people out there that can be saved."

"*Sister.*" The crowd turned in our direction and spoke in one voice. Set's voice. "*Come to me, sister. See what I see and bear witness to the glory of our rebirth.*"

"Dogface is up there on the tower," Noah pointed out.

"That is not my brother. Not anymore." Isis flew up and vanished with a burst of feathers.

"There is still spirit left in him," said Alexandre. "Rewritten perhaps by corrupt prayers of the Infernals, but whatever he is now acts as a conduit for the Infernal Kings."

The crowds opened their mouth in unison and let out a stream of sand that filled the streets. The sand rose to their ankles in seconds and then past their knees. It didn't stop until they buried themselves.

"Get to the first signs of real people and start fighting there," I commanded the Order. "I'll go for Set."

"I'll go with you," Nathaniel said.

"Save the children, Nathaniel." That got through to him. He took off into the air with a look of hardened determination.

The people below crawled out from the sand, more demonic now than human. They retained their humanoid figures, but their eyes and mouths were gone, leaving only holes from which crimson light shone in their faces. Claws replaced fingers and their bodies were stretched over a foot taller. They charged across the sand in all directions, spreading throughout the city.

I wiped the street clean of the creatures with ease that was ultimately misleading. While thousands were reduced to dust, moments later more climbed right back out of the sand to continue their journey.

"Go," I glanced at the Order to dispatch them.

"Don't think I'm leaving you to go wipe their noses," Noah told me.

"I know you better than that—"

A sudden explosion from atop the Eiffel Tower deafened and blinded us. We were sent flying into the street. I felt Noah trying to grab my hand so we wouldn't be separated, but even I couldn't brace us with my powers.

My ears were ringing and vision blurred as I got myself upright. I called for Noah, but wouldn't have been able to hear him if he responded anyway. There were sharp pains coming from my face—glass shards. Of course it had to be glass shards. I pulled them out and was glad I healed instantly.

Once I came to my senses I saw that the explosion had thrown me through a café window, one of the only intact ones left on the street.

"Dor—Dorian?!" I heard Noah's voice and went outside to find him staggering around the street searching for me.

The aurora was gone, replaced by billowing charcoal clouds against a sanguine sky. I thought we had only been thrown across the street, but we were three blocks away. The buildings between us and the park were turned to rubble and the trees were reduced to blackened kindling. The streets were completely empty of the Abhorrent Ones and that worried me. It was never good when your enemies couldn't be seen.

"I don't know how to stop this," I said. My head was still reeling from the blast and so was Noah's when I got to him.

"You're not alone there," he said. The ground began to collapse beneath us as the sand-covered streets of Paris crumbled into pits of magma across the city. I flew Noah with me to locate the Order and provide backup after rethinking our direct assault.

"This is what happened in Yomi," I told him. Closing these chasms was futile; for every one that I sealed on the way, another opened and claimed more buildings to its depths. "Hell has officially taken hold on Earth."

"Where are the angels that are supposed to come down and help? The real ones, with the wings and the halos that Vance used to talk about."

"Maybe there never were any." I had learned in the past that the Infernal Kings—disguised as the Nether Lords that turned Gianluca—also created Christianity, or at least helped push it along in its infancy to get rid of the Old Gods that stood in their way. They could have come up with the whole concept of angels as a ploy to trick mankind into a false sense of security.

The Order had a handle on the situation when we got to them, but the extent of their range was limited. They could only manage one street at a time and the sheer number of the Abhorrent Ones was rapidly overwhelming the rest of the city. What started as hundreds of the hollow demons turned to thousands and was fast approaching numbers in the millions as they sucked out the souls of two and three victims at a time to add to their ranks.

Nathaniel was carrying buses and subway cars loaded with people through the air to safety. He hoisted toppled apartment buildings over his head after clearing them out to open escape routes for survivors and impede the demons' paths from going after them. His strength matched my own, but seemed so much more unimaginable coming from someone using their bare hands.

When facing the demons head on I almost had sympathy for them getting in Nathaniel's way. The light radiating from his being was enough to drive them off in pain, but with the velocity of his punches having the same effect as my telekinetic shockwaves, the Infernals were reduced to little else than dust. He was the perfect demon slayer. Best of all was seeing the people he saved recognize him for it. The thankful cheers were close to drowning out the screams of horror meant for the demons.

"Kid's doing well for himself," Noah said as women of all ages threw themselves at Nathaniel with hugs and kisses of gratitude and children clung to him as their hero.

I went up higher to get a better view of the city. Paris was no small hamlet that could be covered in a single glimpse. The bustling metropolis was packed at every available inch with Abhorrent Ones that needed to climb over each other to get anywhere. The one benefit we had in this was that the demons now stayed dead being that they were within the dominion of Hell. Although finite, the swarm still seemed endless. I brought down destruction on a five-block radius to the east of the Order, but even that was only a small dent to the Infernals' numbers.

"Dogface is still the key to this," Noah said as we descended into the fray and dodged Marianna's giant sword that went spinning past our heads like a boomerang. "We get rid of him and we cut the link to Hell. Then we can go TV shopping."

A twenty-foot ice statue of a man plodded down the broken sidewalk, freezing everything it came in contact with for Alexandre to shatter with his sword.

"He can't be killed..." I smashed the Abhorrent Ones behind Noah as he flipped over me to decapitate the ones at my back. "He needs to be weakened and separated from the Infernal Kings somehow."

Liam and Rafael channeled a spell through their swords aimed at a large group of demons. Time slowed to a crawl around them and any others nearby, allowing the demons to be cut down with greater ease by making a chokepoint to block their escape.

"Got any ideas?" Noah asked.

The area we were in went dark and Gianluca was in front of us in his Roman-knight armor when the shadow cleared. A bolt of lightning struck beside him and Empress Kamakura made her entrance next.

"Tokyo is no more," Gianluca said without his usual warm greeting. "And the New York City too."

"What?!" I shouted. "What about Lyle? Where's Lyle? He was in New York!"

"Yes, he is safe. I go with him to New York, but is too much so he leave. We cannot fight with so little people."

"What do you mean? How can it be gone? New York can't be gone."

"Set is in many place at once. He use the towers in the world to attack the city. The island there is now many pieces and the buildings..."

Gianluca motioned with his hands to show them being flattened. "Tokyo, the same. Maybe more city too. I do not know. We come here to maybe save Paris."

"Paris is already gone," I said. "Look around."

"No, this is not so bad. Set is in many place but only can give a focus to one or two."

This isn't bad? Maybe I didn't want to see how much worse the other cities were. How could New York City really be gone? How could this be happening so fast? There wasn't even a battle over it. We didn't have a chance to stop it.

"The Heavenly Ones demand retribution for the interloper's crimes against our land," said Kamakura. "His strength has grown since our last confrontation."

"Set has been split up and absorbed by the Infernal Kings," I said. "He's their connection to Earth that's letting them do all this. We need to sabotage that connection."

Isis flew down to join us and complete the divine quartet. "What is left of my brother will not be so easily bested."

"We only need to make him useless to the Infernal Kings so they abandon him," I explained. "Then it's time for both goddesses to retake control of your lands so the people have something better to put their prayers in and keep you both with us. We'll need Aurelia to get the militaries of the world to help survivors too."

"It has been agreed upon by the Heavenly Ones that our return shall be ushered by the dawn of peace," said Kamakura. "I will do what I must to smite this menace from the world."

"I walk the path of life and have sworn an oath to the light never to take breath from any being," Isis said. "I wish not to be known as kinslayer, but neither will I see my allies fall."

"Your assistance will be most welcomed. Reserves of aether are plentiful here to sustain us both for a time," said Kamakura.

"My brother's talents in chaos extend beyond ruination," Isis warned. "He has the ability to alter fate itself with infectious entropy. If those who sit behind his throne in shadow are made to feel truly threatened, he could turn our allies' fiercest blows to idle folly or return them from whence they came."

"Fighting him head-on is stupid to begin with," Noah said. "Not every enemy can be defeated in direct confrontation. Not every enemy *has* to be. Dorian made Dogface run away with his tail between his legs by killing a couple of humans and being mean to him. It's his head you've got to mess with."

"We fight him together and show him he cannot win," said Gianluca and called his sword to his hand. "When he has no more pride he will not want to be—ah—embarrassed no more. A warrior with no pride is no enemy to fear."

"How many times are you gonna ram your head into that same wall before you figure out it won't work?" Noah groaned.

"I wonder if we could get him to turn on the Infernal Kings," I said. "All they want is destruction, but all he wants is to bring back Ancient Egypt. Gianni, you turned against them after you realized what they were doing to Rome. What if we got him to fight us where he'd risk destroying the place he loves?"

"Ancient Egypt doesn't exist and current Egypt is an empty desert," said Noah. "And didn't he blow up that temple you were in when he captured you?"

"That was Isis's temple. He would have destroyed it to build one for himself anyway. But you're right; Egypt is empty. Set has nothing in this world to hold on to and take pride in. What if we rebuild it for him?"

"To build the empire will take much time. Time we do not have," Gianluca said.

"Not the entire empire, just a temple maybe. Enough to feed his ego. We only need him conflicted enough to turn on his masters. They'll either kick him to the curb or kill him for us, but either way they won't have a link to Earth any more. At least for a while."

"A sound theory, *if* my brother retains any will of his own," Isis agreed. "The one thing in this world he holds sacred are the lands he felt destined to rule."

"Around ten thousand years between the lot of you and the twenty-year-old kid is the only one to come up with a real plan. I'd be pretty embarrassed if I were you," Noah said and wrapped his arm around me with a kiss to my cheek. "Proudest day of my life and I didn't even do anything."

"Show respect to these goddess or you will lose that tongue again," Gianluca threatened.

"Doubt it."

"Enough, you two," I intervened. "And I'm twenty-four, by the way..."

"The undead one speaks true," said Isis. "We have looked to the past and searched within ourselves for answers where there are none. Age has dulled reason with pride, but there is fortune in our foe's shared folly. The tradition of the old ways are meant as a foundation to build upon, not a wall to impede progress."

"How will you construct such a site?" Kamakura inquired.

"I'm more than destruction incarnate. I can create whatever I think of within reason. The materials are all there in the desert from our battle at Giza. I only have to reassemble them. Someone will need to stay behind to help the Alabaster Order and PROJECT: UNITY keep the demons from escaping the city."

"I shall stand to smite our foes," Kamakura declared and with a clap of thunder her four guardians appeared in the sundered streets below.

"Isis, it would help a lot if you could show me a vision of a temple Set might have had like the time you showed me yours back at Philae. Give me the knowledge you would have given the pharaohs and all I would have to do is fill in the pieces."

"I shall await you there to impart such enlightenment." Isis soared into the sky in a gust of feathers and departed for Egypt.

"That leaves you, Gianni. Take us to Egypt so we can end this."

Chapter Fifty-Six

We exited the shadows to the ruins of Giza where Isis already stood.

"Where's Noah?" I asked Gianluca once noticing it was his hand on my shoulder and not Noah's.

"Ah, I forget him." He gave me a coy smile and squeezed my shoulder. "He is more help to fight the demons in Paris."

"Gianni...He better be all right." I approached Isis and nodded. "Shall we?"

She put her fingertips to both sides of my head and our eyes met in a flash golden light. "See now what divine knowledge hath been lost to the sands—the dreams once bestowed upon chosen pharaohs."

I did more than see a vision of a temple or its construction; my five senses were flooded with information as minute as the formation of the limestone and mud bricks used for the structures and the taste of the dry desert air that blew each grain of sand into the grooves of the hieroglyphs. I started as a separate entity witnessing the creation of an Ancient Egyptian temple falling into place, but then dissolved into the scene as if we were one.

In the past, I had worked hard to learn how to shape objects using my powers by feeling out the materials. I had thought that was a sign of mastery, but it turned out that it was only the first step. I no longer needed to feel and cypher every delicate manipulation like clay, as when I had first transcended. Now it was more of a sweeping exertion of will that molded my surroundings. If I wanted a limestone column or a pillar in the style shown to me, one rose from the rubble without much effort. Temple walls reached toward the moon and statues of Set grew from the sand.

With the scene from the vision completed, my consciousness was returned from its altered state.

"Damn, you're awesome." I heard Noah's voice as my sight was restored last.

"I know!" I gave him a smirk of my own, then looked over at Gianluca to thank him for bringing Noah to me. "It's up to you to get Set here, Gianni. A Roman soldier invading his lands should be the perfect bait to draw him away from the cities."

"I am happy to do this." His smile was almost a bit menacing, but there was no doubt whose side he was on anymore. He donned his dark helmet and was gone to lure our quarry.

I floated around the temple complex in awe of my own work and stopped at a statue of Set. It was so much more elaborate than the one building I had planned. "Isis, do you know the spell to turn others to stone?"

"I do," she answered from atop the main temple with staff in hand. "If what you ask is for my brother, then I may disappoint. A magic catalyst such as the Eye of Ra is needed to inflict a curse upon a fellow god, yet its energy has been drained by misuse."

"The Eye is basically a really powerful aether crystal with an enchantment, right? Set still used it but not at full power because he didn't know Ra's secret name to break the enchantment. What if we get you another really powerful aether crystal to replace it?"

"It should work all the same, but I know not where you would obtain such a crystal of divine quality."

"I do. We need to get Nathaniel here though. Can you send him a birdy messenger?"

"Your herald?" she asked. "Can you not call to him by mind alone?"

"No, I'm not telepathic."

"There is no need to be, Young One. He is the bearer of your soul. Will him to you as you would an object of your desire and he shall feel your call."

"I don't like it," Noah rebuked. "I know how it is to have someone in your head tugging at your leash."

"Don't compare me to Aurelia," I said, closing my eyes, clearing my mind, and calling Nathaniel in my thoughts. I heard nothing in response, yet could feel his presence as if he was standing near me. I assumed that meant it worked, but would have rather practiced at a less critical time.

"Let the Italian take care of Dogface when they get here," said Noah. "We need to keep our eyes opened for any more new tricks the demons taught him."

"I know, I know. Gianluca's been looking forward to this for a while. I wouldn't want to get in his way."

A bolt of lightning split the clear night sky and hit the sand where we were waiting. "They shall arrive shortly," Kamakura said, emerging from the flash. Nobody said anything as we took our positions on a nearby dune to get a vantage point of the temple grounds.

"You okay?" Noah asked me after too many minutes of stillness.

"Given the circumstances, yeah." I held his prayer beads in my hand, rotating each one around the string before moving on to the next in line. "I can't believe New York is gone, and Paris, Tokyo, probably the other four cities too by now. Maybe more. All of Egypt is gone, but it didn't hit me in the same way as places I've been and have memories of. I don't know if it's better or worse that there was nothing we could have done."

"Only good memory I have left from any of those places were with you and there are still plenty of new ones left for us to make," he said and held my hand. "Just keep looking forward, never back."

"Something of great power comes this way," Empress Kamakura announced. The air echoed with the shouts of people we couldn't see. Liam's cabal emerged from a spatial distortion, falling to the sand motionless with Nathaniel flying out after them and landing softly at my feet.

"You're okay," he said in relief and stood before I could reprimand him for kneeling. "I had a terrible feeling you had been hurt. There are so many people dead, so many innocent people..."

"Told you," Noah whispered to me.

"No, I'm fine. I was trying to call to you to fly here—are they going to be okay?" I turned Liam onto his back and checked his pulse. It was weak and his body had gone cold.

"It's my fault," Nathaniel said. "I panicked and had them take me to you since it would be faster. They weren't strong enough to make the trip even with the five of them, but I insisted..."

Isis walked over and with a subtle gesture from both hands she bathed the cabal in a golden light that restored them to health. "Rise, Children of Aether, my sands will not be your final resting place. Arise with vigor renewed and serve your lord once more."

As the light dimmed, their eyes opened without any indication of weakness. I helped Liam up regardless and listened to them comment on how

Isis's magic made them feel revitalized in mind and body.

"Sorry for the mixed messages," I apologized. "It's probably better that you're all here now anyway so we can stick together."

I had just enough time to explain most of the plan to them when the light from the stars and moon went out and left us in pitch blackness. Nathaniel and Isis's personal radiance, however, were as bright as ever.

Gianluca appeared from the darkness with Set pursuing close behind as expected. Set didn't seem to take notice of the new temple in his honor. He attacked Gianluca with a crooked sword from all sides without pause to try and find a weak point in the ebony armor, but there was none.

Set had gotten a dramatic upgrade from the Infernal Kings; he was twice as fast, swapping in and out of his sand form like Noah did with mist. It was close to impossible for Gianluca to strike him without doing something that would level the temple. Six Roman soldiers that Gianluca summoned from the shadows struck Set, but the blow passed right through as he changed to sand on the fly. He conjured waves of hellfire and even the dark lightning from the Underworld in a grim, yet spectacular display.

Gianluca's defenses were proving too much for even a Demon King empowered god to breach, but the maddening struggle was only making Set focus more on Gianluca and not on the temple.

"This is going to go on forever if Dogface doesn't pay attention to what's right under his nose," said Noah.

"Light it up," I told Nathaniel. He made a fist and created a ball of light in his hand that he threw into the sky above the temple. The light exploded like a nuclear warhead sending all of us including the goddesses flying back.

"*RESTRAINT!*" Noah shouted over the ringing in our ears.

"I meant an aurora, not nuke the place!" I yelled. I knew Nathaniel was eager, but that eagerness was turning to rage as he was held back from fighting Set.

"I'm sorry!" Nathaniel apologized as he zipped around to help everyone. I worried that the light would have erased Gianluca's armor, but it seemed he managed to slip into the shadows and use the distraction to get the upper hand on Set by kicking him into a statue from behind. Nathaniel's light remained, making it bright as high noon in the desert.

I saw Set briefly take notice of the statue of himself that he crashed into. It was the first I had seen a clear view of him since his being compromised by Hell. His canine-shaped head was skeletal; his aardvark ears were now curved demon horns. His previously more muscular body was gaunt and alien in a strange biomechanical way like the demon lord back in Yomi with red lines covering his dark skin.

"You think to trick me?" He held up the head of the statue and crushed it in his grip.

Isis flew to him to speak. "No, brother. It is no trick. We have agreed it is best for our land to be reborn. There is naught in our way now that the sands are barren. The Ennead is too weak to lead, but you have the chance to be king and save so many who worship you. Is this not what you have always sought?"

"Foolishness." Set's voice changed and a second pair of fiery eyes opened on his head. He wasn't speaking in our minds anymore with the sound of growls and snarls, but a wholly inhuman voice came directly from his body and not his mouth. "This has been nothing, but a game to test those few that would challenge me. I know everything you have done, are doing, and will do to defy the inevitable. The only reason any of you still exist is because I allow it. You are fulfilling my demands for chaos and providing unending entertainment by your vain endeavors. You kill to serve me. You create to serve me.

"I am eternal. No god is greater than I, no abomination, nor self-righteous mortal. The strongest among you are my servants even in defiance. Your free will is a fallacy. The world needs heroes so that there can be villains. When the time comes to remove you from the field all that will remain in your stead is fear, fear that will breed chaos and hate for me to reap. Then once more will the cycle continue when I abandon this world for another, only to return again. You have no hope—"

A streak of light shot toward Set from the side and when it made contact with him he was sent hurdling through the air for miles until he disappeared from sight. Everyone was stunned and didn't know what to do. I looked to where Nathaniel had been floating next to me, but he was gone.

"Did the kid just—did he just sucker punch a Demon King?" Noah was as befuddled as the rest. I grabbed his arm and he knew I meant to chase after Nathaniel. We found him several miles away by the tremors he caused from pounding Set's face into paste with his fists.

"LEAVE THIS WORLD ALONE OR I WILL RIP YOU IN TWO WITH MY OWN HANDS!" Nathaniel's voice boomed across the desert as he threatened Set, or the Infernal King inside. His aura of light was scorching the demon-god's body enough to cause smoke.

"*Nathaniel*" I shouted. "Get away from him!"

"I'm not afraid of him! I'll protect you, master! Everyone, *everything*, is scared of something and I will be that something to him!" Nathaniel picked up Set by the throat with one hand. "DO YOU HEAR ME?!"

Set disappeared. As amazing as what Nathaniel did was, it wasn't the plan.

"Nathaniel, that was an Infernal King controlling Set—"

"It doesn't matter what he was. I had to do it and I'm not sorry. I could feel your fear when he was trying to get in our heads. I wasn't going to stand for it.

"I've had enough of people being discarded like trash because someone tells them they're unworthy. It reminds me of how I was treated before you came along and I can't stand seeing it happen. I *won't* let it happen, not to you, or our friends, or the world."

No amount of preparation could have helped us fully deal with what we were facing, but out of all of us Nathaniel was the least equipped to handle things emotionally. Gianluca lived and breathed war. The goddesses were brought into existence for reasons like this. Noah had over a century of dealing with the worst the world had to offer. I had experienced more in the past four years of my life than most supernaturals do in a millennia. Liam's cabal was bred for this role and taught how to keep a level head under extreme circumstances. Even Lyle's police training and time with PROJECT: UNITY gave him direction.

Nathaniel had none of that. Inside the body of the invincible man was still the mind of the vulnerable child that knew nothing but suffering. And I had given that child not a gun, but a weapon of mass destruction. It seemed only natural that he would use it to make the pain go away.

"It *does* matter because you can't fight demons with anger, kid," Noah told him. "You're gonna lose every time no matter how strong you think it makes you. Keep your head on straight or you'll only be helping the enemy."

Suddenly, the celestial sky tore open above Egypt as it had during Set's last take over with the large blood moon. Nathaniel might have beaten Set back to his senses and he took the bait to claim his empire. "Back to the temple, quick."

"I do not need you or any Infernal to help me claim what should rightfully be mine!" The good old

Set we knew and loved had returned and was raving like a lunatic at everyone when we got there. The Order took turns teleporting back and forth to slash at him while Gianluca kept him distracted for the most part.

"Nathaniel. Make me the best crystal you've ever made."

The Infernal King must have abandoned Set by how he was acting, but that didn't stop Set from going forward with his plan for total domination. He kicked up a storm of greater strength than he should have been capable of on his own. Kamakura dispelled it with ease, but it was only a smokescreen.

Set appeared from the settling sands to ambush her, but was knocked down by a mighty swing of Gianluca's shield. The two resumed their brawl from earlier, this time aided by Kamakura. There was no telling who was causing what as the elements raged across the battlefield, with the earth and sky being in a constant state of upheaval. The ground had already been split apart more times than could be counted yet there was always room for another chasm caused by one of the three gods rending the bedrock beneath the sand. With the Infernal King's influence gone from Set he lost command over hellfire and dark lightning, making the perilous conditions at least a bit more manageable.

"I can't do it, I can't concentrate!" Nathaniel shouted to me over the mayhem after a dozen pathetic attempts. "Liam—he could—"

"Then fly out of here to somewhere you can!" I yelled back. "It needs to be from a god or close to it."

Noah grabbed him before he flew away. "Stop being a little bitch, man up, and make the fucking rock. You wanted people to count on you and now they are." I felt Nathaniel's determination brought out by Noah's words as he flew up into the atmosphere.

The cabal joined in to land blows against Set when they could, but were kept busy dodging between the storm winds and geysers of sand or rain of mundane fire that littered the area. "Recast your barriers to negate the fire!" Liam instructed them. The translucent spheres that surrounded them changed to a bluish hue, extinguishing the flames that hit it.

"Get to the river and use the aqua barrier to convert the water into aether if you're running low," he added. "One at a time, and call it out so we know we haven't lost anyone to the battle."

Kamakura summoned her guardian spirits into the fray and absorbed them for more power to counter Set's magic. I crushed him to what should have been death more than once, but every time he managed to escape and reappear an instant later. The chaos waves he emitted would frequently redirect and disperse our attacks making it a challenge to hit him at all.

"This guy doesn't play fair! I can't reverse gravity on him!" Marianna shouted.

"What did you expect? He's a *god*, none of our hexes will work on him," Rafael yelled back. He threw out four daggers that nailed Set in the back and then exploded them with a spell. Set didn't seem to mind.

"We have to break his confidence," Noah said and swung me out of the way of a lightning barrage. I caught a glimpse of the statues and got an idea.

If I was to get in his head I'd need to think big like Lyle had told me. I'd need to build big. The Ancient Egyptians were superstitious and there was no better image to channel than that of a rival increased to a nightmarish size.

Starting from the feet I worked my way up using the sand around us to summon a statue of Horus—Isis's son and the rightful king of Ancient Egypt. I had seen plenty of depictions of him through all of the visions, studies, and temple visits to get a decent likeness. When I was done, a massive three-hundred foot replica of the falcon-headed god towered over the battlefield.

I created floating platforms around the statue from sand and rock to lift the Order out of Set's immediate reach so they could rain down spells from above while in relative safety. It wasn't enough to simply have a statue of Set's greatest foe; it needed to move. It needed to attack. I brought the statue to life, manipulating it like a giant puppet and slammed its foot down on Set.

"This is kinda cool. Should've made it look like me though," said Noah, popping up beside me on Horus's shoulder.

"I wanted to scare him, not seduce him." I smiled at Noah's intrigued expression.

Set burst through the head of Horus while I was distracted, but Noah parried his blade and flip-kicked him off the statue at super speed before he could turn to sand and evade.

"What was that you were telling me about being like Horus when you had me chained up in the pyramid?" I jeered at him when he reappeared. "It won't be hard to get people to worship him back to Earth when they see this statue kicking your ass."

"Fool. The demon sorceress has already destroyed all artifacts of the other gods and I have made sure none shall ever leave the pantheon. It would take more power than you could fathom to stir him from slumber." I could feel Set trying to wrestle control of the sand in the statue from me, but my hold on it was stronger.

He pretended not to be rattled by the potential of Horus's return, yet I noticed he was no longer conjuring storms but had instead switched to trying to rush us down with sword attacks and lacerating gales. Noah and I were both sliced and stabbed several times by Set's frenzy until Gianluca stepped in with Kamakura to take the pressure off.

The more that jumped in to help, the more ferociously Set fought back. He was more manageable when only being confronted by one or two at most. Once three and four of us engaged him the chaos peaked and the storms returned.

Our team started to fall one by one. Liam and his cabal were impressive just for being there, yet it was too much for any mortal to face a god of Set's caliber. Isis continually healed them only for them to fall again in a matter of minutes, so I called their retreat. Noah knew he was badly outclassed in this match up and after being knocked around one too many times by the flurry of wide-ranging explosions he decided to pull back and help me dodge by using his speed. Kamakura was burning through energy faster than she could recoup it without any worship or notable aether supply to speak of in the area. Isis sacrificed some of her own strength to keep Kamakura in the battle, but it was only a stalling tactic.

"Do you not see you are destroying our lands, brother?" Isis called out to Set. "There is no glory, no victory to be had in the loss of our home! Do you still not see that the Infernal Kings were only using you? You will be king of nothing! Take Egypt and protect it as you were meant to do!"

"Your offering has been denied," he replied. "It is no better than the corrupt prayers to the false gods that plague this world already."

Gianluca and I were the only ones not on our last leg although our efforts weren't yielding results. Control over the statue of Horus was slipping through my grasp as I balanced negating the storm winds, holding back the rain of fire, and countering Set when he ambushed one of us.

We started this on the offense and now we were playing defense. I reshaped the statue to erect walls to block stray attacks and buffer the storm winds that came and went. Gianluca ensnared Set in a miniature black hole that bent the fabric of space and even tried dumping him in the Nether World for a time, but the chaos god could not be contained. There was too much going on in the world for him to falter.

"If you do not want this land then I take it for Roma!" Gianluca stuck his sword in the ground and the shadows spread like an oil spill. The sky went black and darkness consumed the desert in no time. "You see? Is easy for me. I hold back too long, but no more. Now there is no chaos here, only darkness. I can make this whole world darkness if I like."

"All for naught. Though demons, they still showed me countless worlds, fresh and fertile. Take these dead lands and I will claim a hundred more in this world and the rest!"

Set unleashed an explosion like back in Paris. Noah was ready this time, but didn't make it far enough with me to escape the blast. We went tumbling through the darkness until Gianluca appeared and caught us both, much to Noah's displeasure.

"Where's Nathaniel?" I asked. "Where's Set? Not again..."

"I'm here." Nathaniel's voice came from above as he flew down from the blackened sky. It was dark enough to dim his light, but in his hand was an aether crystal that resembled the Eye of Ra in brilliance and clarity.

"I knew you could do it," I said and caused him to smile. "We have to get that to Isis."

"Get rid of this darkness," Noah demanded. "You proved your point, now it's just annoying."

"Why? You are scared?" Gianluca taunted, but did return the desert to normal. Set had Isis by the throat high up in the air. Nathaniel reacted faster than any of us, zooming up to them before we could reach them. Set let Isis go and disappeared as a cloud of sand in the wind. He tried to run Nathaniel through with his sword, but it clinked uselessly against his chest.

"Not this time," Nathaniel told him. He picked Set up above his head and ripped him in two like a piece of paper.

"Holy shit—!" Noah and I both exclaimed along with Gianluca's version in Latin.

"My, such strength!" Kamakura commented.

Nathaniel handed Isis the crystal and she proceeded to replace the Eye on her staff. Set put himself back together from the desert sand, ready for more.

"Was that all?" he boasted. "The great darkness is gone and so soon? And now you seek the aid of this whelp to make mockery of Ra's splendor in the shape of that forgery? How sad you are, sister. Neither light nor dark can quell chaos. I shall conquer the rest of the broken kingdoms throughout the world. No god or demon can stop me!"

"Forgive me, brother, but I cannot allow you to leave here. The Ennead's departing wish was to see you stopped and now I shall fulfill that." Isis pointed the staff at Set and turned the familiar flash of light against him. I crossed my fingers hoping it would work and let out a scream of joy upon seeing his body begin to harden in stone.

"If I cannot have Egypt then I will make it cost you the world! Down from the heavens! Down from the skies! Celestial calamity will—!" He ranted until the very last moment when his petrified body fell to the ground.

We gathered around the statue, including Liam's cabal that had been watching from afar. "Is it finally over?" Marianna asked.

"No." I crushed the statue into the shape of a baseball. "Throw this into the Rift as deep between the dimensions as you can. I'm sure the parasites there will give him a warm welcome if he's ever revived."

I handed the stone orb to Marianna and the five of them pooled their energy together to banish Set from our world once and for all.

Chapter Fifty-Seven

"What's stopping the demons from retrieving Set from the Rift?" Nathaniel asked me.

"The Infernal Kings wanted us to win. They knew Set's ambitions would get in the way eventually and just used him to get the ball rolling, then used *us* to do their dirty work when they were done with him."

"There is much left to be done before the next battle mounts," said Isis. "We must reclaim and heal our lands."

I fixed up the temple and changed the statues of Set into ones for Isis. "Egypt is all yours and I can help you rebuild it. There are sure to be plenty of refugees from the attacks around the world and there's no better place to find sanctuary than with a goddess of life."

"You better feed me before any of this. I'm hungry," Noah complained and poked me. "And you know I'm gonna want a nap after that, *and* I'll need a bath because you won't let me in the bed unless I'm clean, *and* you know I don't want to sleep alone."

"Stop whining, you big baby." I wiped the blood from under his nose with my sleeve when he leaned in for a kiss. He tried to not grin as he feigned not enjoying the attention from me. "Wait here a minute and be good."

I noticed Gianluca had broken off from the group, so I left the goddesses and the Order to talk amongst themselves to go check on him. "I'm sorry," I said and looked up at the sky with him. "I know it must be hard seeing me with someone else. I didn't mean to rub it in your face like that..."

"No. This is good. I think is the first time I see you are Dorian."

"What does that mean?"

"When I see you the first time...you are so beautiful. You remind me of my love when I am human in Roma. I know you are not him, but I treat you the same. I am sorry for this."

"That's nothing to be sorry about," I assured him. "I understand it must be confusing to wake up two thousand years later in a whole new world."

"I miss Roma," he sighed. "I try to change you to be like my love in the past and when it does not work then I try to change the world. I am very blind like Set. That is the only bad darkness in me."

"You're nothing like Set or you would've done what he did."

"You save me from it before I do, that is why."

"You wouldn't have listened to me if you really wanted to do what Set was doing."

"Maybe is true," Gianluca agreed. "But again I do not know my place. I think I stay in the shadows again until I am needed for the fighting."

"No." Although I knew Noah was watching, I took Gianluca by the hand as a friend to comfort him. "We need you to be a leader and a hero of this world. Don't leave us and hide."

"You are more leader than me. I am a soldier, no more."

"That isn't true. The goddesses respect you for more than your sword. PROJECT: UNITY needs your guidance. People look up to strength and you have a lot of it. Apocatastasis has already started and cities have been destroyed. There's no need to be subtle about things anymore. As long as you aren't wiping out civilizations yourself, there's no reason anymore not to rebuild where people need homes."

"You will help me to build this?" He held my hand and smiled.

"Of course." We hugged and I was glad that Noah didn't burst in to break it up. In fact, I was proud of him.

"I am an honest man so I say to you the truth. Maybe I do not like the man you choose, but I am happy to see he treat you good. He has my respect because I know he is the right man to make you happy."

"Thank you, Gianni." I hugged him a little tighter. "It makes me happy to hear you say that and I'm looking forward to helping you build a new Rome."

"And I am very happy for this. Everybody is happy!"

"Except Set," I laughed with him on our way back to the group. Noah snatched me up as soon as we got close and hugged me territorially, but I knew it was in jest.

"You will take care of him?" Gianluca asked Noah.

"If you know Dorian as well as I do, you'd know he doesn't *need* to be taken care of. But if he ever does, I'll always be there to hold him *up*, not hold him *back*."

"Hm, this is true." Gianluca put out his hand in friendship and the true miracle of the night happened when Noah accepted it.

"Excuse me, Ascended," Claudius interrupted. "Is it me or is that big red moon getting bigger?" We all stared up at the sky to see what he was talking about.

"No...I think it's coming closer— Set had said something about making his loss of Egypt cost us, but I thought he was bluffing! Isis can you seal the hole in the sky?"

"Not like this. The moon is too far for the breach to be sealed. If only Thoth were here to recall it... I fear Egypt is doomed after all. Even in defeat my brother has managed to curse us."

"That thing is going to fuck the whole world, not just Egypt," said Noah. Kamakura disappeared into the sky in a streak of yellow light and transformed into the dragon. The titanic serpent now appeared as a mere thread dancing in the wind against the enormity of the blood moon.

"It's—uh—it's coming down faster," Rafael panicked.

"Gravity is pulling it through the breach," Marianna said. "Our island is going to be underwater from the tide if it isn't already!"

"Get us to the other side of the planet, Italian," Noah ordered.

"It won't matter. If the moon is allowed to make contact it will knock Earth out of orbit and kill us all anyway," said Liam.

Without a word, Nathaniel shot up into the air and headed toward the moon. "Where does he think he's going? To get out and push?" Noah shouted.

"What else is there to do?" I took off after Nathaniel to help. Noah grabbed me and I thought he was about to tell me not to go when the sky became a blur. He used his speed to launch us miles above the ground in the same way we had when flying over the storm wall to escape Set during that first encounter.

"You got this!" Noah shouted and let go to free fall back down to Earth. I didn't know where Nathaniel was, but I could see Kamakura in the distance for a brief moment before the clouds began swirling around her as she used the wind against the moon's descent. I knew that no cyclone would be able to stop something this size.

"It's just one big push," I told myself. Nathaniel had caught up and plowed straight into the moon at full speed. It was already starting to reverse its direction before I did anything. Nathaniel was moving the *moon* all on his own.

I strained and clenched my teeth while slamming all the telekinetic force I could call upon into the moon, but it began descending again. Then I remembered to let go.

I closed my eyes and opened them again when I heard a rumbling crack like thunder. The moon had a new crater in it where I was focusing. I kept my eyes opened this time and imagined myself as the greater force in the struggle enveloping the entire surface of the moon, instead of concentrating on pushing at one point. That was when the rumbling grew louder and started going off in rapid succession.

The moon fractured like a windshield after being hit by a rock. The cracks spread across the surface and I let it have everything left in me. There was an earsplitting explosion as huge chunks of the moon were blasted from its core and then the entire celestial body blew apart.

I was thrown back as pieces of the moon, some the size of mountains themselves, hurtled toward the ground. I was frantically trying to blast the biggest pieces apart before they could hurt anybody down below when Nathaniel came shooting toward me through the meteor shower. He barreled right through the falling rock without slowing down.

"Hurry! We have to—!" I was about to tell Nathaniel to spread out so we could cover more ground when we noticed the pieces of the moon disappearing into their own shadow all across the sky. "Never mind. Gianni's got it."

We flew back down together and looked on as Liam's cabal channeled the nearby ley lines into the aether crystal on Isis's staff. The energy in it became so great that the crystal began to vibrate. Isis raised the staff to the heavens and a beam of light stretched upward beyond the clouds to mend the ruptured sky, shattering the crystal in the process.

Noah tackled me onto the sand as everyone let out cheers. "I love when you blow stuff up," he grinned. "Now go wash the sand out of your butt so we can celebrate."

"Noah!" I laughed and pulled him down to kiss me. Out of the corner of my eye I watched as the Order crowded around Nathaniel to pat him on the back in praise and get a hug from Marianna. I don't think he had ever felt so accepted. That palpable depression he had exuded when we met had been replaced by an unmitigated joy.

"We must venture forth to the other kingdoms and rid them of the Infernal interlopers," said Kamakura. "They will not travel far from their spawning grounds with their masters temporarily purged from this world, but life cannot continue in their presence."

"Vyrlakalos makes a disease for the demons we can use," Gianluca said.

"That's too slow," I said. "We can clear them out in battle faster."

"Hm, yes, I do like the battle," Gianluca smiled.

"You guys go back to the abbey," I told the Order. "Rest up and send everyone that's battle ready to any of the invaded cities to start clearing out the streets. I'll start in New York."

"I'm coming with you," Nathaniel stated without giving me a choice either way and then backtracked when realizing who he was talking to. "Please."

"Okay, Champion," I agreed. "There could still be survivors in the ruins so don't pick up Manhattan and throw it into the sun or anything." He smiled sheepishly and nodded. "Gianni, do us the honors?"

Noah threw me over his shoulder before Gianluca brought us to New York City through the shadows so we wouldn't be separated.

The renowned Manhattan skyline was gone.

The island had been divided into two main land masses with additional smaller pieces splintered off into the Hudson and East Rivers. No point in the city was higher than four stories tall. From where we stood on the remains of the Chrysler Building we had a clear view of the burning architectural graveyard around us.

It was breathtaking in the worst sense of the word. I kept waiting for the landscape to change back and reveal that this was only an illusion, and New York as we knew it still existed.

"Glad you could make it," I heard a voice say from down the pile of wreckage we were on. I was surprised to see Lyle that it was climbing up to us.

"What are you doing here?" I asked and lifted him the rest of the way. "Gianluca said you had left."

"Eh—maybe is a little lie," said Gianluca. "I do not want you to worry and this one is a stubborn man like you. He does not leave when I say."

"I couldn't leave her—the city. This is always gonna be my home."

"Yeah, I thought it must have been bad for you to have left."

"This? This is nothing, man. NYC has come back from worse." He sat on a slab of concrete. He was exhausted by the way he was breathing and dragging his body to move. "Tell me you got the son of a bitch that did this."

"We did."

"I'm sorry I missed it. I would've liked to have put a bullet between his eyes myself, but I knew I could make more of a difference here."

"It's all right, I gave him one for you. Are there... any survivors left?"

"Some. The initial blast that did all this killed pretty much everybody...it was a quick death from what reports came when we surveyed the area. Most of those that survived got turned into those tall things with the glowing faces."

"Abhorrent Ones."

"Whatever. There are still some real people trapped in this mess, but we're running out of steam."

"I'll go find them," Nathaniel told me and was off before the last word left his lips. Noah followed, presumably to drive in the importance of restraint, and Gianluca went off in search of the Abhorrent Ones soon after.

"Have you heard from anyone else on the team?" I asked.

"Rudgar is with Aurelia giving press conferences," Lyle sighed. "She didn't waste a second stealing the spotlight. She made a sweeping pledge that 'her people' would take care of everything, so you can expect all the credit to go to her for what we're doing."

"She'll get hers soon enough."

"Timmons was outside Paris when the explosion went off. She missed it by one block, but she said it wasn't anything like what happened here when I sent her video," he said. "Oh! I ran into the Outsiders. Octavio, Mia, and some other girl."

"I'm glad they're okay. I actually wanted to speak to Octavio about something..." I filled Lyle in on all the details about the Strigoi Ancient's arcanum and finding out that Octavio was once one of them that worked to create me. It was never easy getting a straight answer out of Octavio, but I was hoping that by showing him the book I found his name in that it would jog his memory.

"I don't know where they were headed," Lyle told me. "They had been outside the city, but came back to hand out tin cans full of money and juice boxes to the survivors and first responders to help people get back on their feet."

"Still weird as ever. I kind of want a juice box though." A roving pack of Abhorrent Ones scurried past that I dismembered without interrupting our conversation.

"I want a beer. I can't believe this is happening in my lifetime. I was hoping it wouldn't be until...ah, never mind. Can't let this get to me."

Nathaniel returned with his arms full of children and a woman that must have been their mother. "Do we have a shelter for these folks?" he asked and let them off.

"Bridges and tunnels are out," Lyle said. "We airlifted some to the other boroughs, but the pilots left to refuel."

"I'll make something," I told them. The children were having the time of their lives clinging to Nathaniel's arms and legs and sitting on his shoulders. They didn't want to let go and kept squealing in glee hoping he would fly again. Every time he pried one off, another latched back on like a tick.

"Thank you, thank you!" The mother must have bowed to him and made the sign of the cross at least fifteen times. "Praise the Lord! Heaven has sent us an angel in these dark times."

"Oh, I'm not an angel," he tried to explain. "I'm the Ascended's champion."

"He's not an angel, Mama! He doesn't have wings. He's a superhero!" One of the children exclaimed.

Superhero...?

"Where's your cape?" another child asked. "Every superhero has a cape."

"I left that at home," Nathaniel answered honestly, but it was still funny.

"Where's your secret hideout? What's your superhero name? Do you have a sidekick? If you don't, can I be your sidekick?" The children were at no loss for questions. Nathaniel eventually gave up and sat down while all of them piled on him.

"I don't get it, man. These kids just lost their home, they're surrounded by death, and their world was turned upside down, but they're acting like it's Christmas," Lyle said to me.

"Children are resilient. They can see hope where others only see darkness. All it takes is for someone to give them a chance."

"Speaking of darkness; all else aside, this doesn't really feel like New York with how dark it is. Everything is changing, man... I wish there was *something* that remained constant to hold on to."

"Yeah, you're right," I agreed and pointed to the sky. "Nathaniel! What do you say we give this city some light?"

Epilogue

"Tiger pounce!" Noah appeared out of nowhere and leaped on top of me in bed. "What's up, Tasty One?"

"I got in from another relief mission with Nathaniel a little while ago and was reading through some of the Order's old records to discuss at our next meeting." I put my book to the side knowing I wouldn't be getting much further with Noah around and scratched under his chin as he settled down with his head on my lap. "What have you been up to?"

"Just had a long day of punching kids in the face."

"...What?"

"I was training the brats, Noah sensei style. That Connor kid can really take a beating." It had been about two weeks since we had vanquished Set and every day that went by with Noah remaining in high spirits was a wonder to me. I kept waiting for something to happen that would cause him to shut out his emotions again, but each new day was the opposite.

Sometime last week he had taken it upon himself to start training the Order in his unconventional ways. That caught me off guard, but what really got me was when he began to learn their names. Nathaniel remained as "kid" to him despite being close in size and apparent age, but I knew that it was out of fondness because he connected with Nathaniel the best. I noticed he had a soft spot for the underdogs who struggled to have their voices heard.

From oldest to youngest, The Order took to him well, very well in fact. Some looked up to him because of his martial skills, others liked him because of the unpredictable element he added to their regimented lives, and many saw a side of him that up until now he had only shown me.

He started to take ownership of his role in our new family and became protective over them as if they were all part of his pack. It was the small things I noticed that added up to another real awakening in his personality; helping with repairs around the abbey and leaving before a thank you could be said, offering the rare compliment to others' fighting skills and giving pep talks in his own brash way, or building the little ones a playhouse from the trees on the property.

Whatever the method, the arrogant side of Noah's cocky demeanor drifted away, leaving us with a man whose heart had been mended and who was finally able to be himself. Everyone welcomed him when he was around, but it was me that felt the luckiest because I could say he was mine.

"I hope you weren't actually punching them in the face."

"Only the slow ones." He grinned up at me and kissed my hand. "I missed you."

"I missed you too." I removed his new aviator sunglasses so I could see his eyes and put them on his nightstand by the cowboy hat I had also gotten him.

"I made this for you while I was sparring with the kids." He reached into his pocket to retrieve something. "It's nothing special...I thought you might like it though."

He slipped a braided leather bracelet around my wrist next to the prayer beads that I always wore. "It's just something dumb my mother taught me back in the day to keep my hands busy. I forgot all about it until recently..."

"I love it." I leaned down and kissed him. "Thank you, tiger."

The dynamics of our new life together sometimes caused us to be apart, but it didn't take away from the fact that the time we spent in each other's company was heaven on Earth. Our relationship was based on two strong and independent people that loved one another as equals. Some days we'd wake up together early in the morning and go our separate ways until late at night. I would meet with the new council, composed of Liam, Marianna, and Alexandre, to discuss every aspect of the Order and the direction we wanted to take it while Noah would go to train with the rest. After my meeting I'd leave with Nathaniel to continue our global recovery efforts and if there was a spare moment, it was usually taken up by Lyle coordinating rescues and security.

"I'm starving. Let me get one of those chicken wings."

"What are you talking about—?" I realized what he actually meant when he took my forearm and put it in his mouth. "My arms aren't chicken wings!" I squeezed his nose and jerked free.

"Then gimme a chicken leg." He was cracking himself up and could barely close his lips around my thigh.

"Get your paws off me!" I laughed and shoved him onto his back. "You know Gianluca used to call me little chick, right?"

"Mine's better. I'm respecting you as a full grown tasty bird."

Noah wrapped his arms around me like two big pythons and laughed himself right off the bed, taking me down with him. "I love you so damn much," he whispered with a kiss to my head.

"I love you too."

He turned on his brand new eighty-inch TV, which was powered by an electrically charged aether crystal and mounted on the wall between all the katana I had finished making for him.

"Hey, look, my favorite show is on!" he exclaimed as if surprised and locked his legs around me too. Still surprising to me, Noah loved to cuddle—among other physical expressions of his affection—but half of the time I didn't think he knew the difference from a submission hold. It was either that or he found it funny to nearly squeeze the life out of me. He did give the best foot rubs and learned to make a great cup of coffee, so I forgave him.

"That's because you recorded it and have been watching it on repeat for a week," I said and pulled myself free enough to get comfortable.

"*You're saying that your warriors are the ones responsible for cleaning up the cities so swiftly after last week's tragedies, correct? And they were acting on your behalf?*" The clip playing was from a news segment interviewing Aurelia via video conference during her whirlwind press tour that seemed to never end.

"*Absolutely,*" Aurelia answered. "*I would stop at nothing to guarantee the lives of my beloved human allies and I know that the heroes out there today under my charge feel the same.*"

"*The thing is, there seems to be some discrepancy with your claims. I was on the scene in London and had the chance to speak with one of these heroes, and well, I'll let the clip speak for itself.*"

The report switched to a split screen with a clip halfway through an earlier interview.

"*—you've been seen all across the world saving thousands upon thousands of people, maybe millions. Would you say you're in the millions yet?*"

"*I'm not sure. I don't really count, help whoever I can and do what needs to be done,*" Nathaniel answered with his cape billowing behind him. "*When a city is cleared I put up an aurora to let the people there know that they're safe again.*"

"*Magnificent! The words of a true hero that certainly reflect your selfless actions. Many are even calling you a 'super' hero and have started fan clubs at the shelters. How does that make you feel?*"

"*It's a little embarrassing, but as long as it's giving people hope then I'm fine with that.*"

"*I'd say you've given this world more than just hope, you've handed us a second chance on a silver platter.*"

"*Thank you...*" Nathaniel had deep emotion in his voice upon hearing that. "*I haven't been doing it alone though.*"

"*Yes! As I understand it, you are one of Aurelia's finest warriors. We have been trying to reach her for interview, but of course she must be very busy and we've yet to see her anywhere near the action. Is there any chance you could put in a good word for us? When you aren't carrying us from the brink of destruction in your arms, that is.*"

"*I'm not sure who you're talking about...?*"

"*Aurelia de Saint-Pierre. Your leader?*"

"*I'm sorry, I don't know who that is. The Ascended is my only master.*"

Noah's howls of laughter ripped through the abbey as they had every single time he watched that clip. "Look at her face!" He paused the screen to point out her anger for the umpteenth time. She didn't really change expressions much if you asked me, but he insisted on it. "You can see—you can see her about to explode right on this frame before it cuts to a commercial—!"

"I wish Nathaniel would stop referring to me as his master."

"Too bad that reporter is probably dead..." Noah's roars calmed to a hearty chuckle as wiped tears from his eyes and restarted the clip to watch again. I had seen this interview dozens of times, but it was the first I noticed a birthmark of three dots in a triangle on the side of the reporter's neck. "Damn, that kid is awesome though. This is almost better than offing the bitch."

"I'm glad you're happy." I wriggled out from his embrace and got dressed in my finest, now that I had more than one set of clothes to choose from.

"Where are you going?" Noah asked when I kissed him goodbye.

"I've got a meeting."

"Yeah, with *me*, without clothes! I thought we could go for a swim and then I was gonna get us sushi."

"We will as soon as I'm back. This one is a meeting with the gods," I told him as the shadows from Gianluca encroached to take me to Yomi. "Be good!"

I was brought into the main hall of the golden temple in Yomi where Empress Kamakura, Isis, and Gianluca were assembled. I took a glance around the temple and remembered the first time I had been here and how much I had changed since then.

"'Tis good to see you again, Young One," Isis addressed me from beside the dragon statue. "How fares your champion? Well, I hope."

"He is. He's taken to his role better than I could have hoped, although there's a long road ahead until he can understand the extent of his powers."

I had repurposed the reliquary into a meditation room where I spent a great many hours teaching Nathaniel to master his new abilities. Most of the time he just wanted to talk about life and sought guidance from me that I had only recently learned myself. Being someone's mentor and a leader was strange whenever I reflected on it, considering my own short yet tumultuous journey.

Nathaniel was never able to extend the range of his telekinetic powers despite my attempts at training him, nor could he use them as an added sense of touch or to manipulate matter. He was disappointed, but with encouragement accepted that his unique variation was something to be celebrated.

Much like his eagerness to prove himself, Nathaniel's powers had no "off switch" and still no known limits. Telekinetic energy was perpetually surging through him at its peak, in contrast to mine that I would use for a specific task and then stop. The scientists at PROJECT: UNITY found that Nathaniel's powers fortified his entire body from the cellular down to the subatomic level, granting him theoretical invulnerability to physical harm in addition to his innate aetheric defenses against magic.

"The humans are blinded by his light, granting us the benefit of working undeterred in shadow," said Kamakura. Both metaphorical and literal; Nathaniel's command over light after absorbing the Empyrean Jewel was a power not to be taken for granted. Aside from the novelty of creating spectacular light shows, he practiced using it in combat against the remaining Abhorrent Ones with punishing beams, blasts, and flashes that rivaled my own energy output.

Although he was capable of learning magic, he had told me he would prefer to explore his other options with his powers. The idea of magic left him with a bad taste after growing up around it in such a negative atmosphere and I wasn't about to force him to do something he didn't want.

"That was my plan." Aurelia wasn't the only one who could play the game. The people of the modern world wanted a hero to protect them, not a figurehead telling them what to do. Nathaniel couldn't have been more perfect for the job. He was approachable, obliging, and humble.

We had designed new armor together to fit his change in lifestyle. I insisted on no helmet and he had to wear a cape since it was brought to our attention that superheroes needed those. He didn't want to wear the heavy metal cuirass, so that left us with only the orichalcum greaves and gauntlets. Marianna suggested making a bodysuit out of leather and cloth being that he didn't need the added defense, and in no short time his new superhero persona was born: the Champion.

I had his family banner hung from the ceiling in the main hall of the abbey on the way to the courtyard. Nathaniel was grateful for any small act of kindness, but seeing that brought tears to his eyes. I went a step further and had Liam craft him a medallion exactly like his family crest to fasten his cape so he could have something like the amulets the rest of the Order wore. He still hadn't decided on an enchantment for it, however.

"Has there been word on the other matter we discussed?" Isis asked. "My strength grows with every waking moment as the desert sands fill with those that flock to my light's embrace. Much praise belongs to you, Young One for your work in restoring my temples and building others anew, yet it shant be enough when the true battle comes."

"My spies have been busy gathering information, but as of now there are no solid leads," I said. "We don't want to make the mistake of waking another deity that is likely to turn on us or has close ties to one that will. The druids we've offered membership into the Alabaster Order speak of a 'Goddess' and also a horned god in the north, so that's where we'll investigate next."

The infrastructure of the Order had been reorganized to suit the new laws. Members were appointed to positions based on desire and talents rather than birthright. The transition to a new council was smoothed over by bridging the gap between generations, with the heirs of the old leaders stepping up early.

Liam, Alexandre, and Marianna were already well respected among their peers and their guardians couldn't have been happier to see their lineage remain in power for the time being. I found it easier to work with them than their predecessors, whom I knew would still struggle to break old habits and adopt the new ideals I was aiming toward.

Liam confessed that he was relieved to not have been chosen, as he could never handle the spotlight like Nathaniel did. I couldn't blame him. I preferred to stay out of sight and let Nathaniel take the credit when we toured the cities.

When the need arose for someone that could act with the utmost discretion, no one came to mind sooner than Claudius. The four gods, myself included, came to realize that not only were we currently outclassed, but also outnumbered in our war against the Infernal Kings. The odds would only be further tipped out of our favor should more deities like Set rise, so instead we planned to seek other gods to aid our cause.

To do so we needed to avoid attracting mankind's attention, which was fixated on the supernatural at the moment with all going on in the world. The slightest hint of another god rising would drive humanity into hysteria as they all tried to be one of the first worshippers to get on the new god's good side, totally disregarding the idea of moral alignment (as was the case with Set).

While all eyes were on Nathaniel, Claudius traveled the world in search of any information on other gods, whether they were close to awakening, and their relation to anything that could be deemed a threat. Nothing was off limits for him as he conducted his research undetected. He scouted everywhere from the Vatican's private libraries to ancient monasteries, cultists' hideouts, and even other supernaturals' lairs.

Rafael—who shared a similar skillset—was sent to track down Octavio and the Outsiders to offer them a safe place to stay with me. It was proving to be a rather daunting task, as I had expected, but there were questions I needed answers to and debts of gratitude to be repaid.

"How goes your plight with the Ancients, Dark One?" Kamakura inquired. "I understand them to still be quite an unpredictable factor that should not be ignored."

"I make them think I begin to slip to the demons' side. Now they know fear," Gianluca answered and smiled at me. "For today, no problem. I take a nice rest."

It was a simple yet efficient setup that Gianluca and I decided on. The Ancients were using Gianluca to serve as their middleman and later take the fall so they could rise uncontested with a clean reputation. Castile knew I'd share what I had learned with Gianluca, but was also aware that I had left him for Noah. They counted on Gianluca to uphold his duty to protect them by his honor and then fade away with no other ties to this world once the war ended. They didn't expect me to convince him to stay.

There were always concerns of what would happen if the Infernal Kings manipulated him again. But with me no longer holding his hand to the Ancients' knowledge, he became a liability for them the more he was around. With the world so enamored by Nathaniel and Aurelia vying for their attention, there was little anyone could do to point a finger at Gianluca as a scapegoat. He had agreed to take a step back from trying to rebuild Rome long enough to disappear from the public's eye, so any attempt to vilify him have would come off as paranoid ramblings.

The Ancients were a wild card not to be taken lightly, but with Gianluca's allegiance uncertain and his breath on the backs of their necks they had to constantly watch the shadows, expecting his betrayal at any moment. As much as I would have rather killed them and been done with it, letting their souls get in the demons' claws was still a consequence not worth facing.

"Very well," said Kamakura. "Our focus is better spent on the true enemy."

"To know thy enemy is of utmost importance and I have gleaned the identity of one Infernal King thus far," Isis said. "He is known by many names: Vritra, Ouroboros, Leviathan, Jörmungandr, and the serpent of Eden. In my land he is Apep and it was Set that had kept him at bay for centuries, although many have tried their hand to slay the beast for good. There is no greater evil, and the legends of the immortal serpent coiling around the world is no exaggeration."

"Great—and that's *one* of seven," I bemoaned.

"In war, first is the *legionarii*—the, ah, infantry. The king do not come until a victory is ready," Gianluca said.

"It will take a great deal more to sway the balance of chaos on Earth so that the Infernal Kings could appear," said Kamakura.

"We've stopped them at every attempt to secure vessels too," I said. "That has to be infuriating."

"That may only serve to strengthen their conviction," Isis countered. "They will not hesitate any longer to march their vast armies to their deaths for the chance at discerning a weakness in our defenses."

"Then we keep building and rebuilding while they claw frantically at us from the other side. We're growing stronger the more that people believe in us, one way or another. The only thing is, if we've already seen the infantry, then what in Hell comes next before the Kings?"

"Soon we see, but no enemy is too strong for us," said Gianluca. "We are the new gods of this world and today we make a new pantheon to protect it together."

www.ingramcontent.com/pod-product-compliance
Lightning Source LLC
Chambersburg PA
CBHW031320050726
47500CB00012B/146